THE ADVENTURES
OF MARY DARLING

Praise for *The Adventures of Mary Darling*

"Put the beloved characters of Peter Pan and Sherlock Holmes into the blender of Pat Murphy's prodigious imagination and you have a book that upends, complicates, situates, and explicates the stories we have always known. Full of surprises and deeply satisfying."

—Karen Joy Fowler, author of *Booth*

"Delightfully clever! Pat Murphy has written a page-turner that is both a rousing adventure and an insightful critique of Victorian literary tropes. This is the real story of Neverland."

—Theodora Goss, author of the *Extraordinary Adventures of the Athena Club* trilogy

"The bounty and wit of Pat Murphy's generous imagination kept me reading through the night—just one more page, one more delightful reversal, revelation, surprise."

—Andrea Hairston, author of *Archangels of Funk*

"A fresh new take on both *Peter Pan* and *Sherlock Holmes* that gives new depth and richness to each, unfolding a whole living, breathing world for readers to explore."

—A. C. Wise, author of *Wendy, Darling*

"If you think you have outgrown Neverland, maybe you have. But you don't have to believe in Tinkerbell to love this book."

—Eileen Gunn, author of *Stable Strategies and Others*

"Outstanding characters, a deep understanding of [Murphy's] new fictional world, and clever storytelling round out a novel that's as exciting as it is emotionally satisfying."

—Richard Kadrey, author of the *Sandman Slim* series

"Murphy does a masterful job of subverting Victorian tropes while delivering all the fairies, mermaids, and pirates anyone could desire."
—Susan Palwick, author of *The Fate of Mice*

"A delightful mashup of familiar tales, written by an expert for the reader who hungers for something old, something new, justice borrowed and logical glue."
—Meg Elison, author of *Number One Fan*

"A cracking read, a virtuoso act of gender jiu-jitsu, a Sherlock story like no other, a rough trip to fairyland, and the real, true story of Peter Pan. What a book!"
—Cory Doctorow, author of *Red Team Blues*

"A gem of a novel. I haven't had this much reading fun in ages. A literary mashup that thrilled and tickled me to no end."
—Joe R. Lansdale, author of *The Thicket*

"A clever and delightful secret history of Neverland. This twisty tale full of mystery and fairy magic, grand adventure, and deft character revelations challenges our societal expectations, and causes us to reconsider what it means to be strong."
—Josh Rountree, author of *The Legend of Charlie Fish*

"Pages fly as the mystery unfolds and Pat Murphy gives girls and mothers the thrilling adventures they deserve."
—Wendy N. Wagner, author of *Girl in the Creek*

— Also by Pat Murphy —

NOVELS

The Shadow Hunter (1982)
The Falling Woman (1986)
The City, Not Long After (1989)
Bones (1990)
Nadya: The Wolf Chronicles (1996)
There and Back Again, by Max Merriwell (1999)
Wild Angel (2000)
Adventures in Time and Space with Max Merriwell (2001)
The Wild Girls (2007)

COLLECTIONS

Points of Departure (1990)
Letters From Home (1991), with Pat Cadigan and Karen Joy Fowler
Women Up to No Good: A Collection of Short Stories (2013)

AS EDITOR

The James Tiptree Award Anthology, Vols. 1–3
(with Karen Joy Fowler, Debbie Notkin, and Jeffrey D. Smith)

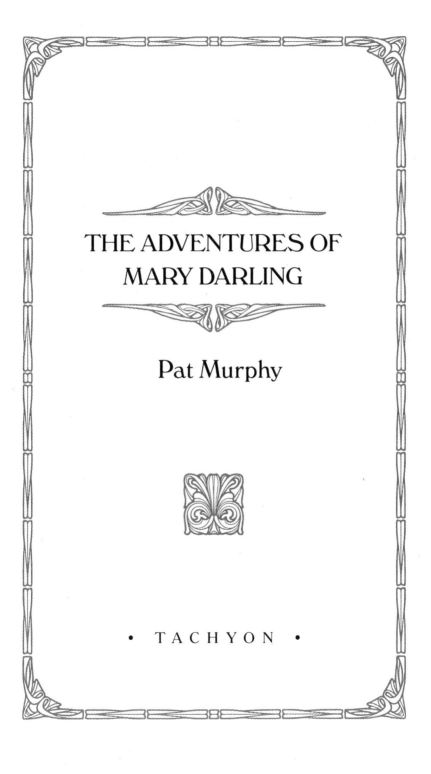

THE ADVENTURES OF MARY DARLING

Pat Murphy

• TACHYON •

The Adventures of Mary Darling
Copyright © 2025 by Pat Murphy

Cover design by Elizabeth Story
Interior by John Coulthart

Tachyon Publications LLC
1459 18th Street #139
San Francisco, CA 94107
415.285.5615
www.tachyonpublications.com
tachyon@tachyonpublications.com
Series editor: Jacob Weisman
Editor: Jaymee Goh

Print ISBN: 978-1-61696-438-2
Digital ISBN: 978-1-61696-439-9
Printed in the United States by
Versa Press, Inc.
First Edition: 2025
9 8 7 6 5 4 3 2 1

For Dave, with love. You are the best.

PART THREE

PROLOGUE

Nosy Boraha, Madagascar
March 8, 1934

Dear Granduncle John,

Here's the book I've been working on. I hope this will set the record straight once and for all. I have always thought it shameful that James Barrie's *Peter Pan* is the only version of my grandmother's story available to the world. He got so much wrong! And he left you out altogether! This book tells the true story.

When I was a child, you complimented me on my vivid imagination. I hope you don't regret those comments after reading this book. I had to use my imagination when writing about what my characters said and thought. Whenever I had to fill in gaps that weren't covered by what friends and family remembered, I made things up—including some things that you said and did and felt.

I respect your opinion—as a writer, as my beloved granduncle, and as someone who was there when all this was going on. I look forward (I think) to any comments or corrections you may choose to share.

Your loving grandniece,
Jane Darling

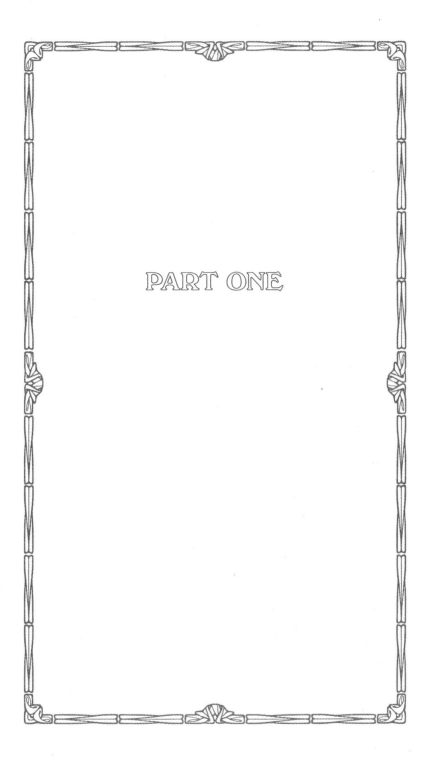

PART ONE

CHAPTER 1
The Events at Number 14
(The Children Are Gone)

I CAN PICTURE it clearly: A light dusting of snow had settled on the cobblestones of a small London street in a respectable middle-class neighborhood not far from Kensington Gardens. The snow was white, a temporary condition for any snow falling in London. The soot of London's smokes would soon blacken the snow, but at that moment, it was still pure and clean.

The year was 1900, the sixty-third year of Queen Victoria's reign. The British Empire ruled over a quarter of the world's population. That's the big picture. But right now, I'm thinking about one small street.

There were footprints in the snow. They led away from the front door of number 14, a tall, narrow house much like the tall, narrow house to its left and the tall narrow house to its right. Two people—a woman in overshoes and a man in ankle boots—had picked their way over the snowy cobblestones to number 27, just a short distance down the street.

I imagine that it was a peaceful scene—except for the dog barking frantically behind number 14. Between bouts of frantic barking, a heavy chain rattled and clanked as the beast threw itself against the restraint that held it captive. The animal sounded desperate—raising an alarm that no one heeded.

On the third floor of number 14, the casement windows were open wide, which was odd on such a cold night. A light flickered in the room—a night light perhaps? No, this light moved about the room quickly, darting this way and that.

From behind the house came the crack of a wooden post giving way. A Newfoundland dog, its shaggy coat soaked with sweat and melted snow, bounded into the street. The dog dragged a chain that was looped through its collar. At the end of the chain was a wooden post that had broken off at the base. The top of the post caught on a cobble, a weak link in the chain gave way, and the chain slipped off the dog's collar.

Free at last, the dog ran down the street and hurled itself at the door of number 27, claws rattling against the wood. A servant girl in a mobcap and apron opened the door. The dog bowled her over. Quicker than you'd think an animal that size could move, the dog was inside.

A few moments later, the dog dashed out again. A woman followed, calling after the beast in a voice as wild and desperate as the dog's barking. "Nana! What is it?"

What is it? By way of an answer, Nana ran toward number 14.

The woman—her name was Mary Darling—ran after the dog. She was a slim woman with high cheekbones and dark curly hair. She wore a light evening dress with a full skirt—last year's style, but she made it look good. She had left her overcoat and overshoes behind.

Her evening slippers were not made for running on snow-slicked cobbles. She slipped in the snow and fell to one knee, but that slowed her only for a moment. She was quickly on her feet again, looking up at the third-floor window of number 14.

A sweet high sound, like the ringing of tiny bells, rang out over Nana's panting.

"No!" Mary cried out as she ran through the snow. "No!"

Mary's husband, George Darling, followed her, a few minutes behind. He had lingered to apologize to the hosts of the dinner party at number 27 for the dog's unfortunate interruption. He had taken the time to put on his woolen greatcoat and to collect Mary's overcoat and overshoes. He stepped carefully to avoid slipping in the snow. As George walked through the snow, he muttered under his breath, "This is what comes of having a dog for a nursemaid."

Mary tried number 14's front door. It was locked. She called frantically to George, who plodded through the snow, fumbled in his pocket, found the key, and unlocked the door.

Mary rushed into the house and up the stairs to the third floor, calling all the while to Liza, the young girl who was their only servant. Nana ran ahead of Mary, leaving a trail of wet paw prints on the stairs.

Liza came up from the tiny room off the kitchen that served as her bedroom, blinking as she pulled a shawl over her thin shoulders. "What is it, m'um?"

"The children!" Mary called. "Where are they?" She didn't pause for an answer, continuing her dash up the stairs to the nursery.

"I went to the nursery not an hour since, m'um," Liza was saying. "The children were sleeping—I heard them breathing softly, the little angels."

Mary stopped in the nursery doorway, frozen. The beds were empty; the bedclothes, thrown back. The windows were wide open. Mary rushed to look out. Below, the snowy street. Above, the dark sky, speckled with stars.

She turned away from the window to stare at the empty beds where she had left her children sleeping. Then she sat on the window seat, as if suddenly unable to stand. Her hands were clasped in her lap, holding onto each other because there was nothing else to cling to.

The nursery was a cheerful room. The walls were a pale yellow. The curtains at the window were printed with bright yellow daisies. Mary had sewn the curtains herself. Over the mantel, she had hung a watercolor painting by her mother: three smiling fairies sat in the shade of a bottlebrush bush, sharing a pot of tea. On the mantel were framed photos of Mary's children—a formal portrait taken in a studio and a photo of the children at the beach, taken when they were on holiday.

Mary had been happy in this room. She had thought this nursery was a place where her children would be safe.

George Darling reached the landing and stepped into the nursery. "Liza says the children are fine," he said. There was an edge in his voice. He had been ready to light a pipe and enjoy a glass of brandy with their hosts when Nana disrupted the party.

"They are gone, George. The children are gone." Mary's voice was bleak and filled with pain.

George stared at the open window and then at the empty beds. "What? This is some kind of joke," he said, in the tone of a man trying to convince himself. "Wendy! John! Michael! Children, this isn't funny." He turned away from the window and looked under the empty beds. He peered inside the wardrobe and swept the curtains aside to look behind them.

Mary wasn't watching him. Once again, she was looking out the window at the night sky. "I closed the windows before we left," she said to no one, or perhaps to Nana, who sat at her feet, leaning against her knee and gazing at her face. "I'm sure of that."

George wasn't listening. He was asking Liza what had happened while they had been at dinner. "The children are gone," he said gruffly, as if Liza couldn't see that for herself.

The girl's eyes were enormous, terrified. "The master had tied Nana in the yard and she was barking and barking. She wouldn't stop. I brought her to the nursery so she could see nothing was wrong. Then I put her in the yard again . . ."

A loud knock at the front door interrupted Liza's recitation. George stomped downstairs to answer and returned a moment later, followed by a police constable. Their neighbors at number 27, alarmed by the Darlings' sudden departure, had fetched the constable from the corner and told him to go to the Darlings' house.

"Our children are gone," George told the policeman. "Vanished."

"Vanished?" The policeman raised his grizzled eyebrows. His gray hair was neatly cut beneath his helmet. Moustache trimmed to a regulation length. Nose red—perhaps fond of a bit of drink, but never on duty. Crystals of melting snow clung to his coat. He had a truncheon on his belt, ready to smack a wrongdoer. But there was no one to smack.

"Could the children be playing a joke?" he asked.

"They wouldn't do that," George said.

The policeman was looking in all the places that George had looked. There were no children under the beds. No children in the wardrobe. No children behind the curtains.

"Kidnapped," the policeman said in a matter-of-fact tone. "I'll tell headquarters."

Mary shook her head in denial, her face wet with tears. George put his hand on her shoulder. "I'll get your Uncle John," he said. "He'll know what to do."

CHAPTER 2
Uncle John and the Great Detective

D R. WATSON SAT by the fire at 221B Baker Street, reviewing his notes on one of the adventures he had shared with his friend, Mr. Sherlock Holmes. Holmes was at the table, working on a monograph about poisons—specifically about deadly potions that could be made with ingredients commonly found in the average household.

Watson gazed out the window. In the snow, Baker Street looked beautiful. So peaceful. Snow hid many things that people would rather not see, covering the soot that darkened the buildings, the horse manure in the gutters, the piles of rubbish in the alleys, and even the beggars that huddled in doorways.

Watson heard the clip-clop of a horse's hooves and the rumble of wheels on cobblestones below. The sound stopped beneath their window. "We have a visitor," Watson remarked. "Someone must be in desperate need to seek out your help on such a cold night."

Holmes put down his pen. "A man, by the sound of it." He glanced at Watson. "I know it's a hansom cab by the pace of the horse and the sound of the wheels—lighter than a growler but not so quick as a dogcart. I hear only one passenger alighting—a respectable woman would not be in a hansom cab alone. And any woman would wait for the assistance of the driver to alight. But our visitor is too impatient for that."

The visitor's impatience was confirmed by a frantic knocking at the door. Watson moved to stand, but Holmes waved him back into his chair. "Don't disturb yourself, Watson. Allow me."

Watson heard a man's voice, speaking loudly, quickly. Watson could not make out the words, but he recognized the voice. It was George Darling, his niece's husband. In an instant, Watson was out of his chair, comfort forgotten.

"What's wrong?" Watson asked, as George entered the room. The man's hands were shaking—from strong emotion, from the cold, or perhaps from both.

"Mary needs you, John. Mary . . . I . . . we need your help."

Though George addressed his appeal to Watson, Holmes answered. "We will do everything we can." Holmes' tone was calm and reassuring. He led George to the chair that Watson had vacated. "But first, you must calm yourself. Watson, get the brandy."

Watson poured George a glass of brandy and draped a blanket over the man's shoulders to ward off the chill.

George Darling was a tall, thin man with regular features and dark wavy hair. He was twenty-nine years of age, but he had the air of a much older man. Watson had always thought him rather dull. George took himself very seriously and expected others to do the same. He worked as a senior accountant in a Capel Court brokerage firm and was always talking about stocks and shares in a deadly earnest tone. Years ago, when George had come to Watson to ask for Mary's hand, Watson had thought him an odd match for Mary, who was a lively, strong-minded young woman. But Watson was glad that his niece had married well and settled down.

"What's happened?" Watson asked.

George downed the brandy. "The children are gone." His voice was low and pained. "The policeman says they've been kidnapped."

"Tell the story from the beginning," Holmes said. He pulled a chair near George and seated himself upon it, leaning forward and giving the man his full attention. "Leave nothing out."

George recounted the events of the evening, ending with the discovery that the children were gone. "Then I came here. I left Mary in the nursery, in case the children returned. Liza is with her. The constable has gone to make a report. Please come back with me, John. Mary needs you."

"You were quite right to come and get us," Holmes said. "We must hurry to examine the crime scene before Scotland Yard shows up to obliterate any clues."

As they rode in the hansom cab to Mary's house, Watson caught flickering glimpses of Holmes' face in the light of street lamps. Clearly Holmes was eager to help Mary in this time of need, but Watson wished he did not look quite so cheerful, delighted to have an intriguing case, even one involving pain to Watson and his family.

Holmes stopped the cab a block away from number 14.

"The house is around the corner," George said.

But Holmes was already out of the cab. He had brought a lantern, which he immediately lit. He began walking slowly toward number 14, leaving Watson and George to follow. As Holmes walked, he studied the street and the houses on either side. When he reached number 14, he continued past the house, frowning down at the marks in the snow. Then he turned and walked back to number 14. "Which window leads to the nursery?" he asked George.

George pointed to the open window on the third floor.

"Here now—hold this." Holmes handed George the lantern, then moved from the doorstep to the ground directly beneath the nursery window. "Come along. I need the light here."

George followed with the lantern. Having inspected the ground, Holmes lifted his eyes to stare at the wall—a brick wall with no ivy, no drainpipe, nothing to cling to.

As Watson watched, Holmes stepped closer, his nose inches from the bricks.

George gave Watson a beseeching look. "We really must go inside," he said. "Mary needs us."

"I'll go up," Watson told George. Watson knew Holmes would be at this for a while. "I'll check on Mary."

"George, keep that lantern up," Holmes said. "I need the light."

As Holmes searched for marks too subtle to catch the attention of anyone less discerning, Watson climbed the stairs to the nursery. There he found Mary sitting on the window seat. The casement windows were open wide. Despite the fire, the room was cold.

Mary's back was straight. She was deathly pale. Her hands were in her lap, her right hand clenched in a fist; her left, wrapped tightly around the fist, as if to restrain it. Her face was streaked with tears. Nana sat at Mary's feet.

Watson set his doctor's bag on the floor and sat beside her. "Mary," Watson said, touching her shoulder. "You will catch your death of cold sitting here." He started to pull the windows closed.

"No! Please, Uncle, leave them open! They must stay open."

Watson shot a glance at Liza. The servant girl stood by the fire, a shawl over her shoulders, her face a picture of misery.

"She won't let me close them," Liza murmured.

"I will leave them open just a bit," Watson said soothingly. "I won't latch them. But you must move out of this draft. Liza, fetch a blanket and brandy."

By the time Watson heard Holmes' footsteps on the stairs, Mary was seated in the chair by the fire. Watson had covered her with a blanket and forced her to sip some brandy.

At the nursery door, Holmes stopped and surveyed the room. "Is this room just as it was when you arrived home?" he asked George.

"Yes," George said. "When we returned home, the room looked just as you see it. We have changed nothing."

"The windows were wide open when I arrived," Watson said. "I pulled them closed."

"Yes, that's right," George said. "Other than that, it was exactly like this."

"Is that the dog's kennel?" Holmes asked, gesturing to the kennel beside the wardrobe.

"Yes, that's Nana's," George said.

Watson stared at the kennel. "Why didn't Nana chase the kidnappers away?" he asked. He knew that dog and a more dedicated animal did not live. She would have given her life to protect the children. "She never would have allowed a stranger to take them."

George put his hand to his forehead, hiding his eyes. "I tied Nana in the yard. She had misbehaved. I was punishing her. It was my fault Nana wasn't in the nursery. It's all my fault."

Oblivious to George's distress, Holmes crossed to the wardrobe, opened the door, and considered the clothing within. "Is any of the children's clothing gone?" he asked George.

George frowned, looking flustered. "I'm not sure. Mary? Is any clothing gone?"

"The boys were wearing their nightshirts. Wendy was in her nightgown," Mary said softly. "All their other clothes are all here."

"They left without jackets," Holmes said. "Without shoes."

Mary nodded, tears running down her cheeks.

Watson moved to stand behind his niece, putting his hand on her shoulder. He could feel the tension in her muscles. "You have the world's best detective working on your behalf," Watson told his niece. "We'll find the children."

Holmes continued his examination of the room. He studied the floor, kneeling to scrutinize the area nearest the wardrobe, lying flat to look under each bed. At the window, he lingered, scrutinizing the window latch, the snow on the sill. There were marks in the snow where some of the loose powder had been pushed to one side.

Holmes pulled tweezers from his jacket pocket. With them, he plucked a leaf from the windowsill, where it had been almost entirely covered by snow. He took an envelope from his pocket, set it on the interior windowsill, and carefully laid the damp leaf on the clean paper.

At that moment, there was a knock on the door below. Liza hurried downstairs, then returned with Inspector Lestrade of Scotland Yard.

"Holmes!" Lestrade said. "How the devil did you get here so quickly?"

"Family connections. And it's just as well that I did get here quickly—I had the opportunity to examine the crime scene before the evidence was trampled underfoot."

"Crime? Have you found evidence of a crime? How do you know the children didn't just run off?"

"If the children ran off, they left in their nightclothes, without coats or boots," Holmes said in a severe tone. "Even a child would turn back for a coat on a night like this."

"Well, then—I suppose it's a kidnapping," Lestrade said, his tone rather peevish.

Holmes smiled. "As I have said before, it's a mistake to theorize before one has data. Just now, the main clue is the lack of clues. I see no children's footprints in the snow. There were no signs of a vehicle, other than the hansom cab that brought us here. No sign anyone scaled the wall. Only a few scuff marks on the windowsill and a dead leaf that may prove to be of interest."

Lestrade waved a hand, dismissing the leaf as irrelevant. "A leaf. Oh, come now, Holmes. Surely you don't believe that a leaf that fell on the windowsill is important."

Holmes cocked his head, still smiling. "At this stage of the investigation, it's difficult to say what might be important."

The inspector looked uncomfortable. "Well, if you choose to waste your time on a fallen leaf, that's your business. There's no need for one of your complex theories here, Mr. Holmes. The constable who reported this incident suggested a simple explanation. The children went downstairs because the dog was barking. Then someone snatched them—perhaps a brothel keeper who had his eye on the girl, perhaps a thief looking for children to train as pickpockets, perhaps a ragpicker who wanted their pretty nightclothes to sell. If we're lucky, we'll find the children in the morning. If we aren't lucky. . ." Lestrade shrugged.

Watson glanced down at Mary. She was staring at the dead leaf that Holmes had carefully collected. Her expression was grim and determined, like a soldier ready for battle.

Lestrade, who had not noticed she was there, saw her then. "But of course we will find them," he said hurriedly.

Mary's expression did not change.

After Lestrade left, Watson, Holmes, and George Darling walked the streets near number 14, searching for anyone who might have seen the children. Holmes was at his best, hailing men who were heading home, unsteady on their feet after an evening at the pub. He enlisted their sympathy for the children and quizzed them about anything unusual they might have noticed. None of them had any useful information to offer.

"We need more data," Holmes muttered. "Someone must have seen something."

On a corner near a pub, two overly friendly women in low-cut dresses were trying to persuade George that he would enjoy their company. When Watson intervened and told the women of their mission, the older of the two, a buxom woman in a flame red dress, shook her head sadly. "Poor babies," she said. "The girl will end up like me and the boys like that one there." She pointed to a ragged lad talking to Holmes. "If your friend still has his wallet at the end of their conversation, I'd say Bing has lost his touch."

When Holmes rejoined them, Watson asked him to confirm that he still had his wallet.

"Of course I do, Watson. I know the tricks. The boy is clever, though. He saw nothing of interest, but he may be of service to us."

Throughout all this, George seemed lost. His overcoat was pulled tight around him, his muffler wrapped twice around his neck, his cap pulled low over his ears. He followed Watson and Holmes, but he asked no questions, made no suggestions.

At last, the pubs closed and Holmes declared that there was nothing more to be learned. They took George home, found a cab, and returned to Baker Street.

Watson was weary, but Holmes was alert, his eyes bright. As their cab jolted through the streets of London, Holmes questioned Watson about Mary and her husband.

Watson provided a brief account of Mary's history. Watson's older brother Henry and his wife Alice went to Australia to seek their fortune in the goldfields. When Henry's efforts at prospecting were unsuccessful, he set up a small store in Cooktown, the closest town to the goldfields along the Palmer River in Queensland.

The store made a living, but not a good one. Alice, an artist who had achieved some success with paintings of flowers and fairies, had supplemented the family's income with sales of her work. Mary had been born in Australia, as had her younger brother Tom.

Like so many fortune seekers, Henry had returned to England poorer than when he left. His wife Alice died in Australia. Watson didn't know all the details, but he knew that Henry had struggled to recover his footing after Alice's death. Eventually, he had decided to return to England.

Henry and his daughter Mary had traveled by steamer from Australia to England, a journey of three months in cramped and uncomfortable quarters. Henry's son Tom had taken a position as a cabin boy on a merchant ship bound for England, with the plan of meeting his father and sister in London. Henry and Mary had arrived in England as planned, but Tom had not.

Tom's ship had gone down in a storm off the coast of Africa. Tom had written that he survived the wreck and had found a berth on a ship sailing for India. After that, there had been occasional letters posted from distant locations. But there had been no letters for the past three years. The boy had never reached London. After all these years without a word, Watson feared that his nephew Tom had died at sea.

These were painful memories for Watson. When his brother had returned after so many years away, Watson barely recognized him. Henry had been eight years older than Watson. He had married and left England when Watson was still a boy. Watson remembered his brother as a good-natured and easygoing fellow—a natural athlete. But the years in Australia had left Henry thin and worn and weary. His health was poor. Watson could not tell if that was because of Henry's drinking or if Henry drank to seek relief from the aches in his bones.

At fourteen years of age, Henry's daughter Mary did her best to be the lady of the house. She put her father to bed when he was too far gone with drink. She chased away creditors who came to the door.

One night, Henry was walking home from the pub. The fog was thick and the night was dark. Henry was crossing the street when he was struck by a hansom cab and killed, leaving his daughter an orphan. Mary became Watson's ward.

Mrs. Hudson, the landlady at 221B Baker Street, had been a great help during this time. Noticing that Watson was ill-suited to care for Mary, Mrs. Hudson had taken a hand in the matter. She found a boarding school that would help the girl—soon to be a young woman—adapt to her new life without breaking her spirit.

"Then she married George Darling," Watson told Holmes.

"What do you know about your niece's husband?" Holmes asked.

"His father was a criminal barrister and a member of parliament—extremely successful," Watson said. "George is the youngest son of five."

"How did Mary come to meet George?" Holmes asked.

"They met at a dinner party, as I recall."

"Who hosted the party?"

"I really don't remember," Watson said, a hint of impatience in his voice. "I was away on a case with you at the time. Mrs. Hudson attended as Mary's chaperone. She might recall."

Watson was baffled by the question. Why this curiosity about George's father and about how Mary met her husband? What difference did a long-ago dinner party make?

CHAPTER 3
Dreams of Flying

THE MORNING AFTER the children disappeared, George Darling woke at first light to find his wife standing at the window, gazing out at the dawn sky. Pale sunlight shone through the clouds. The world was on the border between night and day, between shadow and light.

George sat up in bed quickly. Silhouetted against the sky, Mary looked unreal—an apparition that might vanish at any moment, just as the children had vanished.

He could not think like that, he told himself. Sherlock Holmes would find the children. They had been kidnapped. That's what Inspector Lestrade had said. These men knew what they were doing. And George could help.

The fire in the room had died to coals. The air was cold. Mary wore only her nightgown. Leaving the warm bed, George took Mary's dressing gown to her and draped it over her shoulders. "You'll catch your death," he said.

She turned her face to him. "I dreamed I was flying," she said. "Over the ocean, far from land. I could hear Wendy and John and Michael calling to each other. Wendy was telling the boys to stay close to her, but John and Michael were laughing, as if it were all a game. Just a lark— flying away without a second thought. I tried to catch up to them, but I couldn't fly fast enough. I was afraid I would fall into the ocean and drown. I felt myself falling into the waves. Then I woke up."

George pulled her close, wrapping his arms around her.

If you had asked, he would have told you that he was comforting her. But I think he was really seeking comfort for himself, gathering his wife close to reassure himself that she was there, warm and real, the rock on which his life was built.

"Hush," he said. "That was just a dream."

"But George—"

"No more talk of foolish dreams," he said briskly.

"George, we need to talk—"

"No time for that, my darling. We must help Mr. Holmes gather data. That's what he needs. I have a plan. Come along." He was taking charge, George thought. That was a man's role. "Sherlock Holmes will find them. He is very good at this sort of thing."

George hurried from the room, giving his wife no time to respond. Mary followed him to the nursery. Nana lifted her head when they entered. Her great sad eyes watched George as he crossed the room.

George took the portrait of their three children from the mantel. Wendy, John, and Michael were all dressed in their best. Wendy was smiling sweetly, a perfect little lady. John and Michael were laughing. To make them smile, Mary had stood behind the photographer, playing peekaboo from behind the camera.

"I'm going to the newspapers," George told Mary. "They will run this photo. By noon tomorrow, all of London will be looking for Wendy and John and Michael." He spoke with great conviction, giving her no opportunity to raise an objection. "I will ask that anyone who has seen our children—anyone who has seen anything suspicious—to contact Sherlock Holmes and Inspector Lestrade at Scotland Yard."

Liza came up from the kitchen at the sound of their voices in the nursery. She clutched her shawl around her shoulders and bobbed a curtsey. "I thought maybe the children . . ." Her voice trailed off.

"Mr. Darling must have some breakfast," Mary told Liza. "He has much to do this morning."

After breakfast, Mary straightened George's tie, brushed his hat, and kissed his cheek. She was pale, but she had dried her tears.

"Holmes is counting on me," George said, having quite convinced himself that the detective would be impressed by his efforts. "I won't let him down."

Many years before, when George was courting Mary, she went to Mrs.

Hudson for advice. "We are very different from each other," Mary told Mrs. Hudson. "George says we belong together. He says he wants to take care of me. That's very sweet, but . . ." She hesitated.

Mrs. Hudson finished the sentence for her. " . . . but you think it's more likely that you'll take care of him."

"Just so," Mary said. "Also, we have very different approaches to life."

Mrs. Hudson nodded. There were many practical advantages to marrying George. A young woman needed a husband or a fortune. Mary, orphaned and dependent on her uncle, had neither. George was an excellent match. He came from a good family. He worked in a brokerage firm and made a solid, middle-class living.

"In my experience, few wives agree with their husbands on all things," Mrs. Hudson said. "Your differences will make your marriage more interesting. It would be quite dull if your opinions were all the same."

"There are things he just doesn't want to talk about," Mary said.

"I wouldn't worry overmuch about that. Some men just don't like to talk."

Mary looked thoughtful—so thoughtful that Mrs. Hudson worried that she was considering turning down this promising suitor. "Do you care for him?" Mrs. Hudson asked.

"I do. I know he can be awkward in company, but under all that, he's kind and very sweet."

Mrs. Hudson nodded. "You'll be good for each other. You'll take care of him and he'll take care of you. If there are things he doesn't want to talk about, just don't talk about those things. I learned long ago that it is far better not to tell your husband everything that you think and do."

Mary had taken Mrs. Hudson's advice to heart. She didn't tell George things that she was confident that he would rather not know. She didn't bring up matters that George would rather forget. In general, she and George lived in perfect harmony.

There were, however, two notable subjects on which Mary and George did not agree at all—both of which relate to their current situation. One was Nana and the other was Sherlock Holmes.

Mary thought Nana was a treasure, the perfect nursemaid for the children. George had his doubts about that. "What must the neighbors think of us?" he had asked Mary on more than one occasion. It was a question she chose to ignore. Whenever anything went wrong, he muttered, "This is what comes from having a dog as a nursemaid."

Mary knew what really bothered George about Nana, but it wasn't something she could discuss with her husband. The real problem was this: George felt the children cared more about the big dog than they did about him.

That was, in fact, why Nana had been tied in the yard on the night that the children disappeared. Before leaving for their dinner party, George and Mary had gone to the nursery to say good night to the children. When George turned to leave the room, he had tripped over Nana.

Of course, he had blamed the dog.

Wendy, John, and Michael had taken Nana's side in the resulting dispute, proclaiming loudly that it wasn't Nana's fault. George's feelings were hurt, but he couldn't admit that. So he said, "It's about time this dog understood who's the master of this house." He waved the children back, grabbed Nana by the collar, and chained her in the backyard. Mary tucked the children into bed, whispering that everything would be fine in the morning.

Unfortunately, she had been wrong about that.

Regarding Sherlock Holmes, their positions were reversed. George admired the detective, and Mary, most decidedly, did not. She had formed her opinion of Mr. Holmes at a dinner party when she was eighteen years old—and nothing had happened since to change her opinion.

At the time, Mary was staying with her uncle and his wife while on half-term holiday from school. Mrs. Watson, a warm-hearted woman, had welcomed Mary into their home, treating her like a daughter.

Watson had met the woman who would become his wife when she had asked Holmes for help. Her father had gone missing under mysterious circumstances. Holmes solved the mystery, and Watson fell in love with and married the client. (You can read all about it in Watson's story, *The Sign of the Four*.)

Not long after the wedding, Mrs. Watson arranged a dinner party in the relaxed and convivial atmosphere of her own home. She held Holmes in high regard and wanted to get to know her husband's friend better. It was a party of six—Dr. and Mrs. Watson, Mary, Mr. Holmes, Watson's colleague Dr. Lewis, and his vivacious wife Mrs. Lewis.

For Mary, the party was cause for excitement. It was her first dinner party, and she had a new dress for the occasion. She had never met her uncle's friend, Mr. Sherlock Holmes, though she had read her uncle's stories about him.

The trouble had begun with the soup course. Nothing wrong with the soup itself, a light consommé made from chicken stock and vegetables. But during that course, Dr. Lewis had asked Holmes what he did for a living.

Holmes replied, "I am a consulting detective, sir. On occasion, I assist Scotland Yard, considering their evidence and putting them on the right scent. I also help private citizens, now and again."

"And how is it you do this?" Lewis asked, his curiosity piqued.

"I observe, I analyze, I deduce. A doctor looks at a sick man and spots telltale symptoms that identify the disease that afflicts him. A layman might not even notice those signs, but to the doctor, they stand out. I consider a man, and I see telltale indicators that the detectives of Scotland Yard overlook. I can read a man's history in his fingernails, his coat sleeve, his boots, his trouser knees, the calluses on his hands."

Mrs. Lewis laughed, exclaiming that she had never heard of such a thing. "It's really quite amazing," Watson told her. "When Holmes first met me, he knew immediately that I had just returned from Afghanistan. He deduced it from my bearing, the color of my skin, and my recent injury."

Mrs. Lewis shook her head, still smiling. She was an intelligent woman and a very pretty one. She did not say outright that she did not believe Holmes, but her manner implied it clearly. "Could you tell all my secrets, just by looking at me? Oh, I truly hope that is not so."

Mary noticed as Mrs. Watson glanced at Holmes, the trace of a frown on her face. "I have a lovely fish course," Mrs. Watson said, but it was already too late.

"Not all your secrets," Holmes said calmly. "But a few things are quite evident."

Mrs. Lewis' smile broadened. "Please, tell me what you see, Mr. Holmes."

"Oh, I do think we should serve the fish," Mrs. Watson said, but Holmes was leaning forward, his eyes on Mrs. Lewis.

"You have a careless lady's maid—if you have not already sacked her, I suggest you consider it. You buy your cosmetics from the chemist on Portobello Road. Sometime during the last three days you have been strolling in Kensal Green Cemetery. I also note that you are a follower of spiritualism and have recently attended a séance near Pembridge Square. Of course, none of those things are secret—they are patently obvious to any careful observer."

Mary saw Mrs. Lewis' expression change from mocking disbelief to horror.

Fortunately, Dr. Lewis was watching Holmes, rather than his wife. "You are quite right about the lady's maid," Lewis said. "We discharged her this morning. And you are correct about the chemist and the walk in the cemetery. However did you guess?"

"No guessing was involved." Holmes tapped his nose. "I detected the distinctive scent of aged orris root. Only the most exclusive establishments make use of that scent—and only the chemist on Portobello Road blends it with the arrowroot starch that I see on Mrs. Lewis' cheek. As for the cemetery, I noted a smudge of a pale gray London clay on Mrs. Lewis' shoe and the leaf of a horse chestnut tree caught in her parasol, which is in the umbrella stand by the front door. The only place you'll find that combination is Kensal Green Cemetery. The fact that the shoes have not been properly cleaned and the leaf has not been shaken from the parasol are indications that Mrs. Lewis' maid is careless."

"Very impressive," Lewis said. "But I'm afraid you are mistaken about the séance. My wife used to attend such events, but at my request she has given it up."

Mary glanced at Mrs. Lewis' face, formerly so bold, now pale and frightened. Mrs. Watson had told Mary of the couple's history: a year before, their oldest son—a lad of eight—had died of pneumonia. Mrs. Lewis had attended many séances in the hope of contacting her boy in the world of the spirits. Her husband, as a man of science, had begged her to stop. Mary guessed that Mrs. Lewis had promised to do so, but had failed in that promise.

"I think all this detection is bad for the appetite," Mrs. Watson said, standing with a great flourish and giving her husband a sharp look. "Let us focus our attention on the fish course to come."

"Yes, yes," Mary chimed in hastily. "It's a lovely haddock. It would be a pity to let it get overdone."

"I think you are mistaken, sir," Holmes said to Lewis.

At that moment, Mary knocked over her glass of water, sending a flood across the table into Holmes' lap. She leapt up and began apologizing, while mopping up the flood, effectively ending all conversation.

Mrs. Watson made a fuss about Holmes' suit. Mary hurried to the kitchen to rescue the haddock. Mrs. Watson and Mrs. Lewis talked about how difficult it was to prepare fish and the conversation never returned to the matter of séances.

The next day, at breakfast, Mary told her uncle that she was sorry she had spilled her water on Mr. Holmes.

Watson glanced up from the newspaper he was perusing. "Nothing to worry about Mary. Accidents happen."

Mary thought about telling her uncle that it hadn't been an accident, but thought better of it. She had been glad that Mr. Holmes had been looking at Dr. Lewis when she knocked over her water glass. He would have known that it wasn't an accident. "Mr. Holmes is very good at solving crimes," she said carefully. "But he's not very good with people."

Watson frowned at her. "He pays very close attention to people. That's what makes him a great detective. Through careful observation, Holmes has solved mysteries that have baffled all others. I would say that he sees people quite clearly."

Mary hesitated. Then, impetuously, she went on, "Mr. Holmes observes people as if they were things. As if they didn't have feelings. He didn't see how afraid Mrs. Lewis was. He didn't see how much she was hurting, mourning for her little boy."

Mrs. Watson reached across the table to lay a hand on Mary's. "Mr. Holmes is focused on other things, Mary. His focus on crime allowed him to solve the mystery of my father's murder. Maintaining that focus necessitates an attitude that some might see as cold-blooded." Mrs. Watson smiled across the table at her husband. "I seem to remember you mentioned that in one of your stories."

Mary glanced at her uncle, who was smiling at his wife, and decided to hold her tongue. She did not share her other thoughts about Mr. Holmes. She did not say that he was conceited—though it seemed clear that he was just showing off at the dinner party to impress Dr. Lewis. She did not say that he delighted in fooling others and watching them play the fool, though that was clear in her uncle's stories. She followed her aunt's example and let the matter rest.

After she married, Mary chose not share her opinions on Holmes with her husband. When George read Watson's stories of Holmes' exploits in the *Strand Magazine* and exclaimed about the man's brilliance, Mary kept her thoughts to herself. As Mrs. Hudson had said, she didn't have to tell her husband everything that she thought.

* * *

After George went out to tell the newspaper of their children's plight, Mary looked out the window and remembered her dream of flying. Beneath her, the ocean swells had been dark and smooth. Above her, clouds were illuminated by moonlight. She had felt the joy of flying and the fear that she might fall into the dark ocean below.

Just a dream, George had said. Just a foolish dream.

Mary took a deep breath. She could not allow herself to feel the pain of the children's disappearance. She could sense that pain—a leviathan ready to rise and engulf her, cold and relentless and powerful. If she let it touch her heart, it would stop her from acting. It would sweep her away—weeping and wailing and weak.

She had to act.

She dressed. She told Liza that she was going to the greengrocer at Portobello Road Market to get potatoes for that evening's supper. With her shopping basket on her arm and Nana at her side, she headed for the market.

CHAPTER 4
Mr. Darling Repents

O N THE MORNING after the children's disappearance, Watson woke in his bed at 221B Baker Street. For a moment, he thought he might have imagined the events of the previous night.

Then he saw his overshoes by the wardrobe, still damp and spattered, his clothing thrown carelessly over a chair. He got up, pulled on his dressing gown, and went to the sitting room. Holmes was not there. His overcoat was not on its usual hook. Watson rang for Mrs. Hudson and she came immediately, carrying a pot of coffee and his breakfast.

"Mr. Holmes rushed off to Kew Gardens very early," Mrs. Hudson said. Her face was flushed from the heat of the kitchen. As she spoke, she set Watson's breakfast on the table. "He said he'd be consulting experts about some sort of leaf he had found. Important to this new case, I gather."

Watson hesitated. "Did he tell you anything about the case?"

"Not a word. But it was clear that he was very happy to have a new case."

Of course, Holmes had told Mrs. Hudson nothing about the case. It would not cross his mind—anymore than he would think to curb his enthusiasm for the chase knowing the pain this case brought his friend Watson.

"Sit down, Mrs. Hudson."

She looked puzzled. "Sit down?"

Watson took her hands in his and guided her to a chair. "Our visitor last night was George Darling, Mary's husband."

Suddenly, Watson had her full attention. "Is Mary all right?" she asked. "What has happened?"

"Mary is all right, but the children have been kidnapped."

"The children?" Mrs. Hudson went pale.

Watson told her, as gently as he could, all that had transpired the night before. "Holmes is on the case," Watson told her. "If anyone can find them, he can."

Mrs. Hudson's hands were knotted in her apron. "Oh, the poor children. Oh, poor Mary. I'll make a basket for her. Could you take it when you go to see her?" Mrs. Hudson left for the kitchen in tears.

Watson was finishing breakfast when Holmes returned to Baker Street. The detective was cheerful. "I've had a very fruitful morning. While you were sleeping, I created quite a stir among the botanists at Kew Gardens. At my request, they searched through botanical illustrations and dried specimens to find a match for that leaf. There is only one specimen of this tree that they know of in London. A very rare and interesting leaf." Holmes was clearly delighted that the leaf was something odd and exotic.

"I'll be visiting Mary this morning," Watson said.

"Excellent," said Holmes. "I'll go with you."

Mrs. Hudson returned to the sitting room with a large basket of provisions to take to Mary: freshly baked scones, jars of jam and pickles, cold chicken, and a loaf of bread. Watson was not confident that Mary needed pickles and jam quite so urgently, but Mrs. Hudson seemed to feel that delivering these items was essential to his niece's well-being. It seemed futile to argue.

The morning was bleak and gray. Last night's snow had melted, leaving slush in the gutters of the cobbled streets. Watson and Holmes took a hansom cab to Mary's door.

When Watson rang the bell, Liza opened the door, letting them into the dimly lit foyer.

"I'm so glad you are here, sir." She spoke just above a whisper. "I don't know what to do. The master is out. I don't know how to help my mistress. She . . ."

"Has your mistress had breakfast?" Watson asked the girl.

Liza shook her head. "No, sir. She says she isn't hungry."

"You take this basket from Mrs. Hudson," Watson told Liza. "Make up a tray with a pot of tea, some scones, and fresh bread and butter. You bring that up and leave the rest to me. We'll find our own way to the nursery."

In the nursery, they found Mary sitting in the chair by the fire. The window was ajar and the room was cold despite the fire. Nana sat at Mary's feet.

Mary was knitting when they entered the room. Red yarn—perhaps a cap for John, Watson thought. Such bravery: a suffering mother making a cap for her lost son.

"How are you, Mary?" Watson sat on the window seat.

"As well as a mother who has lost her children can be," she said, her face unnaturally still. "Have you any news for me?"

"Where is Mr. Darling?" Holmes asked.

"He went to the newspapers. He took a photo of the children to show them. He said he would visit the *Daily Telegraph*, the *Standard*, the *Daily News*, and the *Pall Mall Gazette*. He wants people all over London to keep watch for the children."

Watson reached out and took her hand in his. "There's merit to that," he said in an encouraging tone. "Many eyes, keeping watch."

Holmes stood by the window, his keen gaze on Mary. "You went for a walk this morning," he said. "Where did you go?"

Watson stared at Holmes in surprise.

"Mary's boots are by the door," Holmes said, in response to Watson's unspoken question. "They're splashed with fresh mud. From a passing cart, most likely."

"I went out to ask friends for their help in finding our children," Mary said.

Watson shook his head. "Let us do the work. You must take care of yourself and your husband."

At that moment, Liza bustled in with a pot of tea and a tray of food. Watson motioned for the girl to put the tray on the nursery table. He fixed Mary a plate with two of Mrs. Hudson's scones, well buttered and spread with jam.

Holmes was gazing out the window, watching the people in the street below.

"Did you learn anything about that leaf you found?" Mary asked him. "Where did it come from?"

Holmes turned to look at Mary. "The botanists at Kew Gardens say it came from a tree that grows on a small island in the Indian Ocean not far from Madagascar."

"What island?" Mary asked.

Holmes smiled. "I doubt the name would be familiar to you. The French call it *La Réunion*. In English, it's Reunion Island" He waved a hand, dismissing that remote island. "I am far more interested in the sole specimen of the tree that's closer to home. The botanists knew of only one in London—brought here by an orchid hunter. It grows in a garden on Barons Court, just a few miles from here. Do you know anyone who lives in that area?"

Mary shook her head.

"You're sure of that? No friends, no colleagues of your husband?"

"You will have to ask George about his colleagues."

Holmes studied Mary. "Tell me about your daily routine. That might offer clues and connections that will help me unravel this mystery."

Mary detailed how she usually spent her days: taking the children to school, going shopping, walking in the park with Nana and the children, meeting friends at a women's social club on Oxford Street. Watson noticed nothing surprising in her account.

Holmes listened attentively. "I see that you engage in calisthenics and gymnastic exercise. Indian clubs, is it? At your social club? I can see telltale calluses on your hands."

Mary folded her hands, hiding any calluses from view. She was embarrassed, Watson thought. He spoke up to reassure her. "I'm glad to hear you take regular exercise. It is important for you to stay healthy. Your husband needs your support."

Holmes and Watson were preparing to leave when they heard boots on the stairs. George Darling burst into the room, followed by a young man carrying a notebook.

George was talking as he entered. He sounded out of breath, as if he had been talking for some time. His face was red; his eyes, wide and frantic. "This is the nursery. Our children were snatched from this room, taken from these very beds in the dark of night. Wendy and John and Michael—our innocent children! Tell everyone to keep their children safe. Lock the windows, bar the doors. Protect your children!" His voice cracked as he spoke.

The young man glanced at Holmes and raised an eyebrow. "Mr. Darling had not mentioned that Sherlock Holmes had taken this case. I am impressed."

"You have the advantage of me, sir," Holmes said.

"Reginald Bickers of the *Daily Telegraph*," the young man said. "I report on crime. What can you tell me about the case? What thoughts do you have on the matter?"

"None that I can share at this moment."

"And you, Dr. Watson?" Mr. Bickers asked.

"My niece, Mary Darling, is the mother of the children who were taken. I am treating her for shock and for the terrible chill she took last night."

Bickers' eyes fell on Mary. "Mrs. Darling, you must share your story with our readers. A mother's grief melts even the hardest heart."

Sitting by the fire with her knitting in her lap, Mary was the image of British domesticity—the devoted wife and mother, giving all for her family. "What can I tell you, Mr. Bickers?" Her voice was filled with pain. "Last night, I tucked my children into bed and kissed them goodnight. Now they are gone. Sweet Wendy, my precious girl, who likes everything just so. John, who thinks he's already a man, though he is only eight. And Michael, my baby. He still loves to fall asleep on my lap. Where are they sleeping? Are they hungry? Are they cold?"

"Tell me more," Bickers said, stepping closer to Mary. He was trying for a sympathetic tone, but any sympathy he meant to express was overpowered by his enthusiasm for the story. "Our readers will want to know."

Nana stood and stepped between Mary and the reporter. The dog's head was lowered, her ears flattened, her body stiff. She no longer looked like a sweet nanny. A growl rumbled in her throat.

"My niece is exhausted," Watson said, no less protective than Nana. "As her doctor, I can't allow her to continue talking about this."

Bickers had the grace to look embarrassed. He kept his eyes on Nana, taking a step backward, away from the dog. "A formidable beast," he observed. Then he glanced around the room and noticed Nana's kennel. "Is that the dog's kennel? The dog sleeps here? Why didn't the animal bark or attack the intruder?"

"She was chained in the yard last night," Watson told him. "Even so, she broke loose and raised the alarm."

"Yes, she is an amazing beast." George Darling spoke in a voice that was a little too loud. "She would have saved the children if only she had been here." He was watching the reporter. "It's my fault that she was not! I take the blame. I tied her in the yard." He held his head high, like a brave man facing the firing squad.

Then he did the most extraordinary thing. He crouched on the floor and crawled into Nana's kennel. Built for a large Newfoundland dog, it was quite large enough for a man on all fours. George turned inside, curling up so that he could lie on the quilt that padded the kennel floor.

"I will do penance," he announced. "I will stay in this kennel until my children are home safe once again."

CHAPTER 5
An Unusual Tailor

GEORGE DARLING WAS still in Nana's kennel when Watson and Holmes left number 14. He had sworn to Bickers that he would not leave the kennel until his children returned.

The reporter was delighted by this turn of events. He said the photo of the children would be in the morning paper. "On the front page, if I have my say." He promised to send a photographer to take a picture of the distraught father in the dog's kennel.

Holmes and Watson talked with George after the reporter departed, trying to convince him to leave the kennel. Watson told George that Mary needed his help. George could help no one from inside the kennel.

But George would have none of it. He curled up in the kennel, saying sadly, "This is the place for me."

Mary appeared to accept her husband's decision with quiet resignation. Her expression was resolute, determined. Brave women, Watson thought, wore expressions like this as their husbands went to battle.

At last, Watson and Holmes made their departure. As they walked away from the house, a ragged boy ran up to them, tugging on the sleeve of Holmes' overcoat. Watson recognized Bing, the young pickpocket from the night before.

"'Allo, a farthing for a poor boy?" Bing said loudly. His voice dropped to a conspiratorial tone. "I've been watching like you asked. I've seen a thing or two."

"Very good." Holmes jerked his head toward an alley. "Come, Watson. Let's hear what our friend Bing has to say."

Holmes led the way through a maze of streets to a small pie shop. The shop's proprietor greeted Holmes by name and escorted the group past a crowd of men standing at the counter to a table in the back. He recommended the mutton pie.

Holmes ordered coffee for all and, at Watson's suggestion, a mutton pie for Bing. Bing looked like he could use some mutton pie.

Holmes got down to business. "Tell us, Bing. What did you see?"

"I watched the house all night and all morning. First off, a gent leaves in a great hurry and catches a hansom cab. Then a lady goes walking with a dog the size of a carriage horse."

Bing described following Mary down the crowded market street. She had walked past shops and costermongers, not stopping to buy anything, and then turned onto a narrow lane that led to a warren of alleys and shops. "Then she went into a tailor shop that I know."

Watson studied the boy skeptically. Bing's clothing did not suggest he had ever used the services of a tailor. He was dressed in the ragged castoffs of his betters (snatched, Watson suspected, from washing lines). His shirt would have fit a much larger man; his pant cuffs were frayed from dragging on the ground. The boy's story made no sense.

"How do you know the place?" Holmes asked.

"The gents of the swell mob like his wares." The swell mob was a fraternity of thieves and swindlers who styled themselves as gentlemen, with varying degrees of success. "This tailor makes gloves and the like. Not your ordinary gloves. Something special."

Holmes' eyes narrowed as he studied the boy. "Show me these special gloves."

Bing blinked, taken by surprise.

"Come now, Bing. The bulge in your pocket is plain as day."

Frowning, the boy reached into his pocket, brought out a pair of leather gloves, and handed them to Holmes. Holmes examined them— stroking the leather, holding the gloves up to the light, and folding the cuff back to examine the stitching. Having completed his examination, he handed the gloves to Watson. "What do you make of them, Watson?"

Watson considered the gloves, repeating Holmes' actions and doing his best to apply the great detective's methods. "Fine leather," Watson said. "Very thin, very soft. But it's marred here and there." He pointed out a few marks on the leather. "That seems strange, given the quality of the workmanship. Why use an inferior portion of the hide?"

"Strange indeed," Holmes said, clearly enjoying himself. "What animal's skin do you think provided this fine leather?"

Watson frowned. "Lamb, perhaps? Or rabbit?"

"You are on the right track with that last idea. But rabbits are far from abundant in the streets of London." Holmes took the gloves from Watson's hand. "The marks you pointed out are characteristic of a certain small animal—and it's not a lamb or a rabbit. Look carefully and you will see that they are bite marks."

Watson looked at the marks more closely and recoiled. Yes, they were bites. During his service as an army surgeon, he'd seen similar bite marks on a soldier in a particularly appalling field hospital. His stay there had been blessedly brief. At night, he had heard squeals as rats ran and fought in the dark. "A rat," he said with distaste.

"London sewer rat, I'd say. Along the edge here, you can see a few hairs, not removed in the tanning. By the color, I'd guess this rat came from down by the docks. The vermin there tend toward brown hair grizzled with black, as the ships bring in immigrant rats to mingle with the local stock."

"You're saying this leather is made from rat skins?"

"No doubt about it."

"I suppose you're working on a monograph on the subject."

Holmes shook his head. "Hardly worth my time. Identifying leathers rarely figures in solving crimes." Holmes turned the rat-skin gloves over in his hands. "The stitching is quite telling. A sailor or sailmaker stitched these—the manner of fastening the thread at the end of the seam is unique to that trade."

Holmes turned back to Bing. "Do you think it wise to have pinched merchandise from a friend of the swell mob?"

The boy colored. "He don't know it was me. And I won't be going back there."

"How much do you anticipate selling these for?" Holmes asked him.

He named a price, greatly inflated, Watson guessed. Holmes raised an eyebrow.

"They are fine leather," Bing said, his tone confident.

"Rat leather," Watson said with distaste.

"The gents in the swell mob think they're bang-up," Bing observed. "I know I could get that."

Holmes counted out coins to pay for the gloves.

"We must go to visit this rat-skin tailor," Holmes said. "We need to know what business your niece has with him."

Watson and Holmes made their way through a warren of dingy streets and dreary alleys, following the directions that Bing had given them. They passed a pub. The sounds of revelry spilling from the open door made the afternoon seem even gloomier.

A sign on the tailor's shop door read: SAMUEL SMALLS, TAILOR.

Holmes rapped on the door.

A high, cracked voice sang out from inside the shop. "Come in, matey!" The words were followed by hysterical laughter.

Before Holmes could push the door open, a deep and soothing voice spoke from inside the shop. "Belay that, Captain Flint. There's a good fellow."

The laughter stopped and the door opened. The man in the doorway was broad shouldered and tall. His features were well proportioned and handsome. His curly hair was blond; his blue eyes, bright and intelligent; his skin, as dark as the night sky.

He regarded Holmes with interest, then glanced at Watson and smiled. His expression was that of a man meeting an old friend, though Watson was certain he had never seen this man before.

"Good afternoon," Holmes said. "We're looking for the man who made these gloves."

The man looked at the gloves in Holmes' hands. "I'm Sam Smalls and those gloves are my work."

Before Holmes could say another word, the high voice that had called to them through the door spoke again. "Come in, matey! Look lively, matey!"

The tailor stepped back. "Captain Flint is quite right. You should come in." Sam Smalls turned and walked across the wooden floor of the shop. Each time he stepped with his right leg, Watson heard the creak of moving springs and a thump.

In place of his right leg, Sam had an artificial leg. Not a simple peg leg, but an elaborate creation crafted from hardwood and leather and springs by the expert craftsmen on London's Cork Street. Known as a cork leg for its street of origin, this artificial limb, with its articulated joint, allowed a one-legged man to walk with reasonable confidence on smooth ground.

The tailor shop was sparsely furnished. Against one wall, wooden shelves were stacked with cured leather—rat skins, Watson thought with distaste. A worktable was by the window. Four wooden packing crates were set by the table to serve as stools. From a perch in the corner, a gray parrot eyed them and clacked its beak.

"Pretty bird," the parrot muttered in its cracked voice, as if reassuring itself. "Captain Flint is a pretty bird."

"Aye, Captain," Sam said, holding his finger near the perch. "Come and join us."

The parrot fluffed its feathers, stepped onto the proffered finger, and sidled up Sam's arm to his shoulder. Sam took a seat on a crate and gestured to the other crates, inviting Holmes and Watson to sit, and they did.

Holmes laid the gloves that Bing had stolen on the table. "We recovered these from a young man who had taken them in error."

"Is that what you call it? I'd call it thievery, pure and simple. The lad ran in, snatched them from the table, and dashed away. I couldn't hope to catch him. I'm not much for running these days." The man's diction was that of a gentleman; his clothing marked him as a prosperous tradesman.

Watson studied Sam's face and tried to imagine how this black man had come to own a tailor shop in the heart of London. And how had his niece come to know Sam Smalls? Watson could imagine no business that would have brought his niece to this neighborhood, nor to this small shop.

"Bottle of rum," the parrot said. The bird stared at Watson, swiveling its head to regard him with one golden eye, and then with the other. "Bottle of rum." Then, after a moment. "Biscuit."

"Good idea, Captain. It's a chilly afternoon, gentlemen. Best we warm ourselves a bit." Sam leaned over and lifted the top off the packing crate that neither Holmes nor Watson had selected as a seat. Pushing aside some loose cloth, he lifted out a brown bottle and a metal biscuit tin. He set them on the table. His hand returned to the crate and emerged with three glasses.

He gave the parrot a biscuit from the tin, then uncorked the bottle and poured a generous ration in each glass. "I'll offer a toast." He lifted his glass. "To your brother Henry, Dr. Watson. I never met a kinder man."

Watson was thunderstruck.

Sam tossed back his drink. When he met Watson's eyes again, he smiled. "I couldn't keep up the playacting any longer. You look so much like your brother."

"You knew Henry?"

"He was very kind to me when I was an orphan in Cooktown. He took me in. Your niece Mary was like a sister to me; your nephew Tom, like a little brother. They became my family when I needed one most."

The man's praise for Henry touched Watson to the core. Though life had not treated Henry well, he had always been a kind and generous man. Watson was grateful to be reminded of that.

"A finer man I never knew," Sam continued. "When I served as his helper in his Cooktown store, he set me many a problem in maths. 'If a pint of beer costs three pence and you sell four pints, how many pence are due?' He would smile when I got the answer right—so happy for me. I learned my sums to earn that smile."

Watson nodded slowly, remembering Henry's smile. His brother had helped him with his schoolwork when he was a boy. "Henry was a fine teacher," Watson said.

Sam refilled the glasses, still smiling.

"You knew Henry Watson in Cooktown," Holmes said. "Did you come along when he and Mary returned to London?"

Sam shook his head. "Young Tom went to sea, and I went with him. We signed on as cabin boys on a merchant ship, a square-rigger loaded with good Australian wool and bound for England. We waved goodbye to Mary and Henry, saying that we would meet again in England. But our ship met with an ill fate. A storm overtook us off the coast of Africa, and the ship was lost. We were lucky to reach shore in the longboat. We made our way to Cape Town."

"Tom wrote to Henry from Cape Town, saying he had found a berth on a ship bound for India," Watson said.

Sam nodded. "I had a berth on that same ship. A sailor lacks the power to control the where and the when of his journey. Tom and I found our berths where we could and went where the ship took us. We were shipmates until Tom met a captain who willing to take him on as an apprentice seaman. There was no place on that crew for me, so we parted company. When I last saw Tom, he was happy and healthy. But that was years ago."

Sam shook his head sadly. "I would still be sailing if I hadn't lost my leg. I caught a musket ball in a battle, then came down with fever. My leg swelled 'til the skin was like to burst. Finally, my mates took off my leg to save my life. It took three bottles of rum to drive off the pain and three good mates to hold me down so I would not wrestle the fourth man for the saw."

"When I woke, my leg was gone. For a time, I hobbled about on a wooden peg, made by a carpenter and lashed to my thigh." He shook his head. "Then I came to England and bought myself this new leg. It's not as good as my own, but it's better than a wooden peg. Then I put what Henry Watson taught me to good use and opened this shop." He looked at Watson. "Your brother had gone to his rest while I was at sea. I only wish I had returned to London while he still lived. Mary told me how difficult that time was, and I regret that I was not here to help him as he had helped me when I was a boy. I'm sorry that I never said goodbye."

"But you found Mary when you returned to England," Watson said.

"That I did. No need for such a stern look, Dr. Watson. I am no young rake to take advantage of her, not that she would allow it. She's like a sister to me, just as Tom is like a brother. Mary and I are friends, strange though that may seem."

Watson nodded slowly. He believed Sam Smalls.

"This morning, she came to my shop and told me that her sweet children had been snatched. Her tale was enough to break my heart. I told her that I'll do all that I can to help."

"How are you helping?" Holmes asked.

"In much the same way you help people, Mr. Holmes. By finding things out."

Holmes raised an eyebrow. "You recognized me."

"Of course. Mary told me that you and Dr. Watson were helping her. I was glad to hear it—though having a thieving street urchin follow her doesn't seem helpful to me. She pointed out the lad, said that she thought he was one of yours."

Holmes looked put out that his confederate had been detected, but he did not allow this to distract him from his questioning. "I'm sure it's a comfort to Mary to have your help in this matter. Who will you be talking to?"

"I have many friends. Not all of them are as good as they could be. I imagine you know a few people like that, Mr. Holmes."

The tailor poured another round. Though Holmes continued to ask questions, Sam said little more about his friends who were not as good as they could be. He told Holmes that rats from the docks made the best leather and that rat-skin gloves were considered a mark of success among the fraternity of the swell mob. He confirmed that his gloves sold for the price that Bing had named. But he did not elaborate on his strategy for helping Mary. Nor did he discuss how he had come to be glovemaker to the swell mob.

As Sam Smalls talked amiably about his life, revealing only what he wished to reveal, the parrot added a comment now and then. From the parrot Watson learned that dead men tell no tales. The good doctor already knew that, so the information was not particularly helpful.

CHAPTER 6
There Are Many Uses for a Stout Umbrella

WHILE HOLMES AND Watson were interviewing the rat-skin tailor, Bing returned to his post, loitering in the street near number 14. When Mary Darling emerged from the house, he followed her through Kensington Park and the streets of Mayfair to an ABC tea shop near Oxford Circus.

Bing was unaware of the importance of ABC tea shops to the women of London, but I think you should know about it.

Back in the 1850s, Dr. John Dauglish applied his knowledge of chemistry to the baking of bread and determined that it was possible to make bread without yeast. He was convinced that he could make the process of bread making more sanitary by abolishing a practice he considered barbaric and unclean: the hand-kneading of the dough. Little did he realize that decades later his patented mechanical bread-making process would feed a quiet revolution.

In 1862, Dr. Dauglish founded the Aerated Bread Company Ltd. to manufacture his bread. Eventually the company opened a chain of self-service "ABC tea shops." In these humble tea shops, women of the Victorian era could have lunch without a male escort—a radical social innovation. In other eateries, a woman without a man was assumed to be a prostitute and was immediately escorted out.

ABC tea shops provided a safe haven for women of all types—weary shop girls in need of a cup of tea, maids on their day off, respectable housewives lunching with friends, and suffragists discussing militant activity. Mary's social club, the Somerville Club, was located on the floor above the tea shop.

A door to the right of the tea shop's entrance provided admission to the club. The plaque beside the door read: SOMERVILLE CLUB. FOUNDED 1879.

Like the ABC tea shop, the Somerville Club was nothing fancy. The club was egalitarian, requiring only that members be women of a strong intellectual and philanthropic bent. It was named after Mary Somerville, a scientist, writer, and mathematician who had become an "honorary member" of the Royal Astronomical Society back in 1835. (Women were not permitted to be actual members of the Society, no matter what their accomplishments.)

Bing watched from the far side of the street as Mary opened the door to the Somerville Club and headed up the stairs. A few minutes later, Bing watched as a respectably dressed older lady entered the club. Then half a dozen other ladies followed.

But Bing failed to notice something that all the ladies entering the club had in common. Although the sky was clear and there was no threat of rain, every woman entering the tea shop, including Mary Darling, carried an umbrella. All of the umbrellas were sturdily constructed—not a frilly parasol among them.

Had umbrellas been an item with a high resale value, Bing would have been quite interested in them and would have noticed that all the women carried them. As it was, the umbrellas went unobserved, invisible because Bing considered them unimportant. As is true of everyone, Bing's background and predilections influenced what he saw.

From the far side of the street, Bing waited, keeping an eye on the door to the Somerville Club. Had he been closer, he might have heard sounds that did not match what one might expect to hear from a women's club—thumping and grunting, rather like the sounds one might hear outside a boxing gym. Those unladylike grunts were coming from ladies participating in Miss Sanderson's weekly class.

Miss Sanderson's class was not a secret—not exactly. When husbands asked their wives what they did at the Somerville Club, they described Miss Sanderson's class as a program of physical culture and self-improvement. Clearly nothing to worry a husband. That description was true as far as it went, but it was not the entire story.

Miss Sanderson was an expert fencer and a master of baritsu, a martial art that Holmes himself had studied. She had traveled the world studying fighting styles—learning *jiu jitsu* in Japan; *canne de combat,* or fighting with a cane, in France; and dirty fighting tricks in New York from American bare-knuckle fighter Alice Leary. When Miss Sanderson returned to London, she studied historical swordplay and saber fighting with noted swordsman Alfred Hutton.

Miss Sanderson's weekly class at the Somerville Club focused on techniques she had developed for uniquely feminine weapons. She taught how to use a hatpin to dissuade and disable mashers who grabbed and groped women on public trams. She trained women in methods for breaking free when a strange man went beyond impertinent comments and grabbed a wrist, intending to drag the woman away. She instructed women in the many ways to use an umbrella to defend oneself in the streets and parks of the city. When a woman was in a public space, the possibility of physical violence was always there.

The women who attended the class kept their gymnasium attire at the club. When working out, all the women wore loose blouses and split skirts, clothes that were modest and yet allowed for free movement.

Miss Sanderson and Mary Darling met years before, when Miss Sanderson was teaching a physical culture class at Mary's boarding school. In addition to the usual workouts with Indian clubs, that class had included basic fencing, taught with a flamboyance that appealed to Miss Sanderson's young charges.

From the start, Mary had caught Miss Sanderson's attention. In an effort to get Mary and her classmates to relax, Miss Sanderson had suggested that they think of the exercise as a dance—a ballet, perhaps. Mary had regarded Miss Sanderson with a level gaze. "No one dies in a ballet," Mary had said.

Miss Sanderson had returned Mary's gaze and answered, "That's true. Best that you make sure that the one who dies is not you. The first step to excelling is to relax. Thinking of it as a dance might help you do that."

Mary had gone on to become Miss Sanderson's star pupil, but Miss Sanderson never really understood the girl. She was pretty, she was charming, and she had a hidden darkness.

Unlike the other girls, Mary had been comfortable with a blade in her hand from the very first day of class. Occasionally she used a parry or a thrust that Miss Sanderson had not taught her. When Miss Sanderson had asked Mary where she had trained before, the girl said only that a friend had taught her a few moves long ago. She would say no more.

The two women had reconnected when Mary joined the Somerville Club. Mary quickly became a regular at Miss Sanderson's class.

That afternoon, there was no use of swords. Miss Sanderson led her students through a rigorous and energetic series of exercises in which the women responded to attacks by an imaginary opponent wielding a club. In each exercise, the woman used her umbrella to defend herself and dispatch her opponent. After practicing with imaginary opponents, the women paired off and tried the techniques with each other, alternating playing the roles of attacker and defender.

Miss Sanderson moved about the class—demonstrating exactly how to twist an opponent's arm to put pressure on the joint, explaining why it was best to deflect a blow rather than meeting force with force, and praising students for their efforts.

That afternoon, Miss Sanderson noticed that Mary did not seem like herself. She was working with Annie Maunder. Usually, when those two worked together, they were constantly talking—sharing thoughts, making jokes. That day, Mary was silent.

Annie was the attacker, attempting to strike Mary with an overhead blow. Mary blocked the blow with her umbrella, following through with a move that put her behind Annie, ready to counterattack. Mary's moves were technically correct, but they seemed mechanical, lacking her usual style and grace. Her expression was grim.

"Think about flow, Mary," Miss Sanderson said. "Use just enough energy to deflect the blow. When Annie tries to hit you, make sure that you aren't where she expects you to be."

Mary nodded. She had the look of a woman who was maintaining control with great effort. "Yes, Miss Sanderson," she said. She took a deep breath and returned to the exercise, clearly making an effort to focus.

Following combat practice, the ladies dressed in their street clothes, made themselves comfortable in the club's sitting room, and ordered tea sent up from the tea shop below. Miss Sanderson made a point of sitting with Mary and Annie. It was clear that Mary was deeply troubled.

"Are you all right, Mary?" Annie asked. "You are not quite yourself."

Mary laughed abruptly, a sound with no humor in it. "I am not myself. I am someone else entirely."

Miss Sanderson put her hand on Mary's. "What's wrong, Mary?"

"You will read about it in the papers tomorrow." Mary looked down, clearly struggling with emotion. Then she said, "I will be leaving soon. I have to go somewhere. But I don't know how to find my way."

"Surely I can help you find the way," Annie said. "The Admiralty has nautical charts for every part of the civilized world and some that aren't so civilized."

Annie's poor attempt at a joke had a strange effect on Mary. She stared at Annie. "Yes," she said. "I am such a fool. Of course—I need a nautical chart that shows the location of Reunion Island in the Indian Ocean. Can you get it?"

Annie blinked, startled that Mary had taken her joke seriously and that she had such a specific request. But Annie rose to the occasion. "Yes. If it will help in any way, I can get you a chart."

Annie was well-connected to astronomers and cartographers. Her husband worked for the Admiralty as an astronomer at the Royal Observatory. Annie had met him when she was employed there as a so-called "lady computer," performing mathematical calculations to support the astronomers.

"What is all this about, Mary?" Miss Sanderson asked.

"Best not to talk about that," Mary said quickly.

Miss Sanderson nodded. She was accustomed to secrets. Miss Sanderson had helped a woman whose husband beat her. (Best not to talk about how she had helped, but the man never raised a hand against his wife again.) She had arranged for the escape of a woman whose husband had planned to lock her up as mad. (Best not to talk about where the woman escaped to.) The husband reigned supreme at home, and there were many women who had secrets to keep. That power imbalance led to many things it was best not to talk about.

Before Miss Sanderson could pose another question, Mary spoke again. "I also need a sword."

Miss Sanderson was startled, but this clearly fell within her area of expertise. "A sword? A stage weapon?"

Mary shook her head. "A practical weapon, suited to my size. I have a dagger, but I will need a sword as well."

"Mary, what is going on? Why would you . . ."

"Please don't ask. Will you help?"

Miss Sanderson considered the matter, making a mental tally of the weapons in her private collection. "You wish to wield it one-handed, since you'll have a dagger. Not a dueling blade—something practical. Something light, then. Something with an edge as well as a point."

Mary was nodding.

"A light cavalry fighting saber would meet your requirements," Miss Sanderson said. "It's an officer's weapon, not as heavy as those used by the troopers. When do you need this?"

"Soon," Mary said. "Very soon."

That evening, Bing visited Baker Street and reported his observations to Holmes and Watson. After Bing left, Watson told Holmes that the entire operation seemed like quite a waste of time. "Why are you so concerned with Mary? The poor girl needed a cup of tea with friends. I am glad that she has friends to comfort and advise her."

"You think there is no reason to suspect your niece might somehow be involved in the disappearance of her children, but it is a possibility I must rule out," Holmes said. "I once knew a man who claimed his daughter had vanished, when he had in fact sold her into service at a brothel to pay a gambling debt."

"I can assure you that Mary has no gambling debts," Watson said with some heat.

"Calm yourself, my dear Watson. I provide the example only to indicate that one must explore all possibilities."

CHAPTER 7
A Comfortable Chat with the Ladies

THE NEXT MORNING, Watson found Holmes in the sitting room with a fresh pot of coffee and all the morning newspapers. "Bickers kept his word," Holmes told Watson, handing him the front section of the *Daily Telegraph*.

"Children stolen from their beds," the headline read. Below that: "Family dog raises the alarm." The article included a photo of George in the kennel with Nana peering in at him. Bickers noted that Sherlock Holmes was on the case, along with Inspector Lestrade of Scotland Yard. The article hinted luridly of the possible fate of a young girl who fell into the wrong hands. Bickers' article was the most detailed, but all the papers had something to say about the "Darling Kidnapping," as they called it.

"Mrs. Hudson wishes to accompany you when you visit your patient. She is packing another basket of provisions," Holmes said. "I'll be paying a visit to Barons Court to find out who tends the garden where the tree from Reunion Island grows."

"I thought I would visit Sam Smalls again," Watson said. "His business is grisly, but he seems to be an honest man who is quite devoted to Mary. Perhaps he has more information to share."

Holmes chuckled. "You never lose your capacity to surprise me, Watson. Honest is not the word I would apply to Sam Smalls. Surely you noticed that the crates we sat on last night came from Madagascar, a known pirate haven. That rum came from the same region. It was packed in a crate filled with expensive silk cloth, an item with a very high resale value. The man is a pirate—a former pirate, if you prefer, since he is currently landbound. He uses his underworld connections to find a market for luxury goods appropriated by pirates operating in the Indian Ocean. His tailor business provides an excellent cover for his meetings with members of the swell mob."

Watson did not dispute Holmes' conclusion that Sam Smalls was a pirate. But the good doctor had liked Sam Smalls. He wanted to believe the tailor was a good-hearted man—honest in his own way and sincere in his desire to help Mary.

"See what you can find out about the man," Holmes said. "He's a bit of a puzzle. He's a South Sea Islander—that's clear enough. Most likely from the Solomon Islands. The combination of dark skin and blond hair is often found in that area."

It was a cold, dreary morning. The frozen slush in the gutters had been tinted by London soot to a shade that matched the dull gray of the sky. The weak sunlight offered no warmth.

Despite the chill in the air, the street by Mary's house was crowded with gawkers, attracted no doubt by the newspaper articles. At number 14, Liza opened the door a crack in response to Watson's knock, then admitted Watson and Mrs. Hudson quickly, closing the door as soon as they were inside. "The master went to work this morning," Liza said in a scandalized tone.

"That doesn't seem unusual, Liza," Watson said. "Perhaps premature, but—"

"He went to work in Nana's kennel," Liza broke in. "The cabbie and another fellow carried it from the house with him inside. They loaded it in the hansom cab and off he went."

Mrs. Hudson shook her head in disapproval over Mr. Darling's eccentric behavior. She told Liza that she wanted to fix a breakfast for Mary and followed the girl to the kitchen, carrying the basket of provisions.

Watson found Mary alone in the nursery. After greeting her, he took her pulse and temperature. Her pulse was strong; she had no sign of a fever. Releasing her hand, Watson considered how to raise the subject of her visit to Samuel Smalls.

He began awkwardly. "Holmes has a young helper keeping an eye on the house, watching for any suspicious or unusual activity. The boy told us where you went on your walk yesterday. How is it you know Sam Smalls?"

Mary met his gaze. "I told you I went to tell friends about the children's disappearance. Sam is an old family friend. Tom and I met him when we were children."

"I gather he worked with your father at the store. Why did I know nothing of him? Why did you never mention him?" Watson asked her.

"I have many friends that you don't know, Uncle John. It didn't seem important."

"Your old friend is a pirate who associates with the swell mob. He makes gloves from rat skins."

"He is my friend, Uncle. He wants to help."

Watson frowned and wished his wife was with him still. She would know how to talk with Mary about this. His wife had been a wonderful influence on the girl, counseling him not to push her too hard, to let her find her own way. He wondered what his wife would have made of Mary's friendship with Sam. "The man is like a brother to her," he could imagine his wife saying. "With Tom away, it is good that she has such a friend."

"If you must see him, I will accompany you," he said at last. "It isn't right for you to go there alone."

Just then, Mrs. Hudson arrived with a tray. She had prepared a substantial breakfast—poached eggs and grilled bacon, toast with butter and marmalade, and a large pot of coffee.

Watson sat on the window seat, drinking coffee and watching as Mrs. Hudson pressed Mary to eat. It was clear that Mrs. Hudson was settling in for a cozy chat about domestic topics, such as the best foods to serve while George was dining in the kennel and the difficulties in arranging bedclothes in such a limited space.

Watson took comfort in listening to them chatter about household concerns. Even at the worst of times, he thought, the women focused on taking care of the house, fretting about what they would serve for supper and whether the beds were made. Mary had been a wild child, but she had grown up and grown into her role as a woman.

Watson felt he had made his point about Mary's association with Sam. No need to browbeat the girl. He could leave Mary in Mrs. Hudson's capable hands.

He mentioned that he had a few other errands to do. Before he knew it, Mrs. Hudson was seeing him to the door and telling him that she would meet him back at Baker Street.

* * *

Mrs. Hudson closed the door behind Watson with a sigh of relief.

She knew that Dr. Watson loved his niece, but she also knew that he had never really understood her. Mrs. Hudson did not know all the particulars of Mary's early life, but she knew a good deal more than Watson.

Mrs. Hudson had spent many afternoons with Mary. In the warmth · of the kitchen at Baker Street, they had worked together to make new clothes for Mary to wear to boarding school. They had chatted as they sewed a dress, two skirts, and two blouses.

Mrs. Hudson had told Mary about growing up in Scotland, about how she had run away from her childhood home after her mother's death, about her experiences when she first came to London. Though the very picture of respectability now, Mrs. Hudson had been wild in her youth.

When Mrs. Hudson had examined Mary's stitches, she noticed that Mary's needlework was good, but unusual. "Did your mother teach you that stitch?" Mrs. Hudson had asked about the hem of a skirt.

The girl shook her head. "My mother was not much for sewing."

"That looks like a sailmaker's stitch." Mrs. Hudson's late husband had worked in the shipyard, and she knew a bit about sailmaking.

"I learned it from a sailmaker when I was a girl," Mary had said. "I was helping out aboard ship."

Mrs. Hudson was startled. "When was that?"

Mary had looked up from her work. "It's not important," she had said quickly, then added, "It was a long time ago. Best that you don't tell my uncle. He knows little about my life in Australia. He'd probably think using a sailmaker's stitch is unladylike and I should learn to sew in a more proper fashion."

Mrs. Hudson had considered the girl, recalling her own wild youth and all the things that she was glad her relatives did not know. "Sometimes it's best to leave the past in the past," Mrs. Hudson had said in an understanding tone. "No need to worry your uncle with days gone by."

Not long after Watson left, the bell rang, announcing a visitor. It was Annie Maunder. Mary introduced Annie to Mrs. Hudson as a friend from the Somerville Club. Clearly Annie had come to offer Mary sympathy and comfort.

To give the younger women a chance to visit, Mrs. Hudson took charge of hostess duties. She assigned Liza tasks—taking away the breakfast tray, lighting the fire in the dining room, and bringing a fresh pot of tea and plate of scones to that room. When Mrs. Hudson returned to invite the women into the comfort of the dining room, the two of them were examining a nautical chart that Annie had unrolled on the nursery table.

Before Mrs. Hudson could ask what they were discussing so earnestly, the bell rang again. Mrs. Hudson went to the door and welcomed Miss Sanderson, who joined Mary and Annie in the dining room.

Mrs. Hudson listened as Miss Sanderson offered Mary what seemed to be excellent counsel.

"You are a strong woman," Miss Sanderson said. "Stronger than you know. Draw on that strength. And remember that you have friends who will help you in any way that we can."

"The help that you and Annie bring means more to me than I can say," Mary said. "And my dear Mrs. Hudson is keeping us very well-fed. I don't know what I'd do without all of you."

Miss Sanderson—quite a lovely lady, Mrs. Hudson thought—brought Mrs. Hudson into the conversation. She praised the older woman's scones, entreating her to write down the recipe for her. Mrs. Hudson was flattered and pleased to oblige. She was reassured that Mary had the support of friends, as well as family.

After Annie and Miss Sanderson left, Mrs. Hudson asked Mary about the chart that she and Annie had been studying. "What sort of chart was that?"

Mary regarded her with a level gaze. "I love you with all my heart, Mrs. Hudson, but it is best you don't know too much."

Mrs. Hudson studied Mary's face. Like Watson, Mrs. Hudson knew that Mary could be stubborn. Unlike Watson, Mrs. Hudson felt that this stubbornness was an asset, rather than a liability. A woman needed strength of mind to make her way in the world. Even as a girl, Mary had been smart and capable. She knew what she wanted to do, she weighed the risks, and she did it.

Mrs. Hudson nodded. "I only need to know one thing, my dear."

"What is that?" Mary asked.

"How can I help?"

From outside the house, Bing kept watch. He had noted the arrival of Watson and Mrs. Hudson, then Watson's departure. He saw Annie Maunder arrive, carrying a long leather tube—a chart case, though Bing did not know that, having had no past experience with nautical charts.

Bing noticed the tube only as something unusual, and he noted that she did not have it when she left.

When Miss Sanderson arrived, she carried an umbrella—not an unreasonable precaution, given the gray skies. Bing did not take note of the umbrella, and therefore did not notice that when Miss Sanderson left, she did not have an umbrella.

That evening, George Darling returned from work, still in the kennel. The street in front of the house was still crowded. When George's cab pulled up, the crowd cheered. Four strong men happily carried the kennel (with George inside) from the cab into the house.

Mary asked if George would come out of the kennel to dine, but he refused. As Mrs. Hudson had suggested, Mary served him fish and chips in the kennel.

After he handed out his dinner plate, he told her about his day at work. "Everyone had read about the children in the newspapers," he said. "All of London will be looking for them."

"They won't find the children in London," Mary said. "You know that as well as I do, George."

George did not seem to hear her. He was turning in the kennel, trying to get comfortable.

"Please listen to me, George. Come out of the kennel."

He shook his head. He did not look at her. His expression was that of a miserable, yet stubborn child. "I promised to stay here until the children return."

He tugged at the quilt that was beneath him. She had folded it up and used it to pad the kennel. "I feel a draft," he said. "Could you close that window?"

"I'll get you another quilt," Mary said. She did not close the window. She got a pillow and a quilt, then helped him fashion a bed of sorts in the kennel. Nana watched all this with disapproval.

Finally, George curled up with his head on the pillow. "I will stay in this kennel until the children are home. I think that's the very best thing for me to do," he murmured. He reached through the open door of the kennel and took her hand in his. "The children will be all right," he said. "I know they will."

Mary sat by the kennel, holding his hand until he fell asleep.

CHAPTER 8
Do You Mind the Sight of Blood?

W HEN HE LEFT number 14, Watson headed for Sam Smalls'
tailor shop. He turned up his collar against the cold wind
that blew from the Thames. The air from the river carried
the stink of sewage and rot.

"Step here, guv'ner," called the crossing sweeper, a thin, raggedly
dressed boy no older than Mary's son John. The boy stood on the street
corner, holding a broom that was little more than a bundle of twigs.
Whenever a well-dressed person approached, this boy would leap out
into the street and wield his broom with energy remarkable in a child so
thin and pale. He swept away trash and horse droppings, clearing a path
where people could walk without soiling their shoes.

Sometimes, people tossed him a coin, and sometimes they did not
even glance in his direction. Crossing sweepers, many of them children,
were ubiquitous in London. This self-appointed occupation, considered
by many a pretense for begging, was the last resort of those who had no
other way to earn their keep.

Watson thanked the boy and gave him a penny.

London was not kind to poor children. Wherever Watson went in
the city, he saw thin children in ragged clothes, huddling in doorways,
selling matches, sweeping crossings, or simply begging. The sight of these
children reminded Watson of his missing niece and nephews. Were they
being held captive in a tenement, the boys being trained as pickpockets
and Wendy groomed for the brothel? Were they hungry, cold, and frightened? He could not bear the thought—but he had to bear it. He had to

be strong and confident for Mary's sake. He couldn't curl up and hide, like George. He had to trust that Holmes would find the children.

Sam's tailor shop was shuttered, but the stores on either side of the shop were open for business. The tobacco seller next door was doing a busy trade—through the open door, Watson could see men smoking cigars. On the other side, a watchmaker was just setting out a display in his window—ostentatiously large watches, likely to appeal to the young swells who were treating the tobacco shop as their private club.

Before Watson could knock on the door to the tailor shop, the watchmaker, a jovial-looking man, stepped from his store. "No sense knocking," he told Watson. "Sam doesn't open his doors until late in the afternoon. You can find him in the back. Just go along here." He gestured to a narrow passage between his store and the tailor shop. "I hope you don't mind the sight of blood."

In a small courtyard at the back of the shop, three young men—all South Sea Islanders by the look of them—stood at a tall wooden worktable. Even in the winter chill, the air reeked of blood. The men were skinning rats.

Watson stood in the shelter of the passageway for a moment. The man nearest him held the largest dead rat Watson ever cared to see. The rat skinner was making quick work of the beast. He chopped off the rat's paws and tail, then cut through the skin around its neck. Beginning near the head, he pulled the skin loose, working his fingers inside the slit at the neck.

His hands were quick—he had obviously done this many times before. As Watson watched, the rat skinner turned the skin inside out over the body of the rat, just as a man in a hurry might remove a glove. He yanked the skin free and tossed the naked carcass onto a heap of rats in a nearby barrel. Then he turned the skin right side out and laid the pelt on the table to his right.

The carcass of the skinless rat stared at Watson from the pile in the barrel. Watson stared back. The rodent's teeth were bared in a ferocious grin.

The young man turned to pick up another rat from the pile on his left and saw Watson. "Hullo, Sam," he called. "A gent is here."

Sam Smalls emerged from the back of the tailor shop, carrying a bushel basket filled with dead rats still in their skins. "Watson! This is no place for you." Sam set the basket of rats down by the end of the work-table. "Come inside."

Sam led Watson into the tailor shop through the back, closing the door behind him. Watson looked a little ill, Sam thought. Perhaps the good doctor was overwhelmed by the sight and smell of the skinning yard. Sam kept that part of his operation out of public view after seeing a member of the swell mob, a man noted for his brutal ways, turn green at the sight of a pile of rat carcasses.

Sam found it puzzling that strong, brave Englishmen could be overwhelmed by a rat skinning operation. Perhaps it was related to their ability to avoid thinking about unpleasant things. When a man pulls on a pair of light soft leather gloves, he does not think about the animal that died to provide the leather. When a lady adds sugar to her tea or admires the cotton fabric at a dressmaker's shop, she does not think of the plantations where the sugar or cotton was grown. She remains blissfully unaware of the suffering of people forced to work on plantations in the West Indies, the Americas, and Australia. All that was far away and out of sight. But in the skinning yard, you could not avoid the sight of blood.

Sam washed his hands in a basin, then opened the shop's shutters, waking Captain Flint. The parrot shrieked, "Ahoy, matey!" and laughed maniacally.

"Sit down, my friend. I'll make a pot of tea." Sam added coal to the fire and set the kettle to heat, then joined Watson at the table. "Do you have any news? Does Mr. Holmes have any leads?"

Watson shook his head sadly. "Holmes keeps his thoughts to himself while working on a case."

Sam nodded. "I've read of that in your stories. It must make him a trying companion, particularly when the case involves those who are dear to you."

"It does," Watson admitted. "But his detachment is part of what makes him a genius. His judgment is not biased by emotional attachments. He sees each person as another element in an equation. He succeeds where others fail because he can see past superficial appearances to the heart of the matter."

Sam did not agree with Watson's assessment. In Sam's opinion, Holmes never saw to the heart of anything. Holmes lived in a mechanical universe where a gear turns and moves another gear. Sam didn't believe the workings of the world could be reduced to a set of gears and equations. But he kept these thoughts to himself. Right now, Sam thought, Watson needed to believe in Holmes.

The kettle came to a boil, and Sam busied himself with making tea. He poured two cups and set one in front of Watson.

"I don't think you came here to discuss Holmes' methods," Sam said. "I think you came here because it is very difficult to wait at home for news."

"Every beggar boy I see on the street makes me think of John and Michael," Watson said. "Every flower girl reminds me of Wendy. I had hoped you might have news to share."

"I am sorry to say I have heard nothing. I will send word the moment I do."

Watson stared down at his tea. "Holmes did share his thoughts about you," he said slowly. "He says you're a pirate." Watson raised his eyes to meet Sam's.

"To the Spanish, Sir Francis Drake was a pirate," Sam said. "But Queen Elizabeth awarded him a knighthood. It all depends on one's point of view. By some standards, I was a pirate. In any case, I am a tailor now."

"You fence stolen goods for pirates."

"Sometimes, old friends provide me with goods that they would like to sell," Sam said. "I don't ask where those goods came from. I have found it doesn't pay to be overly inquisitive."

"Holmes says you come from the Solomon Islands. But you puzzle him."

"I take it as an accomplishment to have puzzled Sherlock Holmes."

"You puzzle me, too." Watson spoke in a rush. "You make your living skinning the worst sort of vermin and making gloves for criminals. You are a pirate, a fence, and a tailor for the swell mob. But you sound like a gentleman, you knew my brother, and you are an old friend of my niece. How am I to make sense of all this?"

"Sometimes, it's difficult to make sense of the world," Sam said softly.

He studied Watson. What could he tell this well-meaning man? Like his brother, Watson was a kind-hearted man with a narrow view of the world. Watson believed the British Empire was doing the rest of the world a favor by sharing their civilization and its benefits. Watson took it for granted that the original inhabitants of the lands that Britain had annexed were savages. No doubt he thought that Sam was fortunate to have left his island home behind, lucky to have become "civilized."

Sam decided to tell Watson a few truths, but only a few. He addressed Watson's points in order.

"I make gloves because my grandfather made gloves. I skin rats because the leathersellers of London choose not to sell me leather. Criminals like my gloves. I like their money and I tolerate their criminal tendencies. I speak English well because I attended a British boarding school for young gentlemen. Mary and I met when we were children. Mary introduced me to your brother." He shrugged. "Simple enough." If he left enough out, it was simple, Sam thought.

But Sam did not stop there. "What you really want to know, I think, is whether you can trust me." He reached out and laid his hand on Watson's shoulder. "I will tell you this—I will move heaven and earth to reunite Mary with her children. But I warn you that I will do things that a fine and upright man like you would never do. Like your brother, you are a respectable man. I am no such thing. I have led a hard life and I am a hard man." He squeezed Watson's shoulder, then released him. "You can tell Holmes that I am on the case. And I hope you will come and visit again."

CHAPTER 9
A Very Respectable Ailment

OVER THE NEXT week, Watson visited his niece each day to check on her well-being. Number 14 remained the object of great public curiosity. Thanks to George's activities, the story of the children's abduction was still front-page news.

George had sworn he would stay in the kennel until his children were found, and he was keeping that promise. The newspapers reported that he took his meals in the kennel. He slept in the kennel, curled up on a blanket. Each weekday morning, the kennel (with George Darling inside) was carried to a hansom cab and conveyed to his office. A crowd gathered to watch and cheer as Mr. Darling left for work. Each weekday evening, he returned home in the same way.

Watson thought George was a fool, but sometimes he envied the man. George had found something that gave him the illusion that he was helping. Watson had no such illusion. He felt helpless.

Holmes was rarely home. Some days, the only evidence of his presence was the smell of tobacco smoke in the sitting room. When their paths did cross, Holmes asked Watson what he had learned about Sam, but had little to say about his own discoveries. The tree at Barons Court was nothing much, just a small and scraggly bush. The orchid hunter was away on an expedition, and there seemed to be no way to connect him to this case.

Lestrade was swamped with leads about baby farmers, children working in brothels, and pickpocket rings. Investigation of these reports disrupted a number of criminal enterprises, but yielded no useful information about the whereabouts of Wendy, John, and Michael.

Watson was tired, bone tired. His sleep was troubled by terrible dreams. Each dream was different, but in every one, the children were in peril. They were lost in the streets of London—cold and hungry. They were captive in a dark place—a basement, a locked attic, a cave. They were menaced by a shadowy figure. He always woke with his heart pounding, ready to fight the enemy and rescue the children. He was a man of action, but there was no action he could take.

A week and a day after the children disappeared, Watson woke from his uneasy sleep, dressed for his morning visit to Mary, and went to the sitting room. There he found Holmes, drinking coffee and perusing the newspaper.

"Good morning, Watson," the detective said, as if it were an ordinary morning.

"Holmes! What news do you have for me?"

The detective smiled. "Yesterday, I played the part of an idle gentleman for a long and tedious afternoon. Chatting about nothing in particular can be very hard labor indeed, requiring an enormous effort of will."

Watson could tell by Holmes' manner that the detective would take his time sharing what he had learned. "Where did you perform this difficult task?" Watson asked, doing his best to keep his impatience out of his voice.

Holmes named an exclusive gentlemen's club that catered to actors, men of letters, and patrons of the theatrical arts. "A former client is a member. I asked him to invite me as his guest. That gave me the opportunity to talk at length with Mr. James M. Barrie, the playwright in whose home your niece met her husband. Fortunately, Mrs. Hudson remembered who had hosted that long-ago dinner party."

It took Watson a moment to process this. Why was Holmes still wasting his time investigating Mary's past? "I don't see how that's relevant."

"My dear Watson, you seem to have forgotten what your own accounts make clear. Solutions arise from careful observation of trivial details. Your family history is part of the picture. A very important piece of the puzzle."

Watson frowned. "All right. Mary met George there at a dinner party given by James Barrie. Why does that matter?"

Holmes went on. "Talking with Barrie gave me a new perspective on Mary's life. You see, Barrie met her for the first time when she performed with Professor Hartl's Corps of Viennese Fencing Ladies."

"What are you talking about?" Watson was shocked. Professor Hartl was a world-renowned fencer. Watson remembered when his troupe of fencing ladies had toured Europe to great acclaim. Watson's wife had mentioned that she was interested in attending a performance, but Watson and Holmes had been working on a case at the time, and he had to disappoint her.

"One of the ladies in Professor Hartl's troupe had strained her shoulder, leaving the professor short a player for the London performance," Holmes said. "When he was searching for a young woman who could step into that role, Miss Sanderson, a teacher at Mary's school, recommended Mary to Professor Hartl. Mary participated in five performances. The good professor tried to recruit her to join the troupe, but she declined."

Watson stared at Holmes. "That makes no sense. Mary doesn't know anything about fencing!"

"Ah, but she does," Holmes said calmly. "Her boarding school offered a program of physical culture for the girls taught by Miss Sanderson, who promotes fencing as an invigorating exercise for young women. At Mary's club, Miss Sanderson teaches fencing and saber fighting, among other things. In any case, Barrie met Mary at the theater and was quite taken with her. She performed in a few of his plays. . . ."

"Holmes, this is too much! Why are you unearthing Mary's past? How will this help us find the children?"

"It's clear that Mary is keeping secrets," Holmes said. "Her past is vital to understanding this case. Barrie also knew Mary's mother—he has a few of her paintings—ones that are not as cheerful as the one hanging in the Darling family nursery. The paintings that Barrie owns are in the dark tradition of Richard Dadd."

Watson took a deep breath, attempting to contain his fury and frustration. He was outraged—both by the secrets Mary had kept from him and the zeal with which Holmes had pursued those secrets. He objected to the comparison of Mary's mother with Richard Dadd, an artist famous for his madness as well as his fairy paintings. Dadd had done most of his painting while locked up and under the care of doctors in Bedlam and Broadmoor Hospitals.

"My brother's wife Alice was a respected artist," Watson said. "I am not surprised that Barrie values her work. And I fail to see how this connects to the children's kidnapping."

"Perhaps you are unaware that Mary's mother went mad and drowned herself in the ocean."

"Drowned herself?" Watson exclaimed. "That's not true! Alice died in a terrible accident. A rogue wave swept her out to sea. Henry wrote and told me about it. He was heartbroken."

"Perhaps your brother did not share the entire story," Holmes said.

"Perhaps Barrie doesn't know what he is talking about!" Watson was angry and confused.

"I have other sources. The newspaper in Cooktown at the time reported that . . ."

Watson interrupted. "I fail to see how any of this connects with the disappearance of the children. Why are you poking and prying into Mary's past? Why are you digging into the history of my brother's unhappy family?"

"I am gathering data," Holmes said mildly. "It is vital to know what influences are affecting this woman."

"This woman? You mean my niece?"

"Of course. I have learned that her club and the nearby ABC tea shop are frequented by suffragists and anarchists. I know that she consorts with criminals . . ."

"Criminals? Do you mean Sam Smalls?" Watson's voice was shaking.

"He may be an old family friend, but that does not change the nature of his profession," Holmes said. "I have also learned that Mary's husband has a criminal past. As a child . . ."

"This is too much," Watson said. "My family has been torn apart. I need your help and you give me the vilest gossip. I must go tend to the well-being of my niece."

Watson stormed from the room, snatching up his coat. Holmes shouted after him, telling him to wait, but Watson ignored that. He could sit still no longer.

The weather matched Watson's low mood. It was midmorning, but the thick fog that had descended on London the night before lingered—a foul brew of coal smoke from a thousand chimneys and pungent mist from the Thames, spiced with the effusions of gas pipes, tanning yards, breweries, and soap boilers. The air burned his lungs. Filtered through the fog, the morning sunlight was muddy and brown and dim.

Watson walked the two miles to Mary's house. Initially, he was powered by anger. Holmes was wasting his time examining Mary's life. She was a young mother with a foolish husband who was living in a dog kennel.

As Watson made his way through the thick fog, his anger gave way to melancholy. The fog was enough to make a person doubt his senses. *Am I losing my way? Am I losing my sight? Am I losing my mind? Maybe all three.*

He was happy to reach number 14. Liza opened the door. The gaslight in the front hall was lit, casting a warm light, a welcome relief after the gloom of the street.

"I'm so glad you've come." Her face was pale; her young voice was trembling. "I will tell the master you're here."

"But I am here to see Mary."

"You must see the master," she said, then fled before Watson could say more.

She left him to hang his hat and coat on the rack by the door. He noticed an unfamiliar hat and coat already hanging on the rack. He studied them for a moment, attempting to calm himself by applying the principles he had learned from Holmes.

Both articles of clothing were well-made. The greatcoat was of dark wool, no signs of wear. The hat was fashionable, but not foppish. The owner, Watson surmised, was well-to-do, respectable, probably middle-aged. Watson knew that Holmes, given the same hat, would immediately discern the wearer's occupation, marital state, and what he had for breakfast.

Liza returned. "The master will see you. Please come." There was a note of urgency in her voice.

"I am glad you're here," George said from the kennel, craning his neck to gaze up at Watson's face. "I was just consulting Dr. Hill."

George did not look glad. His expression was that of a man who has resolved to do something that terrifies him. "Dr. Hill, this is my wife's uncle, Dr. Watson. He has been a great support to us since the children vanished."

The man who sat by the fire was middle-aged and obviously well-to-do. The doctor's bag at his feet was made of fine leather.

"Pleased to meet you." Hill stood and greeted Watson with a small bow. "It is clear from what your niece has told me that she values your opinion enormously."

George spoke again. "Dr. Hill is an alienist. He specializes in rest cures for patients with neurasthenia."

Hill nodded. "I have a private clinic where my patients stay—a lovely house in the country designed to serve those whose senses have been overtaxed. Very quiet; very secluded."

Watson looked at George Darling in his kennel. It had been obvious for some time that the man needed help, but Watson was surprised that George had recognized his need. George was a proud man, quick to take affront, always concerned that others might be looking down on him. Not a man to accept the taint of nervous weakness easily. Watson was impressed that George would bring in professional help, that he would consider a rest cure.

"What do you think, Watson?" George asked.

Watson hesitated before answering. How would his niece fare if her husband withdrew the very limited emotional support he gave her? "What does Mary think?" he asked.

"She opposes it," George said dolefully. "She doesn't think she needs help at all."

Watson straightened in his chair, staring at George in disbelief. "I beg your pardon. You think Mary needs a rest cure?"

"Of course. What did you think I meant?" George looked confused.

Watson was shocked, shaken to his core. "Mary has held this house together while you retreated to that kennel. While you have indulged yourself in an ostentatious display of grief, she has been a rock of stability. I can't believe . . ."

"I have to keep her safe," George said in a desperate tone. "I don't know what she might do. She visits that tailor without my permission. She keeps the nursery window open, whatever the weather. It's not safe. It's my duty as her husband to keep her safe. Dr. Hill's rest cure will help her."

A word here about the rest cure, a treatment devised by neurologist S. Weir Mitchell in the 1870s for the treatment of nervous diseases. For a period of at least six weeks, the patient (almost always a woman) was isolated from family and friends and confined to bed for twenty-four hours a day. All activities—reading, writing, sewing, and even conversing with others—were forbidden. All stimulation was withheld.

A special nurse turned the patient in bed, cleaned her, and fed her a high-fat diet of milk and raw eggs. Patients who rebelled against this diet were force-fed. The nurse massaged them and activated their muscles with "electrotherapy" administered by devices that supplied high-voltage electricity at low current levels.

The goal of the treatment, Mitchell noted in his writing, was to render the patient unable to make decisions or act independently, ensuring a childlike acquiescence. In Mitchell's opinion, too much "brain work"—thinking, reading, writing, and decision-making—was unhealthy for a woman, imposing nervous strain and interfering with her "womanly duties." The doctor—and ultimately the patient's husband—would take charge of the brain work.

Many patients considered the cure to be far worse than the disease that it was meant to treat. Some even said that there was no disease to be treated. But who would listen to such patients—afflicted as they were with mental disorder and a severe discontent with the status quo?

Certainly not Dr. Hill. In a calm and professional tone, he explained, "I have interviewed the lady. It is clear to me that the children's disappearance has strained Mrs. Darling's nerves. My diagnosis is neurasthenia. A very respectable ailment, nothing to cause the family the least embarrassment. Many patients suffering from neurasthenia are persons of considerable intelligence and fortitude. A rest cure will do her a world of good."

Watson kept shaking his head. "Mary is unhappy, it's true. That is natural. Her children have vanished and her husband is living in a dog kennel. But I have seen no sign of the lethargy associated with neurasthenia. There is no paralysis of the will."

Hill would not be dissuaded. "Hers is an atypical presentation. Her disease is in its early stages. As a medical man, you appreciate the need for prompt treatment to prevent her disorder from growing worse. She is confused, distraught, hallucinating."

"My niece has been bearing up well under a considerable shock," Watson retorted. "I have visited her daily since the children were taken, and I have seen no indication of hallucination."

Hill remained unperturbed. "With all respect, Dr. Watson, her husband has reported her problems to me in detail. He is, of course, in the best position to notice the changes in his wife. He has the right, and also the duty, to seek appropriate treatment for her."

Watson turned to George. He looked miserable as he met Watson's gaze.

"I know you think I'm a fool," George said. "And maybe I am. But I love my wife. I will do what I must to keep her safe."

"Her nerves are shattered," Hill continued. "You do your niece no favor by opposing her treatment. I have the best equipment available. Just last month, I imported one of the most advanced electrotherapy devices, an Oudin resonator known to be far superior to the apparatus developed by Tesla. . . ."

Watson stopped listening. Proponents of electrotherapy talked endlessly about their machines and the high frequency currents they could deliver to their patients with a carefully tuned "oscillation transformer." In Watson's opinion, it was quackery. But clearly George Darling and Dr. Hill did not care about Watson's opinion any more than Holmes did. A husband had the right to have his wife committed—all he needed was two doctors willing to sign the papers.

"I've drawn up the necessary papers," Hill continued. "I hope you will sign them with me. The sooner we begin treatment, the better for the patient."

"I need to speak with my niece," Watson said stiffly.

From Hill's expression, Watson guessed that he was considering how much trouble Watson could make for him.

"I would not oppose a brief visit from her uncle," Hill said to George. "It will calm her to have a sense of normalcy."

Mary sat at her dressing table in the bedchamber, sewing a button onto a pair of Mr. Darling's trousers. Her back was ramrod straight; her eyes were fixed on her work. Nana was at her feet, a constant guardian.

"Mary," Watson said, and then he didn't know what else to say. He wanted to comfort Mary and tell her that he would protect her from Dr. Hill. He also wanted to confront her and ask her about fencing and performing on stage and keeping secrets from him—because he was sure that Holmes was right about that, as he was about so many things. Watson sat on the edge of the bed.

"Is that doctor gone?" Mary lifted her eyes from her sewing. Her expression was grim.

"He's talking with George now. "

"Dr. Hill wants to lock me up." She stabbed the needle through a hole in the button with unnecessary ferocity. "George wants me to be calm. I have been calm. The time to be calm is over. It's time for action. If I'm locked away, I will never find my children."

Watson took a deep breath. "Holmes is spending night and day looking for the children. He will find them," he told her, professing a confidence he didn't feel.

Mary shook her head. "Holmes doesn't understand what's happening here."

"But you do?" Watson studied his niece. "Do you know something that will help us find the children?"

Mary shook her head. "If I told you all that I knew, I fear you will agree with Dr. Hill. I know that Holmes would."

"Do you trust me so little?"

"I trust your heart, Uncle John. I trust you to love me and care about me and do what you think is best for me. But I do not trust that what you think is best will match what I know is best."

"Tell me what you know, Mary," he said. "I want to help you."

She took a deep breath, then spoke quickly. Her tone was that of a person who is telling a secret that has been kept too long. "There is a boy named Peter. The children have flown away with him to a place called Neverland. I must go there and bring them back."

The anguish in her face broke Watson's heart. "What are you talking about, Mary? You say the children flew away? You know that makes no sense."

Perhaps Dr. Hill was right. Perhaps the pain of losing her children had strained her nerves beyond what they could bear. But even so, surely it was best for her to stay in her own home, in familiar surroundings.

"Please, Mary, I will do my best to keep you here at home, but you have to help me. Be calm. Take care of your husband. He's worried about you."

"My husband is worried? Poor George has taken refuge in a dog kennel." Her face twisted in anguish.

Watson put his hand on her shoulder, thinking of how alike they were in temperament. He sympathized with her frustration, her need to act. In every case in which he had assisted Holmes, he had felt that same frustration.

"I am here and Holmes is working on your behalf. When the time comes, Holmes and I will act swiftly. You can be sure of that."

Mary did not appear to be reassured.

When he returned to the nursery, Watson was deeply troubled.

"So, Doctor, what is your professional opinion?" Dr. Hill asked.

"I will consider the matter tonight and give you my answer tomorrow," Watson said. He needed time to find a way to help Mary. "Can you wait until then?"

"We must act quickly. It's for her own good." George spoke with the manic energy of a man who is trying to convince himself he is doing the right thing. "I don't know what she might do. She talks of flying away. Flying away! So dangerous, so dangerous. She can't go. I will not allow her to go. Dr. Hill will help. She is my wife. I must protect her."

"She is calm now," Watson said. He looked at Dr. Hill. "You will only agitate her if you take her away now. Please do nothing until you hear from me. I can make this easier."

He did not say that he would make it easier for Hill. Watson allowed Hill to assume that. Watson wished, of course, to make things easier for Mary.

Hill nodded. "Indeed, it would be better to have your assistance." He spoke to George. "Perhaps we can wait until tomorrow. If Dr. Watson is unwilling, I'll call on one of my colleagues to assist." He smiled, a confident man who knew that he could get his way.

CHAPTER 10
An Unexpected Departure

WATSON HURRIED HOME to Baker Street. Snow was beginning to fall—delicate flakes driven before the wind.

He was hoping to enlist Holmes' assistance. Whatever Holmes thought of Mary's sanity, he would surely see that she was better off at home than in the care of Dr. Hill. And George respected Holmes; he would value the great detective's opinion.

Holmes was not in the sitting room. Mrs. Hudson said Holmes had left an hour before. "Did he say where he was going?" Watson asked.

Mrs. Hudson shook her head and studied Watson's face with concern. "Has something happened?" she asked.

Watson told her about Dr. Hill and the rest cure. Mrs. Hudson's eyes widened. "Her husband can have her locked up," she said. "He has the right. She is not mad now, but being locked up may well drive her mad."

"I convinced him to wait until tomorrow," Watson said. "Perhaps Holmes can convince George to change his mind."

Mrs. Hudson's expression was grim. "Dr. Hill won't wait. He relies on patients like Mary for his bread and butter. It's a profitable business, locking women up. He will act as soon as he can." She paused, thinking things through. "Bring her here. She can stay downstairs with me. You must tell everyone that she has gone to the country for her health. To the seaside, perhaps. Make sure she takes clothes for a holiday at the sea. That will send Dr. Hill looking elsewhere."

Watson stared at Mrs. Hudson, startled. Mrs. Hudson was the ideal landlady, a good cook, and remarkably tolerant of Holmes' propensity to keep odd hours and treat the flat like a chemical laboratory. But this was a side of her he had never seen.

Mrs. Hudson had many sides that she had never revealed to Watson and Holmes. Watson had never suspected that she was anything more than the perfect landlady. He knew nothing of her wild youth, nor her current efforts in the women's suffrage movement. No doubt Holmes could have deduced them, had he ever thought to apply himself to the task. But why would he bother?

"When did you leave her house?" Mrs. Hudson asked.

"Eleven o'clock, I would guess."

Mrs. Hudson's eyes went to the clock. It was just past noon. "You must get her away now. There's no time to waste."

"Then I must go," Watson said. Wearily, he went down the stairs to the front door. Mrs. Hudson followed.

At the door, he heard a dog barking. A very large dog, by its bark. The dog was tied to the metal post beside the front door. It was Nana—no question of that. When the big dog saw Watson and Mrs. Hudson, she stopped pulling against the rope that held her and looked up at them with beseeching eyes.

An envelope had been tucked under Nana's collar and secured with a bit of ribbon, the sort of ribbon Mary used to tie back Wendy's hair. Watson squatted beside Nana and pulled the envelope free.

The note was in Mary's handwriting.

Dear Uncle,
    I am going to get the children and bring them home. It will be a difficult journey. I am sorry that I must leave Nana behind. Please take care of her and take care of George. I will bring the children home or perish in the attempt.
    All my love, Mary

Watson gave Mrs. Hudson the note. When she read it, she cried out in distress, "Oh, Mary!"

"I must find her. When I do, I'll bring her here," Watson said decisively. "Give this note to Holmes when he returns. Tell him I have gone to find Mary. Take care of Nana."

The snow was thick on the ground and still falling. The walkway beside the dog bore the traces of many footprints—some partly filled by falling snow, some almost completely obliterated. Perhaps Holmes could have made sense of the footprints, but Watson could not. People hurried past, heads down.

A hansom cab was at the corner, waiting for a fare. Watson stepped closer and called up to the cabman, "I'm looking for the person who brought this dog to my door. Did you see anyone come this way?"

The man had his nose buried in the great muffler that encircled his neck. He lifted his head to glance at Watson, then at Mrs. Hudson, who stood at the door to the flat, holding Nana's leash. "Is that a dog? I took it for a pony." He chuckled at his own witticism. "A young woman led the beast past me. That's all I know."

"I saw her," said a hoarse voice. It was the crossing sweeper who worked on the corner.

"What did you see?" Watson asked the boy.

"A young woman. She tied the dog there." The boy pointed at 221B.

"Where did she go?" Watson asked.

"She asked me where to catch the horse tram to Kensington. I showed her where the stop was."

"What did she look like?"

"She was dressed in a blue coat. She was crying. I wanted to help her. She was so sad."

Watson knew that the tram stopped just a few blocks away from Mary's home. But it seemed unlikely that she would go home. What other reason could she have to go in that direction? He remembered George's words: "She visits that tailor without my permission."

Watson tossed the boy a penny and shouted to the cabman, giving him the address of Sam Smalls' shop. "Make it quick, and there's a half sovereign in it for you."

Whenever it snowed, the perpetually bad London traffic grew even worse. At every intersection, there was a problem: two cabmen in an altercation over a fare; a delivery wagon with a broken wheel; a coach caught in a rut. It seemed that every vehicle in London conspired to slow Watson's journey.

When Watson finally reached the tailor shop, he stepped inside without stopping to knock. From the perch by the window, Captain Flint whistled loudly and shrieked, "Ahoy, matey! Look lively!"

"Watson," Sam said, emerging from the back. "What a surprise! Sit down for a moment and I'll be right with you."

Before Watson could speak, Sam disappeared into the back room, fast on his feet for a man with an artificial leg. Watson hesitated for a moment, looking around the shop, hoping to spot clues that Holmes would have seen in an instant. Had Mary been here? He saw nothing that caught his attention.

Watson went to the back door to look into the courtyard behind the shop. A man in a red knit cap and an old canvas coat was walking away, barely visible through the falling snow. He carried a battered canvas seabag on his shoulder; the collar of his coat was turned up against the cold.

"Step sharply now, Marty," Sam shouted to the man. "The tide won't wait. Away with you." Sam turned to Watson without a backward glance. "An urgent delivery," he said. He laid a hand on Watson's shoulder as he escorted him back into the shop. "What's the trouble, my friend? You look like you've had a shock." In the shop, Sam brought out the rum bottle and glasses and waved Watson to a seat at the table.

Watson sat down. The old injury in his shoulder was aching and he felt very tired. He accepted the glass of rum Sam offered. "Mary has run away. I thought she might be here."

From its perch, the parrot eyed Watson. "Look lively," the bird said in its scratchy voice.

"Run away? Why? What has happened? Tell me from the start, my friend," Sam said.

Watson told him about Dr. Hill. "She said she would not let them lock her up. She said she had to find her children. I tried to reason with her, but she was determined." He shook his head. "Mad or not, she would be better at home than locked away by Dr. Hill. I tried to reason with George too."

"George has decided the course he will take," Sam said. "There will be no talking him out of it. Where is Holmes?"

"I don't know. I asked Mrs. Hudson to give him Mary's note when he came home."

"Would he go to Mary's home to look for you? Perhaps you should look for him there."

"Yes," Watson said. "We'll go to her house. Perhaps Holmes will be there."

"You look pale, my friend," Sam said. "Have you eaten today?"

"There's no time for that. We must go quickly."

"You'd best go on without me," Sam said, frowning. "I am not welcome under George Darling's roof."

Watson laid a hand on Sam's shoulder. "I need your help. Mary needs your help. Please. You must come."

At Watson's insistence, Sam accompanied him to number 14. They did not go as quickly as Watson would have liked. Sam—so sure on his feet in his shop—moved slowly on the snowy streets. He had to stop twice to adjust the straps that held his artificial leg in place.

When they reached number 14 at last, Liza responded to their knock on the door. Her eyes were red, as if she'd been crying. "Mr. Holmes is here," she told them. She dropped her voice to a whisper. "I don't understand what he is doing."

She took them to the bedchamber where Holmes was conducting his investigation.

Watson stopped in the doorway, gesturing to Sam and Liza to stay on the threshold. From there they watched Holmes at work.

Two wardrobes stood side by side against the far wall of the room. The doors to both were wide open. In the wardrobe on the left, below the hanging dresses, one of the drawers was pulled out.

Holmes was considering the contents of this drawer. He lifted a handkerchief from the drawer and set it to one side. He peered into the drawer, leaning close to examine the contents with his magnifying glass. He reached into the drawer and took something out—a coin of some sort. Taking an envelope from his pocket, he placed the coin in it, then lifted out another handkerchief and shook something—dust or sand or ash—into the envelope.

He turned then to the second wardrobe, in which Mr. Darling's clothing hung. Watson saw nothing amiss, but it was obvious that Holmes noticed something Watson did not. The detective sank to his hands and knees in front of the wardrobe door. First, he peered at the floor of the wardrobe—then at the floor of the room. He crept across the floor, examining it minutely. He was in the middle of the room when he looked up at Liza.

"When was this floor last washed?" he asked the girl.

She had been watching from the doorway, her mouth agape, clearly astonished at the sight of a gentleman crawling on the floor. "Yesterday, sir," she said.

Holmes nodded. He straightened up and looked at Watson for the first time. "When did you see your niece last?" he asked.

"I visited her this morning."

"Describe your visit."

Still standing in the doorway, Watson gave a careful account of his meeting with George Darling and Dr. Hill, followed by a description of his conversation with Mary. "She sat right there." He gestured at the dressing table, where Mary's sewing box was still open, the pincushion on the table. "I saw no sign she was going to run away. She was fixing a pair of her husband's trousers." He shook his head in puzzlement. "Why would a woman who was planning to run away fix her husband's trousers before she went?"

"Why indeed?" Holmes asked. "What have you been doing since you left here?"

Watson felt ill from lack of food, from stress, from anger, from sorrow. But he carefully recounted all that had happened since he left Mary. "She brought Nana to Baker Street," he said. "And then . . ."

Holmes waved a hand. "That's enough, Watson. No need to say more. Mary did not bring the dog to Baker Street."

"Of course she did," Watson protested. "The lad described the woman who left the dog—a young woman wearing a dark blue wool coat."

"Liza," Holmes interrupted. "Mary gave you her coat to wear, did she not?"

"She didn't want me to be cold," Liza said, her voice trembling. "She asked me to take Nana to Dr. Watson and she feared I'd catch a chill. She put the coat on me and wrapped her very own muffler around my neck to keep me warm."

Holmes nodded. "You should have asked the crossing sweep about the young woman's shoes," he told Watson. "The boy notices shoes, since he earns his pennies helping his clientele keep them clean. And he certainly knows the difference between a servant's shoes and a lady's walking boots."

Watson's eyes went to Liza's well-worn footwear. "Mary wasn't at Baker Street at all."

"Quite so," Holmes said. "And here is something else of note: Mary is gone, but her boots are still here. What do you think she was she wearing when she left the house?"

Watson looked in the wardrobe. Mary's walking boots were there. Holmes waved a hand toward Mr. Darling's wardrobe. "Look at the shoes, Watson."

Watson wearily stared at the shoes on the floor of Mr. Darling's wardrobe, but they revealed nothing to him. "I see a pair of shoes and a pair of boots," he said.

"Not the shoes that are there. Think about the shoes that aren't there."

Watson peered at the space Holmes indicated, right beside the shoes that were there. He saw an empty space.

"There are minute scuff marks on the polished wood of the wardrobe," Holmes continued. "The soles that left those scuff marks were well-worn." He glanced at Liza. "Did Mr. Darling have a pair of old boots?" he asked.

"Yes, sir," she said.

"Mr. Darling is not wearing those boots now—his bedroom slippers are his footwear of choice when he's curled up in the kennel. And here on the floor I've found traces left by those old boots. The marks are separated by the length of Mrs. Darling's stride. Consider the clothing, Watson."

Watson looked at the shelves of the wardrobe. He felt exhausted, defeated, but he did his best. One of the lower shelves had empty space. "Some clothing is missing. Maybe the clothes that go with the missing boots."

Holmes nodded. "Those trousers you said she was mending, Watson—more likely she was adjusting them for a better fit. And of course you noticed that the lady left her wedding ring behind."

Watson looked at the dressing table. A hairbrush and a scattering of hair clips were strewn across the table top beside the pincushion. Beside them was Mary's wedding ring, a simple gold band.

"She's coming back," Liza said. "She said she would find the children and bring them back." Liza's hands were knotted in her apron, her eyes red rimmed and sorrowful.

"Did you help her cut off her hair before she left?" Holmes asked.

Liza shook her head. "She did that herself. All her lovely curls. She cut them all off."

Holmes nodded, smiling in satisfaction. "Then she put on her husband's clothes, dressed you in her coat, and sent you on your way with Nana."

"She looked like a handsome young man," Liza said.

"Bing saw Liza leave with the dog," Holmes said. "Sharp lad that he is, he noticed her shoes and knew that it wasn't Mary. Then he saw a man leave the house. Bing didn't follow. He was looking for Mary, not a man."

Watson stared at the floor. He had failed his niece, he thought. He had failed the children. "Where could she have gone?" he said, half to himself.

"You rushed away this morning before I could tell you all that I had learned from Mr. Barrie," Holmes said. "He told me more about that long-ago dinner party where Mary met George. It was a gathering of actors, artists, poets, and playwrights—including such notables as Oscar Wilde and Lillie Langtry. Barrie invited each dinner guest to tell a story. George Darling begged off, but Mary told a fairy tale about Peter Pan, a magical boy who refused to grow up.

"Peter Pan takes children from their homes and flies away with them to a place called Neverland, the island where the fairies live. That would explain how Wendy, John, and Michael left the house without leaving any footprints. They flew out the window with Peter Pan to the island of Neverland."

Watson stared at Holmes, startled. "You can't believe . . ."

"I can't, but Mary can." Holmes' smile was sardonic. "Overcome with the shock of the children's kidnapping, she cast about for an explanation and remembered her mother's story of Peter Pan. She has set off to find this fairy-tale island. We'll find Mary at the docks, looking for a ship that will take her to Neverland."

"I'll spare you that trip," Sam said. "Mary's ship sailed with the tide. It's too late to catch her."

"Gone?" Watson stared at Sam, suddenly thinking of the man who had been leaving the yard behind the tailor shop just as Watson arrived. "Marty," Sam had called him. A short, slight young man with his collar turned up and a seabag on his shoulder to hide his face.

"Marty, the man who was leaving . . . that was Mary, wasn't it?" Watson realized that he had been betrayed, played for a fool by his niece who did not trust him and by this soft-spoken pirate who pretended to be his friend. "I came to you for help, and you lied to me." His hands in fists, Watson took a step toward Sam.

Then, overcome with the stress of the day, Watson fainted.

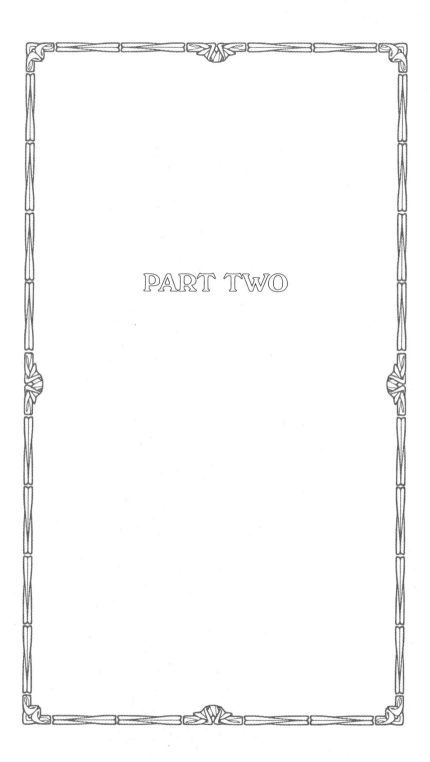

PART TWO

CHAPTER 11
Who Are You, Marty Watson?

WESTFERRY ROAD WAS crowded with slow-moving wagons making their ponderous way from the docks to the warehouses. They were laden with barrels of sugar and rum, sacks of coffee and cocoa, bales of wool, baskets of cotton, and crates of tea—all imported from far-flung British colonies to satisfy the needs of the great metropolis of London.

The air stank of horse manure and sweat. And it was loud, so loud—with wagon drivers shouting abuse at any who blocked the way, a drunken sailor cursing as his shipmates ushered him back to his ship, draft horses huffing in the cold winter air, and wagon wheels rumbling on cobblestones, a deep bass note that played beneath it all.

Sailors who had just made port were eagerly hurrying toward the city, pockets filled with money earned on a long voyage. Other sailors, pockets empty, headed toward the docks, ready to ship out again. One group, determined to enjoy every moment ashore, passed a bottle as they walked, singing a bawdy song (if the discordant bawling in a vague semblance of a tune could be called singing).

Such a crowd of men from all over the world—British, Scottish, and Irish, to be sure, but also men from Asia and Africa, the South Sea Islands and the Caribbean, Australia and the Americas. Every shade of humanity. A cacophony of shouting and cursing and joking in a dozen languages.

Among them, Mary walked alone—seabag on her shoulder, short curly hair peeking out from under her red knit cap. She was dressed as a man and she walked like a man. She alone knew she was a woman surrounded by rough men.

Was she afraid? Her heart was beating fast; her hands were sweaty. But even so, her blue eyes appraised the world around her like the eyes of a young man who knew what he was about.

Did she want to turn back? Not for a moment. The docks were no place for a lady, but apparently she was not a lady. She no longer knew what or who she was.

Years ago, when she had been in boarding school, she had sometimes masqueraded as Marty Watson, a young man who could escort her schoolmates to places where young ladies could not go unattended. Marty took one friend to a play in the theater district, another to an art exhibition at the Royal Academy.

Had they been caught, it would have been a great scandal. But Mary did not see the harm in it. The girls all went to places they had good reasons to be—but could not go without a male escort. Over the course of several such escapades, she had learned to stand like a man, walk like a man, swear like a man, and even, on a few occasions, stare another young man down. Mary had done it for a lark. Just a lark. Nothing more.

But this wasn't a lark. This wasn't a schoolgirl prank.

Mary Darling strode through the mud in her husband's old boots. Ever since her children had been abducted, she had thought of them constantly. How could she not? She missed little Michael, the youngest, hugging her each morning, his small warm body against hers, his face lighting up to see her. She missed John, quite the little man, and Wendy, already earnest and ladylike at nine years of age. But though Wendy tried to be quite grown-up, she always held her mother's hand as they walked down the street, as if wanting to be sure that her mother was still there.

Their absence left an emptiness that only finding them could fill.

But at that moment, on her way to rescue the children, Mary was not thinking of them at all. Making her way down the crowded street, stepping out into the world, leaving the place she had been assigned by society, breaking all the rules—she felt she was right where she belonged. She was grimly determined to do whatever she had to do to find her children. At the same time, she felt like she had been let out of a box where she had been trapped for far too long.

Sam had arranged for passage to Madagascar for himself and Marty Watson on the *Honest Trader*, a wooden brig that Sam described as "a sturdy vessel, but no beauty." He had told her where the ship was berthed, and had planned to take her there and accompany her on the voyage. Watson's unexpected appearance had upset that plan.

But Mary was prepared to go without Sam. She had taken time to consider the role she was assuming. Marty Watson was a bit younger than Mary's own age of twenty-nine. He was a smart man and more than a bit of a rogue—he knew how to sweet-talk a young woman into letting him take liberties that she hadn't ought to allow. He was not entirely honest and lately he had been up to no good—something involving a young lady with a rich father—and it was best he leave town.

Mary turned off the road at the Middle Dock, following Sam's instructions. Halfway down the dock, she found the *Honest Trader*. The ship's figurehead was a smiling mermaid, unabashedly bare-breasted. Around her waist, just above where her human torso became a scaly fish tail, she wore a belt on which she carried a knife. One hand was extended in what appeared to be a greeting. Her other hand was on the knife. From what Mary knew of mermaids, that pose seemed very much in character.

"Hullo," she called up to a sailor standing at the ship's railing. "I'm Marty Watson. I've booked passage to Madagascar."

When Mary Darling set foot on the deck on the *Honest Trader,* she became Marty Watson.

Marty stood at the ship's railing, watching the dock below and thinking about George, huddled in Nana's kennel. George was very good at pretending—so good that he actually fooled himself. He pretended that he was in the kennel to do penance, but he was really in the kennel because he felt safe there. He pretended to believe that Holmes could find the children in London, but he really knew better.

George pretended to be a hardheaded realist, but he was really a man with far too much imagination. When he thought about doing something, he immediately imagined all the things that could go terribly wrong. He tried very hard to act the part of a strong, brave, and confident husband, but he was quite bad at it. He fooled no one but himself.

These thoughts were interrupted by a gruff voice. "You must be Marty Watson." Captain Jack leaned against the rail beside Marty.

Marty had not met the captain before, but recognized him from Sam's description. "Captain Jack is a grizzled old sea dog with a wicked grin, a gold tooth, and the bluest eyes you've ever seen," Sam had said.

"We'll be sailing with the tide," Captain Jack told Marty. "Casting off soon. If Sam's not here . . ." He shrugged. "The tide won't wait."

Marty met the captain's gaze boldly, as any confident young man would. Marty knew that Captain Jack was taking his measure in the way that men had with each other.

"Aye, Captain Jack. I know that." Marty let a hint of an Australian accent come through. This was no time to talk like a British lady. Marty spoke with the rough accent of an Australian miner. "If Sam's not here in time, he'll find his own way."

"What the devil is keeping him?" the captain asked.

"When I left his shop, a gent had just stopped by. I'd guess that's delayed Sam for a bit. No worries for him, but it's best that I leave. Sometimes, it's wise to make a quick exit."

"So you left Sam behind?" There was a challenge in Captain Jack's voice.

Marty nodded. When Sam had heard Captain Flint shrieking in the shop, he had whispered, "If I'm delayed, don't wait. Make your escape."

"It's me they're after," Marty told Captain Jack. The captain could decide for himself who "they" might be. "With me gone, he'll have no trouble. He sent me along, with orders to be gone."

Captain Jack nodded thoughtfully. "Sam can take care of himself."

"I know that well enough. Sam and I are old friends. We sailed together on the *Jolly Roger* under Captain Scratch."

Marty took a quiet pleasure in watching Captain Jack's change of expression. He regarded the young man with a new respect. Captain Scratch was notorious.

"It was a long time ago," Marty said. Having established himself as a man to be reckoned with, it was best to downplay his history. "And we were only cabin boys."

When Mary was growing up, her family lived in Cooktown, a settlement at the mouth of the Endeavour River in Queensland, Australia. The town was named for Captain James Cook. In 1770, that famed explorer beached his ship by the river mouth for repairs.

More than a hundred years after Captain Cook's visit, prospectors discovered gold in the sandy bed of the Palmer River. Would-be gold miners flocked to Cooktown, the nearest port to the newly discovered goldfield.

Henry Watson's store was on the edge of town, with a storefront facing the street and living quarters tucked away in the back. Henry still went prospecting—taking supplies overland to the miners and lingering to search for the precious metal. Whenever Henry was away, Mary's mother, Alice Watson, managed the store.

Alice Watson was a better artist than she was a store manager. When she was just eighteen, one of her watercolors had been exhibited in the Royal Academy Summer Exhibition. A reviewer had praised her work as "an elegant joining of accurate botanical illustration with fantastic imagery. Her mischievous fairies look as real as the flowers behind which they hide." When Alice was nineteen, her father—owner of a small London printing house—had created a line of Valentine cards that featured reproductions of her fairies and flowers.

In the spring that Alice turned twenty, she met Henry Watson at a dinner party given by a family friend. Henry was a dashing young man with more panache than prospects. He was on his way to Australia to make his fortune prospecting for gold. But he lingered in London to woo and win Alice. They set out for the Australian goldfields together, ready for a great adventure.

In Australia, Alice had continued her work as an artist. She painted fairies among the local wildflowers, including several native orchids. Inspired by Cooktown's scenic coastline, she painted seascapes and lagoons with mermaids lounging on the rocks.

Sales of Alice's work provided a welcome addition to the family income. She shipped many paintings to a London gallery. Others decorated the walls of the store and occasionally sold to the local gentry.

Mary's childhood in Cooktown was happy enough. She and her younger brother Tom helped out in the store and played in the wildlands on the edge of town. But in the summer that Mary turned twelve, when her father was in the goldfields delivering supplies to miners, something surprising happened.

It happened on a day when Mary's mother had a visitor in the shop—Mrs. Charlotte Walker, the wife of a well-to-do businessman in town. Mrs. Walker had written a children's book about a little girl who visits the fairies. This was Mrs. Walker's first book, and she wanted Alice to illustrate it. Mrs. Walker told Alice that this was a book that would elevate the morals of Australia's children.

To prepare for Mrs. Walker's visit, Alice had taken down one of Mary's favorite paintings—a group of mermaids basking in the sun by a tropical lagoon. The painting was a favorite among the miners who visited the store and Alice was confident that it would sell in London, but she said that Mrs. Walker would disapprove of the mermaids' bare breasts.

Mrs. Walker was a woman of very firm opinions—on fashion, on literature, on art, and on morals—and she was accustomed to having her opinions taken very seriously. As she walked about the shop and studied Alice's fairy paintings, she shared her opinions freely.

In Alice's paintings, not all the fairies were sweet and happy. Mrs. Walker didn't like that. She scowled at the picture that showed three fairies setting out on a hunting party. Two carried spears; the third, a bow and a quiver of arrows. All three had brown skin and black hair. They wore clothing made of animal skins—mouse fur, Alice had told Mary. They looked competent and fierce. Mary particularly liked the girl fairy. She looked like she knew how to use that spear.

Mrs. Walker lingered at a painting of a blonde, blue-eyed, pale-skinned fairy dancing in a meadow. "This is the sort of fairy you must draw for my book. So pretty. Such a good example for children. Smiling and happy. Fairyland is a very happy place, you know."

Mrs. Walker said that fairyland was filled with flowers. The fairies had picnics with many lovely things to eat. "Little cakes and biscuits," she said, in a tone that made Mary think that Mrs. Walker was very fond of cake.

"Will you draw pictures for her book?" Mary asked her mother, after Mrs. Walker had left the shop.

"If she chooses so, I believe I will. It will pay well." Alice did not look happy and she sounded angry. "And all the fairies will be blonde and pretty, sweet and happy." Her tone was derisive. "As if fairyland is a perfectly lovely place. She thinks she knows so much. Fairyland is not a happy place filled with cakes and biscuits, no matter what Mrs. Walker thinks."

"I like your fairies," Mary said, stoutly defending her mother. "I like the mermaids, too. Everyone likes them. And I think it would be fun to go on an adventure to fairyland."

"No," her mother said abruptly. "It wouldn't be fun. Mermaids aren't nice and neither are fairies. And adventures are not as much fun in real life as they are in stories."

"It would be lots of fun," Mary said, with the confidence of the young.

Her mother pressed her lips together, as if keeping a bitter retort from escaping. After a moment, she said, "Why don't you and Tom fetch me some water? The shop needs a good cleaning."

Mary's mother was out of sorts—irritated by the heat, by the wind, by dust that blew in from the street, and by Mrs. Walker's firmly held opinions. Tom carried water, Mary mopped the floor, and Alice scrubbed the counters. Sometimes, when they cleaned, Alice made a game of it, singing as they worked. But there was no singing that day.

At the end of the day, the children submitted to being scrubbed themselves. After supper, they all went to bed, cranky and tired. Mary said no more about fairyland, but she thought about it. In fairyland, she thought, there were no floors to mop or counters to scrub.

Late that night, Mary woke to the tinkling of bells. Opening her eyes, she saw a flickering light that darted about the room, as bright as the fireflies down by the river. Moonlight shone through the open window. The twinkling light flew past her bed—so close she could hear the whir of wings.

She sat up, rubbing sleep from her eyes. That was when she saw the boy. He was just her size. He stood in the middle of the floor, staring at her.

"Who are you?" she asked the boy, only half awake.

"I'm Peter Pan," he said in a tone that suggested she should already know that. He seemed to think he had every right to be in Mary and Tom's bedroom—as if he had every right to be anywhere he chose. "Who are you?"

"Mary Watson." She stared at him. He wore a tunic made of animal skins and grubby trousers torn off at the knees. "Where did you come from? What are you doing here?"

"I flew here from Neverland. That's where I live." He smiled at her, as if he expected her to be impressed by this.

She blinked at him—still in that twilight region between sleeping and waking where anything is possible. Again she heard the sound of bells. The twinkling light flew around Peter's head.

"What's that?" she asked. "Some kind of trained firefly?"

The light landed on Peter's shoulder. As the light flickered, the bells jangled. Now that the light was still, Mary could see that it was a tiny winged woman, a fairy like the ones her mother drew.

"This is Lucibelle," Peter said.

Mary studied the fairy. She wore a scrap of cloth—it looked like it came from an old flour sack. The cloth was tied around her waist with some string to make a sort of dress. She had black hair, brown skin, and green eyes that regarded Mary with disdain.

The bells rang again. "Why does she make that sound?" Mary asked.

"That's how she talks. She says you ask too many questions."

Lucibelle's jangling had roused Tom, who sat up in bed. "Is it a burglar?" he asked, rather calmly, considering the question. Tom was a fan of adventure books for boys in which characters confronted pirates, thieves, and other villains. A burglar in the bedroom didn't seem unreasonable. Based on his reading, he was confident he could handle the situation.

"I don't think so," Mary said, standing up and moving to her brother's side. As the eldest, she was protective of her brother. She had read many of the same books and was also quite confident in her ability to handle the situation. "It's a boy named Peter Pan. He says he comes from Neverland."

"Huh." Tom eyed Peter with suspicion. "Never heard of Neverland." He was a practical sort of boy, who felt that anything he hadn't heard of couldn't be important.

"He says he can fly," Mary told her brother.

Tom frowned at Peter. "Do you take me for a fool?" he asked, a phrase he had picked up from miners who shopped at the store.

By way of answer, Peter rose from the floor, did an elegant backflip in midair to show off, then flew around the room.

Well, that changed matters.

"I'll teach you to fly if you want to come to Neverland with me," Peter said. He smiled and did another backflip.

Once Peter had sprinkled them with fairy dust, it wasn't hard to lift off the ground. It took longer to gain control. Mary whacked her head against the ceiling the first time she took off.

They went outside to practice flying. That was Peter's idea, but Mary and Tom agreed enthusiastically. They didn't want to wake their mother and the ceiling kept getting in their way.

Mary could hear music and voices from the pub in the next block, but their street was deserted. The moon and stars were brilliant in the dark night sky.

Mary soared high above the store. The air grew cooler as she climbed higher. It was exhilarating—an adventure. Her mother, she thought, was wrong about adventures. This was wonderful fun.

"Neverland is this way," Peter shouted. "Come on!"

"Is it far?" Tom asked.

"Not so far! Follow me." With a glorious swoop, Peter headed for the harbor.

Unable to resist, Mary followed. Gliding down from a height was like running downhill, without the running. She was as fast as a diving hawk; she was as free as a floating cloud. The cool wind blew back her hair, cleansing her of the long grimy grumpy day.

Peter leveled out and spun in the air. "Can you do this?"

She spun—seeing stars and moon above, the lights of the town below, then stars and moon again. She laughed as her nightgown wrapped itself around her legs, then glanced back to check on Tom. He was right behind her, spinning and grinning.

"Follow me!" Peter called again.

Following Peter, they climbed higher as they flew over the harbor—high above the tallest mast of the biggest ship, so high the ships looked like toys. The water below was silver; the town, a sprinkling of lights like stars on the ground.

Peter dove, swooping low over the ocean. Lucibelle flew beside him, her twinkling light marking his path. Mary followed on another long, glorious glide, and Tom came along after her. They skimmed just above the water, disturbing a flock of seabirds that had been resting on the ocean swells. The birds took flight, shrieking their displeasure, and Peter gave chase, with Mary and Tom right behind him. The birds were fast, but Peter could match their speed, darting this way and that, much to the annoyance of the birds.

Mary and Tom were amused by Peter's antics until the birds led him into a low cloud. Mary and Tom followed him, and suddenly there was no following.

Entering the cloud was like stepping into the thickest pea soup fog you can imagine. Mary could hear the birds shrieking, but couldn't tell which way to go. She called out to Tom, "Dive down. Let's get out of this."

She dove down and out of the cloud. For a moment she was alone above the waves just below the dark cloud. "Tom," she called, afraid that he might be lost. "Over here."

Tom burst from the cloud, his eyes wide.

The two of them skimmed along below the cloud. There was no land in sight. The ocean waves had looked cheery in the moonlight. But the cloud blocked the moon, and the waves were dark and sinister, rising and falling as if great beasts lurked just below the surface of the water. Mary shivered in her thin nightgown.

"I think we should go home," Tom said.

"Yes," Mary agreed, then she realized she did not know which way home lay. She spun in the air, looking in all directions, but could see no land, no lights. Peter's flight had twisted and turned, a random path she could never retrace. "I don't know the way."

"We can use the stars to guide us," Tom suggested, calling on information gleaned from one of his books. People always used the stars to guide them.

"Can't see the stars," Mary said. The clouds were solid above them.

"Where did Peter go?" Tom asked.

As if summoned by the mention of his name, Peter swooped out of the cloud, laughing. He was holding a feather in his hand. Mary guessed he had snatched it from one of the birds in flight. He dropped the feather and she watched it fall, fluttering this way and that before it landed in the water. Watching the feather fall reminded her, for the first time since they had left the house, that she too could fall.

"We need to go back home," she told Peter abruptly.

"But we're going to Neverland." Peter looked confused and a bit disappointed.

"That sounds lovely. Perhaps some other time." Trying to be polite, Mary used words she had heard her mother use when declining a social invitation. "We really must go home now."

"All right," Peter said. "Go on back if you must. I'm off to Neverland."

"But we don't know the way home."

Peter waved a hand at the horizon, a gesture so vague it was useless. "It's over that way."

"We need you to show us."

He frowned. "The Lost Boys are waiting for me." Then he echoed her polite phrase. "Perhaps some other time." Mary could not tell if he was mocking her. "I really must go to Neverland. You can come if you like."

CHAPTER 12
She Is Alone and Unprotected

WATSON WOKE UP on the bedchamber floor. A pillow was under his head; a blanket covered him; a cold cloth was on his forehead.

Watson blinked, confused. "What . . .?" he muttered. "Where . . .?"

He removed the cloth from his forehead and sat up. Sam was in a chair by the window, watching with concern. Watson glared at the man. "Where's Holmes?" he asked.

"I am sorry I had to lie to you, my friend," Sam said. His voice was genuinely sorrowful. "Mary needed my help, and I could not refuse."

"And now she is alone, unprotected." Watson's voice trembled with emotion.

The sound of footsteps on the stairs forestalled any response from Sam. "Watson," Holmes said from the doorway. "So glad to see you are recovering. You gave me quite a start when you keeled over. I've asked the girl to bring coffee and something to eat."

Moments later, Watson was seated in a chair with a cup of coffee and a plate of cold chicken, with bread and cheese. He had eaten nothing that day, having left the flat in a rush after talking with Holmes. He had anticipated breaking his fast with Mary. The presence of Dr. Hill had upset that plan, and in the rush of events all thought of food had been banished.

As Watson ate, Holmes paced and explained his observations and deductions. He was intent, focused, keen as a hound on a scent.

"I had noticed that the stitch on the hem of the curtains was a sailmaker's stitch. But I dismissed that as a mere oddity, something your niece had learned from her brother, or perhaps from Smalls here." He cast a glance at Sam. "I noticed that her kitchen was set up in the fashion of a ship's galley—pots hung so that they might sway, rather than falling when the ship rocked. But there are cooks who prefer hanging pots in a small kitchen. I dismissed these observations as irrelevant.

"Your tales paint me as infallible, Watson, but I have blundered. I knew that Mary was keeping secrets, but I did not realize the extent of those secrets. Your niece has been lying to us from the beginning. While playing the grieving mother, Mary was preparing for her departure. Consider the note that she sent you by way of Nana. It was written with a steady hand, not the work of a sudden impulse. No doubt Dr. Hill's visit accelerated matters, but Mary had already made plans. I am still gathering information, but I am confident of this: Mary knows where the children are and she's gone to find them."

"I don't understand," Watson said. "I can't believe . . ." He shook his head, unable to finish the sentence.

"The situation is complex," Holmes said. There are many threads to untangle. I am gathering data, making inquiries. But I must go where the evidence leads. The next step is clear. We must follow Mary. The leaf I found on the windowsill came from a tree native to Reunion Island. The nearest major port to that island is the city of Toamasina in Madagascar. I believe that is Mary's destination. What do you say to that, Sam Smalls?"

Sam did not answer immediately. He had found it difficult to remain silent while listening to Holmes disparage Mary, but he had held his temper.

"Please, Sam," Watson said. "Tell me where she has gone."

Sam took a deep breath, then spoke slowly. "Mary's destination is a small island off the coast of Madagascar. The French called it Île Sainte-Marie, but the Malagasy, those native to the island, call it Nosy Boraha. And the people you refer to as pirates call it home."

"Perhaps," Holmes said, "you could also shed some light on how a Spanish doubloon came to be in the drawer where Mary kept her handkerchiefs."

Sam regarded Holmes with a steady gaze. "I would assume that Mary missed that coin when she was retrieving the other Spanish gold she had hidden there."

"Can you tell us how she came by that treasure? A gift from you, perhaps?" Holmes asked.

Sam shook his head. "That story is Mary's to tell. I can only say that she came by the coins honestly."

"I don't know that you would be the best judge of honesty," Holmes said to Sam. "Who can trust the words of a pirate?"

Sam shrugged. "There are honest pirates and ones who are not so honest." He was addressing himself to Watson, not to Holmes. "I would place myself in the first group. But even those of us who are honest are not entirely so. You must make your own decision as to whether you wish to trust me or not. Just as I must decide whether to trust you. But I will tell you this. Unlike her husband and Dr. Hill, I value Mary's wishes. I believe that she has the right to control her own destiny.

"I will also answer one other question that you raised," Sam continued. "Where did Mary learn to sew like a sailor? I didn't teach her. Mary learned to sew in the same place that I did—on the deck of the *Jolly Roger*."

"Mary has set sail in search of the children," Holmes told George Darling.

After his revelation that Mary had learned her sewing skills aboard a notorious pirate ship, Sam had returned to his shop. George was in the nursery, curled up in the kennel. His face was set in an expression of misery as he watched Holmes pace the room.

The detective continued, "Sam tells us that she is going to a small island called Nosy Boraha. Through my contacts at the London docks, I will confirm that information by checking on the destinations of all merchant vessels that sailed with the tide this afternoon."

Holmes was enjoying this, Watson thought, as he listened to the detective. Just as a foxhound loves the chase, Holmes loved solving mysteries. He also loved explaining how he did it. The client was merely an excuse. It was the mystery and the clever solution that mattered.

So much had changed in the last week. A week ago, the nursery had been the happiest room in the house. Now, bereft of its usual inhabitants, it felt abandoned, empty. The three fairies in the painting above the mantel eyed Watson with malevolence.

"Watson and I will book passage on the first available ship to Madagascar," Holmes said. "We will find your wife. I am certain of that."

The kennel door banged open. George wriggled out of the kennel with greater speed than Watson would have ever thought the man could manage. Moments later, George stood on the hearthrug, his hair disheveled, his shirt spotted with porridge from breakfast.

He straightened his back and held his head high, almost losing his balance in the process. The days spent curled up in the kennel had left him weak. "I will go with you," George proclaimed. "It is my duty as a husband and a father. My marriage vows supersede my vow to stay in this kennel. You need my help. We must rescue my wife."

Watson stared in amazement as George collapsed into a chair.

"Liza," George called. "Come here at once."

The serving girl hurried into the room, then froze, her eyes on George, her face a mask of confusion.

"I need coffee," he said. "And a real breakfast—eggs and bacon, none of that gruel I've been eating. I must prepare for an ocean voyage. I am going to Neverland. It will be quite terrible and I am certain to be seasick, but that doesn't matter. I am going to rescue Mary."

"No need to exert yourself," Holmes said. Even the great detective was surprised by George's burst of activity.

"You are in no shape to travel," Watson said, recovering from his astonishment. "You need to be here in case the children come home."

George fixed Watson with a stare. He meant it to be intimidating, but he did not succeed. He had lost weight while confined in the kennel and his eyes looked enormous in his thin face. His look was one of pathetic determination, like that of an angry child who will not be denied his way.

"I must go," he said. "You need my help."

"Really, George," Watson began. "I don't know what you could do to help. I—"

"I know where Neverland is. I've been there. It's a horrible place." George's voice faltered. His face was pale and grim. His eyes focused on the painting of fairies above the mantel. He shuddered and looked away.

This was a side of George that Watson had never seen. Watson knew that George had never been a soldier. But the man's expression reminded Watson of soldiers who had returned from war, unable to forget all they had seen and done. George was staring into the distance, as if seeing terrible things beyond the nursery walls.

George took a deep breath, visibly pulling himself together. "You need me. I will go with you to bring Mary and the children home." His voice faltered, but he continued. "If you will not accept my help, I will book my passage and proceed alone."

At that moment, George was worthy of our respect. He was determined to rescue Mary, even though he was terrified and he knew it would be horrible. Most people only think about the jolly parts of an adventure. George had an unnaturally clear-eyed understanding of adventure and exactly how miserable it could be. For George, there were no jolly parts. Just terror, pain, and danger.

Liza arrived with a pot of coffee and a tray of eggs and bacon. George turned away from Watson, clearly welcoming the interruption. "I must regain my strength," George said and addressed himself to the food.

Watson and Holmes left George Darling to his breakfast.

"I will go to the docklands to trace Mary's ship," Holmes said as Liza closed the door behind them. "I suggest you pay another visit to Sam Smalls. We need to keep an eye on that fellow. I believe he can tell us a great deal more about where Mary has gone, and he is more likely to share that information with you than with me."

Watson made his way down Portobello Road and through the labyrinth of alleys to Sam's shop. The sun was setting and the street was filled with shadows. A light glowed in the tailor shop's window.

Sam opened the door in response to Watson's knock. For a moment, Watson stood in the doorway, feeling awkward and at a loss for words.

"Come in, Watson," Sam said. "Sit down. I'm glad you're here."

Soon Watson was seated at the table, drinking a glass of beer. "George is coming with us," Watson told Sam. "He claims he has been to Neverland."

"Ah! He admitted to it, then," Sam said.

"He sounded quite mad. He said we would need his help to find the place. I don't know what to think," Watson said. "When I saw Mary, she also spoke of things that seemed quite mad, but when she looked in my eyes and asked for my help, she did not seem mad. She seemed angry and determined."

"I don't think Mary is mad," Sam said.

"Holmes says that Mary's mother went mad and drowned herself."

"And how would Holmes know anything about that?" Watson heard the anger in Sam's voice. "No one was there when Mary's mother died." Sam took a deep breath. "No one knows what happened. Her death was a tragedy."

Watson hesitated. "Do you believe in this Neverland place, too?"

"I will state no opinion on the matter." It was clear from Sam's expression that he would say no more.

"Holmes is looking for a ship that will take us to Nosy Boraha. He wants to pick up Mary's trail."

"Nosy Boraha is not an easy place to get to," Sam said. "You need to know the right people."

"You know the right people," Watson said.

"I do."

"You're planning to go and help Mary." Watson gestured to the seabag on the floor in the corner of the shop. "Can you help us find our way there?"

Sam studied Watson's face. "Would Holmes trust a pirate to be your guide?" he asked.

Watson thought a moment before answering. "Holmes wants to keep an eye on you. And I trust that you want to help Mary—though I know that we may not agree on what is right for her."

"I trust Mary to know what is right for her." Sam reached across the table and clapped Watson on the shoulder. "I will welcome your company, Watson. If Holmes and George choose to come along . . ." Sam shrugged. "Better they come with us than try to get there on their own, I suppose."

Sam went on. "There won't be another merchant ship going directly to Nosy Boraha for a month, but merchant ships regularly travel to Toamasina in Madagascar. From there, I can find a local who will take us to the island of Nosy Boraha."

"And once we are there?" Watson said.

"That's when things will get interesting," Sam said.

CHAPTER 13
There Is No Turning Back

MARTY WATCHED THE docklands of London recede in the distance. The shouts and curses of dockworkers and the rumble of cartwheels on cobbles had been replaced by the shouts and curses of the *Honest Trader*'s first mate and sailors.

The setting sun had painted the sky with streaks of crimson and gold. Clouds of coal smoke rising from the chimneys of London's factories made dark streaks on the brilliant colors. The air still stank of London's smoke and sewage, but there was a touch of brine in the mix, a promise of fresh sea air.

Marty surveyed the traffic on the river behind them, looking for any pursuit. There was none. The *Honest Trader* moved swiftly, carried down the Thames by the river's flow, the wind, and the outgoing tide.

When they passed the Chapman Lighthouse, Marty began to relax. Right or wrong, the decision had been made. There was no turning back now. In the blue light of twilight, the *Honest Trader* passed out of the Thames estuary. The lights on Southend Pier vanished in the distance.

"Mr. Watson?" A young sailor stood at Marty's elbow. "The captain invites you to join the officers in his cabin for supper."

There were three men in the captain's cabin: Captain Jack and two other men. Marty greeted their curious stares with a carefully calibrated smile. It was not the soft smile of a lady, but rather the confident grin of a young man.

"Mr. Watson," Captain Jack said. "Glad you could join us. Meet Mr. Carter, the quartermaster, and Mr. Davies, the sailing master."

"The captain says that you sailed on the *Jolly Roger*," said Carter.

"Many years ago," Marty said. "And only for a short time."

Carter was a burly man who looked like he knew how to hold his own in a tavern brawl. He studied Marty, narrowing his eyes. "You didn't care for the life of a pirate?"

Marty shrugged. "I had business to attend to elsewhere." A roguish young man, Marty knew, would not share overmuch as he sized up his shipmates. "But I am glad to be heading out to sea again." That last was certainly the truth. "London wears on a man."

Carter nodded. "Too crowded."

Over a simple meal of beef, biscuits, peas, and beer, the three men attempted to satisfy their curiosity about Marty Watson. Marty knew what they were doing and took care to supply affable answers that revealed little: Yes, Sam was an old friend. They had worked together, on and off on this and that. Why such a hurry to leave London? Some things better left unsaid.

The men nodded. Marty mentioned that it was very good that the *Honest Trader* was a fast ship, noting with a grin that speed came in handy under certain circumstances.

Marty was careful to remain in character—a brash young man of dubious honesty. "I'll be needing to practice with my sword," Marty told Captain Jack. "I got lazy in London and I need a bit of work. I don't suppose you'd mind if I practice on deck?"

The captain nodded, looking thoughtful.

"Why do you need to practice?" Davies asked. He was a small, tidy man who looked more like a clerk than a sailor. "Do you plan to do some fighting?"

Marty met Davies' gaze. "Perhaps you've noticed that I'm rather small in stature. Sometimes my business requires that I explain rather forcefully that size is no indication of my ability in a fight. A good sword can be very convincing when one is trying to make that sort of explanation."

Marty continued to stare at Davies for a moment, as if challenging the older man. Then Marty suddenly grinned impudently. Davies laughed. The captain and Carter joined in.

From Marty's point of view, the supper went quite well. Only once did Marty decline to answer a direct question. When Carter asked how Marty had come to be on the *Jolly Roger*, Marty said, "That's a very long story. Quite tedious really. I'd rather not bore you with it."

You already know the beginning of that long story: Mary and her brother Tom flew away with Peter Pan. A few hours into their flight, high over the ocean waves, Mary had asked Peter Pan to show them the way home. He declined and flew on.

In that moment, young Mary had weighed her options quickly: she and Tom could be lost at sea, or they could follow this strange boy. She followed Peter and Tom followed her.

It was a long flight to Neverland. Peter quickly regained his good humor, forgetting that they had wanted to go home. He showed off, flying on his back, effortlessly aloft. He told them tales of Neverland. The Lost Boys, as he described them, were a band of adventurers that had a jolly time fighting with pirates and hunting wild beasts.

Tom happily listened to Peter's tales. They were like the adventure books he loved. Tom managed to forget Peter's willingness to abandon them, but Mary could not. Mary feigned interest in Peter's tales of his adventures in order to keep him nearby. She feared he might fly off and forget them.

Peter seemed to take it for granted that she would be fascinated by his stories and happily kept talking. Occasionally, she made a comment like "Really?" or "Is that so?" but he was quite ready to go on without encouragement. Keeping him talking slowed him down, and that was good, because Mary and Tom couldn't fly as fast as Peter.

"Are there any Lost Girls?" Mary asked Peter.

"Oh, no," Peter said. "Girls don't get lost. I came looking for you because we need a mother."

"A mother?" Mary had never been inclined to play games that some girls are rumored to enjoy, where they pretend to be the mother of a family. Being a mother seemed like too much work and no fun at all. "I'm not a mother," she said flatly.

Peter didn't seem to hear her. "Look! There's a mermaid," he said. Quicker than she could follow, he dove down to skim just above the waves. He returned after a bit, laughing. He said the mermaid had told him a very funny joke, and he told them the first part, which had to do with a pirate, a sea turtle, and a flounder. But he couldn't remember the rest. He just kept saying it was very funny. They never got back to the question of mothers.

When Mary said she was hungry, Peter pursued a seabird and snatched a fish from its mouth. Mary tried to be polite, but she couldn't bring herself to eat raw fish. When she said she was thirsty, Peter showed her how to fly into a cloud and catch the droplets of water on her tongue. That didn't satisfy her thirst, but it helped a little.

The moon set and the sun rose. At first, the sunshine provided a welcome warmth, but then it became too hot. The light glittered on the waves, blinding in its intensity.

And still they flew. Questions like "How far is it?" got the useless answer "Not far at all," which was clearly not true. Or it reminded Peter of a time that he had flown a very long way in pursuit of pirates and that led into yet another of Peter's stories.

Mary was tired, hungry, and thirsty when she spotted a small ship on the waves below. "Look!" she shouted, pointing at the ship. "They might have food."

"Oh, yes!" Tom said and headed for the ship without hesitation.

"Let's go visit!" Mary called to Peter. "It will be a jolly adventure!" She had realized that he would do just about anything if it was a jolly adventure.

Lady Emily Hawkins was having tea on the aft deck of her steam yacht. She and her husband, Lord Robert Hawkins, were en route to the port of Toamasina on the island of Madagascar. From that port, they would ship several crates of orchids and other plants to London, specimens they had collected on the island of Mauritius.

Lord Hawkins enjoyed traveling in exotic lands. He had met Miss Emily Taylor on a journey to San Francisco a few years before and had recognized her immediately as a kindred spirit. The only child of a man who had struck it rich in silver mining, Miss Taylor was an adventurous young woman who was heir to a great deal of money. Lord Hawkins was a member of the British aristocracy, with a venerable name, a large rather rundown estate, and no fortune to speak of. It was a perfect match.

They married and returned briefly to London. Lord Hawkins wished to explore islands in the Indian Ocean, and his new wife was eager to travel with him. She had grown up in the rough-and-tumble environment of a mining camp. As a young lady, she had lived in San Francisco society, which was given to opulence. The combination had given her a flexible attitude toward travel. Though she could rough it if she had to, she preferred to travel in comfort and style. Thanks to her father's wealth, she could afford it.

She commissioned the construction of a steam yacht—the very ship Mary had spotted in the distance. Lady Hawkins christened the yacht *Salacia*, after the Roman goddess of the sea. The happy couple sailed to the Indian Ocean to hunt for orchids.

Though American, Lady Hawkins had happily adopted certain British customs—such as the light meal known as afternoon tea. She and Lord Hawkins were having tea on the aft deck when Mary, Tom, and Peter landed beside them.

"Excuse me," Mary said ever so politely. She wanted to grab a handful of biscuits and fly off, but her mother had taught her to ask nicely for what she wanted. "My name is Mary Watson. This is my brother Tom and our friend Peter. I'm sorry to intrude, but we're very thirsty and hungry."

Lady Hawkins stared at the children, cheerfully astonished. She was a woman of boundless imagination, willing to believe in extraordinary things. As a result, extraordinary things had a way of finding her.

The children were not looking their best. Mary's hair was a terrible tangle from being blown this way and that. Her nightgown was crumpled and sweaty. When Tom was learning to fly in the bedroom, his nightshirt had caught on a bedpost and ripped when he jerked it free. Peter was smiling a lovely smile, but he looked even worse than the other two in his animal skins and ragged trousers.

It was probably just as well that Lucibelle was not there. The fairy had chosen that moment to have a conversation with a mermaid who had been following the yacht in hopes that someone might fall overboard. Mermaids rather enjoy watching people drown.

"Where did you come from?" Lady Hawkins asked.

"Cooktown, in Queensland, Australia," Mary answered, feeling it best to stick to the essential facts.

"How did you get here?"

"We flew," Mary said. "Peter showed us how."

"You flew?"

"Indeed they did," Lord Hawkins said. "Quite nicely, in fact. I saw them land." He shared Lady Hawkins' love of the unexpected. "You were pouring tea at the time, darling."

"Can you show me?" Lady Hawkins asked.

Tom, who had been staring at the biscuits and tea with an expression like a hungry dog looking in a butcher shop window, rose from the deck and hovered a few feet above it, his feet kicking a bit. From this position, he asked, "Could I have a biscuit?"

"Please, ma'am," Mary said, an edge in her voice. Manners were all very well, but she was getting impatient. "We are very hungry."

"Of course," Lady Hawkins said. "Let me make you each a plate and you can tell me more about your journey."

"I must take a photograph of this," Lord Hawkins said, his eyes fixed on the hovering boy. Lord Hawkins had recently acquired a dry plate camera and he delighted in experimenting with it. He headed into the cabin for the camera.

For a time, the children were busy with tea and biscuits and jam and butter. Lord Hawkins returned with his camera and proceeded to set it up and take photos of the children.

"Tell me," Lady Hawkins said as the children devoured biscuits, "how did this adventure begin?"

"Peter came in our bedroom window," Mary said. "He comes from a place called Neverland. We're going there with him." Mary leaned closer and spoke more softly. "We've been flying for a very long time."

"If you started in Australia, you have come a very long way," Lady Hawkins said thoughtfully.

"Where are we now?" Mary asked.

"In the Indian Ocean. Lord Hawkins and I were visiting the island of Mauritius and now we are heading to Madagascar."

Mary's knowledge of geography was limited. "I don't know those places," she told Lady Hawkins. "I wonder if you have a map I might see. I need to figure out the way home." Mary glanced toward Peter. "Peter won't show us," she said quietly. "He insists we go to Neverland."

Peter and Tom were listening to Lord Hawkins. He had his camera set up and he wanted them to hover so he could get a photo.

"Stay here with me," Lady Hawkins said decisively, taking the girl's hand. Like Mary, she spoke in a low conspiratorial tone. "Your friend Peter does not seem reliable. You and your brother can travel with us. I would love your company. We will get you home, though it may take some time."

"There's a whale!" Peter shouted just then, pointing to the horizon.

"Where?" Tom was excited. He knew about whales from having read a book whose author had borrowed heavily (without attribution) from Jules Verne's novel, *Twenty Thousand Leagues Under the Sea*.

"Right there! Follow me." Suddenly, Peter was in flight, with Tom right behind him.

"Wait," Mary called, but her cry was too late. The boys were flying away. "I must catch my brother! I'll come back."

Mary took flight. Peter and Tom were barely visible in the distance, skimming low over the ocean. The boys vanished for a moment in a cloud that appeared from nowhere, just over the water's surface.

The cloud disappeared, and Mary could see the boys again. "Tom," she called. "Come back!" The wind snatched her words, carrying them away. She saved her breath and continued the chase.

The boys did not follow a straight course. Rather, they flew this way and that. Their path was marked by strange clouds that seemed to rise suddenly from the sea. She caught up at last.

"Look down!" Tom shouted as she came alongside him.

She looked down and saw something enormous in the water—something as smooth and shiny as a polished boot. It broke the surface and suddenly she was enveloped in a cloud of warm steam that smelled like dead fish and ocean brine. It was the breath of a whale.

When the warm moist air blasting from the animal's blowhole met the cold air above the ocean water, it made a sudden cloud. Sun shining on the airborne water droplets made a brilliant rainbow that lingered in a moment. Then the rainbow vanished and the stench of dead fish faded as the cloud of whale's breath dissipated.

The whale's tail lifted from the water, then the enormous great beast dove below the waves, only to be followed by another whale. Over a dozen whales were swimming together.

"There's a mother and a baby," Tom told her in a babble of excitement. "The baby is as big as a coach!"

Mary had to see the baby. Indeed, the young whale was as big as a coach. It was following its mother, a whale the size of a tram. As Tom and Mary flew low over the water, the mother surfaced again, rolling in the water to look up at them with one dark eye, barely visible above the curve of her mouth.

Mary forgot about the fishy stench. "She's looking at us," Mary cried, just as excited as Tom.

They followed the mother whale and her baby, flying low over the water when the whales submerged and watching to see where the animals might surface again. The great beasts seemed as curious about the children as the children were about them. Each time the mother whale surfaced, she rolled in the water to eye them.

To Mary, the whales seemed just as magical as Peter's fairy. So enormous, so calm, spouting rainbows as they traveled to some mysterious destination. She and Tom followed them until the mother whale dove deep, followed by her baby and the other whales. Then Mary looked around and realized that she had no idea where Lady Hawkins' ship was.

"Where's the ship?" she asked Peter.

"The ship? Oh, I don't know. Come on! Follow me!" And he was off again, flying fast. Tom took off after him.

Mary hesitated for a moment, then realized that once again she had little choice. She followed. Maybe, she thought, they'd find another ship.

They didn't. No more ships, no more whales, just a long flight above the ocean as the sun sank toward the horizon.

Mary noted that they were flying toward the setting sun, which meant they were flying west. She remembered a map of the world that her father had once shown her. North of Australia, the ocean was crowded with a mess of islands, packed together like puzzle pieces ready to be joined. But the Indian Ocean was an empty expanse of blue.

When the sun dipped below the horizon, Venus, the evening star, shimmered in the deep blue twilight sky. The moon rose behind them, its light glittering on the ocean swells. Her father had taught her to find the Southern Cross and she looked for it as the sky darkened. She found the four bright stars of the constellation in the sky to her left just as Peter called out, "There's Neverland."

The island was a dark shape on the horizon. As they flew closer, Mary could make out details: a lagoon on the eastern shore, a dark mountain to the north. Peter flew low over the island with Mary and Tom.

Mary heard a chorus of strange sounds from the trees below—the mingled songs of birds and frogs, the coughing growl of a leopard, a terrifying howl that she later came to know was the call of a monkey. She was suddenly filled with a sense of danger.

They skimmed over the dense canopy of jungle trees. Here and there, she caught a glimpse of a clearing or a path snaking beneath the branches.

Peter swooped down into one of these clearings, landing with a shout. "I'm back!" Mary and Tom landed beside him, grateful for the feeling of land under their feet.

Half a dozen boys emerged from the shadows. In the moonlight, Mary could see that they were dirty and ragged, clad in animal skins and clothing that was little better than rags. They looked hopefully at Peter.

"I've brought a mother for you at last!" he shouted, gesturing to Mary.

"I'm not a mother," she said loudly, just as she had when Peter had raised the subject before. But her words were lost beneath a chorus of cheers from the boys.

There were seven Lost Boys just then. Six of them—Tootles, Curly, Nibs, Slightly, and the Twins—were British boys, with pale skin beneath the dirt and suntan. The seventh, a tall boy with dark skin, blue eyes, and curly blond hair, was Sam Smalls.

CHAPTER 14
The Cannibal King

S AM SMALLS WAS born on an island about a thousand miles northeast of Australia. His father was a missionary; his mother was a woman of the islands.

Sam's missionary father, Matthew Smalls, taught Sam to speak English and told him about the Ten Commandments and the Holy Trinity—God the Father, God the Son, and God the Holy Spirit. His mother, Kepa, taught him to speak like everyone else in the village, to have a good heart and to respect his ancestral spirits and the wild spirits of the bush. She also taught him to listen to his father enough, but not too much. She taught him to listen to his grandfather more than that.

Sam's grandfather, Biuku—along with Sam's uncles and cousins— taught him how to fish in the sea, how to climb trees to get coconuts, how to sail a canoe, and how to find his way from island to island. Biuku was the best navigator in the village.

One day, when Sam was eight years old, a ship called the *Black Dog* anchored in the bay by Sam's village and sent a launch to shore. Sam's father and grandfather went to meet the sailors.

"We have cloth to trade," said the biggest sailor, a bearded man with golden hair. He had a length of bright red cloth. "We want to trade for water and fruit."

Matthew Smalls translated what the man said to Biuku—adding a warning that they needed to be careful of these men. They could be pirates.

But the cloth was a beautiful color and there was enough of it to make bright clothes for all the village grandmothers. So Sam's grandmother brought out a basket of bananas and coconuts, and Biuku pointed out the path to the river where the sailors could fill their barrels. The golden-haired man smiled and agreed to the trade.

The golden-haired man stayed on the beach while the strongest young men in the village went with the sailors to fill the barrels with water. Sam followed the young men, hanging back and listening to the sailors talk.

A skinny sailor wearing a red shirt seemed to be in charge. "These are the kind of fellas we're looking for all right," Redshirt was saying. "Strong boys—just what we want."

Redshirt pulled a flask out of his pocket and called to Sam's cousins. "Have a drink, boys," he said. "It's rum—very good stuff. Plenty more for you on the ship if you help us." He took a swig from the flask to demonstrate, then offered it to Sam's oldest cousin.

"What is he talking about?" Sam's oldest cousin asked.

Sam translated. The cousins gathered around and drank. Soon the cousins were laughing and talking as loudly as Redshirt.

The cousins filled the barrels, rolled them along the path to the beach, and loaded them into the launch. The grandmothers were still examining the cloth. Matthew Smalls and Biuku were watching the women, smiling at their pleasure.

When all the water barrels were in the launch. Redshirt motioned Sam's cousins aboard. The boys were not so steady on their feet, and the sailors were telling them, "Come on! More rum for you!" The golden-haired man had returned to the launch.

Before Sam realized what was going on, his cousins were in the launch and the launch was in the water. His youngest cousin, still laughing, moved to jump out of the boat, but the golden-haired man pushed him back in. When he tried a second time, the golden-haired man hit him with an uppercut to the belly that left the boy doubled over and gasping for breath.

The sailors were rowing for the ship as fast as they could. Other sailors were hitting Sam's cousins, knocking them down into the bottom of the boat and striking them when they tried to get up.

Sam shouted for his father, for his grandfather, for his uncles. The men came running. There was shouting and confusion and the older men gave chase in their canoes. By that time, the launch had reached the ship. From shore, Sam watched the sailors haul his unconscious cousins onto the ship, hoist the launch, and raise the anchor.

As the islanders' canoes neared the ship, Sam heard the sharp crack of pistol fire and saw his grandfather drop his paddle. Then the ship's sails were up. The afternoon wind filled the sails.

The ship sailed and Sam's cousins were gone.

The sailors were blackbirding, a term that sounds far friendlier than abducting and enslaving innocent people through trickery, force, or a combination of the two. They took Sam's cousins to a Queensland sugar plantation where the boys became workers with no way home. Sam's grandfather Biuku died, wounded by the pistol shot.

But that wasn't the worst of it. The sailors left behind the red cloth. Along with it, they left another gift of the civilized world: a disease called smallpox. One of the sailors was recovering from the disease, but was still contagious.

The disease spread through the village. Three of his uncles and two of his aunts died. His mother died. His favorite cousin, a sweet girl just a year younger than Sam, died. Her name was Kariomae, her eyes were as blue as Sam's, and her smile always made him smile.

Sam's father tended the sick until he fell ill himself. By the time the disease ran its course, more than half the villagers were dead, and Matthew Smalls was a broken man. His beloved wife was dead and the life he had built for himself in the village was gone. The next time a missionary ship visited the island, Matthew Smalls returned to England, taking Sam with him.

For Matthew Smalls, the return to England was a return to his former life. For Sam, it was a trip to a strange foreign land filled with pale people who stared at him.

In London, Sam and his father lived in the house of Sam's grandfather, Samuel Smalls. This grandfather was a pale, gray-haired man who never smiled. He was a glovemaker and leatherseller.

In London, there was no ocean, no beach, no coconut palms to climb, no canoes to sail, no cousins to play with. The weather was damp and dreary. Sam's grandfather arranged for Sam to go to boarding school. "This boy has so much to learn," he said sternly.

Sam was sent to Dr. Plummer's Academy, a small school for about forty "select young gentlemen," all of them sons of London businessmen. Sam's father had attended the academy many years before. He spoke fondly of the good chums he had made there. Sam would have great fun at school, his father said.

Alas, Sam did not have great fun at school. He read books and wrote letters home and learned maths. He learned to play cricket. He was good at these things. Reading and writing and maths were no harder than navigating by remembering where the stars rose and set. Sam was a strong and agile boy, so playing cricket was not hard, once he learned the rules.

What was hard was understanding the other boys. On Sam's first day at the school, a popular boy named Arthur Howard had laughed derisively when he met Sam. "Who is this?" he had asked. "The King of the Cannibal Islands?"

The other boys had laughed too, and Sam's fate at school was sealed. Teachers called him Sam, but Arthur called him "King," snickering whenever he said it. The other boys followed suit. The boys did not want to play with Sam. Outside the supervision of adults, when the boys put together a cricket game, there was no place on either team for Sam. No one wanted to be Sam's chum.

Sam didn't understand it. For a time, he tried to be friendly, then he gave up and spent his free time reading in the library.

On the day before the boys left for the half-term holiday, Arthur Howard gave Sam a book. The two boys were alone in the dormitory, all the others having already departed. Arthur had packed his bag and was walking toward the door. Then he stopped, set his bag down on the bed beside Sam's, opened his bag, and took out a book. "I think you should read this," Arthur said. "All the boys have read it."

Sam took the book, surprised at what seemed to be a gesture of friendship. "Thank you."

"Oh, don't thank me." Arthur smiled. It was not a friendly smile. It was an arrogant and superior smile. "I think it will help you understand where you belong."

Then Arthur picked up his bag and hurried away.

On his first night back in London, Sam began reading the book. The title was *The Coral Island*; the author, R. M. Ballantyne. The story told of three British boys who were shipwrecked on a tropical island. The book's author seemed to think that the boys were heroic, but they seemed quite foolish to Sam. They did not know the first thing about fishing or boat building, but even so, everything they tried turned out very well for them.

Then the boys saw two war canoes approaching their island. One of the boys said, "all the natives of the South Sea Islands are fierce cannibals . . . We must hide if they land here."

The canoes landed and the boys hid. From hiding, they witnessed a battle between two groups of native men. The men in both groups were almost entirely naked and they fought with enormous clubs.

The leader of one group was described as "a most extraordinary being . . . His hair was frizzed out to an enormous extent, so that it resembled a large turban. It was of a light-yellow hue, which surprised me much, for the man's body was as black as coal, . . . Altogether, with his yellow, turban-like hair, his Herculean black frame, his glittering eyes and white teeth, he seemed the most terrible monster I ever beheld." By the end of the chapter, this yellow-haired monster is killed by the shipwrecked boys.

Sam closed the book, unable to read any more. He was sitting by a warm fire in his grandfather's house, but he suddenly felt very cold and very alone. He understood the origin of his nickname at school. Arthur had given Sam the book so that Sam would understand that he was a monster and he did not belong at Dr. Plummer's Academy.

At the front of the book, the author had included a short message to the reader: "If there is any boy or man who loves to be melancholy and morose, and who cannot enter with kindly sympathy into the regions of fun, let me seriously advise him to shut my book and put it away. It is not meant for him."

"It is not meant for me," Sam thought.

The next day, Sam talked to his father about his life at Dr. Plummer's Academy. "The other boys call me King of the Cannibal Islands," Sam told his father. "They don't like me. One of them gave me this book to read." He handed his father *The Coral Island*. "It says that all the natives of the South Sea Islands are cannibals."

Matthew took the book from his son, frowning at it with a distracted air. "Well, that's just foolish," he said. "Clearly the author of this book is quite ignorant. He should know better than that. But I'm sure the boys don't mean anything by it. Just a bit of fun. They do like to tease. Did I tell you what my nickname was at school?"

He had told Sam, several times in fact, but that didn't stop him from telling Sam again. "Because my name is Smalls, they called me Weeny. Sometimes it was Teeny Weeny; sometimes it was Teeny Weeny Weiner." He shook his head. "That's just how boys are."

"I have no friends," Sam said. Perhaps it was bad to be called Teeny Weeny, but Sam guessed, from his father's rueful smile, that he had been friends with the boys who teased him.

"Now, now," Matthew said. "You told me one of the boys gave you this book to read."

Sam nodded slowly. "Yes, Arthur gave me the book."

"Maybe Arthur would like to be your friend," Matthew said. He studied his son's dejected expression. "You know, there's a festival this week with a fun fair. I'll take you to it. When I was a boy, I loved riding on the roundabout. I'm sure we'll have a wonderful time."

"What is a roundabout?" Sam asked.

"Oh, it's quite exciting!" his father said. "You'll ride a beautiful horse as it gallops in a circle and the music plays."

Sam nodded as if he understood. He wished his father would read the book, rather than just tell him it was foolish.

The next day, they went to the fun fair. Sam clung to his father's hand as they made their way through the crowd. Wherever he looked, someone was staring at him.

A pale, towheaded boy at a candy stall gaped at Sam. The boy's voice cut through the din of the fair as he asked his mother: "Why does that black boy have yellow hair?"

An apple seller pushed his cap back on his head to reveal a face tanned by the sun. He remarked to his customer, "Will you look at that child?! Blue eyes and skin as black as coal."

Two young women at a fortune teller's stall looked up from cards spread on the table and stared at Sam, wide-eyed with wonder. They were so pale and thin, Sam thought. They looked washed out, unhealthy. The brown-skinned fortune teller smiled at Sam, the only one of all the crowd to do so.

So many people, and no one who looked like him. Sam felt his face get hot as his father led him through the crowd. He did not belong here.

They passed a street where a band was playing. Showmen shouted to be heard over the banging of drums and the discordant tootling of trumpets. Down that street, Sam saw banners made of sailcloth painted with glorious pictures in brilliant colors. The banners showed a cow with six legs; two people joined to make one body with two heads, two arms, and four legs; a woman with a beard; a scowling dark-skinned man with blue eyes and golden hair. Above that last picture, the banner said: "See the King of the Cannibal Islands!"

That made Sam stop and stare. "Wait!" he called to his father. But his father didn't hear him over the din. Sam, clinging to his father's hand, was pulled along, leaving the street with the enticing banner behind.

They turned down an alley with stalls offering oysters, oranges, pastries, gingerbread, and penny toys. A gnarled old man was playing some kind of game with three upended cups and a pea on a little round board. A crowd had gathered around him, and he was talking quickly: "One little pea—Catch him if you can. Put your wager on the table. Them as don't play can't win. . ."

Then suddenly the crowd was parting to let someone come through. The crowd carried Sam with it as an ocean wave might carry away a swimmer. Sam lost his grip on his father's hand.

Women were shrieking and children were laughing and a man was shouting, "Follow me! "Follow me!" Sam, looking in that direction, saw a bear towering over the crowd. A bear! The animal was standing on its hind legs, waving its front paws in the air. It wore a lace collar and a cap with a feather. The cap was attached to a leather muzzle that kept the beast from opening its mouth. There was a ring in the bear's nose; a rope was tied to the ring.

A stout, red-faced man held the end of that rope. He had a staff in his other hand, holding it like a weapon, ready to smack the bear if he needed to. "Follow me to the Dance Pavilion," the man shouted. "This fierce beast from the wilds of Russia will dance for your amusement. Follow me!"

Sam could not stop watching. The bear was stronger than the man. In the forest where the bear belonged, the man would run away from the beast in terror. But this was not the bear's world. This was a world that belonged to the pale Londoners. That's why they all laughed. The mighty beast had become a clown. The more the bear roared, the funnier it was.

As Sam watched, the man tugged on the rope. The bear dropped to all fours and shuffled forward, looking sad and hungry.

Sam looked for his father, but could not see him anywhere. Sam was surrounded by strangers—laughing, shouting strangers. Sam was grateful that they were, at that moment, staring at the bear, rather than at him.

Struggling against the crowd, Sam pushed and squeezed and shoved his way to the side of the street, where he found a spot to stand between a stall selling penny toys and another selling gingerbread. His heart was pounding as he scanned the crowd for his father. He saw only strangers, so many strangers.

"Hullo, boy," said a girl's voice. "You lost?"

The girl who stood beside the penny toy booth was studying him as if he were as exotic and strange as the dancing bear. He returned her stare. He had never seen anyone quite like her. Her skin was a warm healthy brown, unlike the pale Londoners. Her dark hair was curly and wild, barely contained by a red scarf that was wrapped around her head like a turban. She had bangles on her wrists and gold hoops in her ears. He thought she was very pretty.

"My father is lost," he said.

She studied him. "You speak like an Englishman."

"I am an Englishman."

She smiled at that. "Are you now?"

"I need to find my father," he said.

She nodded briskly, as if coming to a decision. "My uncle can help you. Follow me."

She ducked through the small space between the stalls. Sam hesitated, then followed. It was nice that she had offered to help and he didn't really know what else to do.

Just behind the stalls was an area where women were cooking sausages over a fire for the sausage vendor. Other vendors were talking and laughing and exchanging insults. Sam didn't have much time to wonder about where they were going. The girl was hurrying on and he had to keep up.

They turned a corner, still separated from the crowds by a row of stalls. Sam could hear the noise of the street, the shouting of vendors.

"Hey, who's this?" someone called to the girl.

Sam was startled when he saw who was asking the question. The speaker sounded like a woman and wore a dress, but she had a luxuriant beard.

"A lost boy. I'm helping him."

"Of course you are," the bearded lady said. "Good luck, lost boy! Be careful."

As he followed the girl, Sam noticed other unusual sights: a very tall man standing with a group of very short people, two men juggling flaming torches, a cow that stood on four legs but had two extra legs growing from its back.

"Here we are," the girl said. She ducked into the back of a tent and he followed her. Curtains separated the back of the tent from the rest of it.

Sam could hear a man speaking on the other side of the curtain. "A wild man, straight from the Cannibal Islands," he was saying. "Nurtured on the flesh of his enemies! He has a tattoo for every man he has eaten. I try to content him with pork, but I know by the look in his eyes that he's hungry for something more."

The showman's words were drowned out by a roar—a man shouting. Sam realized suddenly that he could understand what the man was saying. He was shouting in the Pijin language that the men of Sam's village used to talk with visitors from other villages. "I want to eat that fat man," the man shouted.

"Stay back, sir," the showman cried. "The Cannibal King is measuring you for his stewpot."

Sam moved to where he could see through a gap in the curtains. He saw the audience first—more than two dozen fairgoers, all staring at the stage where the showman stood beside a large metal cage. A dark-skinned man with curly blond hair was in the cage, grinning through the bars at a fat man. As Sam watched, the fat man took a step back, bumping into the people behind him. The man's eyes were wide; his mouth turned down in an expression of fear.

The showman was talking about what would happen if the Cannibal King got loose. "He has a taste for the delicate flesh of ladies. And children, of course—such tender morsels. Keep your distance."

"Give me the women!" shouted the Cannibal King in Pijin.

Sam was appalled and confused. How was this going to help him find his father? What was he doing here? He looked at the girl. She was smiling slyly. He had seen that look on the faces of the sailors when they asked his cousins to load water into the ship's hold.

She laid a hand on his. "You will do very well for yourself here," she said in a whisper. "The Cannibal King makes good money doing this—and you're his spitting image. Such an act you'll have. You'll be rich." Her dark eyes shone.

Sam turned away from her, ready to run. Then he heard a voice that froze him in his tracks. His father's voice, shouting over the showman and speaking to the Cannibal King in Pijin. "Hello, friend," Matthew Smalls called over the crowd. "Have you seen my son?"

Sam ran—through the gap between the curtains and onto the stage. "I'm here, Father!" he cried. A woman screamed as Sam jumped off the stage. The crowd scrambled to get out of his way. They feared him, he realized. The audience could not exit the tent fast enough.

"They'll be talking about this show all over the fair," the showman said after the crowd had fled. Sam and his father were alone in the tent with the showman, the Cannibal King, and the girl. "It will be great for business." The showman studied Sam. "Would you be interested in touring with me? I'll make it worth your while."

The Cannibal King had climbed out of his cage and was sitting on the edge of the stage. Sam stared at the Cannibal King. Could he pretend to be like this man? He would bare his teeth, growling and grimacing. Women would scream and men would back away.

Sam's father glared at the showman. "You will never put my son in a cage and call him a cannibal!"

The showman shrugged. "He'd ne'er be short of money, working with me. And there needn't be a cage. I'd bill him as an educated cannibal. He could dress smart—as long as he can deliver a hungry look when called on."

The Cannibal King laughed. Then he gave the showman an impressively hungry look: teeth bared, eyes gleaming.

"That's the ticket," the showman said. "Oh, the ladies do scream when they see those teeth. The man's a natural."

"Make them fear you," the Cannibal King said to Sam in Pijin. "It's easy. And it teaches them respect."

"How did you come to be here?" Sam asked him. It felt strange but good to be speaking Pijin again.

The man said that he had taken a berth on a whaler that was short-handed. That had been more than a decade ago. He was a skilled navigator, a valuable man to have aboard in the South Pacific. But over the years, whaling in the South Pacific had become less profitable. His last ship ended its voyage in London—and he hadn't found another ship that needed his expertise. He had no way to get back to the islands.

The showman had found him in the Strangers' Home for Asiatics, Africans and South Sea Islanders, a lodging house set up by Christian missionaries to provide temporary shelter for stranded sailors. Captains of ships headed for Asia or Africa or the South Seas went there in search of crew. And so, apparently, did showmen in search of exotic performers.

"I miss the sea," the man told Sam. "But the food here is better and the work is easy."

"But they're making fun of you," Sam said.

The man laughed. "You heard the women scream. You saw that fat man back away. I am not the one who is the fool."

Sam and his father went back home as soon as they left the tent. Sam's father kept a firm grip on his son's hand and Sam did not stray from his side.

When Sam returned to school two weeks later, he took *The Coral Island* and his memory of the Cannibal King's words with him. At school, he waited and watched for the opportunity to talk with Arthur. A few days after school began, he found Arthur alone in the library, finishing an assignment.

Sam stood by the table where Arthur sat. He set the book in front of the boy. Arthur smiled at him, a nasty sort of smile. "A ripping tale, don't you think?" he asked.

Sam's expression was serious as he stared at the grinning boy. "The man who wrote it knows nothing of life in the islands," Sam said, his voice low. "He's a complete fool."

"Oh, come now," Arthur said, still grinning. "What makes you say that?"

"It's clear that he doesn't know the first thing about butchering a body for a feast." Sam kept his eyes fixed on Arthur. "Anyone knows that the first thing you do is cut the throat." He gestured toward Arthur's throat. "You want the blood to flow. The blood makes the meat taste gamey."

Arthur's smile faltered. Sam stood close to the desk, looming over Arthur. The boy was caught between the library wall and Sam. He had nowhere to go.

"It's best to cut the throat while the heart is still beating," Sam said softly. "When the heart stops beating, the blood stops flowing. The sweetest meat comes from a man with a strong heart, a man who clings to life. I've wondered sometimes what it feels like as your blood leaves your body, each heartbeat hastening your death." Sam smiled then—showing his teeth.

He had prepared this speech carefully, considering the best way to strike fear into the heart of his enemy. Arthur's eyes were wide and his face was pale.

"Now what's going on here?" The school librarian had come over to the two boys. "You know there is no talking in the library, Sam."

The librarian knew Sam as a diligent student. "Sorry, Mr. Williams," Sam said easily. "Arthur lent me this book. He thinks it's a ripping tale, but I can't overlook its inaccuracies. I have to say it's really not for me."

"Ah, a literary discussion," Mr. Williams said. Before Arthur could move to stop him, the librarian picked up the book that Sam had set on the desk. He read the title and author, then shook his head and frowned at Arthur. "I commend you on your superior taste, Sam. This is not a book I would recommend. A waste of time, I think."

After that, Sam stopped trying to make friends. He was still lonely, but the boys no longer teased him. They left him alone, and that was a relief of sorts.

About a week after Sam's discussion with Arthur, the headmaster called Sam into the office and said his father had fallen ill with a fever. Sam went back to his grandfather's house to sit by his father's bed as he died.

Sam went with his grandfather to his father's funeral. They stood by the grave and watched men shovel dirt over the coffin. People came to talk softly to his grandfather and say how sorry they were. No one spoke to Sam. The boy stood quietly at his grandfather's side, aware that everyone was staring at him.

That evening, after the funeral, Sam's grandfather called him into the sitting room. His grandfather sat in an armchair by the fire. Sam stood on the hearthrug.

"Tell me who you are," his grandfather said.

Sam looked at his grandfather with surprise, but answered, "I am Samuel Matthew Smalls."

"Who was your father?"

"My father was Matthew Turner Smalls."

"That will do," his grandfather said. He had closed his eyes when Sam started speaking, but he opened them now. "When I close my eyes, you sound like a British gentleman. When I open them . . ." Sam's grandfather shook his head. "Well . . . never mind that. The headmaster tells me you are doing well in your lessons. He says you have some skill on the playing field, that you have the making of an excellent batsman." He studied Sam, still frowning. "You'll return to school tomorrow."

That evening, in the gloomy bedroom where he slept when he was at his grandfather's house, Sam thought about running away. He didn't want to go back to school. Going to school had been bearable when his father was alive. Now his father was dead. His mother was dead. His relatives in the village were dead. He didn't belong anywhere. Perhaps he could find the showman and work with the Cannibal King. He didn't want to pretend to be a cannibal, but even that would be better than returning to school.

At that moment, he heard someone tapping on his window.

CHAPTER 15
You Can Be My Big Brother

O N THE *Honest Trader,* Mary slept in a narrow bunk in a storeroom near the galley. Her bunk was surrounded by kegs of
salted beef and sacks of onions and potatoes. When Sam had
booked their passage, he had arranged for her to bunk there, giving her
privacy that was rare aboard a merchant vessel.

In the privacy of that storeroom, Mary could stop being Marty
Watson. She could release her breasts from the binding she wore to smash
them flat. She could relieve herself in the chamber pot she had packed
in her seabag.

In the cabin, she could be Mary Darling—though she sometimes
wondered who Mary Darling really was. She did not feel like the same
person who had packed a seabag in London. She was a mother determined to rescue her children. She was a bold adventurer on a quest. She
was a Victorian wife, freed from constraints at last. Mary felt confused
because she was not sure which role suited her best.

In her cabin, she allowed herself to think about times past.

Neverland was not the paradise that Mary had imagined when Peter
invited her to fly away. The Lost Boys slept in a cave that smelled of dirt
and rotting leaves, and there was never enough to eat.

Adventures are uncomfortable. No one thinks much about that when
they are setting out on an adventure. They think about the excitement.
They think they'll be a hero, have some fun, and be home in time for
dinner. They don't think about how dangerous adventures can be.

Here is a list of some of the dangers that the Lost Boys faced during their time on Neverland:

1. Illnesses caused by poor sanitation (something rarely mentioned in tales of adventure),
2. Starvation when hunting wasn't good,
3. Mauling by wild beasts when the wild beasts did not want to become dinner,
4. Saltwater crocodiles that lived in the mangrove swamp and thought children were tasty,
5. Mermaids, who were not as sweet and friendly as they are described in children's stories,
6. Fairies, who are not as bad as mermaids but may get you killed anyway,
7. Pirates, who also aren't as bad as mermaids, but may kill you if you get in their way.

There were other dangers, but that's a start. The number of Lost Boys on the island changed as boys were killed and Peter brought in new recruits. Many Lost Boys died. It was not that Neverland was more dangerous than other tropical islands. Any tropical island can be dangerous to those who are careless or ignorant, and most of the boys were both.

When Mary arrived, the Lost Boys on the island had survived longer than most. In large part, that was because of Sam. Having grown up in the Solomon Islands, he was familiar with all the dangers listed above except for numbers 5, 6, and 7. His prior knowledge of dangers 1 to 4 had been important to the Lost Boys' survival rate.

When Mary woke up that first morning on Neverland, she told Peter, "I'd like to go home." She had spent most of the night swatting mosquitoes that wanted to feast on her blood. "My mother will be wondering where I am."

"Your mother? Oh, she's forgotten you already," Peter said. "Mothers are like that. Would you like to go to the mermaids' lagoon?"

Mary really didn't believe her mother would forget her so quickly, and she wanted to go home. But she also wanted to see mermaids. So she went to the lagoon with Peter and the Lost Boys.

The beach by the mermaids' lagoon had smooth white sand shaded by coconut palms. Peter, Tom, and the other Lost Boys hurried down to the water to play, but Mary stayed in the shade of the trees with Sam.

Three mermaids lounged on Marooners' Rock, a wide flat rock in the middle of the lagoon. They basked in the sun and combed out their long hair, looking just like the mermaids in her mother's painting. The water was the same impossible blue. The scales on their mermaid tails glittered like jewels in the sunlight.

Over the sound of the lapping waves, Mary could hear the mermaids' high, sweet voices. She couldn't make out what they were saying, which was just as well. The youngest mermaid was telling the others about a sailor who had jumped off his ship when she called to him from the water. The man had drowned, of course, and all the mermaids thought this was terribly funny.

From the beach, Mary watched them. As one of the mermaids lifted her arms to push back her hair, Mary saw her bare breasts glistening in the sun. The mermaid was beautiful—and it was clear she knew it. The creature was sublimely confident—not proud exactly, since that would imply that she cared what others thought and that was not the case. But she was comfortable in her smooth brown skin and scaly fish tail. She did not care what anyone thought of her. Mary was fascinated.

"It's no use trying to talk to them," Sam told Mary as she gazed at the mermaids that first day. "You won't get a civil word out of them. They tolerate Peter, but they don't care for anyone else."

"They're so beautiful," she said. "But my mother says they aren't nice."

"Your mother is right about that," Sam said. "They think it's funny that we can't breathe underwater like they can. They'll promise you whatever they think you want most, just to get you into the water. Then they'll grab your feet and pull you under, just for the fun of it. They pretend it's a game, but it's not." He shook his head.

"My mother says fairies aren't nice either."

Sam nodded. "They aren't as bad as the mermaids, but they'll steal your food if you don't watch it. Sometimes they pinch you if you say something they don't like." Sam glanced at Mary. "How does your mother know so much about mermaids and fairies?"

Mary frowned. She had never asked her mother that. "She just knows."

Sam was curious about this strange girl. "Why did you come here?" he asked her.

He had asked that question of each new boy. The answers seemed to depend on what adventure books a boy had read—but they generally focused on treasure and fighting. The boys all wanted to look for treasure or explore the jungle or hunt wild animals or fight pirates and outlaws and Indians.

"Peter showed us how to fly," Mary said. "That was wonderful until we flew into a cloud. Then I wanted to go home, but I didn't know the way. Peter wouldn't show us the way home, so we had to keep going. Why did you come here?"

Sam was surprised. None of the boys had asked Sam that.

"I was in my grandfather's house in London," Sam said. "I didn't belong there. No one wanted me there. I wanted to go back to the village where I grew up. When Peter told me about Neverland, it sounded like my village. So I flew away with him."

"Is it like your village here?" she asked.

"In some ways. But my friends and family aren't here."

"Maybe Peter could take you to your village." Mary was touched by how sad Sam suddenly looked.

"I can't go back to my village."

"Why not?"

Sam told her about the ship that had taken his cousins and brought the disease that killed his family, about Dr. Plummer's Academy and his father's death. As he talked, he stared out over the blue water of the lagoon. He had never told anyone before, because no one had asked. "I have no family," he said. "I have no village."

He glanced at Mary. Her eyes were wide. She was thinking about how she would feel if her family was taken from her. "You can be my big brother," she said impulsively. "I have a little brother, but I've never had a big brother."

Sam studied Mary. She reminded him of Kariomae, his cousin who died of the smallpox. She too had been small, but totally fearless. "I never had a little sister," Sam said slowly. "I didn't have any brothers either. But I had lots of cousins. We played together and looked out for each other."

"That's what brothers and sisters do," Mary said.

Sam nodded. "I'd like that," he said.

Mary slipped her hand into his. "All right then," she said. "I'll be your little sister and you'll be my big brother."

"Peter said that he brought you here to be mother for all the Lost Boys," he said.

"That's wrong," she said flatly. "I told him I'm not a mother."

"He seems to think we need a mother," Sam said. "He talks about how our mother would tuck us in at night and tell us stories."

Mary shook her head. "Peter is very strange, don't you think?"

Sam pondered this for a bit. The other Lost Boys seemed to think of Peter as a boy who had a few more powers than they did. Sam didn't think that Peter was a boy at all. Peter pretended he was a boy—maybe he even really thought he was a boy. For Peter, pretend and real were very much the same.

Sam thought that Peter was a spirit—one of the wild nature spirits that lived in the bush. Those spirits, like Peter, sometimes looked like people. Everyone in his village had recognized those spirits as a part of the world, a part of nature, a part of daily life.

But Peter was a spirit that belonged to the pale British people. He could go to London and then return to this island. It was strange that the British children did not recognize Peter for what he was. Not a person, but a different sort of entity altogether—powerful and unpredictable. But then, Sam had noticed that the British people—even his father— were often blind to what was going on around them.

Sam thought of Peter as being like the wind blowing over the water in the lagoon. Wind could push a sailing canoe along, helpful and pleasant. Or the wind could pick up speed and swamp a canoe or tear down a house. It wasn't that the wind was good or evil. The wind was indifferent to human needs. It didn't care about you or your canoe. Peter was like that wind—indifferent, uncaring, neither good nor evil.

Despite Mary's protests, Peter continued referring to her as the Lost Boys' mother. When it was time for dinner, the Lost Boys asked Mary when they would eat. When any of them were unhappy, they looked to Mary for comfort. When their clothes were torn, they asked Mary to mend them.

An aside here: maybe you've had this experience. You set out with friends on a great adventure—but someone has to make dinner and everyone looks at you. Somehow, they all think you are the mother, the grown-up, the one who will take care of things. You didn't sign on for it, but somehow everyone thinks it's your job. Eventually you give up and do it. After all, someone has to. But you aren't happy about it and you are always aware that it isn't really your job.

It's bad enough to be designated the cook when there's food to pre- pare. It's even worse when there's never enough to eat. And there was never enough to eat on Neverland. Peter liked to go hunting, but he couldn't be depended on to put food on the table (not that they had a table). He could snatch fish away from seabirds and fly to the treetops for coconuts, but he was easily bored with anything that seemed like work—and getting food seemed like work. He never seemed to get hungry, and he didn't really care about food.

Fortunately, Sam worked hard to keep the Lost Boys fed. He climbed palm trees to get coconuts and showed the other boys how to do it. He built a fish trap near the reef. When the tide was high, the fish swam in. When the tide went out, the fish were trapped.

He taught the Lost Boys how to dig up taro roots and boil them in an old pot—blackened with soot, stained with rust, but the only pot they had, and therefore a treasure. After boiling the roots, he would roast them in the fire. The roots tasted a little sweet and a little nutty and absolutely wonderful.

But Peter didn't care about all that. What Peter liked best was having adventures and telling stories about his adventures. Listening to those stories, Mary was struck by how many of his adventures sounded like the games she and Tom had played with other children in Cooktown. Cops and robbers, cowboys and Indians, brave sailors and wicked pirates—they were all about fighting.

Peter often talked about fighting pirates. He never said why he was fighting them. Like the games she and Tom had played, it seemed like it was enough just to be fighting. But sometimes, when Peter described a battle with pirates, it didn't quite sound like a game. "I killed a dozen men in that battle," he said, smiling happily.

"It must be a game," Mary thought. "He couldn't really have killed anyone. It was just a game."

CHAPTER 16
A Different Point of View

TWO WEEKS AFTER Mary's departure, Watson and Holmes were aboard the *Golden Dawn*, a ship bound from Southampton to Madagascar, carrying cargo and passengers. They were accompanied by George Darling, Sam Smalls, Nana, and Sam's parrot Captain Flint.

Mrs. Hudson had insisted that Watson take Nana with him. "The dog is pining away," she told Watson. "She needs to help." Nana sat at Mrs. Hudson's feet, gazing at Watson in mute appeal, her sad eyes pleading for useful work. Watson felt he had no choice but to give in.

Mrs. Hudson also took charge of Liza, the Darlings' young servant. The girl couldn't stay in the Darlings' house alone and did not want to return to the workhouse. So she joined Mrs. Hudson at Baker Street, where the very capable landlady trained her to make excellent biscuits.

Sam had made the travel arrangements. The *Golden Dawn* was a three-masted barque with an auxiliary steam engine for times when the winds were contrary. They would make good time, Sam said.

Sam came aboard with a well-worn seabag slung over one shoulder and Captain Flint perched on the other. Sam was quite at home aboard the ship—sure on his feet, despite his artificial leg. He presented a bottle of rum to the captain. He discussed the ship's speed and power with the mate.

Nana quickly became a favorite with everyone aboard, even the ship's cat, a surly old tom. The cat's initial hostility was overcome by Nana's amiable nature. By the end of the first week, the cat curled up to sleep with the big dog on chilly evenings.

After dinner on the first day, George retired to his cabin, afflicted with the queasiness that would be his constant companion while aboard. Holmes and Watson lingered on deck.

Watson took out his pipe, ready to smoke and relax. For the past week, his time had been filled with preparations for the trip, with no time to spare. He was grateful to be on the ship at last.

"What do you make of our fellow travelers?" Holmes asked.

Watson did not reply immediately. He was tired and he had not given much thought to their fellow travelers. He wanted to smoke in peace and perhaps hear a bit of praise for his hard work. As soon as Holmes spoke, Watson knew he would get neither peace nor praise. Holmes wanted to share his astute observations on the other passengers.

"What are your thoughts on Benito Salini?" Holmes asked.

Watson shrugged. He had no thoughts on Benito Salini. The thin young Italian man had introduced himself as a businessman, but had not disclosed the business he was in.

"Surely you noticed his watch fob?" Holmes said.

Watson had not, but Holmes was happy to describe what Watson had missed. "A silver disc adorned with a coiled serpent intricately carved from hematite and set with ruby eyes. Compliment him on it, and I expect you'll learn that it is his own work. His hands have calluses characteristic of an engraver. He's a jeweler, and he will be purchasing gems in Toamasina. Madagascar is known for its sapphires."

Watson nodded.

"John Dawson and his son are orchid hunters," Holmes said. Dawson had said he was a botanist. "Dawson has the air of a gentleman, but I noticed that he and his son are both carrying sidearms. Orchids are lovely flowers, but collecting them can be a cutthroat business."

Watson nodded again. He was not in the mood to be told about the importance of seemingly insignificant details. All of this seemed irrelevant to their pursuit of Mary, but he knew better than to say that to Holmes.

"And what do you make of Richard Rumbold?" Holmes asked.

Rumbold had introduced himself as a ship's surgeon. He was returning to Madagascar to rejoin his ship after visiting his elderly and ailing mother—then staying to attend her funeral.

"Rumbold's an interesting fellow," Watson said. "We chatted a bit about his days as a navy surgeon."

Watson and Rumbold had talked shop. Rumbold had a wealth of knowledge on tropical diseases. He also knew a great deal about amputating limbs and treating the resulting stubs to keep the patient alive. A ship's surgeon in the Royal Navy always kept his bone saw sharp, since injuries that required amputation were common.

"He left the navy some years back," Watson said. "Given his tales of the work aboard ship, I can understand why he chose to leave."

"His departure from Her Majesty's service was not his choice," Holmes said. "He was drummed out of the navy."

Watson was taken aback. "Why do you say that?"

"Have you ever known a military man who has absolutely no memento of his service somewhere on his person? A pin, a key fob, a tattoo? Rumbold has none of that. He lacks any hint of military bearing. Instead, he affects an Eton slouch. I imagine he loses that upper class accent when he's sailing with pirates," Holmes said.

Watson had not noticed any flaws in Rumbold's diction; his accent was that of an educated man. "What makes you think he is associated with pirates?"

"I overheard him chatting with Salini about jewelry. Rumbold's knowledge of the values of various gems was very specific—the sort of knowledge useful to a pawnbroker, a fence, or a pirate. Given his destination, pirate is the obvious choice. You might ask your friend Sam if he knows the man."

Later, after Holmes had retired to the cabin, Watson lingered on deck, smoking his pipe, watching the moon on the water. Now, in this moment of quiet, he could wonder where Mary was, what she was doing, whether she was safe. He could not talk about such things with Holmes, who would dismiss his musings as a waste of time.

"Dr. Watson, may I join you?" It was Rumbold.

Watson nodded. Pirate or not, he rather liked the man.

Rumbold leaned on the rail, looking out over the water. "I wanted to tell you how much I have enjoyed your tales in the *Strand Magazine*. Your understanding of human psychology and motivation is impressive."

"You mean Holmes' understanding of psychology," Watson said. "His knowledge and observations of human behavior are unmatched. I only tell the tale."

Rumbold shook his head. "You misunderstand me. It is your observations of Holmes that impress me. You filter his disdain for others through the lens of your affection and friendship. Your perspective brings humanity to the stories—and to Holmes himself. Without that, the case studies would not be compelling, no matter how brilliant his deductions."

Watson stared at the man, momentarily struck silent by his praise. He recovered enough to say, "Thank you. Holmes doesn't see it that way."

Rumbold chuckled. "Holmes considers the world as if it were a crime scene and regards each person as a possible criminal. He ignores observations that are irrelevant to that view. There are many things that Holmes is blind to—but he would never acknowledge it. I'm sure that makes him a difficult companion at times."

Watson nodded, cheered by the man's sympathy and praise for his writing. "It does," he said. After a moment, he added, "By the way, Holmes says that you are a pirate."

Rumbold nodded, still smiling. "That, I would say, is a question of perspective. I sometimes sail with pirates, but they would not count me as one of them. They would say I was a doctor." He shrugged. "It all depends on your perspective."

They smoked in silence for a bit. Then Rumbold said, "I noticed that your friend George is suffering from seasickness."

Watson nodded. "That he is. I advised him to drink ginger tea to ease the symptoms."

Rumbold puffed meditatively on his pipe. "I've found that some patients dismiss commonplace remedies. For those, I have found that medication can be more effective if it is exotic, foul tasting, and somewhat difficult to obtain. These attributes seem to increase their belief in the medicine—and their belief makes the remedy more effective. Do you think George might be such a patient?"

"It's possible," Watson said.

"If ginger tea does not solve the problem, I'd like to offer him another remedy—with your permission as his physician, of course." Rumbold turned to face Watson. "It will involve ginger tea, combined with some foul-tasting ingredients that Chinese healers use to treat nausea."

Watson smiled. "I welcome the experiment."

Richard Rumbold had studied medicine because his father was a doctor, an honest country practitioner who wished his son to follow him in his chosen profession. Rumbold was driven by curiosity, eager to know about any manner of things. He would have willingly pursued a career as a chemist, an engineer, a naturalist, or anything else involving arcane knowledge, exploration, and experimentation.

After completing medical school, he worked for a time at Leith Hospital in Edinburgh. He left after a scandal (which Rumbold would have described as a "misunderstanding") regarding morphine supplies in the hospital infirmary.

He went on to become a ship's doctor in the Royal Navy. That promising career came to an end when he was dishonorably discharged for pawning his surgical instruments for gambling money. At his tribunal, he argued that he had planned to reclaim the instruments with his winnings, as he had done many times before. (He had worked out a system of counting cards that allowed him to do quite well in friendly games with other gentlemen.)

The judge regarded Rumbold's calm description of his intent to redeem the instruments with gambling winnings as an impertinence. Rather than congratulating Rumbold on his past successes, the judge slammed down his gavel and ended Rumbold's career in the navy.

Rumbold was more competent at doctoring than most naval surgeons. He kept his instruments in excellent repair. (After all, instruments in top condition could be pawned for more.) He was drunk less frequently than most. In fact, he was rarely drunk as he disliked the way alcohol dulled his senses. He preferred other drugs.

Rumbold's dismissal didn't dismay him overmuch. He found a berth on a scientific expedition to the South Pacific. The food was better than what was served in the navy, and the company of scientists was more congenial than that of naval officers. Rumbold was interested in all manner of natural oddities and unusual customs, and the expedition offered the opportunity to collect the former and experience the latter.

On a remote island, Rumbold's curiosity led him astray. When the ship's officers met with the villagers, the captain focused his attention on a tall, well-built man that he thought was the chief. The man was, in fact, an excellent hunter, but he had no significant power in the village hierarchy.

While the captain was talking to the hunter, Rumbold hung back, considering the other villagers who had gathered. It seemed to Rumbold that several others among the group were more likely to be the village's leader. Perhaps the older man who sat by the door of a hut, watching the proceedings with interest. Or the tall woman who stood nearby, staring at the captain with an expression of disdain.

As he perused the natives, Rumbold met the gaze of a wiry old man who was studying him with great curiosity. The man grinned as his eyes met Rumbold's, recognizing in him a kindred spirit.

After the captain had completed his discussion with the hunter, Rumbold sought out the old man. The old man invited Rumbold to join him on a journey to see something special in the island's interior. At least, that's how Rumbold interpreted the man's gestures. Communication about anything that was not concrete and immediate was difficult.

Rumbold knew the ship would remain on the island for several days as the scientists collected specimens, the crew replenished supplies, and the navigator mapped the island's shores. Thinking the proposed journey with the old man would take just a few hours and believing he might learn of useful herbs or local medicines, Rumbold joined the old man on a trip into the jungle.

Rumbold was in the island's jungle interior for two weeks. During that time, he twisted his ankle and smoked the leaf of a powerful hallucinogen that took him on a much longer journey. During Rumbold's absence, the crew finished renewing the ship's stores. The scientists gathered samples of many interesting plants and insects. The navigator completed his mapping.

Eventually the captain despaired of Rumbold's return from the island's interior and set sail without him. The captain had never cared for the ship's doctor in any case. Rumbold's bedside manner was brusque at best. He had dismissed the captain's constant bellyache as a consequence of the man's rich diet.

When Rumbold finally straggled out of the jungle with the old man, the ship that had brought him to the island was gone. In its place was a pirate ship, stopping at the island for water and fresh fruit. Rumbold introduced himself to the pirates and made himself useful by tending to a few medical issues—a stab wound that was festering and a case of bellyache.

When the pirates set sail, Rumbold sailed with them.

A few days later, on the *Golden Dawn*, Rumbold offered George a remedy that might ease his seasickness. George told Watson that it tasted dreadful and caused him to break out in a sweat. But it eased his nausea and made him a little less miserable, a minor but significant improvement.

That evening, in their cabin, Watson shared the conversation with Holmes.

"Rumbold seems a little too willing to laugh at his patients' afflictions," Watson said. "Very good at diagnosis, though."

"Rumbold seems to be well stocked with useful remedies," Holmes mused. "A good man to know."

Within the week, Holmes had found, in Rumbold's well-stocked medical kit, relief from the boredom that beset the great detective during periods of idleness.

"It is a stimulant that I first encountered in the Maldives," Rumbold told Watson, as they smoked on the deck one afternoon. "Chinese healers use it to cure bad breath, to purify the body, and to kill tapeworms. It induces alertness, increases stamina, and gives the user a sense of well-being."

"How does it compare to cocaine?" Watson asked, always alert to his friend's weakness for that drug.

"By comparison, this is quite benign. The natives in the Maldives use it rather like we use tobacco or coffee, sharing it among friends. The natives chew it, but I've found a way to make it into a palatable drink."

Watson nodded, somewhat reassured. "How is it you came to learn of this stimulant?"

Rumbold chuckled. "I collect knowledge—specifically knowledge of medical treatments and cures used by native healers. There are potent remedies in some of their concoctions of herbs, roots, mashed beetle larva, and whatever. If I were on a tropical island, deathly ill with a fever, I'd consult the old woman who lives in a hut and has been curing the villagers for decades. I'd value her opinion above that of the most respected British doctor. Odds are the old woman has seen that fever before. She'll call on local deities, dance around and sing songs, and feed me an awful paste of mashed ants, jungle roots, and Lord knows what else. Then she'll attribute the cure in equal parts to the deities, the dancing, and the dosing. I'd credit it to something in the ants and the roots. But never mind that. The important thing is, I'd get better."

Listening to Rumbold, Watson was reminded of Holmes: analytical, precise, cold-blooded, and somewhat startled that everyone else did not approach the world with that same scientific frame of mind. Rumbold was, Watson thought, more relaxed and amiable than Holmes on initial acquaintance. He was less apt to challenge a person. He did not reveal his knowledge with a theatrical flourish. An easy man to join for a smoke or a drink, but perhaps, like Holmes, a difficult man to know well.

CHAPTER 17
The Secret of Neverland

MARY WOKE SUDDENLY in her small cabin aboard the *Honest Trader*, awake and alert as if someone had stuck her with a pin. She lay still, her heart pounding, listening in the onion-scented darkness. A sound had awakened her—something more than the water against the ship's hull, the wind in the sails.

Though the night was warm, she pulled the thin blanket around her. She wanted to stay in bed, but she couldn't. What was that sound? She pulled on boots and clothes, then stepped onto the deck.

The moon was up—a waning crescent low in the eastern sky. The wind was steady and the sails were full. She saw Davies, talking with the sailor who was at the helm.

She leaned on the railing. The ocean water by the ship's hull glowed with a soft blue light. The sound that had awakened her was louder here—but still soft. Just a whisper in the dim light. There was movement in the depths—brighter points of light, rising toward the surface.

Then she saw the mermaids—smiling as they rose through the water, holding their arms out to her. She could not make out the words of their song, but somehow, she knew what they were saying. "We have been waiting for you. You don't belong there—always pretending to be something you're not. Pretending to be a docile and obedient wife. Pretending to be a man. Come with us, where you don't have to pretend."

They were as beautiful as she remembered. They danced beneath the waves in an intricate ballet, surfacing, raising an arm to beckon to her, then sinking beneath the water. One mermaid lazily rolled in the water to smile up at her, then dove with a flick of a silvery tail. Their song grew louder as she watched them, a sound that she realized was only in her mind.

She gripped the railing, remembering how Sam had warned her about the mermaids in Neverland.

"Come with us," the mermaids sang. "You can be free."

Freedom, she thought. Yes, that had once been her heart's desire. She remembered a moment in London, backstage with Professor Hartl's Corps of Viennese Fencing Ladies. She had just completed a choreographed fight with a taller, stronger woman. When she was on stage, all eyes had been on her. So many men watching her every move. She could feel the heat of their gaze; she could feel their desire. In that moment on stage, she felt strong, powerful, unstoppable.

When she left the stage, she was exhilarated. All the women smiled and congratulated her. Professor Hartl had laid a hand on her shoulder.

"There is a place for you in the troupe," he had said. "Come with us to Paris, to Vienna." He had smiled at her, his teeth very white in the darkness backstage.

She had turned him down. Why? Perhaps it was that proprietary hand on her shoulder. Perhaps it was the thought of Uncle John, recently widowed and so sad. Uncle John had taken care of her when she needed it. She could not leave him now.

Later, when Mary told Miss Sanderson of Professor Hartl's offer, her teacher had smiled and said, "Wise choice, my girl."

The mermaids promised her freedom and power. Was that really what she wanted? "Men fear us," the mermaids sang. "They yearn for us and they fear us, because we are strong and free."

"Quite a show, isn't it?" Davies was at the railing by her side.

She started, surprised. "I didn't hear you coming," she said, wondering that he could speak of mermaids so casually.

"Mesmerized by the light," he said, chuckling. "Very pretty. Darwin wrote about it. The light comes from tiny marine insects agitated by the ship's movement."

Why was he talking about insects? Didn't he see the mermaids?

"Insects? I thought I saw something larger in the water." She could still see movement in the depths, but the mermaids did not surface.

"Dolphins, perhaps?"

The mermaids' song was fading. Davies, she thought, had driven them away with his talk of Darwin. He did not see the mermaids. He did not yearn for them. He did not believe in them. He was thinking of insects.

"I thought I heard a sound," Marty said. "Almost like singing."

"The wind plays tunes on the sails and the lines," Davies said.

"Ah, that must be it," Marty said, turning away.

Mary's memories of Neverland were complicated, as memories of childhood often are. Neverland was the place where Mary first picked up a sword. It had been a short sword—rusty and badly in need of sharpening. Holding the weapon made her feel simultaneously powerful and terrified. This was a weapon designed to kill people. She didn't know how to use it, but she knew she had to learn. Peter had decided to attack a pirate ship.

Peter loved adventures—and all of his adventures all seemed to involve killing. He thought of death as part of the game. It was all a jolly good time—and someone had to die. The attack on the pirate ship was a particularly bloody adventure. Not a memory that Mary enjoyed thinking about. She preferred adventures that did not involve killing—like the time she met Chief Laughing Bear.

That was Tootles' doing really. Tootles was a smart boy—the kind of smart that came from reading books rather than doing things. By reading books written by folks who had never ventured far from London or New York, Tootles had gained his understanding of cowboys and Indians, Arctic explorers, pirates, and South Pacific islanders.

When Peter Pan had tapped on Tootles' window, the boy was sure he would enjoy an adventure. On the flight from London to Neverland, he realized that he liked flying, but did not like being rained on, or hungry, or cold. But at that point it was too late to turn back.

Tootles was a gangly, clumsy sort of boy. When he tried to help Sam with the fish trap, he put a foot wrong and fell in the water. When he tried to help Mary with the cooking, he dropped the fish in the fire, or burned his hand and required comforting. He could never manage to do it right, with "it" being just about anything practical.

Tootles didn't really fit in with the other Lost Boys. They liked to rush through the jungle in a noisy pack, but Tootles preferred to stop when he noticed something that he wanted to examine—or when he heard a sound that might be something dangerous. So he often went on solitary walks.

On one such walk, Tootles saw a patch of plants that he recognized as taro. There had been a patch of taro near the cave—but the boys had dug up every plant and had eaten every root. Now, there were no taro roots anywhere near the camp. The discovery of a new patch of plants was very good news. Tootles returned to camp, eager to tell the others of his find.

Peter was off somewhere on an adventure. Sam was checking the fish trap. The other Lost Boys had gone hunting, something they did most days when Peter was gone. (They rarely brought back anything to eat.)

Mary was alone in the camp, weaving a sleeping mat from palm fronds. Tootles told her about what he had found, showing her the taro roots. "There are lots of plants," he told her. "Lots and lots."

Mary looked at the roots Tootles had gathered. Not enough to split among all the Lost Boys. "Let's go get more," she said.

She found a canvas sack in the back of the cave, where the Lost Boys tossed stuff they didn't use but didn't want to throw away, and took that along. Tootles led the way through the jungle to the far side of the island.

The taro was growing in marshy ground along a stream. By the time they got there, Mary was hot and out of sorts. She began digging up roots as quickly as she could, using a stick to dig and doing her best to stay out of the muck (with no success at all). Tootles started working nearby, but Mary quickly left him behind as she worked her way up the stream.

The tropical sun was hot. Sweat dripped into her eyes. Her bare feet squelched in the mud, and each squelch released the odor of rot. She was near the jungle trees, just stepping forward into the shade, anticipating a bit of cool relief from the hot tropical sun, when she heard something—a rustling in the leaves. Then she saw the serpent, just inches from where her foot was about to land.

On the pirate ship raid—the one that Mary did not like to think about—she had seen just how easily a person could die. The slash of a cutlass could split a man's belly, releasing his inner secrets—a river of blood, a terrible spill of guts. In a moment, a person could go from being a person to being nothing. Not a person. Just blood and flesh and bone and guts with no one there.

Peter had caught the pirates unaware, swooping down from the sky to land on the deck. There he fought three men at once, laughing with each parry and thrust of his blade.

Inspired by Peter's example, Curly and Nibs had attempted to do the same. Curly, who was always telling stupid jokes and had a very good opinion of himself, was sure he could kill a pirate or two. Nibs, who was quieter, was always willing to follow Curly's lead.

Mary remembered the smell of blood, the ringing of steel on steel, the cries of the injured and dying, men and boys wailing in pain as they breathed their last. Mary had heard Curly cry out—a shriek cut short by a swift slice across the throat. Then Nibs had wailed—a terrible cry of fear and pain, stopped by a blow to his head with the butt of the same cutlass that had silenced Curly.

Tom had been cornered by a pirate wielding a dirk in one hand and a cutlass in the other. Determined to save her brother, Mary had swooped down and smacked the man's head with the flat side of her rusty sword. That smack distracted the pirate long enough for Sam to slice the man's leg from behind. As the man fell forward, Tom lifted his blade. The pirate, most obligingly, fell on the point, leaving Tom pinned beneath the man's lifeless body. When Mary and Sam rolled the pirate off Tom, he was uninjured, but weeping, and drenched with the dead pirate's blood. But she knew that her brother could have died.

After the battle was over and done, they flew back to Neverland, short a couple of Lost Boys. Later that week, Peter flew off and came back with two new boys, lured by the promise of adventure. Peter called the new boys Curly and Nibs—the same names as the boys who died. The new boys objected at first, but eventually got used to their new names.

In stories, the hero never dies. And every child thinks of themself as the hero of their story. But children could die. She could die. Tom could die. Sam could die.

That was one of the secrets of Neverland. There were fairies and mermaids. You could fly away on adventures. And you could die.

At the sight of the serpent, Mary cried out, a sound that was part surprise and part terror. The serpent could bite her; she could die. She tried to step back, but she had committed her weight to stepping forward and she could not easily change course.

She twisted and fell. At just that moment, she heard another sound, a soft hiss and a thud. An arrow had pierced the serpent just behind its head, pinning the creature to the marshy ground. The serpent's body— as thick as Mary's arm and marked with stripes of black and midnight blue—thrashed in its death throes.

The arrow had come from somewhere in the shadows. Dazzled by the sun, Mary could not see clearly, but she stared in that direction. She saw a movement. She blinked. Someone was coming toward her from the shadow of the jungle.

She tried to scramble to her feet, but a sharp pain in her right foot stopped her. Then the figure emerged from the shadow: a girl, just a little younger than she was. The girl's dark hair was in braids. She had a bow in one hand with an arrow ready in the other. Right behind her was a boy about the same age.

"I thought it would bite you," the girl said, gesturing toward the snake. The snake's body continued to writhe, but more slowly now. "So I killed it." She spoke carefully, as if English were not her native language.

Mary struggled to catch her breath, trying to make sense of the situation. She looked at the snake, then at the bow in the girl's hand.

Just then, Tootles came running through the marsh, stumbling and splashing, almost falling, then recovering and running again. It could have been a moment of triumph for Tootles. He intended to rescue Mary from whatever danger had caused her to cry out.

But Mary was no longer in danger and Tootles was not given to moments of triumph. He slipped in the mud and fell headlong into the marsh a few yards from his destination. He scrambled to his feet, panting and covered in mud, trying to regain the dignity he never had.

Mary spoke quickly then, realizing that Tootles was there to protect her even though she no longer needed protecting. "There was a snake," she told Tootles. "I screamed and this girl shot it with an arrow."

Tootles stared at the strange children, taking in the girl's bow and arrow, her long braids, and the boy's dark hair. He frowned at the children. "You're Indians!" he said abruptly.

Mary frowned at Tootles, who seemed unaware that he was being rude. At the very least, he could introduce himself. "Thank you for saving me," Mary said to the strange children. "My name is Mary Darling. This is Tootles. What's your name?"

"I'm Princess Tiger Lily," the girl said. "This is my cousin, Ben."

"You're a princess?"

"My grandmother is Chief Laughing Bear, so that's my name in the show," the girl said, as if that explained everything. "My everyday name is Polly. You can call me that, if you like."

Mary decided to set all that aside for the moment and deal with her immediate problem. "I've hurt my foot," she said. "Can you help me up?"

She spoke to Tootles, but Polly and Ben helped too. At awkward moments it is always good to have something practical to do. Working together, the children lifted Mary to her feet. Or rather, to her left foot. She could put no weight on her right foot.

They helped Mary hop to a boulder where she could sit down. Tootles splashed water from the stream onto her right foot, washing off the mud. Her ankle was red and starting to swell.

"I can't walk on it," Mary said. "How will I get back to camp?"

"My grandmother will help," Polly said. "I'll stay here with you. Ben can take Tootles to my grandmother."

CHAPTER 18
Pretending to Be Indians

ABOUT A YEAR before Mary met Polly in Neverland, Polly's grandmother, Julia River, was sitting on the porch of her house on a warm summer day with her sister Anna. The two women were weaving fancy baskets from sweetgrass and black ash splints. The sisters were known for their skill in basketmaking, and the sale of their baskets provided an important source of income for the family. But at that moment, Julia's mind was not on the baskets nor on the income they would bring in.

"I'm guessing they'll be coming for Polly soon," Julia said to her sister. She spoke quietly, even though the sisters were alone. This was a conversation she didn't want anyone to overhear. "Polly is almost as old as Nelly was when they took her." Nelly and Polly were Julia's grandchildren.

Anna nodded grimly. "They'll be after Jesse and Ben, too." She also kept her voice down. Jesse and Ben were her grandchildren.

There was no need to say who "they" were. Anna knew. Julia knew. Everyone knew. "They" were the agents of the government that controlled life in this small community that straddled the Saint Lawrence River, half in Canada and half in the United States. Two years before, without warning, despite the family's protests, government agents had taken Julia's granddaughter Nelly to a residential school run by missionaries.

It was essentially a government-sanctioned kidnapping, perfectly legal according to the laws of the colonial governments. Nelly's attendance at a residential school was required by law. If her parents did not comply with the law, they could be sent to prison.

That's because the sisters and their families belonged to the Kanien'kehá:ka nation. In the parlance of the time, they were Indians. More specifically, colonists called them Mohawks—a name that came from the Narragansett people. In the Narragansett language, Mohawk meant "man eater" or "cannibal." Since it seems rather rude to accept a name provided by someone's enemy, I will use the name that Julia and her family used for themselves: Kanien'kehá:ka, which means "People of the Flint."

But let's get back to what happened to Nelly. Being taken to a residential school was similar in some ways to becoming one of the Lost Boys in Neverland. Here's how the two experiences are similar:

1. You were assigned a new name, whether you liked it or not. You had no choice in the matter.
2. You could not go home, no matter how often you asked.
3. You were always hungry.
4. You could die.

All that sounds bad enough, but being taken to a residential school was far worse than flying away with Peter Pan. At the school, everything familiar was taken away from you. Sometimes, school administrators could not be bothered to give you a new name—so they simply assigned you a number. You had no name. Your traditional clothing was replaced with a school uniform. Your hair was shorn—braids cut off, heads shaved. Even your native language was forbidden—you were punished for speaking it. You were also punished for failing to follow orders given in English— even if you knew no English. Every effort was made to strip you of your identity and to sever your connection to your families and your culture.

I could go on, but you get the idea. At the school, children were punished for being Indian. Richard Henry Pratt, founder of a particularly notorious residential school, described the school's goal clearly: "Kill the Indian . . . and save the man." Nicolas Flood Davin, a politician who helped design the residential school system, put it even more baldly: "The aim of education is to destroy the Indian."

The mandatory, missionary-run schools were the government's solution to what members of the United States Congress and the Parliament of Canada referred to as the "Indian Problem." Put simply, the Indian Problem was this: Indians, the people who had lived in North America for tens of thousands of years before the colonists arrived, were getting in the way of progress, as defined by the colonists. The Indians were living on lands that colonists wanted. The Indians were insisting that colonists abide by treaties negotiated decades before.

Politicians in the colonial governments maintained that colonists had the right and responsibility—a God-given right, in fact, and a God-given responsibility—to spread across the entire North American continent, bringing their version of civilization to lands they perceived as wilderness and to people they perceived as savages. The Indians disagreed.

Proponents of the residential school system claimed that there would be no more Indians—and therefore no Indian Problem—after a single generation was forced to attend residential school. Certainly, there would be broken and traumatized children, but that was just the price that must be paid. Certainly, some children would die from starvation, mistreatment, and disease. The government realized and accepted that. As one deputy superintendent of Indian Affairs explained, "Indian children in the residential schools die at a much higher rate than in their villages. But this does not justify a change in the policy of this Department, which is geared towards a final solution of our Indian Problem."

Julia and Anna did not know that they were part of an Indian Problem. But they did know that they would do anything they could to keep any more grandchildren from being taken to a residential school.

"We have to protect the children," Anna said. "We can't let them be taken away."

"I've been thinking about that," Julia said. "They can't take the children if the children aren't here."

Anna frowned. "You want to take the children where they can't be found? Difficult to manage that without a travel pass." Inhabitants of the reservation were required to have a government permit to travel outside the reservation.

"Suppose I take the children with me to the Kickapoo Medicine Show," Julia said. "Frank works for them sometimes. I've sold baskets there."

Anna considered that. Even as the governments were doing their best to erase Native cultures, colonists happily attended shows featuring Indians. The colonists loved Indians—as long as those Indians were portrayed as noble, brave, and ultimately doomed to oblivion. Bravery and nobility were optional, but oblivion was mandatory.

The Kickapoo Medicine Show—which featured war dances, sharp-shooters, and trick riding in the service of selling a patent medicine called Kickapoo Indian Sagwa—was just one option. There were also Wild West shows that had all of the above entertainment, plus some dramatic "reenactments of frontier life" with whooping and shooting and Indians falling from the saddle.

Some members of the Kanien'kehá:ka nation had successfully circumvented governmental interference by signing on with a show. The white showmen ran interference for their performers. As long as you stayed with the show, you had some measure of protection from the authorities.

"Too easy for them to find you at the Kickapoo Medicine Show," Anna said. "And you'll be working for white men."

Julia nodded. "Hard to get around that."

"Suppose you started your own show," Anna suggested. "Uncle Jack could help."

As a young man, their Uncle Jack traveled to Britain and Europe with the Great United States Circus. Under the stage name of Chief Running Elk, Uncle Jack had demonstrated his impressive skills with bow and arrow.

When he returned home, Uncle Jack set up a small show that traveled by horse and wagon throughout the northeastern United States. Anna traveled with the show for a time, selling baskets and beadwork after each performance. Uncle Jack eventually stopped traveling, but he still had all the costumes and props. And he knew people in the circus business.

Julia nodded slowly. "That might work."

"It would be best to go where they can't follow," Anna said.

Julia was skeptical. "Not easy to do."

"There are ships that sail from Quebec to London," Anna said. "Uncle Jack said the circus did very well in London."

"Yes," Julia said. "They wouldn't find us in London."

The scent of the sweetgrass hung in the air as the sisters worked and talked. They made a striking picture—two older women, their skin darkened by the sun, their heads close together in conversation. Had a government agent happened to see them, he would never have suspected the subversive nature of their conversation. But then the white men had never understood the power of women among the Kanien'kehá:ka. White men paid attention to the chiefs, unaware that the women selected the chiefs. The women made all decisions related to property and family.

Though the chiefs spoke as the nation's voice when dealing with outsiders, they remained in power only with the support of the women.

Over the course of that afternoon, while weaving baskets for trade, the two women sorted out the details of a plan. A traveling show would need someone who could talk to white folks and make arrangements. Julia could do that. She and her sister both spoke English well, having learned from their mother, who had worked in the ginseng trade, brokering the sale of wild ginseng root to Irish merchants in New York.

The show needed a name and a man who could appear to be in charge, since white folks expected that. Julia's husband Frank—a big man with a noble bearing and a deep voice—was perfect for that role. Julia consulted with Frank and he approved of the plan. After much discussion, the women settled on a name: Chief Laughing Bear's Amazing Indians. Frank would be Chief Laughing Bear.

Everyone would play a part in the show. Frank would deliver the final speech from the stage play *The Last of the Wampanoags*—the dying words of a noble Indian chieftain whose people were vanishing into oblivion. Frank made fun of the speech, written by a white man back in 1829, but could deliver the lines with somber conviction. The children—Julia's granddaughter Polly and Polly's cousins Jesse and Ben—would sing and dance, led by Susan, Julia's daughter and Polly's mother. Polly would demonstrate her skills with the bow and arrow. There would be trick shooting and trick riding.

Through Uncle Jack, the sisters made contact with a middling-sized circus that was traveling to Birmingham, England for a show. The promoter was interested in an Indian act, and arrangements were made for Chief Laughing Bear's Amazing Indians to travel with the circus and perform with them in the major cities of England.

Uncle Jack brought out the teepee he had used with his traveling show and the women cleaned and repaired it. He explained why the Amazing Indians had to have a teepee. "The audience really doesn't want to see you," he told Julia. "They want to see the Indians that they believe in, the ones that they've read about in books by people who have never met an Indian. Those Indians all live in teepees. In the show, you have to pretend to be those Indians."

In the dead of night, when no one would ask inconvenient questions, Chief Laughing Bear's Amazing Indians left. A thick fog hung over the *Kaniatarowanenneh*, the great river that colonists called the Saint Lawrence. Julia loaded their trade goods—baskets, beadwork purses, and trinkets designed to appeal to Europeans. Frank and Uncle Jack loaded the teepee and the props for the show. Uncle Jack would go with them as far as Quebec, then return home with the canoe.

In the bottom of the boat, Julia's daughter Susan made a nest of blankets for the children.

Polly, Jesse, and Ben settled down in the blankets. Julia and Susan sat on either end of the children's bed of blankets. Then Frank and Jack pushed the canoe into the current. Susan's husband Joe was already in Quebec with his brother Will, who had decided to join them.

As the current carried the canoe east toward Quebec, the fog embraced them. Julia looked toward the shore. Through the fog, she could barely see the outline of the mission building and the agent's office for the Bureau of Indian Affairs. Dark and quiet—no indication that anyone was aware that the River family was leaving the reservation, no one to see the canoe headed east.

Julia had put out the word that she was headed south to join up with the Kickapoo Medicine Show. It would take a while for the bureau agent to realize that they were gone, and it was best to ensure that any pursuit would be headed in the wrong direction.

As the river carried them eastward, the fog lifted. Julia could see the farms of family and friends. These were poor farms—not because the Kanien'kehá:ka were poor farmers, but rather because the land where the government had grudgingly allowed them to live was poor land. The Kanien'kehá:ka had lived here for thousands of years, yet the colonial government acted as if this land were a gift they should be grateful for, rather than the return of what was rightfully theirs.

This was the land of her people, Julia thought. This was her river. She belonged here. She was leaving it all behind. When would she be back?

Just then, she felt movement in the blanket beside her. Polly took Julia's hand. "We're going on an adventure," Polly whispered.

Julia looked down at the child's smiling face. Polly looked so much like her sister Nelly that sometimes it made Julia's heart ache. Nelly had never returned from school and she never would. About a year after she was taken, Julia had asked the bureau agent to write to the school to ask about the girl, giving him one of her best fancy baskets in return for the service. The reply from the school said Nelly had died of tuberculosis. When asked for more information, the agent shrugged, a gesture of complete indifference. So many Indian children—what did one girl matter?

Looking at Polly, Julia knew that she was doing the right thing. "Yes," she said to her granddaughter. "We are going on an adventure."

Chief Laughing Bear's Amazing Indians took England by storm. Frank was impressive as Chief Laughing Bear. His deep voice reached the farthest seats in the tent when he delivered his speech, a settler's interpretation of an Indian chief's last words: "Though numbers overpower me and treachery surrounds me, though friends desert me, I defy you still!" He died beautifully, a perfect portrayal of the stoicism the audience expected of an Indian chief.

Joe and Will showed off their skills in knife throwing, trick riding, and shooting. Julia and Susan sang and danced. Ben, Jesse, and Polly amazed the audience with their archery skills.

The show always ended with the Friendship Dance. Frank, the lead singer, played the water drum. Ben kept time with a cow horn rattle. Susan demonstrated the steps. Everyone else danced and sang. The children invited the audience to dance with them. Who could resist that?

Chief Laughing Bear and his Amazing Indians performed with the circus throughout England, then accompanied the circus on its tour of Europe. Their association with the circus came to an end in Paris. The circus would be returning to the United States, but Chief Laughing Bear and his Amazing Indians would travel on.

Just after their final performance in Paris, Frank and Julia met with a French promoter who suggested extending their tour to South Africa. The promoter offered to arrange first-class transportation on a merchant ship with the auspicious name, *Bright Destiny*. He promised large audiences and a very profitable run.

An agreement was struck. Then, while the performers were enjoying a week of rest in Paris, Frank came down with a fever. Perhaps it was scarlet fever; perhaps it was typhus; perhaps it was one of the dozens of other diseases that were common in Europe at the time. Whatever the disease was, it was deadly. Frank died a few days after he fell ill.

Julia had little time to mourn her husband's death. She conferred with the others about their options. The troupe could continue their tour without Frank or they could return to America, to the reservation they had left. It was a hard discussion—they all missed home and family, but the threat of the residential schools outweighed their longing to return. They decided to continue their tour.

They needed to replace Frank as Chief Laughing Bear. The show would not be complete without his speech and death scene. Since Julia knew all his lines, she adopted her husband's stage name and assumed his role in the show.

The troupe set sail for South Africa on the *Bright Destiny,* which was not quite the first-class transportation that the promoter had promised. En route to South Africa, a storm overwhelmed the ship. The crew lowered the lifeboats. Joe and Will had just enough time to release their horses. The performers took a lifeboat and the horses swam for it.

The lifeboat was taking on water when Neverland appeared mysteriously in the storm. The waves pushed the boat toward the shore, then slammed it into the reef. The lifeboat was lost, but everyone aboard made it to shore. Even the horses made it, swimming through the waves to the beach. A day later, two steamer trunks filled with the troupe's belongings, including props for the show, washed up on the beach— along with wreckage from the ship.

CHAPTER 19
Feeling Like the Elephant

EAVING MARY WITH Polly, Tootles followed Ben to the beach. As they walked along the beach, Tootles noticed hoofprints in the sand. Then he heard the rhythm of galloping hooves. He turned toward the sound.

A horse was galloping along the beach. It passed within a few yards of Tootles, close enough to give him a good look at the rider—a young man who lifted a hand to wave as he passed.

Then another man on a galloping horse came into view, apparently in hot pursuit of the first. As Tootles watched, the second man raised his hand and shouted very loudly: "Bang! Bang!"

At that moment, the first rider fell.

Tootles gasped. The man did not fall to the ground—it looked like his foot was caught in the stirrup or tangled in the reins. He fell to one side of the horse, his body limp and his head just inches from the sand. Dead, Tootles thought, most certainly dead. Though how the man could have been killed by a shouted "Bang!" was a mystery. The horse kept galloping.

Ben called out to the men in a language that Tootles did not understand. The man who had shouted "Bang!" pulled up beside them. He seemed unconcerned about the dead man. "Hullo," he said to Tootles.

"This is Will," Ben said. "That's Joe." He pointed in the direction of the dead man. Tootles looked at Joe just in time to see the horse slow and the fallen man pop up again, regaining his seat on the horse's back. He turned the horse and trotted back to join them.

"You fell," Tootles said to Joe. "I thought you were dead."

"It's a trick," Joe said. "Will and I decided to practice some tricks on our way back to camp."

When Tootles looked puzzled, Joe gestured inland. There was a canvas banner tied between two palm trees to make a large patch of shade over a blanket, where three people were sitting. The banner read: CHIEF LAUGHING BEAR'S AMAZING INDIANS! TRICK RIDING! ROPING! FRONTIER DRAMA! THE REAL WILD WEST!

"Will and I are the trick riders," Joe said.

The two women and the boy who had been in the shade of the banner came to join Joe, Will, Ben, and Tootles on the beach. All the performers considered Tootles with great curiosity. Ben was speaking quickly in the language that Tootles didn't understand. The only words he could understand were "Mary" and "Tootles."

Tootles remembered going to the London zoo with his parents to see the elephant. There had been dozens of people crowded around the elephant's enclosure, all talking about the animal. Now Tootles thought he knew how the elephant had felt. It wasn't a good feeling.

At last, the oldest of the women spoke. "Hullo, Tootles," she said. "I'm Chief Laughing Bear."

Tootles nodded, his eyes wide. He had so many questions. How did these Indians get to Neverland? How could a woman be a chief? Why didn't she talk like the Indians in the adventure books he'd read? He froze, not knowing which question to ask first.

"Ben says your friend needs help," Chief Laughing Bear said.

Tootles nodded. "Mary hurt her foot. She can't walk."

Chief Laughing Bear regarded him steadily. "And where would Mary walk to, if she could?"

"Back to our camp on the other side of the island."

"We can help with that," Chief Laughing Bear said.

Polly sat on the boulder beside Mary. She studied Mary's canvas sack filled with uprooted taro plants, lying on the ground where Mary had dropped it. "Why are you gathering those plants? Do you eat them?"

"Oh, yes. They're very good." Mary explained how to boil and then roast the roots, happy to share what she had learned from Sam.

Then Mary asked about something that had been puzzling her. "You said your name was Princess Tiger Lily in the show," Mary said. "What show are you talking about?"

"Chief Laughing Bear's Amazing Indians. It's a show where we pretend to be Indians."

Mary struggled to make sense of this. "But you are Indians, aren't you?"

"We are Kanien'kehá:ka. White men call us Indians." Seeing that Mary was confused, Polly repeated what her grandmother had told her when they left the reservation. "White men made up a story about Indians. They think all Indians live in teepees and carve totem poles and hunt buffalo and shoot arrows. They don't remember making up this story. They think it's true. To make a show that white people will pay money to see, we pretend we fit their story."

"You don't live in teepees?"

"Not at home. But we have a teepee for the show. We're living in it now."

"How did you get to Neverland?" Mary asked.

"Neverland? I don't understand."

"This island is Neverland. How did you get here?"

"Our ship was caught in a storm. Our lifeboat brought us here. How did you get here?"

"Peter Pan brought us." Mary told Polly about how she and her brother had flown to Neverland. Mary was glad to have another girl to talk to. The Lost Boys were very talkative, but not that good at listening. "I want to go home, but Peter won't take us, and I can't find the way without him."

"Why won't he take you home?"

"He says my mother has already forgotten me," Mary said sadly. "He says mothers are like that." She bit her lip thinking about the main reason she wanted to leave. "Peter likes to fight—he thinks it's a game. We fought pirates and Curly and Nibs died. They really died. It wasn't a game. And now Peter has forgotten Curly and Nibs."

Polly frowned as she tried to make sense of all this.

Thinking about Peter and the pirates, Mary remembered when one of the Lost Boys mentioned the Indians in a penny dreadful novel he had read. Peter had listened with great attention. Then he said, "Maybe someday we'll have Indians on Neverland. Then we'll have a good fight." The memory made her shiver.

"Peter wants to fight Indians," she said slowly.

Polly saw her grandmother in the distance. "Look! My grandmother is coming."

Chief Laughing Bear—or Julia River, if you prefer—was leading a horse. Tootles walked beside her. They were accompanied by Polly's parents, Susan and Joe.

"I've brought help!" Tootles called to Mary. "You can ride home on a horse. The Indians will help us get back to camp."

Julia sat on the ground and took Mary's ankle in her cool hands, gently examining it. As she worked, she talked to Mary softly, a running commentary of diagnosis, reassurance, and explanation—a soliloquy that was a variation on a medicine show pitch. "Just a sprain," she said. "Your ankle twisted where it should not have twisted. You tried to do too much too quick." She took a bottle of liniment from the pouch at her belt. "But I have the medicine that will fix the problem right here." She opened the bottle and waved it under Mary's nose. "Breathe deep and smell that sweet healing scent."

The smell made Mary sit up straight. It smelled like a mixture of pine trees, mint, licorice, and ginger.

"It's made from healing herbs that will ease your pain and bring down the swelling." Julia applied the liquid to the ankle, gently rubbing it into the girl's skin.

Mary's skin tingled and she felt better immediately. It was wonderful to be taken care of like this. At the Lost Boys camp, she was the one everyone looked to when they needed mothering, but there was no one to mother her. Julia's gentle care made her realize how much she missed that.

Julia wrapped Mary's ankle tightly in a cloth bandage. "This will help you heal by stopping your ankle from bending and twisting."

"Thank you," said Mary. "That feels much better already."

Having remained quiet as her grandmother worked, Polly spoke to Julia in their native language. Mary understood just two words of what she said: "Peter Pan."

Julia looked at Mary. "My granddaughter says that you flew here with Peter Pan. Is that so?"

Mary nodded.

Julia considered this. She wondered how Peter Pan flew. Her people had stories of the Kanontsistóntie's, a ferocious spirit that took the form of an enormous flying head. But it did not seem likely that Peter Pan was one of those. The girl did not seem fearful or eager to escape him. Perhaps Peter Pan had some sort of flying machine. She would have to find out more about this.

* * *

When Peter Pan returned to camp late that afternoon, he found the Lost Boys gathered around the fire, roasting taro roots. For once, they were not interested in hearing about what Peter had been doing. They were listening to Tootles, which was strange because no one ever listened to Tootles. Tootles was telling them about the people that he and Mary had met on the far side of the island. Tootles said they were Indians.

Peter saw Mary sitting by the fire, her foot bandaged and propped up in front of her. "They attacked you?" His hand was on his knife, ready to dispatch whoever had caused this injury.

"No!" Mary said. "They saved me!"

Tootles started his story over, beginning with the taro roots and ending with the horseback ride to the Lost Boys camp. "They have a teepee," he told Peter. "Chief Laughing Bear fixed Mary's ankle. Then Joe and Will brought her home."

Curly spoke up then. "I bet they'll go on the warpath," he said enthusiastically. "Indians always go on the warpath."

"We'll fight them," Peter said with enthusiasm.

"No!" Mary said loudly. She spoke without thinking. She glared at Curly and at Peter. "These people are friends of mine. We will not fight them."

All the Lost Boys stared at her. Peter blinked, startled by Mary's tone. No one, not even Sam, said no to Peter.

To be honest, Mary had startled herself, too. Until that moment, she had never directly opposed Peter. She had never told him flat out that he could not do something. But now she looked at him with an unwavering gaze and said, "No!" She did not smile. She was remembering the battle on the pirate ship. She was thinking that fighting was not a game. She knew that people could die.

"We will not fight them," Mary repeated firmly.

CHAPTER 20
People Believe What They Want to Believe

L ATE IN THE night, Peter Pan woke from uncomfortable dreams. In his dreams he sometimes remembered things that he had forgotten in waking life, things like pain and loss and death. Usually, when he had bad dreams, Mary comforted him in a motherly sort of way.

But that night he did not wake Mary. Peter did not want to talk to Mary. He couldn't have told you why he didn't want to talk with Mary, but maybe you can guess. He wanted a mother who was sweet, self-sacrificing, and completely devoted to making him happy. But at the same time, he knew that mothers weren't really like that.

Mothers were a dangerous force—more dangerous than wild animals or pirates or Indians. Because you couldn't really fight mothers the way you fought those things. Given half a chance, a mother would make you grow up—and that he would never do.

When Mary had stared at him and said, "We will not fight them," Peter didn't know what to do or say. He felt a shift in the world around him—everything was the same, and yet everything was different. Mary was acting like a grown-up, and that was terrifying.

So when Peter woke in the night, he quietly slipped out of the cave and flew away. At sunrise, he was on the far side of the island, perched in a tree overlooking a large teepee. He wanted to see Chief Laughing Bear and the other people that Mary said he must not fight.

When the sky was beginning to grow lighter in the east, Julia left the teepee, followed by the others. In the clearing beside the teepee, Julia began to speak in a language that Peter did not understand. She seemed to be reciting something. Something about the way she said the words, and the way the others listened, made him realize that these words were important.

As she spoke, Peter noticed something changing in the forest. From the trees around him rose a chorus of whistles and warbles, squawks and trills, hooting and honking. At that moment, as Peter looked down at these strangers that Mary said he must not fight, he interpreted the raucous dawn chorus as a reaction to Julia's words. The island, he thought, was listening to Julia and answering her.

This was, of course, totally wrong. Every day, as the sky brightened, the birds and animals of the forest began to wake up and comment on the coming of the light. Parrots whistled and squawked, frogs croaked, flamingos honked. It happened every morning. Being a rather self-centered boy, Peter had never paid much attention to it. But when Julia spoke, he was very aware of the chatter of birds and animals—and he wondered what was going on. What was the woman in the clearing below saying? What sort of magic was she working in the world?

Julia was reciting the Ohèn:ton Karihwatéhkwen, the words the Kanien'kehá:ka used to open any meeting. Literally translated, Ohèn:ton Karihwatéhkwen means "what we say before we do anything important."

Julia's words were intended to bring the minds of everyone at the gathering together as one—in harmony with each other and with the natural world around them. To that end, she expressed thanks to all the forces in the natural world—the earth, the waters, the sun, the moon, the winds, the plants, and the people. She asked that everyone come together to talk about the children they had met the day before. How should they interact with Mary, the Lost Boys, and Peter Pan?

Everyone told the group their thoughts. Polly repeated what Mary had told her about Peter Pan and how he wanted to fight Indians. Joe and Will described the Lost Boys camp.

"Those boys are no threat to anyone but themselves," Will said. "Peter Pan wasn't there, so we didn't meet him."

Susan wanted to check and see how Mary was doing.

Julia mentioned that Peter Pan and the children had flown to Neverland. Everyone agreed that was strange and worth learning more about.

* * *

Watching from the tree, Peter saw only the results of the discussion. The group ate breakfast. Then Susan, Polly, and Joe set out on the horses in the direction of the Lost Boys camp. Will, Ben, and Jesse left to go fishing. After the others left, Julia sat in a patch of shade near the teepee. She picked up the half-finished basket she had been weaving the day before, when Tootles' arrival interrupted her work.

Peter flew down and landed gracefully just a few feet from her. "I'm Peter Pan," he said. "I'm looking for Chief Laughing Bear."

Julia regarded him with a steady gaze. "I'm Chief Laughing Bear."

There is tension and uncertainty when one spiritual system collides with another. Missionaries deal with this tension by asserting that their system is the only true way of thinking. But Peter Pan was not a missionary. It's hard to say what he was—a spirit, a god, or an idea that somehow became real. In any case, Julia River and the Ohèn:ton Karihwaté́hkwen puzzled him.

Julia was not what Peter Pan had expected. He had imagined Chief Laughing Bear to be a big man wearing a headdress of eagle feathers, not an older woman with her long hair in braids and a basket in her hand.

Peter Pan was not what Julia had expected. When Tootles had said Peter Pan was the leader of the Lost Boys, she had imagined a man, not a child.

"I thought you'd be a man," Peter said.

"I thought you'd be a man, too," Julia said.

"Are you an Indian?" he asked.

Julia studied this child thoughtfully. From what Polly had said, she knew he wanted to fight Indians, and she had no desire to wage war on a child. On the reservation, she was called an Indian, a term that was applied to her whether she liked it or not. There, she had no choice. In the show, she called herself an Indian, because that was part of the show. But now she was not on the reservation nor playing a part in the show. She did not have to use the label that colonists had applied to her people.

"I am Kanien'kehá:ka," she said.

"Oh, that's all right then," he said.

Suddenly Peter felt much better. Tootles was wrong about these people being Indians. If they had been Indians, he would have had to fight them no matter what Mary said. But they weren't Indians after all.

Julia was still studying him. Under her gaze, Peter grew uneasy. He was meeting, perhaps for the first time, a force even more powerful than a mother. Because Julia was not just a mother. She was a grandmother.

Children can win their mother over with a smile, but grandmothers can see right through all that. All children are susceptible to the grandmotherly gaze. Peter felt she was looking past the façade he presented to the world. He felt she could see all the things he had forgotten and she knew the dreams that woke him up at night.

Among the Kanien'kehá:ka, women are strong, thoughtful, and powerful. Grandmothers are the most powerful of all women. A Kanien'kehá:ka grandmother was no one to trifle with.

"How is it you fly?" she asked him.

"Fairy dust," he said. Peter was thinking just then that flying away might be a good idea. Julia's matter-of-fact scrutiny made him uncomfortable. He was used to being met with admiration and amazement.

"I had thought you might have flown here in a balloon airship," Julia said.

Peter was intrigued. "A balloon airship? What's that?"

"I saw one once," Julia said. While traveling through New York State, the Kickapoo Medicine Show had arranged for a balloon ascent as part of the show. "A lady aeronaut flew away in a balloon airship that was as round as the moon and as light as a cloud."

Peter did not know what an aeronaut was, but he could imagine a beautiful lady floating away in a basket tied to the moon. That image made flying with fairy dust seem so dull.

"As round as the moon," he said, in a voice filled with wonder.

When Mary woke up that morning, she could not walk more than a few steps. Had Peter been there, he could have sprinkled her with fairy dust so she could fly, rather than walking. But Peter was gone.

Mary and the Lost Boys ate leftover taro roots for breakfast. Then Curly, Nibs, Slightly, the Twins, and Tom went to the mermaids' lagoon, saying they would look for Peter. Mary knew that task would slip their minds as soon as they left camp and they would end up playing on the beach.

Tootles and Sam helped Mary to a comfortable place to sit near the cave. They tried to cheer her up, but she wasn't in a mood to be cheered up. Her ankle ached and she kept wondering where Peter was. That was when Susan, Joe, and Polly rode in.

Susan examined Mary's ankle, removing the bandage, applying fresh liniment, then gently rewrapping the injury. Mary felt much better immediately. It was wonderful to have a mother's kind attention when you were unwell, even if Susan wasn't her mother.

While Susan tended to Mary's ankle, Tootles had a question for Joe. "How did you stay on the horse when you fell? After Will shot you."

"He didn't shoot me. He shouted, 'Bang!'"

"I know he didn't really shoot you. But how did you stay on the horse?"

"It's a trick I learned from a Cossack while I was working for the Kickapoo Medicine Show. At least he said he was a Cossack." Joe shrugged. "Hard to say for sure. People say lots of things."

Tootles was puzzled, and you can't really blame him. There was so much about America and the people who lived there that his books had failed to touch upon.

"Joe doesn't sound like an Indian name," Tootles said. "All the Indians I've read about have better names than that. Why don't you have a name like Tiger Lily or Laughing Bear? Those sound like Indian names. In my books, all the Indians have names like Laughing Bear."

Sam spoke up then. "Those books aren't true, Tootles."

"What do you mean?" Tootles asked.

"People have wrong ideas sometimes," Sam said. "They write books full of wrong ideas." Sam noticed that Joe was watching him closely, focused on him in a new way.

"So why doesn't anyone tell them they're wrong?" Tootles asked.

"You can try," Joe said. "But it doesn't work."

"Why not?" Tootles was determined to figure this out.

"People believe what they want to believe," Sam said. "When I went to school in England, there was a boy who believed all kinds of things that were very wrong."

That was how Sam found himself talking about his experience at Dr. Plummer's Academy. He talked about the book, *The Coral Island,* and about seeing the Cannibal King at the fun fair. He told them that he had explained to Arthur, in grisly and imaginary detail, how he would kill a man he meant to devour. Then Sam grinned his Cannibal King grin.

Susan and Joe laughed. Tootles didn't.

"A good joke," Joe said. "A very good joke."

"You fooled him," Tootles said uneasily. "You lied to him."

Joe grinned. "That boy fooled himself. Sam made a trap and then that boy fell into it."

CHAPTER 21
I Hear the Mermaids Singing

ACH EVENING ON the *Golden Dawn*, Watson walked on the deck, trying to exhaust himself so that he would sleep. Nana paced solemnly after him as he walked from bow to stern and back again.

One night, after walking for the better part of an hour, he stopped at the ship's bow to lean on the railing for a moment and smoke his pipe. The night air was cool, a welcome respite from the heat of the day. The ship's sails were full. Water whispered against the wooden hull as the ship rushed forward. Wood creaked as small changes in the wind shifted the sails ever so slightly, changing the pressure on the mast.

The bow wave was proof that the ship was moving steadily through the water. They were following Mary and he took some comfort in that. Right now, there was nothing to do but wait, and he was ill-suited for waiting.

As Watson idly watched the water, he noticed something strange. The bow wave was glowing with a pale blue light. As Watson watched, the glow grew brighter, making ribbons of light in the water.

Were there shapes moving beneath the water, outlined in shimmering light? Hard to say. The light shifted and changed, but he thought he saw something moving down there. Dolphins sometimes swam beside the ship for a time, surfing on the bow wave. Could those shapes be dolphins, he wondered.

It seemed to him that a new sound had joined the creaking of the sails and the rush of water against the hull—some sort of music, barely audible. The faint sound reminded him of his dear departed wife. Sometimes, while doing chores, she would sing to herself—so soft and sweet. Ah, how he missed her! That sound—those mysterious half-heard voices—made him long for her. He thought he could hear her in the chorus of voices, singing a song that called to him.

Nana growled, a rumble low in her throat. She stepped toward the railing, ready to protect this foolish man who seemed so oblivious to a threat.

Watson paid no attention. He leaned out over the rail, straining to listen, wanting to hear his wife's sweet voice again. He could feel cool drops of ocean spray on his face.

"Watson, come away from there!" He felt a hand grip his shoulder, pulling him upright, turning him away from the railing.

Watson tried to pull away, but Sam held him firm.

"I heard music," Watson said. He tried to turn back toward the water, but the music was fading. The light was fading too.

Sam said, "Don't listen."

Watson felt disoriented and confused, as if he were waking from a dream. There was no music, just the creaking of the sails in the wind and the rush of the water against the wooden hull of the ship.

He stared at Sam. "What's down there?" he asked.

Sam did not release his grip on Watson's shoulder. "What did you hear?"

"I heard my dead wife's voice," Watson said. "She was calling to me."

"You must not listen," Sam said. "They want to lure you into the water. They want to watch you drown."

"What are you talking about?" Watson asked. "Who are they?"

"Mermaids." Sam's tone was matter-of-fact. He didn't like talking about mermaids or Neverland, but he had to help Watson understand the dangers they faced. "Mermaids swim in the lagoon in Neverland."

Watson stared at Sam. "You're talking about Neverland as if it were a real place. As if you've been there."

"Yes," Sam said. "I've been to Neverland. That's where I met George, Mary, and her brother."

"You didn't tell me that in London. When I told you that George talked of Neverland, you said—"

"I said I would state no opinion on the matter. George is an upstanding citizen with a respectable job. He can talk about Neverland and be regarded as merely eccentric. As a dark-skinned tailor with dubious connections . . ." Sam shook his head. "I have no interest in being locked up in Bedlam as a madman."

"You think the children are in Neverland?"

Sam nodded slowly. "In London, fairies and mermaids are the stuff of children's fairy tales. But we are no longer in London." He regarded Watson solemnly. "Things are different here."

Watson turned to look at the dark water rushing past the hull of the ship. There were no lights; no distant singing. "A dream," he said. "It must have been a dream."

"You can believe that if you like," Sam said. "You don't have to believe in mermaids. But be careful. Things you don't believe in can still kill you."

On his first morning aboard, Holmes had created a routine that allowed him to endure the tranquility of the ocean voyage. He had selected a place on deck that was sheltered from the wind. There he set up two deck chairs and settled in—initially with his pipe and tobacco pouch, and later with a pot of Rumbold's special tea as well.

From this comfortable vantage point, Holmes observed other passengers strolling on the deck. Occasionally he drew one into a long conversation. (That was what the second deck chair was for.)

The morning after Watson's late-night encounter with mysterious blue lights, the good doctor found Holmes in his usual spot and took the deck chair beside him. Nana, who had been keeping a close eye on Watson since his late-night observation of lights in the water, sat beside him and leaned against his leg as if to remind him that she was there.

"Join me in a cup of tea?" Holmes asked. When Watson shook his head, Holmes smiled. "My dear doctor, don't look so grim. Rumbold assures me that this beverage will do me no harm. I'm pleased to say that this tea has helped me stave off boredom for a time. I have whiled away these long afternoons taking advantage of the expertise of our fellow passengers. Dawson has educated me about the value of orchids. Benito Salini has taught me about gems. Rumbold has added to my knowledge of exotic poisons."

"I've had some interesting conversations as well," Watson said. "Sam told me where he met Mary and George."

"Excellent! What have you learned?"

"You won't like it."

Before Watson could speak again, Holmes held up a hand. "Don't just tell me what he said. Tell me when you talked, where you were, and what was happening when he told you. Include every detail, however trivial."

"It was last night," Watson said. "I was at the bow of the ship, watching the moonlight on the water. As I stared at the water, I became aware of light below the surface, ribbons of blue light that shifted and flowed. I could see moving shapes under the water. I heard sounds that blended with the rush of the water against the hull and the wind in the sails. Almost like music."

Holmes was listening intently. "Go on," he said, as Watson hesitated.

"Sam found me there and told me not to watch the lights and not to listen to the sounds." Now, in the bright light of afternoon, Watson felt foolish. Experiences of the night before felt like a dream.

"Did he give you a reason for this warning?"

Nana put her head in Watson's lap, encouraging him with her presence. "Sam said that mermaids were trying to lure me into the water so they could watch me drown. He told me they came from Neverland." Watson hesitated, then went on. "Sam said that he met Mary and George in Neverland."

Holmes nodded. "I am glad that Sam has acknowledged that he has a long acquaintance with George. I had deduced as much."

Watson stared at his friend, astounded. "You believe that they met in Neverland?"

Holmes chuckled. "They met as children—but not in Neverland. They met in a thieves' den in one of London's most squalid slums."

"What are you talking about?"

"On that long-ago morning when you stormed out of the flat, I told you that George has a criminal past," Holmes said. "When George was twelve years old, he was kidnapped and trained as a pickpocket. Eventually, he escaped and returned to his family."

Watson shook his head in disbelief. "How could you possibly know that?"

"The story was reported in several newspapers at the time," Holmes said with a smile. "It was quite a sensation. Interest in the matter died away after Scotland Yard was unsuccessful in locating the ring of thieves that kidnapped the boy—but I retained the articles in my archives.

"Unraveling Sam's history took a bit more effort. Fortunately, you provided me with two facts from your chat with Sam: his grandfather was a glovemaker and Sam attended a school for young gentlemen. I arranged for an introduction to the current master of the Worshipful Company of Glovers. That gentleman put me in touch with an elderly glovemaker willing to reminisce about the old days. It turned out that he had been friends with a glovemaker named Samuel Smalls, whose son Matthew had been a missionary in the Solomon Islands.

"My elderly friend remembered meeting Smalls' black-skinned, blue-eyed grandson at Matthew's funeral. He said the boy was very well spoken—apparently Smalls had sent the boy to Dr. Plummer's Academy for young gentlemen. I confirmed that with a visit to the school. The school librarian remembered Sam—and was sorry that the boy had not returned to the school after his father died. The librarian remembered hearing that Sam had run away from his grandfather's home."

Holmes smiled. "There's no need to invent a magical island to explain how Sam and George met. Sam ran away from his grandfather's home and was recruited by a gang of pickpockets. George met Sam among the pickpockets. When George escaped and returned home, Sam did not. In search of adventure, he found a berth as a cabin boy—on a smuggler's ship, perhaps. Eventually, he joined a pirate crew.

"Neverland is as fictitious as the hound from Hell that was reputed to plague the Baskerville family," Holmes continued. "Fairy tales can be an excellent distraction for those who wish to conceal the truth."

"That doesn't explain the blue light in the water," Watson said.

"That blue light in the water is as natural as a firefly," Holmes replied. "Ask Rumbold about it. He'll tell you about tiny marine creatures that glow when disturbed and dolphins that surf on the bow wave of a ship. Nothing supernatural about it."

Watson nodded, uneasy, but trying to feel reassured by Holmes' explanation. He could still remember the sound of his wife's voice, calling to him from the water.

Later that day, Watson joined Rumbold for a smoke by the railing.

"I saw the strangest thing last night," Watson said. "The water by the bow of the ship looked like it was glowing."

"Ah," Rumbold said. "There are a number of marine organisms that glow like fireflies under the right conditions."

"What sorts of organisms?" Watson asked.

"Microorganisms too small to be seen with the naked eye. There are also squids and jellyfish that can glow."

Watson nodded, relieved to hear Rumbold repeat Holmes' rational explanation for the light he had seen.

But Rumbold didn't stop there. "It's worth noting that I have heard other opinions. My friend James, an experienced sailor, has advised me to be careful about observing lights in the water too closely. He says they are made by mermaids whose dearest desire is to watch you drown."

Watson stared at Rumbold. "Do you believe that?"

Rumbold shrugged. "I'm aware that many sailors claim to have seen and heard women in the ocean's depths. Are those sailors just longing for the women they left behind? Does that longing make them imagine mermaids? Hard to say. But James' advice made me cautious about watching lights in the water."

Watson shook his head. "You are a man of science. How can you entertain such ideas?"

Rumbold smiled. "Curiosity is what makes me a man of science. Science begins with the unknown. There are so many things in the sea we know nothing about. We investigate, we explore, and we discover. Did you know that there are fish that attract smaller fish with glowing lures? Could there be larger creatures that do the same? It's possible. It's a great wide world, Watson."

CHAPTER 22
Between the Old Wolf's Teeth

WHEN MARY'S ANKLE healed, she and Sam went to visit the Kanien'kehá:ka camp as often as they could.

Sam went hunting with Ben and Jesse. Ben taught Sam to throw a knife and shoot a bow and arrow. Sam taught Ben and Jesse the best way to climb a coconut palm tree.

Mary helped Susan and Polly collect grasses and palm leaves for making baskets. They gathered shellfish to bake in the fire. Mary found it comforting to be around Susan and Polly and Julia. But being with them also made Mary think about how much she missed her own mother.

"Why are you sad?" Polly asked her one day. The two of them were spreading basketmaking materials in the sun to dry.

"I miss my mother," Mary said. "I miss my home. When I flew away with Peter Pan, I didn't know I'd be away so long."

Mary remembered the last time she had seen her mother. They had both been tired and out of sorts. Even so, her mother had combed Mary's hair and hugged her good night. "Tomorrow will be a much better day," her mother had said.

Mary had given up on asking Peter Pan to take her home. The last time she asked, Peter had shaken his head. "I tried to go back to my mother once and the window was barred," he told her. "There was another little boy sleeping in my bed. She had forgotten all about me."

"Sometimes I wonder if my mother has forgotten me," Mary told Polly.

"I don't think she would," Polly said.

"I left without saying goodbye. Maybe she's angry with me."

Susan, who was sitting nearby working on a basket, spoke up then. "Your mother is waiting for you to come home. She is wondering where you are, worrying about you." She spoke quietly, but there was something in her voice that caught Mary's attention. Her hands had been busy just a moment before, but now they were still. "Your mother will never forget you."

The thought of her mother being worried alarmed Mary almost as much as thinking her mother had forgotten her. Her mother might think she was dead. She might be in mourning. Her father would have returned from the goldfields and found Mary and Tom gone.

Her father talked sometimes about returning to England. Maybe he would convince their mother to go back to London. When Mary and Tom finally went home, they'd find an empty house, an empty store.

"I need to go home," Mary said.

After that conversation, Mary became serious about finding a way home. Sitting by the fire with the Lost Boys while Peter was off on some adventure, she talked about escaping Neverland. Most of the boys didn't want to talk about it, but Sam was interested in her plans.

"We need a boat," Mary said.

Sam agreed, but they didn't have a boat. He and Mary talked about building a boat, but the idea never moved beyond the talking stage. Sam had watched his uncles build a boat, and he knew it was a big job. That's where the matter stood until one morning, when Sam returned to camp with news.

"I've found a boat," he told Mary.

Sam led Mary and Tom to the other side of the island, where a forest of mangrove trees grew close by the water. These were mangrove giants with a thick canopy of leaves and branches and great mats of tangled roots that held the trees above the water.

"Follow me," Sam said, stepping onto a root and climbing up into the tangled branches.

Mary and Tom followed him through a maze of branches that led out over the water. Tree-climbing crabs skittered away at their approach, heading down toward the water, but stopping short to watch the children's progress.

"Don't fall in that water," Sam said. "The crocodiles like it in the mangroves, you know."

Mary hung onto the branches tighter after that and kept watch for crocodiles in the water below. She had seen them before, while flying with Peter. Floating half-submerged, they looked like scaly logs with hungry eyes and too many teeth.

"There's the boat," Sam said.

A wooden boat was caught in the roots of the mangroves. Its bow rested on a clump of roots, half in and half out of the water. Mary stared down at the boat from her perch in the tree. "There's a man in it," she said.

"I think he's dead," Sam said.

"Hullo!" Mary called down to the man. "Ahoy there!"

"Ahoy!" said a strange scratchy voice. It didn't come from the boat, but from above. Mary turned so quickly to look for the speaker that she nearly fell from the branch.

"Ahoy, matey," the voice said again, following the words with a loud whistle.

It took a moment for Mary to find the source of the voice: a small gray parrot with yellow eyes. The bird twisted its head to consider the children with one bright eye and then with the other. It sidled closer to them, stepping along a branch.

"Hullo, bird," Sam said to the parrot in a friendly sort of way.

"Ahoy, matey," the bird repeated, eyeing Sam. "Captain Flint's a pretty bird."

"Hullo, Captain Flint," Sam said. "Good to meet you." The bird clacked his beak.

Sam turned his attention back to the boat. "The branches get thinner lower down," Sam said. "I haven't climbed closer. They might not support my weight."

"I'll try," Mary said.

Carefully, she climbed lower on the mangrove branches, stopping each time a branch sank beneath her, then continuing when she was confident it would hold. All the while, she kept watch on the man in the boat. He didn't move when she dropped into the boat beside him.

The man was dead—done in by thirst and hunger, by the look of him. His skin had dried and drawn tight to his skull. His lips, as black and dry as old leather, had pulled back, showing his teeth in a fierce grin that revealed a gold tooth. He had a kerchief wrapped around his head and he wore gold earrings in the leathery remnants of his ears.

"He's dead," Mary called up to the boys in the tree.

"Look lively, matey," the parrot said.

"How's the boat?" Sam asked, ignoring the bird.

Mary examined the craft. The hull looked sound—at least, all the parts she could see.

Gingerly, she pushed on the body with her foot—nothing but the pirate's ragged clothing between her bare foot and the corpse. It didn't feel like a real person at all; it was more like the straw dummy of Guy Fawkes that they burned on Bonfire Night.

With the corpse pushed to one side, Mary could see that the boat was dry, the planks solid. In the bottom of the boat were two oars, a couple of wooden boxes, and a wooden keg.

She looked up. A torn sail hung limply from the mast, which was leaning against a mangrove branch. She looked at the roots that supported the boat's bow. The tide was rising, and she felt the boat rock a bit in the gentle waves. "It looks like a sound craft," she said. "We need to get it free of the trees."

Tom climbed down to join her. Sam followed, carefully testing each branch before trusting it with his weight. They pushed the corpse to the back of the boat, where it sprawled over the boxes, out of their way. Then they set to work.

It wasn't easy to get the boat loose. Each time a wave came in, the boat rocked with the water's movement, but the rope tied to the boat's bow was tangled in the mangroves, holding it fast. The bow was cradled between two clumps of roots, able to rock, but little more.

Mary untangled the rope, standing on the clump of mangrove roots while she worked the rope free.

Tom offered advice from the comfort of the boat and the parrot offered advice from the comfort of the branches above her. Tom's advice was marginally helpful. "It's caught on that snag," he observed, as she tried to untangle the rope from a snag. Captain Flint's advice was more colorful, but less relevant. "Look lively, matey," the parrot said.

Sam found a nearby clump of roots that would support his weight. He figured out how to use one of the oars as a lever to lift the boat's bow, wedging the blade under the boat. A thick mangrove branch that hung low over the water served as a fulcrum.

When the rope was free at last, Mary and Tom sat in the boat and used the other oar to push against the mangrove roots when Sam lifted. Whenever an incoming wave lifted the boat a little, Sam pushed down on his oar to lift it still more. Mary and Tom pushed with their oar against the roots, moving the boat toward open water.

With each wave, the boat moved a little. Finally, it came free of the roots. "Look lively, matey," Captain Flint suggested again. Sam followed that advice and jumped aboard. He used the oars to guide the boat out of the mangroves and into the open water of the cove.

In the open water, Sam fitted the oars into the oarlocks and rowed for the beach on the far side of the cove. When the bottom of the boat scraped against the sand, Mary and Sam jumped out and pulled the boat up onto the beach.

For a moment, Mary considered the boat. When they were pushing it out of the mangroves, it had seemed very large, always catching on a root or a branch. Now, on the empty beach, it seemed very small. Could they really travel across an ocean in that?

Captain Flint interrupted her thoughts, flying from his perch in the mangroves to land on the side of the boat. The bird clacked its beak, then bobbed his head, his eyes on Sam. Sam held out his hand, and the bird jumped onto his finger, then sidled up his arm to his shoulder.

"What do you think of the boat?" Mary asked Sam.

"She looks seaworthy."

"Seaworthy enough to cross the ocean?"

Sam studied the boat. He glanced inland, in the direction of their camp. "It'd be easier if we could fly."

"That's so," Mary agreed. "But I don't think that's likely anytime soon." She glanced at Tom. "And waiting seems like a bad idea."

Peter had been restless lately. He wanted to attack another pirate ship.

"It will be dangerous to go," Sam said, interrupting Mary's thoughts.

"It's dangerous to stay." Mary's voice was firm.

"That's true," Sam agreed.

And with that, the decision was made.

Sam knew the trip in the small boat would be difficult, but he also knew it was time for him to leave the island. He had been in Neverland for the better part of a year. He was twelve years old—the oldest of the Lost Boys.

Peter had been treating him differently lately. Sam attributed the shift to changes in himself. When he came to Neverland, he had been just as tall as Peter Pan. But now he was a few inches taller—and wider as well. His arms were muscular. He was still a boy, but he was becoming a man.

Yes, it was definitely time to leave.

* * *

Sam and Mary lifted the pirate out of the boat—Sam was up by the grinning leathery face, and Mary was down by the feet. Mary noticed that the booted feet were surprisingly heavy. After they laid the corpse on the beach, Mary pulled off the dead pirate's boots to find out why they were so heavy. In the right boot, she found a leather sack filled bright golden coins. She held the coins out for Sam and Tom to see. "Look at this," she said.

"We're rich," said Tom.

Sam didn't even look at the coins. He knelt by the corpse and drew a knife from the sheath on the man's belt. The bright blade flashed in the sunlight—sharp and free of rust. "We can use this," he said. Sam took the belt and sheath as well. "He doesn't need those clothes either."

The shirt and trousers came off easily. Mary washed them in the warm ocean water and pulled them on, replacing her tattered nightgown. She rolled up the trouser legs to make them shorter and used a length of rope as a belt.

Tom had turned his attention to the other items in the boat. He opened the larger of the two boxes and the children blinked in astonishment. The contents made the gold coins in the boot seem like nothing. The box was filled with gold and silver—bright coins and jewelry set with precious stones.

"Now we're really rich," Tom said. He picked up a handful of coins, then let them trickle out through his fingers. "You can keep all those other coins, Mary. We have plenty to share."

Mary took a ring from the chest and held it up to the light. A brilliant ruby set in gold glittered in the sun. "I'll take this home to Mother," she said.

While Tom was admiring the coins and Mary was pocketing the ring, Sam opened the second box. This one held items that Sam knew would be useful: a fishhook and line, a tin cup, an empty bottle that had once held rum, a machete, a sailmaker's needle, a spool of sturdy thread, and a magnetic compass.

Sam considered the boat and its contents solemnly. He had traveled with his uncles on more than one trip to the farthest island in the archipelago, and he had some idea of what they would need to survive.

"We will need all the water we can carry," he said. "And all the coconuts we can gather. We can drink coconut milk and eat the nut's meat."

"We'll catch fish," Tom said brightly.

"If we are lucky, we'll catch some fish." Sam eyed the box of treasure. "You can't eat gold and there's nothing to buy in the middle of the ocean. Better we take a few coins and leave the rest here. In the middle of the ocean, you'd rather have a coconut than gold."

Tom looked dubious, then his face brightened. "We could bury the treasure."

Sam nodded. "That we could."

"I'll find a good spot," Tom said, turning away from the boat.

Mary put the ring in her pocket and picked up the compass. "Will this help us find our way home?" she asked.

"It'll help," Sam said. "But we'll also watch the stars. My uncles showed me how to find the way home to my island using the stars. You look for where each star rises, and that tells you the direction."

"What about when it's daytime?" Mary asked.

"You pay attention to where the sun rises. You look for the path that its light makes on the water." Path wasn't the right word, but it was as close as Sam could come in English. "Then you watch the waves and sometimes the birds." Sam couldn't keep the excitement out of his voice. He was remembering what it was like to be in a canoe, out of sight of land. Like being at the center of the sky—a sky that showed the way, if only you could read it.

"I wonder," Mary said. "Should we ask the others if they want to come?"

Sam looked at Mary, waiting for her to answer her own question. Mary hesitated. When she thought about the other boys and Peter Pan, she felt an emotion she couldn't quite define.

There was something in it of sorrow—she felt sad that the Lost Boys were hungry and in danger from Peter's whims. But there was also anger—Peter kept telling the boys that she was their mother. She wasn't really anyone's mother. But somehow, maybe because Peter was in charge and he kept saying she was the mother, the boys looked to her for comfort that she couldn't give. That wasn't fair.

And there was something of fear, too, a strange sort of fear. The boys wanted so much from her, and she couldn't give it, and that made her feel torn up, as if each boy that needed something tore a piece out of her heart. They would take all of her and leave nothing.

"I think I have to ask," Mary said reluctantly.

"You'd best tell them the truth of it," Sam said. "It'll be a hard journey and we might not make it. You know they would rather stay with Peter."

"I also have to say goodbye to Susan and Polly."

Sam looked at the waves. "The tide will be turning soon. That would be the best time to go."

"Do you want to come and say goodbye?" Mary asked.

Sam shook his head. "There's work to be done on the boat. I'll be busy here."

"I'll help Sam," Tom said.

Mary went to see Polly and Susan first, since their camp was closer. Joe and Will were there, but Julia, Susan, and the children were in the jungle, gathering medicinal herbs.

Joe invited her to wait for a time, but she declined. "Sam and Tom and I are going home," she told Joe. "We found a boat tangled in the mangroves. We'll set sail when the tide goes out. Will you tell them that I came to say goodbye?"

"Where is this boat?" Joe asked. "I'd like to take a look at it."

"On the beach near the mangroves." She waved a hand in the right direction. "I have to go to camp and tell the other boys."

When she reached the Lost Boys camp, she found it deserted except for Tootles. Peter was off somewhere. The other boys were hunting.

"Sam found a boat," Mary told Tootles. "Sam and Tom and I are going to leave the island when the tide turns. You can come with us, if you like."

Tootles' eyes widened. "Leave the island?" he repeated.

"Sam says that it'll be dangerous. He thinks he can find the way, but he can't be sure."

"You can't go," Tootles said. "You'll die of hunger. Or pirates will capture you. You must stay here, where you can be safe."

Mary frowned at him. "It's not safe here."

"Safer than being on a boat in the middle of the ocean! And what about Peter?"

"Peter isn't ever going to take us home!"

"Don't go," Tootles said. "You can't. If you go, I'll never see you again."

"How do you know that? You told me you live in London. Maybe you'll get back there and maybe I'll go there."

"You won't remember me," he said gloomily.

Mary was growing impatient. "Of course I will. I'll get to London and I'll ask everyone 'Where does Tootles live?' And I'll knock on your door . . ."

"Tootles isn't my name," Tootles said.

"What is your name then?" Mary asked.

"My name is George. George Darling."

"All right, then I'll ask everyone where George Darling lives. And I'll knock on your door and say, 'Hullo, George!'"

"You'll never find me. You can't go."

"I most certainly can," Mary said. She gathered her things. She didn't have much: a fishing line she had made of threads extracted from palm fronds and twisted together, a sharp-edged shell that she used for scraping the scales off fish, some fishing hooks that Sam had made from fish bones. She took some of the fish that she and Sam had dried, leaving the rest for the Lost Boys. Then she headed back to the beach.

Tootles—or George, if you prefer—followed her through the jungle, talking about crocodiles and sharks, about drowning and dying of thirst. By the time they reached the boat, Mary was heartily sick of listening to him.

"I'll fight a crocodile with my bare hands before I'll stay another day on this island," she told him.

When they got to the beach, Joe was already there, talking with Sam. George went to join their conference, while Tom told Mary about all that he and Sam had done while she was gone.

He and Sam had buried the box of coins, which Tom referred to as the "treasure chest." They had buried the dead pirate with the box. Mary agreed that seemed like the right thing to do.

"We buried it right beside the tallest palm tree," Tom said proudly. "When we come back for the treasure, we can find it easy enough."

Mary glanced up at the palm tree. Not the best marker, she thought. Palm trees grew—in a few years, one of the other trees might be taller. In fact, a few of the ones nearby were almost as tall as the one Tom had chosen. And palm trees died—from where she stood, she could see a couple that had toppled in past storms.

Near where the treasure was buried, Mary noticed a large boulder—a gray triangle, pointing at the cloudless sky. It made her think of a tooth—a wolf's tooth maybe. Wind and waves had worn it down, rounding its edges. An old wolf, Mary thought. A few yards on the other side of the treasure spot was another boulder, like another tooth—smaller and more rounded. "Between the old wolf's teeth, the treasure lies," she said aloud. She had read a book or two herself, and she knew that you had to draw a map or, failing that, create a cryptic saying that would identify the spot. "That's a better way to remember it."

But Tom wasn't interested. He was still talking about what he and Sam had done. "We took down the sail and sewed up the tears in it. We put lots of coconuts in the boat. But we still have to get water."

While Mary was listening to Tom, George was telling Sam that they couldn't go. "You'll die of thirst! You'll be eaten by sharks! You'll get lost!"

Sam listened calmly, then looked George in the eye. "My people have crossed oceans in their canoes. My uncles taught me to read the skies and the waves, to watch for the birds and the clouds. We won't get lost."

"I believe you will find your way," Joe said.

Joe helped while they finished their preparations, filling the wooden keg and the rum bottle with fresh water at a nearby stream, gathering more coconuts to pile in the bottom of the boat.

At last, they were ready.

"Are you coming?" Sam asked George.

George shook his head, looking panicked.

"The tide is turning," Sam said. "Time to go."

Joe and George watched as Sam pushed the boat into the water. Mary and Tom climbed in. Just before Sam got into the boat, he looked up at the parrot. During all the activity, the bird had watched with great attention from a perch on the boat's mast. "Are you coming with us, Captain Flint?"

The bird flew down and landed on Sam's shoulder. It eyed George, sizing him up. "Dead men tell no tales," Captain Flint said in a conversational tone.

"Goodbye, George Darling!" Mary called. "Goodbye!"

George took a step forward, as if to follow them. Sam put up the sail and adjusted it to catch the wind. Joe lifted a hand in farewell.

CHAPTER 23
You Can't Trust a Fairy

E ACH NIGHT, WATSON tossed and turned in his cabin on the *Golden Dawn,* disturbed by dreams of Mary. The circumstances of his dreams changed each night, but Mary was always there.

A dream: Mary stood on a rock in the middle of a roiling sea. Watson had no body; he was just a presence floating above the water—but he could feel the chill breeze that tousled Mary's curls. There were creatures in the water—women with flowing hair and fish tails. They reached for Mary, tugging on her skirts and trying to pull her into the sea. He could do nothing to stop them.

Another dream: Mary was in the nursery at number 14, standing by the open window. Her hair was cropped short. She wore trousers and a man's loose shirt. It was night and Mary was staring out at the stars. He called her name. She turned to look at him, her face pale, her eyes filled with sorrow.

"You must listen to me," she told him.

"What's wrong, Mary?" he said. "How can I help you?"

"You have to believe me."

Before he could say anything, she stepped up onto the window seat and dove through the open window.

He woke from that dream with a start. He was suddenly alert with a sense of certainty that something terrible was happening, not just in his dreams, but in reality. Nana sat by his bunk, gazing at him with grave concern.

Needing fresh air, Watson slipped from his bunk, pulled on his clothes, and left the cabin. Nana followed close behind, her toenails clicking on the *Golden Dawn*'s wooden deck.

Watson and Nana were alone on deck. The sails, pulled taut in the wind, blocked them from the view of the sailor at the helm. Moonlight silvered the ocean swells.

As Watson stepped toward the railing, he heard an odd sound— the thump of something hitting the deck, followed by a high-pitched jingling, like Christmas bells. Nana, quicker than Watson to respond, bounded toward a large crate on the deck.

Watson saw the ship's cat crouched beside the crate. He surmised that the thump he had heard had been the cat leaping from the crate to pounce.

Something was pinned beneath the cat's paws. It glowed with a golden light, flickering like a gigantic firefly. Some tropical insect, Watson thought. The Christmas bells jingled with an urgency akin to panic.

Nana stepped closer to the cat. The cat glared at the big dog and growled.

"What is it you've caught, you old villain?" Watson asked, approaching the cat. The bells rang with a desperate fury. As the light under the cat's paws glowed bright, Watson got a clear look at what the cat had caught. It was a creature with the body and face of a woman and wings like a giant dragonfly.

"Get away from there." Watson shoved the cat aside with his boot. The cat knew from experience that attacking a booted foot was futile. The beast hissed, but backed away, wary of a kick.

Nana moved to stand between the cat and its prey. Watson knelt to examine the strange creature that lay on the wooden deck. It was not glowing now. The crate blocked the moonlight, and Watson could not see it clearly. He took his handkerchief from his pocket, folded it to make a small pad, and laid the pad on the deck.

While Nana watched, Watson carefully, almost tenderly, lifted the creature onto the pad. He touched it with his hands, an impulsive action given the propensity of tropical insects to sting. But he couldn't leave it lying on the deck with the cat so near. His urge to examine it overcame his natural caution.

He picked up the pad and laid it on top of the crate where the moonlight was bright. Yes, it was a winged woman—pale brown skin, jet black hair, a curvaceous body, and wings like a giant insect. She wore a tunic of sorts—short enough to show off her legs, tight enough to show off her bosom.

"What are you?" Watson murmured. "Surely not an insect."

The creature opened her eyes and regarded him. She spoke then, flickering with the golden light he had seen earlier. Her voice was the jingling of Christmas bells.

The fairy's name—and yes, she was a fairy—might be translated as Aribelle—*ari*, which can mean gold or breeze or earth, depending on the language of origin you prefer, and *belle*, which can mean beautiful and can mean "bell."

"An insect?" Aribelle snapped, offended by the thought that anyone could mistake her for an insect. "Certainly not, you silly ass."

Watson could not understand a word she said. He did not realize that she had been shouting for help, cursing the cat, and promising to grant a wish to anyone who saved her from that vicious beast.

Her terror forgotten, Aribelle sat up carefully. A few bruises—nothing worse. The cat had knocked her down and stunned her momentarily. Truth be told, fairies are much tougher than they look. She stood up, stretched out her arms, and fluttered her wings. Nothing broken.

Watson blinked at her. "So beautiful."

Aribelle was always pleased to be admired. Her emotions were mercurial, changing swiftly from fear to anger to pleasure. She smiled at him like a coquette at a dance. "You are a fool, but you have good taste."

"You understand me," Watson said in a tone of wonder.

"Of course, you bacon-faced noddy!" Aribelle smiled as she said it. Watson heard only the sweet jingling of bells.

Like most fairies, Aribelle thought humans were rather stupid. Easily tricked. Usually greedy. Great hulking oafs stumbling through life, missing most of the beauty and all of the fun. She never hesitated to let humans know how she felt about them. In fairy speech, all her insults sounded quite sweet and merry.

Aribelle studied Watson, considering how he might be useful. Fairies are opportunists, always looking for the angle that will turn a situation to their advantage. They like gifts. They enjoy chaos and they like to make trouble.

Contrary to what some believe, fairies' powers are quite limited— they can fly and use fairy dust to give you the temporary ability to fly. They can glow in the dark. (They can't give you the ability to glow; you'll have to take a flashlight along for that.)

Aribelle saw no immediate value to an ongoing friendship with Watson, but she smiled at him anyway. You never knew when a gullible human might come in handy.

She took flight then, circling Watson's head and giving him the opportunity to admire her again. She called out "Goodbye, my dear chuckleheaded chub!" in a cheery jingle and flew away, leaving Watson standing on deck with his mouth agape.

He took a step after her.

That is—he tried to take a step. But the foot that swung forward to step did not land. Watson found himself floating above the deck, drifting slowly toward the railing.

Remember that fairy dust? Watson's hand—the hand he had used to move Aribelle from the deck to his handkerchief—was covered with the stuff. When Watson attempted to step toward the railing, the push of his foot propelled him upward on a trajectory that would, unchecked, carry him over the railing and out to sea.

This could have ended very badly. Fortunately, Nana was watching. The dog lunged forward, determined to save Watson.

It was also fortunate that Watson had never gone in for fashionable slim-fitting trousers. He wore loose trousers that reached below the ankle. The late Mrs. Watson had deplored those trousers as ill-fitting and baggy. But in this situation, Watson's complete lack of fashion sense became his salvation.

Just before Watson's feet passed over the rail and followed the rest of him out to sea, Nana's jaws clamped down on the cuff of Watson's trousers. At the same time, Watson, a man of action, reacted to his peril by flailing wildly in midair. Despite the erratic movement of his legs, the stout cloth of his trousers did not tear. Nana held steady, anchoring Watson in place and halting his seaward progress. Crouching low to the deck, Nana pulled, hauling him back on board the ship.

Twisting in midair, Watson grabbed the railing with both hands. Confident he had the situation under control, he called to Nana, "Let go! Nana, let go."

Against her better judgment, the big dog released her grip. For a moment, Watson clung to the railing—feet lifting toward the sky. His body was flying, rather like a flag in the shape of a middle-aged British gentleman.

Momentarily secure in this rather peculiar position, he took a deep breath. When he inhaled, his body rose. His right hand, the one covered in fairy dust, tingled. The skin felt like it had been drenched in peppermint oil—a strange sensation of heat and cold. His hand sparkled as bits of fairy dust caught the moonlight.

Watson had always been a very solid sort of man—down-to-earth, no-nonsense. But now he could feel his body respond to the wind. He could feel every breeze, every breath of air. For a moment, he wondered what would happen if he let go. How lovely it would be to let the wind carry him aloft, soaring above the waves. Where in the great wide world would the wind take him?

But Watson was a practical man. As he clung to the railing, he realized that it was ridiculous to think that he could fly. He considered what Holmes would make of this situation. It was quite impossible—that's what Holmes would say. As Watson thought about Holmes, his body lost its buoyancy and his feet sank toward the deck.

When he felt the deck beneath his feet, he used his grip on the rail to pull himself to a standing position. Nana stood close by his side, ready in case he took flight again. As he stood there, the wind carried away the fairy dust that clung to his hand. His body regained its former weight.

Moving carefully, one hand still clutching the railing, Watson crouched down so that he was eye to eye with Nana. "Thank you," he said to the big dog as he tousled her ears. Nana accepted his thanks with her usual dignity.

Watson straightened up and cautiously relinquished his grip on the railing. His feet remained on the deck. He turned to the crate where his handkerchief lay. He picked it up and fairy dust fell from the cloth, sparkling in the moonlight. Oblivious to the power of the fairy dust, Watson shook the handkerchief, tucked it back into his pocket, and returned to his bed.

When he woke in the morning, he was convinced that his meeting with the fairy had been a dream. Quite convinced. He was sure of it. No question. He could not possibly have taken flight—though he distinctly recalled the unsettling feeling when his feet had left the deck.

Later that day, Watson joined Sam at the rail when he was having a smoke. After a bit of chitchat, Watson raised the subject of tropical insects. "I've heard there are some strange fireflies here in the tropics."

Sam nodded thoughtfully, curious about Watson's sudden interest in insect life. There was something tentative in Watson's tone, a sense of uncertainty, as if he were asking a question he wasn't sure he should ask.

"Yes," Sam said, "there are several different fireflies. Rumbold could probably give you a list of them."

Watson hesitated, then asked, "Do you know of any fireflies that make a jingling sound, like Christmas bells?"

Sam scrutinized him. "That description sounds more like a fairy than an insect."

Watson was silent for a moment. "A fairy," he repeated in a dubious tone. "Like the ones in fairy tales?"

Sam had read some books of British fairy tales in the library at Dr. Plummer's Academy. To Sam, the fairies in those stories seemed like a watered-down and misunderstood version of the wild spirits that lived in the bush. Meeting fairies in Neverland had not changed his view. He did not know exactly where they fit into the pantheon of ancestors and spirits, but he was confident that they did.

"They have some similarities, I suppose," Sam told Watson. "The fairies I've met are not to be trusted."

At that moment, George came upon them, on one of his endless promenades around the deck. "Hullo," he said. "I am feeling much better today. I think perhaps my digestion is finally accustomed to the motion of the ship."

"Watson met a fairy last night," Sam said.

George's eyes widened. Suddenly, he was alert. "Where did you see it?" he asked.

"Maybe it was just a dream," Watson said.

"Tell us what you dreamed then," Sam suggested.

Watson described what had happened, from chasing off the cat and picking up the fairy to the fairy's departure. "She flew away and . . ." He hesitated, not certain he wanted to talk about the moment when his feet left the deck.

Sam filled in the gap. "And you flew."

Watson stared at him. "How did you know?"

"I imagine you got fairy dust on your hand when you picked up the fairy. Fairy dust lets you fly," Sam said.

"You can fly as long as you believe," George added.

"Believe what?" Watson asked him.

"Believe in a different world, one that you don't understand," Sam said. He studied Watson for a moment. "You saved this fairy, so she owes you."

"But it's a good thing you didn't follow her when she flew away," George said. "You can't trust a fairy."

"I wanted to follow her," Watson confessed. "I thought I would soar like a bird." He glanced down at Nana, who regarded him gravely. "Nana held me back."

"Good dog!" George said.

"You can fly with the fairies as long as you believe you can," Sam said. "But suppose you had looked down and suddenly thought, 'This is not possible.' Then you'd fall. George and I both flew with the fairies as children. It was easy to believe back then."

"You both believe that you flew to Neverland?" Watson looked from Sam to George and back, not knowing what to think. He wanted to say all this was impossible, but he still remembered the moment when he felt his body respond to the wind, when he fought the urge to let go of the railing.

"For a long time, I tried not to believe." George wrapped his arms around himself, as if suddenly chilled. "Peter Pan took me there. It was not such a bad place when Sam and Mary and Tom were there too. But then they sailed away."

"How did you get home?" Sam asked. "I've always wondered."

"I told Peter about going to a fun fair in London," George said. "I told him it would be a jolly adventure. I talked about riding on the roundabout and seeing the dancing bear and watching a Punch and Judy show. The next time he flew to London to recruit another boy, he took me along so I could show him the fun fair. When we got there, I landed in a park and found a policeman to take me home."

"That was clever," Sam said.

"But there was a problem when I got home," George continued. "When I told my mother where I'd been, she wept and said I'd been driven mad by my kidnappers. She found an alienist who said he could help. The alienist said I had been kidnapped by a gang of thieves and put to work as a beggar or a pickpocket. He told me that I had to forget this fantasy of Neverland and live in the real world. He was very sure of himself. So I did my best to forget."

George gazed into the distance. "I didn't talk about it anymore. A newspaper reporter interviewed me for a story about kidnapped children and I told him about learning to pick pockets, since the alienist told me that's what really happened. I grew up and became an accountant. I liked working with numbers. Numbers are right or wrong, and everyone believes in them. Then I met Mary at a dinner party and she called me Tootles."

"Tootles?" Watson said.

"That was the name Peter Pan gave me. When Mary called me Tootles, all the memories came back—the good and the bad. I had never forgotten Mary—not really. I dreamed of her, even after I had packed all my memories of Neverland away. At that party, she told a story about Neverland. She talked about all the things that the alienist told me to forget.

"Now my children are in Neverland and my wife has gone there to save them." He met Watson's eyes. "I know you think I'm a fool. But I love Mary. I can't bear to think of her there, all alone. I have to help her. I'm no good at this sort of thing, but I have to try."

Watson put his arm around George's shoulders. "Cheer up, old man," Watson murmured. "Sam and I are here to help. We'll do this together."

Think about your own childhood. Do you remember it? All of it? Are you sure you are remembering it the way it really happened?

Maybe you were afraid of the dark because you heard sounds in the night. There were mysterious footsteps, or claws scratching at your window, or someone (or something) groaning in your closet. You told your parents about the sounds. You thought the sounds came from robbers or monsters or ghosts, but your parents dismissed these concerns. They explained away the sounds: the footsteps were floorboards creaking as the house settled; the claws were branches rattling against the window; the groaning was the rumble of the furnace.

You tried to believe your parents. It was best to believe them, because they got annoyed if you persisted in talking about the noises in the night. They reassured you that there were no robbers, no ghosts, no monsters. You wanted to believe them. Over time, you came to accept what your parents said. You too dismissed the fantastic possibilities and believed that there was a rational explanation for every sound. It's comfortable to believe in the rational explanation. It means that you are safe.

To get by in the world, to feel safe in the world, George stopped believing in Neverland. Then his children disappeared and his illusion of security disappeared with them.

Watson did not mention his encounter with the fairy to Holmes. He did not tell Holmes that Sam and George were confident that fairies existed, or that they believed a person could fly when dusted with fairy dust. Watson did not reveal that he had taken flight . . . or even that maybe he had dreamed of taking flight.

The time never seemed quite right to bring up the subject. Holmes spent much of his time indulging in Rumbold's drug or recovering from its influences. And even if he had found the perfect time, Watson was not sure how he would raise the subject.

He considered asking Rumbold whether any tropical fireflies made a sound like jingling bells, but decided against it. His conversations with Rumbold focused on more practical matters—like their travel plans.

"Sam tells me that you'll be looking for a ship to take you from Toamasina to the island of Nosy Boraha," Rumbold said one evening as they strolled together on the deck. "Nosy Boraha is my destination as well. I thought I would offer my assistance. I'll be looking for a ship headed down the coast to the island. I could arrange transportation for all of us."

"That would be very helpful," Watson said.

"I confess that I am curious about what brings a group of British gentlemen to the island of Nosy Boraha," Rumbold said. "Most visitors to the island are interested in purchasing merchandise of dubious provenance. You know the sort of thing—'It's a lovely silk and I'm sure those bloodstains will come right out.' But you don't seem like the type for that."

Watson remained silent, wondering how Holmes would feel about taking Rumbold into their confidence.

Rumbold went on. "In any case, I could make a few introductions to help you get your footing. Sam mentioned that you were looking for a woman named Mary Darling."

Watson nodded. "Mary Darling is my niece. She left London on a ship bound for Nosy Boraha. We need to find her."

"And why would she be going to Nosy Boraha?"

"That is a much longer story. But we have reason to believe she visited the island when she was a child and sailed on a notorious pirate ship— the *Jolly Roger*."

"Fascinating." Rumbold studied Watson, as if reevaluating his opinion of the doctor. "Let me tell you about some of the people you're likely to meet on Nosy Boraha."

CHAPTER 24
Aboard the Jolly Roger

MARY'S FAVORITE PLACE on the *Honest Trader* was the crow's nest. High above the deck, she was alone in a way she could never be alone in London. Mary had not realized it before, but she valued being alone, where she could relax and think her own thoughts.

She looked out over the water. Nothing to see but waves and the wake spreading behind the ship. She looked for ships on the horizon. That had been her duty the last time she had spent any time in a crow's nest.

You remember, of course, that Mary and Sam and Tom left Neverland in a small boat, planning to sail across the Indian Ocean to Australia. That's a voyage of over four thousand miles in an open boat. It would have been an amazing feat had they managed it—but they didn't.

Sam set the course, sailing the boat as his uncles had taught him. To his credit, he set a good course, but the winds were against them and their progress was slow.

About two weeks after they left Neverland, they ate the last coconut, sharing it between the three children with a bite for Captain Flint. Sam had caught a fish, which they ate raw. They shared the last cup of water left in the wooden keg. The rum bottle had been emptied long since.

Mary lay in the bottom of the boat, looking up at the sky and wishing for clouds. Maybe a kindly cloud would appear from nowhere and rain on them. She imagined raindrops pelting her sunburned skin, the water filling the bottom of the boat. But the sky was relentlessly blue; not a cloud in sight.

Maybe Peter Pan would come to rescue them. She wasn't too proud to wish for that. But if Peter were coming, surely he'd have arrived already.

Maybe Lady Hawkins would sail by and offer them tea. Mary vividly remembered the tea and biscuits and jam she had eaten with Lady Hawkins.

Maybe . . .

"I see a ship!" Sam said. "Over there!"

There are different sorts of pirates in the world. Some want fame and adventure, glorying in the freedom of the sea. Some are experts in psychological warfare and theater. Blackbeard, for example, was known to twist fuses into his hair and beard and set them alight before battle, so that he appeared to his foes wreathed in smoke like a demon from Hell. Some pirates have a more political outlook. Arabic pirate Khayr al-Din Barbarus battled various Christian enemies after the Knights of St. John killed one of his brothers and imprisoned another.

Captain Scratch of the *Jolly Roger* had no religious zeal, no sense of theater, and no desire for revenge or adventure. He was a rare sort of pirate: a businessman who tallied profits from each ship he took with the enthusiasm of an accountant, which he had been before going to sea. Where other pirate captains might revel in the glory of battle or the terror of their victims, Scratch was pragmatic, viewing fighting and killing as a necessary part of doing business.

He was far ahead of his time in terms of marketing. In casual conversation when the ship was in port, he took care to mention wanton acts of cruelty, which had never, in fact, occurred. That built his reputation without all the screaming victims and blood to clean up. The captain's dispassionate delivery when telling tales of atrocities added to his reputation, so his very mildness contributed to his notoriety.

When the lookout of the *Jolly Roger* spied a small boat carrying three children who were waving at the ship frantically, James, the clever young man who was first mate, alerted the captain.

Scratch was tallying the expected profit from their latest prize. He looked up from his accounting long enough to tell James to retrieve the children and hold them until he had time to assess their value. Captain Scratch was always interested in opportunities for additional revenue. If the children could be ransomed or put to work, he'd keep them. If not, it would be simple enough to toss them overboard.

The deck hands lowered the dinghy, dispatching James and Zakri to fetch the castaways. Zakri rowed, pulling hard against the wind. As the dinghy approached the children's boat, Tom called out, "Do you have water? We're nearly dead of thirst."

James tossed a rope to the boy. The children gripped the rope and pulled their boat alongside the dinghy. James eyed them, wondering what their fate on the *Jolly Roger* would be. If they came from wealthy families, they might be ransomed. More likely, they would be pressed into service as cabin boys.

The ship's last cabin boy had washed overboard in a storm and the one before that had caught a cannonball during a battle with a merchant vessel. Cabin boys on the *Jolly Roger* had a rather low survival rate, but some did well. James himself had started as a cabin boy.

"I'm Sam," said the first child as he clambered aboard the dinghy. An islander, James thought. The gray parrot that perched on the boy's shoulder eyed James with suspicion and clacked its beak.

"I'm Tom," said the second child, the smallest of the three.

"I'm Mary," said the third.

James stared. He would not have known her for a girl. She was dressed like the others, filthy and ragged, burned brown by the sun. She could pass for a boy, but that name revealed she was not.

James was not your typical pirate. He came from a good family. He had attended a well-respected British boarding school. He shook his head. His dismay at learning that she was a girl showed on his face.

"What is the matter?" Mary said.

"A pirate ship is no place for a girl," he said. "A woman on a ship is bad luck. Any girl we capture would be cast adrift, at best." He did not speak of the worst that might happen.

She stared at him, then spoke again. "A girl? What do you mean? My name is Marty, short for Martin. And my brothers and I would like nothing better than to be cabin boys on a pirate ship."

He nodded slowly, holding her gaze. "Very good. I misheard you. Marty it is then." He knew he had not misheard. "Marty, Tom, and Sam."

James glanced at Zakri. The big man's native language was Malay; he spoke just enough English to get by. He had paid no attention during this exchange, being occupied with holding the boat beside the dinghy as the children came aboard. Even if he had been paying attention, James was confident that he would not have understood the discussion.

"Look lively, matey!" said the parrot on Sam's shoulder.

James took the parrot's advice, hurrying to get the children back to the ship.

The cook on the *Jolly Roger,* a round-faced man who was known to all as Cookie, immediately took charge of the castaways. He gave them water, advising them to sip rather than gulp. He gave them biscuits to eat.

As pirates go, Cookie was a soft-hearted man. He also had work that needed doing. In one of Captain Scratch's efforts to maximize efficiency, Cookie had been put in charge of mending the sails, as well as cooking. Two sails had been torn by enemy fire in the *Jolly Roger*'s last battle.

By the time Captain Scratch had completed his accounts, the three children were sitting on deck and helping Cookie mend the sails. Marty was particularly handy with the sailmaker's needle.

Scratch studied the three children, weighing their value against their expense. "Where did you come from?" he asked.

"My father's ship was blown off course and we stopped at an island for water and food," Marty told him. "We were attacked by savages. My father and the crew were killed. We escaped, and the savages didn't bother to chase us." She had made up the story on the spot, having decided that a tale involving fairy dust would not go far with this grim-faced man, even if it was the truth. Tom and Sam nodded their agreement.

Scratch considered this. "Your father . . . a missionary, was he?" Scratch had little use for missionaries. They were usually poor and always annoyingly pious. A waste of time in his estimation.

Mary heard the disdain in his voice. "No, sir," she said quickly. "He was a merchant."

Scratch nodded. James was standing nearby. He knew that the captain was calculating the ransom value of the children and finding it lacking.

"Helpful to have small hands to work those seams, ain't it, Cookie?" James asked.

"You have the right of it, James." Cookie was canny enough to know what James was about. "These ones are quick to learn, too."

"They are light enough to climb higher in the rigging than any sailor," James added. "And small enough that they don't need much in the way of food. No grog ration either."

Scratch was always grumbling about the cost of rum and its effect on the ship's efficiency. He could not curtail the men's drinking without facing a mutiny, but he'd be glad to have some crew members who did not drink.

"You don't drink, do you, Marty?" James asked.

"Only water, sir," Mary said quickly. "That's enough for us."

"Are you willing to work hard?" Scratch asked.

"Grateful for the opportunity, sir," Mary said, smiling easily. The other children nodded.

The captain was in a passably good mood. The ship was returning to her home base—the pirate haven on the island of Nosy Boraha. It had been a very profitable voyage. Scratch nodded to Cookie. "Keep them as long as they're useful. If they're not useful, throw them overboard." He returned to his cabin, leaving Mary, Tom, and Sam determined to demonstrate how useful they could be.

As the *Jolly Roger* made its way to Nosy Boraha, the three children were eager and willing helpers, stitching the sails, swabbing the decks, and climbing the rigging. Captain Flint made friends with the cook and spent his time on a perch in the kitchen. James kept his eye on Marty, who was always willing to help, never hesitating to climb high in the rigging.

It may sound strange, but the children enjoyed being on the pirate ship. It was exhilarating to climb into the rigging to adjust the sails or to keep watch from the crow's nest. Such a view from up there—miles of sparkling ocean waves under an endless sky. Sometimes, there was a puff of steam in the distance, a sign that a whale was surfacing. Sometimes an albatross kept pace with the boat for a time.

After the starvation rations on Neverland, the wretched food of the pirate ship was as good as a feast. There were weevils in the biscuit, but at least there were biscuits. There were beans—very filling, and the children were happy to feel full. Salted pork, rice, sometimes even cheese—it was all good.

Tom learned to splice rope and spent his days assisting with repairs. There were always repairs to be made.

Sam worked with the ship's carpenter, a dour Scot who was always grumbling and swearing that the ship would go down in the next storm. The fearful thing was—Sam thought that most likely he was right. Sam's job was to pack oakum, scraps of old rope too worn to be reused, into the cracks between the ship's boards to keep the vessel watertight. He ladled hot pitch into the seams to seal them.

Mary helped Cookie in the galley. She was quick and handy, always willing to scour a pot or cut the rotten bits out of the potatoes before they went in the pot. The cook slipped her extra rations, which she shared with the other children.

One sunny afternoon, she was cutting up potatoes to be boiled for supper. Cookie was watching her—a rare moment when he wasn't busy. "You've a good hand with the knife when you're cutting potatoes," the cook said thoughtfully. "But to get by in this world, you need to know how to fight with it."

Mary agreed. Her days on Neverland had convinced her that there was much she needed to learn to get on in the world. "So how do I do that?" she asked.

Cookie scratched his head, thinking of the best fighters among the crew. Irish Jack relied on his size and strength—the cook had seen him pick up an opponent and hurl him overboard. Zakri was an excellent man with a scimitar, but that was largely because of his long arms. He could get inside another man's guard.

Then he thought about James, a young man of average height and weight. Cookie had seen him fight with sword and dagger—the sword for the initial attack and the dagger for delivering a killing strike in close quarters. James had a pretty fighting style that fooled many opponents into dismissing him, a fatal mistake.

"Ask James if he will teach you," Cookie suggested.

So that evening she asked James—politely and respectfully—if he would teach the children how to fight with swords. She mentioned Cookie had said he was the best fighter on board, which was not entirely true. The cook had said James would be the best teacher for her, which was not really the same. But she could tell that James was flattered.

The lessons started that evening, after the cooking chores were complete. All the children gathered—Sam and Tom were eager to learn as well. James began with the basics. Giving each child a belaying pin in place of a sword, he showed them how to hold it, taught them a solid stance (knees bent, ready to move), and drilled them on moving across the deck, sword ready.

Crew members who were not on duty gathered to watch. They drank their grog ration, smoked their pipes, and called out encouragement and instructions: "Keep your sword up, lad!" "Head up there. Keep a sharp eye out."

The lessons became a nightly ritual. The children were sore after each lesson—bruised, muscles aching, heads swirling with new ways of thinking. But they persisted. Mary was quick as a cat, darting in and away. Sam was stronger, with a better reach. Tom was the smallest, but he made up for his lack of size with enthusiasm.

James taught them to use a dagger in combination with a sword. "A weapon for each hand," James said.

They worked on fighting as a team, all three children against James. "Is that fair?" Tom asked, and the pirates jeered.

"Fight fair and be gutted," Cookie called.

They learned to fight dirty—grab an ear, gouge an eye, trip a man to bring him down, then kick him in the head.

They got advice from the spectators. "Kicking's better than punching," one young pirate observed. "'Specially if you're wearing boots."

"Stomping is good," agreed Irish Jack. "Stomp a man's hand and he won't be picking up that sword right away."

The children learned to be aware of their environment, using the crates and barrels on the deck to their advantage. The assembled pirates applauded when Mary leapt over the extended legs of Irish Jack, who was sitting on the deck and leaning against a crate. When James followed her, Irish Jack tripped him. James landed on another pirate, spilling his grog. In the ensuing melee, Mary made her escape.

It was a terrifying sort of game, but the children learned to defend themselves with sword and knife and elbows and knees and fists. Mary loved it.

After one particularly successful session, Mary stood by the rail with James as the sun sank into the ocean. She was exuberant. "They'd never believe this at home," she said.

"Where is home, Marty?" James asked.

"Australia."

"Do you want to go home?"

A wary look came into her eyes. "Yes, but I don't know how to get there."

James nodded. "I think there's a way," he said. "We are heading for our home port on the island of Nosy Boraha. Australian traders sometimes call on Nosy Boraha. They are, for the most part, on the dodgy side of honest, but they are merchants, not pirates. Perhaps we could find a ship that would take you back to Australia."

He kept his voice low. Captain Scratch had mentioned that he was considering how to best profit from the children. James had pointed out that the crew seemed to like having them aboard, and the captain had allowed that he might keep one—but he mused about where he might sell the others. Perhaps to a brothel or to a business that needed some young helpers.

Scratch thought of the children as a valuable asset, part of the ship's plunder. Though they helped out on the ship, they were not part of the crew. They had not signed the ship's articles, the document on which each crew member had scrawled his signature or made his X. They were not entitled to a share of the plunder. They were not entitled to anything and could be disposed of at the captain's whim.

"How would we find a ship?" Mary asked.

"Let me see what I can do," James said quietly. "Keep this a secret between the two of us. The captain . . ." He hesitated, not wanting to frighten the child. "The captain might not like it."

The next evening, James visited Cookie in his galley, ostensibly to discuss provisions to be purchased on Nosy Boraha. The two men chatted about the captain's insistence on including citrus fruits in the crew's diet. James observed that the crew preferred oranges over lemons or limes. Cookie responded that lemons and limes were cheaper.

Cookie knew that James had not come to him solely to chat about provisions, and James knew that the cook knew it. But they were careful in their approach to the real subject at hand.

"You may be losing your helpers," James said. "The captain says he's thinking of finding another place for two of those children."

"The captain is always looking for the best profit," Cookie observed.

James nodded. "The children would like to go home to Australia," he said.

Cookie nodded. "I wonder if you might have time to visit Ruby first thing after we make port. It would be good to have a chat with her before the captain pays her a visit. Tell her about the children. She may be able to help. I would go myself, but the captain insists that I arrange for provisions before I take leave."

James nodded. "I'll pay a call on Ruby first thing."

CHAPTER 25
An Island of Women

E ACH NIGHT, IN her tiny cabin on the *Honest Trader,* Mary Darling slept and dreamed.

Sometimes she dreamed of London—of shopping on Portobello Road, of dinner parties where the men smoked cigars and talked about politics and the women talked about servant problems and fashion. It seemed unreal—so far away, so very strange. Did she really wear all those petticoats? Did she really spend so much time doing the wash, cleaning the house, fretting about what they would have for dinner? She woke from dreams of London feeling confused.

Sometimes, she dreamed of being a child in Neverland. In those dreams, she remembered how to fly. It wasn't difficult at all. It was as easy as breathing. How could she have forgotten what it was like to let the wind lift you up and carry you away? She had felt free—but that sense of freedom was touched with fear. Anything could happen.

And sometimes, she dreamed of Nosy Boraha, of Ruby's place, and the comfort Mary had found there. She woke from those dreams feeling calm and comfortable, secure in the knowledge that Ruby would help her.

Nosy Boraha is a small island, just off the east coast of Madagascar. Nosy means "island" in Malagasy, the language of the people of Madagascar. The French, who had claimed Madagascar and the nearby islands as their territory, called the island Île Sainte-Marie. The French, when they thought of Nosy Boraha at all, thought of it as an island of pirates. The pirates also thought of it as an island of pirates. But they were both wrong.

Nosy Boraha was an island of women. The pirates came and the pirates went, but the women were always there. You might think the women spent their time waiting for the pirates to return, but you'd be very, very wrong. It's true that particular women pined for particular pirates, but most of the time most of the women were happy to work in the company of other women, with occasional visits from men they favored—or men they welcomed for economic reasons. Piracy was the economic engine that made Nosy Boraha thrive. It was an island of women who provided services for pirates.

Women gardened and raised chickens and goats. They hunted for game in the forest. They built houses, brothels, saloons, shops, and all the other structures that made a town. With their carpentry skills, they repaired leaky barrels, leaky ships, and broken masts. They cooked meals, catering to the pirates' cravings for good food with fresh meat and tropical fruits.

Of course, women satisfied the pirates' other cravings as well—there were several brothels in the port. They ranged in elegance and price from back rooms in the harbor tavern to Ruby's, an elegant bordello up on the hill behind the town.

The women in the brothels did much more than provide sexual favors. They listened to the men in ways that their crewmates wouldn't. They nodded and smiled as pirates complained about their lot, explained how they had been wronged, or recounted what had happened (in excruciating blow-by-blow detail) when their ship captured a merchant vessel. The women provided a softness that many a hardened pirate craved. They talked to the men sweetly and gently, admiring them, praising their valor, their sexual abilities, their generosity. They made every pirate feel like a hero.

Nosy Boraha was an island owned by women, but no woman would tell that to the pirates. It would have hurt the men's feelings, confused them, and perhaps even embarrassed them. A hurt, confused, embarrassed pirate could be quite dangerous, so best to avoid all that. Ruby, the owner of Ruby's bordello, would never tell a pirate that she was in charge, though she was very much so.

Ruby was a beautiful Malagasy woman. The pirates called her Ruby, but her Malagasy friends called her Raza, an abbreviation of her real name, which began with Raza and continued for far longer than any European cared to remember or pronounce. Malagasy names incorporate the mother's name, the father's name, and something about the individual's history and prospects. For example, consider the famous Malagasy king named Andrianampoinimerinatompokoindrindra, which meant "the prince who was given birth to by Imerina and who is my real lord." (His nickname was Andrianampoinimerina the Wise.)

Raza had been born on the island of Madagascar and educated by Catholic missionaries from the age of thirteen, when her parents had died of typhoid. Even as a young woman, she was confident, capable, and very aware of her sexual power. Men—even supposedly devout Catholic bishops—wanted her. They spoke to her as if she were a child and lusted after her as a woman. Women—even pale and proper missionary wives and French nuns—treated her with scorn (and sometimes lusted after her as well).

Despite the missionaries' best efforts, Catholicism didn't sit well with Raza. She felt sorry for that skinny man on the cross wearing thorns on his head, but she thought him a fool to get himself in that situation and she saw no reason to worship him.

Raza was both smart and clever (which are not at all the same thing). Because she was smart, she learned to speak fluent English and French. She also learned a bit of Spanish, Portuguese, and Latin. This last she had picked up from a lonely French priest who valued her companionship in his bed and her silence outside the bedchamber.

Because she was clever, she did not let it be generally known that she could understand multiple languages. This gave her the advantage of learning far more about what was going on at the mission than any of the Europeans realized.

One day, she overheard the head nun making arrangements to send her to Toamasina, the center of the French occupation of Madagascar, to serve in the household of a high-ranking French official. That same official had leered at Raza and slapped her bottom when he had visited the mission. He was, she thought, a very rude and arrogant man. She had no interest in serving in his house as a maid and quite likely his unwilling mistress.

So Raza slipped away in the night, making her way through the jungle trails to the coast with the help of a young hunter who was a cousin of hers. She found a fisherman willing to take her to Nosy Boraha, where her aunt and several cousins lived.

In the harbor town on Nosy Boraha, Raza began calling herself Ruby and started building her brothel. She had the capital she needed—the head priest at the mission had kept a store of gold coins in a box beneath his bed. She had found them when she was cleaning his room, and she took three before she left. There had been many coins and she took just a few. She knew he would not notice immediately if a few were gone. Besides, a few coins were fair pay for all her work at the mission.

Ruby had been eighteen when she escaped the mission. She was twenty-five when the *Jolly Roger* sailed into the harbor with Mary, Tom, and Sam on board. Over the years, Ruby had created an economic empire. Not only did she gather a group of beautiful courtesans (many of them relatives of hers), she also used her fluency in French, Spanish, Portuguese, and English to make connections with merchants who could fence the pirates' plunder.

She had a purchasing agent who met the ships as they came in and provided an on-the-spot evaluation of a cargo's value. For more involved negotiations, she met with pirate captains in her office at the bordello.

When the *Jolly Roger* made port in Nosy Boraha, James was the first one off the ship. He did not linger at the harborside tavern. He followed the winding dirt track that led through town and up the hill to Ruby's.

A high, red-mud wall with a tall wooden gate separated the brothel's garden from the path. James paused by the gate. It was late morning, a quiet time of day in the brothel. Birds called from the trees on the other side of the fence. He could hear the murmuring of women's voices within.

James rang the bell that hung beside the gate. A moment later, a young woman opened the gate and smiled at James. "My apologies, sir," she said softly. "We are not open for business just now. If you return tonight, you will be very welcome."

"I have business with Ruby," James said, meeting the woman's eyes. "My name is James. I am from the *Jolly Roger.*"

"One moment." The gate closed and James waited.

The young woman returned and led him through the garden. Jungle trees shaded the path. Clusters of brilliantly colored orchids clung to the trees, filling the air with fragrance. Ruby's home was behind a fence in a remote area of the garden—close enough to the brothel to make a visit easy, but far enough to be quite separate.

Ruby met James at the door. She was a tall dark-skinned woman who carried herself with a regal grace. Her hair was tied up in intricate braids; her eyes were bright and discerning.

She waved him to a seat. "A pleasure to see you again, James," she said, pouring him a cup of tea. Ruby made a habit of remembering names and faces and always had tea while conducting business with British pirates. "How is Captain Scratch?"

"He'll be here to see you soon," James said, then hesitated, uncertain of how to proceed.

Ruby considered him thoughtfully. "You have hurried ahead to talk to me about a private matter," she suggested.

James nodded slowly. "I have come to seek your advice," he said. He told her about the children and about Captain Scratch's interest in profiting from the youngsters. "I want to find a way to help these children return home."

Ruby studied him. "You think that I, as a soft-hearted woman, will sympathize with their plight and assist you in cheating your captain of his profit."

"That's not it at all," James said hastily, though he had thought she'd be sympathetic. "I would never cheat the captain. I just thought . . ."

Ruby waved a hand, her expression softening. She was glad this young man had had the sense to seek her advice. "I am sympathetic, James. But this is a tricky problem." She paused, considering the situation. "Are these children popular with the crew?"

"Very much so."

"Did you have a successful voyage?"

"Yes, very successful."

She nodded. "I'll see what I can do." She rang a bell and the young woman who had brought James to the office appeared in the doorway. "Tatamo will take you to the garden where you can have tea with one of the ladies."

James frowned.

Ruby smiled and thought for a moment. "Felana would be a good choice," she said to Tatamo. "Felana is very sweet and could use practice speaking English," she told James. "I noticed that your accent is excellent. It would be a favor to me if you would chat with Felana. If that conversation leads to more . . ." She smiled and shrugged.

James nodded. "It will be my pleasure," he said.

"Please escort Captain Scratch here as soon as he arrives," she told Tatamo.

Ruby's profession required that she understand the secret desires of those with whom she did business. Often, a man's secret was buried so deep that even the man himself did not know it.

Take Captain Scratch, that hardheaded business-minded pirate. James assumed, as did many others, that Scratch was motivated solely by his quest for riches. Not an unreasonable assumption—the captain claimed that his goal was to amass a fortune, return to England, buy a country estate, and become respectable. He wanted land and a wife (preferably a woman of title). People would tip their hats when they met him in the street.

But riches were not his only motivation. The captain's hero was Blackbeard, the most famous pirate of all time. Celebrated in the popular press for both his ferocity and his generosity, Blackbeard was feared by his foes and revered by his crew. He had hobnobbed with governors, a man of power among men of power.

Captain Scratch wanted respect—and not just the petty grudging respect that he earned as a hardworking captain who made his crew rich. He wanted to be celebrated as a great man, to be admired by all.

Ruby had realized this. And Ruby had ways of making use of what she knew.

James was drinking tea with Felana when Tatamo came to escort him back to Ruby's office. There he found Captain Scratch with Ruby. The captain was sipping a glass of wine, which was quite out of character. "Did you know," he asked James, "that Blackbeard released any children that he captured?"

James nodded. He knew very little about Blackbeard, but he was ready to play along. "I have heard that. He was known to be fierce in battle, but always generous to children."

"Generosity is the mark of a great man," Ruby said.

The captain nodded gravely, then gave James his orders. He was to go to the ship and tell Cookie to bring the children to Ruby's.

"Instruct the children on what to say when newsmen ask them about where they've been. They must say that they were very grateful to be taken aboard by Captain Scratch. They were treated very fairly. Tell them to say that."

"Yes, sir," James said. "Very fairly."

"Captain Scratch was fierce but fair," the captain said. "And generous. Kind to orphans."

"Yes, sir," James said. "Generous and kind."

* * *

Cookie led the children through the town—past brothels and taverns where rowdy pirates drank, sang, fought, and engaged in other activities best not mentioned in front of the children.

As they followed the winding path to Ruby's, Mary could hear drunken singing, shouting, and shrieks of laughter. She stayed close to Cookie, and Tom stayed close to her. She kept one hand on the short sword that she wore at her belt, a parting gift from James. Sam walked a bit apart, peering into the open doors as they passed.

"Why such a hurry?" a woman called down to them from a second-story window. She was wearing a low-cut blouse that barely covered her large breasts. "Bring those boys to me! I'll make them men!"

"We're going to Ruby's," Cookie said, and that was enough.

"Have a good time, boys," the woman called.

Near the top of the hill, they left the taverns behind. The air was fresher, touched with the scent of flowers. As she took a deep breath, Mary realized that she had grown used to the stink of the pirate ship—a mix of sweat, tar, dirty clothes, and food on the edge of going bad. The sudden absence of stink and noise was disconcerting.

When Cookie rang the bell at the gate, a woman answered and led them into a wonderful place. Was it a room or was it a garden? Mary wasn't sure, and it really didn't matter. There were trees, there were flowers. Sometimes there was thatch overhead and sometimes open sky. There were walls made of cloth that shifted and swayed in the light breeze.

There were women—such women! These were not women who flashed their breasts and called out promises from a high window. They wore silk gowns—low cut to be sure and artistically slit to show off a fine leg. There were pale-skinned women and dark-skinned women, thin women and large, curvaceous women. All of them were smiling, relaxed, and welcoming.

They were not all beautiful. But there was something about them: a quiet strength, a regal confidence. They sat at ease among the flowers. They had been talking among themselves before the pirates arrived, and Mary was sure they would continue talking among themselves after the pirates left.

"We're going to meet Ruby," Cookie told the children. By the way he said it, Mary knew that meeting Ruby was something special.

The courtyard by Ruby's house was shady and filled with flowers. Ruby was waiting for them. She took Cookie's hand. "Abraham," she said. "So good to see you again."

Mary stared at the cook. Abraham? Everyone called him Cookie. Abraham ducked his head like a schoolboy, smiling and looking down.

Ruby studied the children thoughtfully. "I'm Ruby," she said. "What's your name?"

She was looking at Mary when she spoke, so Mary answered. "I'm Marty. This is my brother Tom and my friend Sam."

Ruby smiled. "Very glad to meet you all. Would you care to join me for a cup of tea and some cake?"

Before Mary could say a word, Tom answered for all of them. "Oh, yes, please."

Ruby turned her attention back to Cookie. "You're welcome to join us for tea, Abraham," she said. "Or do you have another engagement?" She leaned closer to the cook, one hand still holding his, the other on his shoulder.

Mary could not hear what Cookie said, but she saw Ruby beckon to the woman who had brought them from the gate. "Tatamo, will you show Abraham the way to the salon? I know Kintana will be very glad to see him."

Tatamo took Cookie's arm. As they walked away, Mary realized that they were alone with Ruby. She stood very still, like a wild creature caught in a trap.

"Let me get the tea," Ruby said.

"And cake," Tom said.

Mary shot him a look. She had long since decided that at times of peril you had to remember your manners. "Tea would be lovely," she said. "Thank you very much."

Soon they were sitting on rush mats, sipping tea and eating cake. While Tom and Sam were occupied with the food, Ruby leaned close to Mary. "James suggested that I might be able to help you and your friends."

"We don't need any help," Mary said. There was a brittle edge in her voice. She could take care of herself. She had to take care of herself. She had to take care of Tom.

Ruby nodded thoughtfully. "You don't need help, but perhaps there is something you want. What is it you want, Marty?"

What did she want? At the question, with its suggestion that anything was possible, something in Mary let go. "I want to go home," she said. Now tears were leaking from her eyes. She couldn't stop them, but she tried to ignore them.

Ruby's comforting arm was quickly around her shoulders. "Of course," she said. "Of course you do. If you like, you can stay here with me for a while. I'll find a ship to take you home. I'll even call you Marty, though I don't think that's the name your mother calls you."

Ruby sent out inquiries through her extensive network of friends and family, in search of the right sort of captain with the right sort of ship bound for Australia. The captain had to be dishonest enough to be dealing with pirates, but honest enough to be trusted to deliver the children.

While Ruby looked for the right captain, the children slept in a room in Ruby's house, quite separate from the brothel. James and Cookie came to say goodbye just before the *Jolly Roger* sailed. "Don't forget us," James said, and Mary said she never would.

After that, James did not often think of Marty, Tom, and Sam, but when he did, he counted his role in their escape as a good deed that could be credited to his account, if anyone was keeping accounts.

The children were happy at Ruby's. She set them small tasks—like sweeping the path by the front gate or helping tend her small garden.

Life took on an easy rhythm. Every morning, before Tom and Sam were out of bed, Mary went to the courtyard where a stream ran through a great stone basin. This was where the women went to bathe. Mary went there very early, so that she could bathe in privacy.

One morning, she took the time to wash her hair. She had forgotten to bring a comb, but she used her fingers to comb out her unruly curls. For a moment, she sat naked on the side of the basin. Her bare feet were in the cool water. Her hair was loose and her eyes were closed as she leaned back and enjoyed the warmth of the morning sun on her skin.

"Good morning," said a soft voice.

Mary was instantly alert, startled, aware that she was naked. Felana, a tall, beautiful, pale-skinned, young woman, smiled at her from just a few feet away, on the other side of the basin.

Mary saw the cloth she had been using to scrub herself clean on the edge of the basin. She grabbed it and laid it in her lap. Her clothing was out of reach. Maybe Felana hadn't seen.

"Relax, my dear," Felana said, her voice low and soothing. "We all have secrets here. I won't tell." She spoke English very well. Ruby's claim that she needed James' help had been a pretense.

Mary sat frozen, the cloth in her lap. Felana had seen. Mary knew that Ruby had guessed her secret. But Ruby was different; Ruby knew everything about everyone. Mary had continued to dress as a boy, valuing the freedom and sense of safety it gave her. But now that Felana knew, everyone would know.

Felana set down the basket she carried. She undressed and gracefully took a seat on the other side of the basin. Mary blinked and stared. Felana was not a tall, thin, beautiful young woman. She was a tall, thin, beautiful young man.

Mary was confused. "I thought you were a woman."

Felana was still smiling. She nodded. "Yes, I am a woman."

Mary glanced at Felana's penis, then at her face.

"There are many ways to be a woman," Felana said. "There are many ways to be a man. There are many ways to be a person."

Mary nodded, thinking about this. Felana dipped water from the basin and bathed herself. She took a wooden comb from her basket and combed out her hair. Then she offered to comb out Mary's curls. The two of them sat in the sun as Felana combed Mary's hair.

"Do you like being like a boy?" Felana asked.

Mary frowned, thinking about it. She had become Marty so quickly and easily, almost without thought. It was safer to be Marty. It was easier wearing trousers—she couldn't imagine climbing the rigging in a skirt. When everyone thought she was a boy, no one expected her to be their mother.

But there were things about being a boy she did not like so well. When she hurt herself, she couldn't cry. And she wasn't really a boy—she knew that.

"I like dressing as a boy," Mary said. "I like doing things that boys can do, things that girls aren't allowed to do. And if people knew I was a girl, they'd make me wear a skirt."

"Yes, they would," Felana agreed. "On a pirate ship, it is best to be a boy."

"Ruby is looking for a ship that will take us home to Australia," Mary said. "I'll be a boy until I get home."

When she put on her trousers, she became Marty again.

A few days later, the children set sail for Australia on the *Safe Passage,* a merchant freighter carrying pirate plunder to market.

CHAPTER 26
Welcome Home, Mary Watson

THE VOYAGE FROM Nosy Boraha to Brisbane, Australia was uneventful. In Brisbane, the captain of the *Safe Passage* used funds provided by Ruby to book tickets for the children on a steamship traveling to Cooktown.

There was a bit of trouble about Sam—the head steward on the steamship balked at having Sam travel in the same cabin as Marty and Tom. But Marty (Mary was still in the guise of a young boy) insisted that Sam was his brother. And when Sam spoke up for himself, the upper class British accent he had learned at Dr. Plummer's Academy made it clear that he was not a field laborer. And so Sam was allowed to travel with them.

Ruby had provided the children with clothing that would pass muster in polite company, packing both dresses and trousers for Mary. Before they disembarked in Cooktown, Mary put on a dress, knowing that her mother would like that. She combed her hair and tied it back in a braid. In her pocket, she carried the ruby ring from the pirate treasure that they had buried on Neverland. She was eager to tell her mother of all she had seen and all she had done. She knew she was in for a scolding, but she also knew her mother would forgive her for running away.

Mary felt uncomfortable leaving the steamship and walking down the street toward her family's store. The once-familiar street seemed strange—so many people, such noise and confusion.

They were almost home when Mary heard someone calling her name. "Mary? Mary Watson! Is that you?"

Mrs. Hall, who lived just down the street from the store, stood by her front door, broom in hand. She had been sweeping the porch when she saw the children. A heavyset woman with six sons, Mrs. Hall had always been kind to Mary and Tom.

"It is you! Oh, Mary! Where have you been?" Mrs. Hall set her broom aside and hurried into the street. "And Tom, too! We feared you were dead. Your poor father! Come along, come along! This will do him a world of good."

Before Mary knew what was happening, Mrs. Hall had her by the hand and was hustling her toward the store. "Mr. Watson!" she called. "The children are home! Mr. Watson!"

Henry Watson stepped through the open door of the store. He was so thin and sad that Mary almost didn't recognize him.

"Hello, Papa!" Tom shouted.

"Tom?" Henry's voice was faint. "You've come back. And Mary? Mary is here, too?"

"We've been on an adventure!" Tom said.

Mary was glad that Tom began chattering about all that they had seen and done—a blast of babble about pirates and crocodiles and sailing ships and leopards. The sight of her father looking so careworn quite took her breath away.

"This is my friend, Sam," Tom said. "We took good care of Mary—well, mostly I did, but Sam helped."

Mary saw the tears on her father's face as Mrs. Hall shooed them all into the store. Henry sat down in a chair by the counter, as if walking to the door had taken all of his energy. Mrs. Hall made tea, while Tom prattled on.

Mary noticed that the floor needed sweeping. Every day, people tracked in dirt. The wind blew in dust. Every morning her mother swept out the dust that the wind blew in and washed away the dirt that customers tracked in. But now there was dust in the corners and the marks of miners' boots on the floor.

"Where's Mother?" Mary asked, when Tom paused for breath.

It was then that she learned all that had happened since they had flown away. Mrs. Hall told most of it, with her father filling in gaps in a soft voice, the voice of an invalid. Her father had come down with fever in the goldfields—typhoid most likely. In a distant mining camp, he had fallen sick with a hacking cough, a painful rash, and a terrible fever. It had taken weeks for him to recover and make the trip back home.

When Henry Watson had returned to Cooktown, sad news awaited him. His wife was dead and his children were missing.

It was unclear what had happened. Mrs. Hall told of Alice Watson coming to her door and asking if Mrs. Hall had seen Mary and Tom. Their beds were empty, unmade. The children were gone.

Mrs. Hall had helped Alice search for the children. They asked every neighbor on the street if they had seen the children. They questioned Mrs. Hall's sons and all the other children that Mary and Tom played with. Then they looked more widely, asking all the merchants downtown, travelers staying at the hotel, sailors in the port.

There was no sign of the children anywhere. The town rallied and search parties went out to look for the children in the wildlands outside the town. After a time, they stopped looking for the living children and instead searched for their bodies.

After a few weeks, the community stopped searching. The children's disappearance was a mystery. As with any mystery, people speculated— saying that the children had been kidnapped by a band of aborigines, that they had gone for a morning swim and been swept away by the sea, that they had been taken by a mysterious stranger, perhaps a miner on his way out of town.

There were even darker speculations—some calling into question Alice's account of the children's disappearance. How could the mother have slept while her children wandered off or were taken away? Did Alice know something that she wasn't saying? And where was their father?

Mrs. Charlotte Walker, to her credit, weighed in on the matter— vehemently disputing any suggestion of neglect on Alice's part. Mrs. Walker said she had seen the children the day before their disappearance. They were well-behaved, she said. Polite and well cared-for. Alice, Charlotte said, was a fine artist and an upstanding member of the community. But still there was speculation. What did Alice know?

Alice took to wandering the hills and beaches outside town. "She never stopped looking for you children," Mrs. Hall said.

One day, when Alice did not return in the evening, Mrs. Hall rallied the town and people searched for her. They found Alice's body, still fully clothed, washed up on a rocky shore. Some people speculated that she had drowned herself, but Mrs. Hall didn't believe it. She thought Alice was the victim of a rogue wave that swept her out to sea. "She was a good swimmer," Mrs. Hall said, "but who can swim with skirts tangling around your legs and a wave that drags you out to sea?"

Mary wept to hear this terrible story. She was still crying when Mrs. Hall asked the inevitable question: Where have you children been? Mary buried her face in her hands, unwilling to answer with the truth. They had flown away without a thought for their mother.

Surprisingly, Tom came to her rescue. "We were captured by pirates," he said. "We went to the river, early that morning, to pick wildflowers for Mother. We saw a pirate ship in the harbor and a boat on the beach."

Mary stopped listening to Tom's story. She was thinking about her mother, trying to absorb the news of her death, waiting for someone to say it wasn't true. She was looking at her father—so worn and tired. If he had died while they were gone, she and Tom would have become orphans, alone in the world.

When Mary started paying attention to Tom again, he was talking about how he had stood up to the pirates to protect his sister. They had met Sam on the ship. He had been captured by the pirates, too. Sam and Tom became friends. They stole a boat from the pirate ship and slipped away in the dead of night.

They were navigating by the stars, Tom said. They would have made it—but they were picked up by another pirate ship. That ship, the *Jolly Roger,* had a British captain—Captain Scratch, who took them to the pirate island of Nosy Boraha. There he arranged for their passage home. "He treated us very fairly," Tom said. "He is fierce in battle, but always generous to children."

It was a totally unbelievable story. But Mary saw her father and Mrs. Hall nodding, their eyes wide as they listened to Tom's tale.

"You were so brave," Mrs. Hall said. "Protecting your sister. Standing up to those pirates. What a brave boy!"

Tears in his eyes, Henry pulled his son into an embrace.

How could they believe all that, Mary wondered. It sounded like one of Tom's adventure novels, with Tom as the hero, Mary as the lovely maiden, and Sam as the loyal Indian scout.

But she didn't contradict Tom. In his story, she and Tom were heroes, rather than heartless children who flew away to have fun while their mother suffered. Thinking of that, she wept again. Mrs. Hall comforted her. "It's all over now, dearie," the good woman murmured. "You're safe now."

When word spread, others believed Tom too. The newspaper published his story—edited so it made a bit more sense. The reporter contacted Captain Eddie of the *Safe Passage,* who confirmed that Captain Scratch of the *Jolly Roger* had arranged for the children's passage from Nosy Boraha. Mrs. Charlotte Walker took up the cause, writing about how the town needed to fortify itself against a pirate attack.

Over time, Mary came to realize that the good people of Cooktown believed Tom because they wanted to believe him. There was a reason that adventure novels were popular. They told the stories that people wanted to believe—tales of terrifying savages and bold British explorers. People wanted to believe that plucky children could stand up to pirates and survive. They wanted to think that a British pirate captain like Captain Scratch would send the children home.

Mary also realized that her mother was dead and someone had to make dinner every night. That first night, Mrs. Hall helped her assemble a hasty meal. But after that, the cooking and cleaning fell to her as the only girl in the household.

Sam helped Henry in the store every day, putting his maths lessons from Dr. Plummer's Academy to work. He slept on a cot in the store that was put away each day. Mrs. Hall set that up on the first night.

Tom helped in the store sometimes, but more often he went to town, supposedly on errands, but actually to reap the benefits of being a young hero. He told Mary about those benefits. If he happened to be near the sweet shop, people bought him sweets. If he was near the pub, men asked him to tell his story and bought him sweet lemonade to drink.

Mary noticed other things, too. Mrs. Hall advised her not to be too friendly with Sam. She frowned when Mary said that Sam was like an older brother to her. Mary overheard a miner asking her father what that boy was doing in the store. The man sounded very angry that Sam was there.

Once, when she and Sam were standing outside the store, a wagon drove past. It was filled with *kanakas,* Pacific Islanders who worked in sugar plantations to the south of Cooktown. Sam called out to the workers in a language that Mary didn't understand. He ran along beside the wagon until the driver threatened to whip him if he didn't stop. Sam stopped, but he stood in the street, watching until the wagon was out of sight.

When Mary asked Sam about the men in the wagon, he said the men were slaves, captured just as his cousins had been captured and working because they had no choice. They had to work or starve. Those men were not from his village, but from another island. He had spoken with them in the Pijin that the men of his village used to talk with visitors from other places.

Later, when Mary asked her father about the *kanakas*, he shook his head. "An unfortunate situation," he said. But he went on to say that many of the islanders had agreed to work in exchange for passage to Australia where they could have a better life. Later, they thought better of it, but the deal had been made and there was no going back.

"Most of them are ignorant brutes," he told her. "They are not like Sam. His father was British and he was brought up right."

When she asked more questions about the *kanakas*, her father waved them away. "These are complex matters," he told her. "Wise men in the government are working to figure them out."

Mary settled back into life in Cooktown. She took care of her father, and some of his strength returned. With Sam's help, the store's business picked up. Tom spent most of his time down at the harbor, hanging about with sailors.

Sometimes Mary went walking near the beach where her mother's body had been found. She wondered about what had happened there. Had her mother heard the mermaids' voices calling to her from the waves? What promises had they made to lure her into the water? Mary stayed as far from the sea as she could, wary of the waves.

When her father decided to ship all her mother's paintings to the London gallery for sale, Mary was happy to send the painting of the mermaids away. She asked to keep just one painting as a memory of her mother—the three smiling fairies sitting in the shade of a bottlebrush bush.

Gradually, Neverland faded in Mary's memory. She had no time to dwell on the past. She was always busy with day-to-day chores: cooking, cleaning, laundry, and all the other things that keep a household running.

Then one day, Mary's father made an announcement at dinner. "We're going home," he said.

Mary didn't know what he meant. "What do you mean, Papa? We are home."

"We are going home to England."

Henry had a list of reasons. A well-to-do Cooktown businessman had offered to purchase the store for a handsome price. Henry wanted to see his brother again—John, the uncle Mary had never met. Mary was becoming a young woman; she would benefit from the civilizing influence of London society.

The real reason, Mary knew, was that Henry was sad. He missed his wife, just as Mary missed her mother. He wanted to go back to a place that felt like home to him.

Plans were made. Mary and her father booked passage to England. Tom and Sam found a ship bound for England and signed on as cabin boys. Mary went home to a land she had never known. She wasn't sure she liked the idea of becoming a civilized woman, but it seemed she had no choice in the matter.

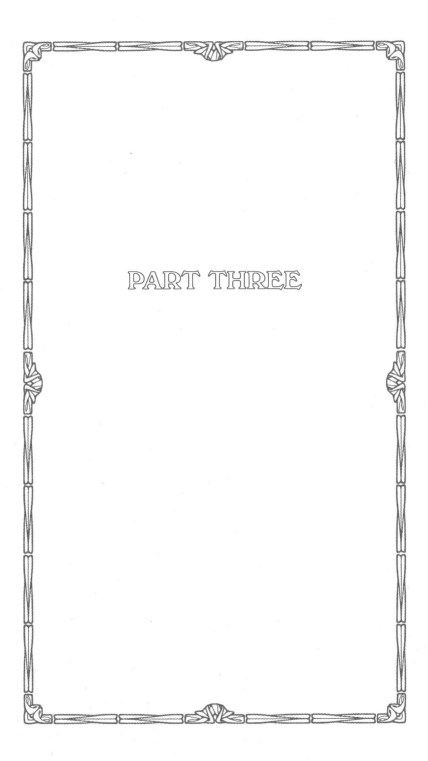

PART THREE

CHAPTER 27
The Wild Australian Girl

MARTY STOOD BY the rail as the *Honest Trader* sailed into the harbor on Nosy Boraha. Though Marty was still dressed as an adventurous young man, let us consider, for a moment, the feelings of the woman behind the masquerade. What was Mary Darling feeling just then?

She was very different from the woman who put her children to bed and left for a dinner party on a snowy evening in London. Here are the questions that had preoccupied her at that time:

1. What will I make for dinner tomorrow?
2. When will I find time to do all the mending?
3. Is George happy?
4. Michael sneezed this morning. Is he coming down with a cold?

She was also quite different from the woman who had escaped her home at number 14 and found a berth in a tiny cabin on the *Honest Trader*. A different set of questions preoccupied her at that point.

1. When will my husband come out of Nana's kennel?
2. Will the alienist lock me up for a rest cure?
3. How are the children? Are they well? Are they hungry?

By the time the *Honest Trader* reached Nosy Boraha, she had narrowed her questions down to just one:

1. How will I get to Neverland and rescue my children?

Mary was tanned, lean, fit, and focused. She was ready to act. She wore her sword at her belt. When she drew that sword to fight, the blade felt like an extension of her arm.

On the long voyage, she had rediscovered the version of herself that she had somehow lost during the time she was in London—the wild Australian girl who could do or try anything. Strange that she had to dress as a young man to find that girl, but no mind—that girl was back, though no longer quite so wild.

She was brave and bold and ready for anything—but there was a part of her that knew adventures could go very wrong. She was no longer the innocent girl who had told her mother that it would be fun to go on an adventure with the fairies.

The *Honest Trader* reached Nosy Boraha late in the morning, sailing into the harbor town when it was looking its best. The day before, a passing rainstorm had washed the town clean. The morning sun was shining and a fresh breeze was blowing.

"Glad to get here?" Mr. Davies asked, leaning against the rail beside Mary.

"That I am," she said.

"And where will you be going, now that you're here?" he asked, careful in the way that men are when they ask after each other's plans. He would have had a different tone had he known she was a woman. He would have been giving her advice, she thought. Davies would have been telling her where to go, what to do. It might have been good advice; it might have been bad advice. It might have been welcome; it might have been annoying. All that didn't matter. Had he known she was a woman, he would have been very generous with suggestions whether she wanted them or not.

"I'll be going to the same place I went on my very first visit to this island," Mary said.

"And where would that be?"

"To Ruby's."

"Ah," he said. "Of course you are."

Mary walked up the hill, following a winding path past brothels and taverns and stores. A stout woman swept the wooden porch in front of her store, where broken glass from a rum bottle sparkled in the morning light. In a large wooden chair on a brothel's porch, a young pirate, not yet sixteen years of age, slept soundly. His beatific expression contrasted with his snoring.

Mary remembered following Cookie up this path. Back then, she had been frightened by the scantily clad women who called to them. Now Mary carried herself like a young man—brash and confident. She nodded a greeting to the woman sweeping the porch. When women called to her from the brothels, she grinned and replied as Cookie had so many years ago, "I'm going to Ruby's!"

At last, she reached the wooden gate in the wall of red mud bricks that surrounded Ruby's establishment. Many years ago, she had said goodbye to Ruby at that gate, hugging her fiercely. Mary had been glad to be going home to Australia, but so sorry to be leaving Ruby behind.

Mornings had been Mary's favorite time at Ruby's. Late in the morning, the women were relaxing in the garden. Business was slow, and this was the time for bathing, drinking tea, laughing, and chatting. When she had lived in the brothel, Mary would fetch tea for the women, and they would make much of her. She had dressed as a boy, and at the time she thought she had fooled everyone. But now she realized that the women had guessed the truth. They saw through her disguise, but allowed her to believe that they didn't.

The women had advised Mary on how to make her disguise more convincing. When she bumped into a small table and apologized, the women laughed. "No, no, no," one said. "Boys don't say 'I'm sorry.' They say, 'That table was in the wrong place.'"

Mary had listened and learned. In the afternoons and evenings, when men came to Ruby's, she had watched them. She paid attention to how the men walked, to how they talked to each other, and to how they talked to the women. Mary practiced being a boy—unapologetically taking up a lot of space, talking loud, laughing loud, and (though always being respectful as befit a young lad) never apologizing.

Mary rang the bell that hung beside the gate. A young woman opened it just a little and smiled at her. "My apologies, sir," the woman said softly. "We are not open just now. If you return tonight, you will be very welcome."

"Please tell Ruby that I need to see her," Mary said. "We knew each other long ago."

The young woman still smiled, but there was a studied hint of regret in her expression. "Ruby can't see you now, sir."

"Just tell her that Marty is here," Mary said. "She helped me out many years ago. She will want to see me." Mary spoke with more conviction than she felt. Suddenly she wondered: Would Ruby remember her after all these years?

The woman closed the gate. Mary knew that she would be telling the other women that some poor lovesick fool was at the gate, thinking that Ruby would remember him. Mary only hoped that she would tell Ruby, too.

Mary waited. Birds called from the trees on the other side of the fence. She could hear women's laughter.

After what seemed like an eternity, Ruby opened the gate.

When Mary had last seen Ruby, she had been a beautiful young woman with a great mane of dark hair and a laugh that echoed across the garden. Now middle-aged, Ruby was still beautiful, but her beauty had a majesty to it. She held herself like a queen—back straight, head high.

Looking at her, Mary felt like a child again. "Ruby," she said, and then stopped as words failed her. She pulled the kerchief off her head, releasing her hair—cut short, but just as curly as it had been when she was a child. "It's Marty. You helped me get home, so many years ago." She took a deep breath, fighting back tears. "I need your help again."

Ruby reached out to touch Mary's cheek, then pulled her into an embrace. "I never thought I would see you again, child. Captain Eddie said he had delivered you to Australia. He brought back a newspaper article about how you had been captured by pirates. Captain Scratch was quite pleased by what Tom said about him.

"Sam came back—a grown man, he was. He said that you'd gone to England. But you are here now—dressed as a young man. Am I dreaming? Come—we will have tea. You will tell me all that has happened. And then I will help you. Of course I will."

Ruby led Mary through the garden. They went past the big house, where a group of women sat on the broad veranda. Their conversation fell silent as Mary drew near, only to revive when she was past them. Through a gate, past a fountain, behind a screen of tall tropical trees, she followed Ruby to her house.

In the courtyard that served as her kitchen, Ruby heated water on the fire. Mary sat at a wooden table and watched her. The air was scented with wood smoke, with the peppery aroma of last night's sweet potato stew, with the perfume of flowers from the garden. Mary breathed deep, remembering what a comfort this place had been after her time on the pirate ship.

"Drink your tea," Ruby said. "Tell me about your life these last twenty years."

Under the tropical trees, surrounded by birdsong and flowers, Mary summarized the years since she had last seen Ruby: her trip home, arriving in Cooktown to find that her mother had died, the journey to England, and her father's death—painful memories. Ruby shook her head sadly, her eyes filled with sympathy at Mary's troubles.

"My Uncle John and his wife took care of me after my father died," Mary said. "They tried to raise me as a proper English girl."

Mary told Ruby about marrying George and about her children. "Wendy is all that I wasn't as a child: tidy and polite and sweet. Such a little lady. She likes pretty things. John is the adventurer, trying so hard to be all grown-up, though he is only eight. Michael is the baby. I worry about him the most, though I know Wendy will take care of him."

On the long voyage, she had kept these memories sealed away. Talking about George and the children tore at her heart. Mary told Ruby about the terrible night when she came home and found that the children were gone. "The window was open. I knew they had flown away and I knew where they went." She hesitated for a moment. "I never told you how I had come to be on the *Jolly Roger*. There is an island called Neverland and a boy named Peter Pan who takes children there."

Ruby waved a hand, dismissing Mary's hesitant explanation. "James told me about this island. I had heard of the place before, though not by that name. Sailors tell stories." She waved a hand again—not dismissing the stories, but suggesting there was no need to retell them. "James told me of this boy—not really a boy, I think. A spirit—a very old spirit who is used to getting his way in all things."

Ruby considered Mary, her face still wet with tears. The poor child. Mary was lost, Ruby thought. All of the British people who came to Nosy Boraha were like this. They were an uprooted people, wandering the earth in search of their home. They kept claiming places that were not theirs, places that they said they had "discovered"—ignoring the people who had lived in those places for many generations.

Ruby took Mary's hand. "What is it you need, child? How can I help you?"

"I need a ship that will take me to Neverland. Sam told me that James is captain of the *Jolly Roger* now. Perhaps he will take me there."

Ruby refilled Mary's teacup. The young woman was very determined. "James is not the young man you remember. And you must understand: a pirate captain is not the lord and master of the ship, like the captain of a merchant ship. The crew must agree with James' decision to go to Neverland. If they don't like his decision, they will find another captain. Pirates are motivated by gold. There is no profit to be had in battling Peter Pan to rescue your children."

"You're wrong about that." Mary fumbled in the pouch that hung at her belt and brought out the ring that she had carried back from Neverland to give to her mother. The ruby glittered blood red in the sunlight. "Sam and Tom and I buried treasure there. This ring is from that treasure. Plenty of gold and jewels to reward those who help me."

Ruby took the ring from Mary and held the gem to the light, examining it for flaws. "Yes, this will certainly interest James and his crew." Ruby returned the jewel to Mary.

"I thought the pirates could take half the treasure and I could split the other half with Tom and Sam," Mary said. "That would be fair, I think."

"You will be entering a business arrangement with scoundrels," Ruby said. Her tone was grim. "They are scoundrels I regularly do business with, and I know them well. If you are acting on your own, there is nothing to stop them from taking the treasure and tossing you overboard." Ruby shook her head and frowned. "You would be wise to have me negotiate an agreement for you regarding the division of the treasure. My involvement will offer you some protection."

Mary blinked, then remembered how casually Captain Scratch had talked of tossing the children overboard. "James wouldn't do that. At least, I don't think he would. I . . ."

"James might not, but the crew could toss both you and James overboard, if it was worth their while. You're an outsider—someone they don't need. They can't dismiss me so lightly. If they return without you, I will ensure that Nosy Boraha is closed to them. They will lose access to the best market for their goods, the best port for reprovisioning and repair—and the best place to enjoy the company of women. I will make the consequences of betrayal quite clear."

CHAPTER 28
The Battle of the Coconuts

J AMES, THE MAN on whom Mary was pinning her hopes, had been born to a respectable family. If he had remained in London, he probably would have grown up to become a Member of Parliament. But he did not remain in London.

When he was ten years old, he was home from boarding school for the Christmas holidays. His sister, a lovely young woman of eighteen, had recently become engaged. His parents were dining with the parents of her fiancé.

"They've gone out to dinner?" he asked the maid, when she came to his room to bring him a slice of cake as a treat.

The maid, a sweet-faced girl of sixteen, busied herself with adding coal to the fire. She felt uncomfortable around the boy, who was quiet and melancholy by nature. "Yes, young master."

"My mother did not come to say good night," James said. His tone was matter-of-fact. "I suppose they were in a great hurry." His mother was a beautiful woman, more suited to attending dinner parties and looking lovely than to mothering an awkward child. In the excitement of preparing for the party, she had quite forgotten that James was home from school.

His father was a barrister and a businessman, chairman of the Great Western Railway, and an investor in a timber import business. James was the youngest of his six children—at age ten, he was not yet old enough to be of much interest to his father.

James listened to the maid's footsteps on the stairs as she hurried away. In the kitchen, the servants were having a small party—celebrating with leftovers from the Christmas feast.

James sat in the chair by the fire to read *The Coral Island* by R. M. Ballantyne. One of the boys at school had pronounced the story "ripping," so James was giving it a try. From what he had read so far, he wasn't impressed.

James didn't have much in common with the boys at his boarding school. They all cared about sports, and James was terrible at sports. Sitting alone in his room, James focused on his book to avoid thinking about his inevitable return to school.

Just then, Peter Pan tapped on the window.

It was a second-story window. James peered through the glass and saw a boy flying—flying!—just outside. The boy was dressed in animal skins and his hair needed cutting. James opened the window and Peter flew in, accompanied by a blast of cold air.

Peter circled the room (just to show off, James realized later) and landed in front of James. "Hullo. I'm Peter Pan." His tone implied that James should immediately recognize the name. Peter was eyeing the slice of cake that the maid had left on the table. "What's this?"

"That's my cake. Would you like some?" James was a polite boy.

"Yes," said Peter. Without another word, Peter picked up the slice of cake and ate it all. He ignored the fork that was on the table beside the plate. Peter was not a polite boy.

He wiped his hands on his tunic and took flight again, circling the room while somersaulting in midair. That distracted James from the outrage of having his cake devoured without a word of thanks.

"What are you doing in here?" Peter asked James.

"Reading a story about some boys shipwrecked on a desert island. They fight pirates and have adventures."

Peter nodded. "Just like Neverland. I live there with the Lost Boys. There are mermaids and pirates and we have jolly adventures every day."

"Neverland? Where is that?"

"Not far at all, if you know the way. Do you want to go there?"

James frowned, recognizing that the boy's answer wasn't an answer at all. "How would we get there?"

"We'll fly. I'll teach you how." Peter reached into a bag that hung from his belt and pulled out a pinch of glittering dust that he sprinkled on James. "Now jump."

James, feeling foolish, gave a little jump. Rather than landing on his feet, he slowly rose in the air until he bumped into the ceiling.

"You fly like this." Peter demonstrated.

Imitating Peter, James leaned forward and lifted his feet. That sent him into a forward glide.

The winter before, when his family was visiting his grandparents in the country, one of James' older brothers took him sledding and showed him how to steer the sled by leaning. James tried the same technique in flight, spreading his arms and leaning to one side to make a lovely swooping. He swooped around the room once, twice, three times. It was wonderful. He felt competent in a way that he never had while playing sports. He couldn't trip over his own two feet while high in the air.

"Let's go!" Peter said. "We can hitch a ride on the wind and we'll be in Neverland in no time."

James hesitated. Later he looked back on that moment as a pivotal point in his life. He could hear laughter drifting upstairs from the servants in the kitchen, a distant merriment that made his own life feel even more empty and Peter's invitation even more inviting. "Yes, I'd like to have an adventure," he said.

He said it just as he might have said he'd like a sweet or another piece of cake. He did not know what a real adventure was like. A real adventure takes your life and shakes it, like a terrier shakes a rat. Your life may be better for it or it may be worse—as it was for the rat. But it won't be the same.

"Come on!" Peter called, and he dove through the open window. James followed and they soared over the city. Gas lamps glowed on the city street beneath them and stars shone above.

It was a long journey to Neverland—a night and a day and another night. James, like every other child who flew off with Peter, was surprised and dismayed by the distance.

Eventually, James sighted Neverland just as a slim crescent moon was rising. The island was an irregular shape in the glittering ocean waters—a dark mass of jungle, with a few tall palms rising above the rest. As they flew lower, James could hear a strange wailing coming from the water below. The sound filled him with fear and longing.

"The mermaids are singing to the moon," Peter said carelessly.

James followed Peter down, down, down to land in a jungle clearing. The Lost Boys emerged from the shadows. They were gaunt and filthy, their eyes hollow and hungry. "Did you bring any food?" they asked Peter.

"No," Peter said. "But I brought a new boy. This is Tootles."

That was the moment when James began to wonder whether he had made the right choice. He frowned. "My name is James," he said.

Peter shook his head, smiling. "Here, your name is Tootles."

So James became Tootles. He didn't like it, but Peter insisted.

You really don't want to hear about the long weeks that James spent in that jungle camp with the Lost Boys. No one is interested in the bloodthirsty mosquitoes, the constant gnawing hunger, the pervasive dampness of the underground room. Mold grew on James' shoes.

James had been on the island for about a week (though it seemed much longer) when Peter announced that he had spotted a pirate ship, a brig called the *Wicked Mistress*. "Today, we will fight pirates," he said.

James frowned. "What's the plan?" he asked Peter.

Peter grinned. He was always happy when he was about to do something frightfully dangerous. "The plan? To kill as many pirates as we can."

The Lost Boys had an assortment of knives and swords and cutlasses, collected over a number of years. They were stored at the back of the cave with predictable results. Every one of them was rusty and dull. James took a short sword that he carried awkwardly, thrust into his belt.

They flew over the ocean, and that part was wonderful. Then Peter spotted the pirate ship, drew his sword, and shouted, "Have at them, boys!" The ragtag band of Lost Boys followed Peter as he dove toward the deck of the ship.

There was a certain sameness in Peter Pan's battles with pirates. Remember Mary's account of a raid on a pirate ship? Like that battle, this was a bloodbath, and most of the spilled blood belonged to the boys. The pirates were a battle-hardened crew, veterans of many a fight against Royal Navy ships. The boys were untrained and untested. There was much screaming, much bloodshed, and some impressive swordplay by Peter.

By the time Peter had enough, the Twins had gone down in a pool of blood. Back at camp, Peter told the story of the battle as a glorious victory. The dead boys were forgotten.

A few days after the battle, Peter arrived at camp with two new boys. Peter called them the Twins, though they did not look at all alike. Like the other boys, the new Twins accepted their new name reluctantly and with some bewilderment.

A month later, when Peter once again announced that he had spotted a pirate ship, James was ready. He had made a plan that would let him stay a safe distance from the battle while appearing to participate. In an improvised sack made of an old shirt, he brought a dozen coconuts along on the flight out to sea.

When Peter shouted, "Have at them, boys!" James swooped low, but did not land. From above the deck, just out of reach of a swinging sword, James hurled coconuts at the pirates.

His first few coconut missiles missed their intended targets. The coconuts rolled about the deck. The Lost Boys flew over them, but the pirates tripped and stumbled. Cursing and kicking at the rolling coconuts, the pirates moved away from that area of the deck.

Then something unexpected happened.

A hatch opened. A small wiry man popped out and snatched up two coconuts that were rolling across the deck. He retreated to safety through the opening from which he had emerged, pulling the hatch closed behind him. As the battle moved toward the bow, the deck near the hatch was momentarily empty.

James threw another coconut, bouncing it off the deck beside the hatch. Again, the small man emerged, grabbed the coconut, and retreated.

James flew down and lifted the hatch. From a dimly lit galley at the bottom of a ladder, the wiry man stared up at him. The aroma of onions and biscuits and limes mingled with the scent of tar and old wood. Not the best combination of smells, but James had been hungry since he arrived in Neverland and the smell of any sort of food was attractive.

The man—the ship's cook—stared up at the boy. "Come on, then," he called to James.

The cook could hear running feet pounding the deck as the battle above them shifted. He saw James as the lesser danger. James climbed down the ladder.

Years later, James would say he had spared the cook. Truth be told, the cook had enlisted him. By the time Peter shouted for the Lost Boys to follow, James was eating his third biscuit. It was not a great biscuit—his mother's cook would have tossed it in the bin—but it was a remarkably good biscuit by pirate standards. The cook—known as Cookie, of course—was the pirate equivalent of a five-star chef. He kept his flour relatively free of weevils and he was the proud owner of a keg of butter, a substance he cherished and protected.

The ship was the *Jolly Roger*. The captain was Captain Scratch. Scratch accepted James as Cookie's helper because Cookie insisted on it, and Captain Scratch liked his cooking.

Cookie enlisted James as an assistant. When he wasn't working with Cookie in the galley, James made himself useful in other ways. In school, he had been at the top of his class in maths. His ability to do sums and long division came in handy when the pirates divided their plunder. His aptitude for math also attracted the attention of the ship's navigator, and James became an assistant navigator of sorts, helping keep the ship's log up to date.

Seven years later, when the *Jolly Roger* picked up Mary, Sam, and Tom, James was seventeen and an indispensable member of the crew. After arranging to get the children home, he continued to develop his skills as a sailor and a pirate. He had a cool analytical streak that served him well. Pursuing merchant ships under sail was a strategic game. You had to know the winds and the sails and how to use them to your advantage.

He even made use of his family connections. James recognized one of the passengers on a captured ship as a timber trader, a colleague of his father's. James interviewed the man—not about treasure exactly, but rather about the trends in trade and industry. How were innovations in the weaving industry affecting the value of silk? Were sapphires still the most popular stone for jewelry?

Through the timber trader (released unharmed with a letter to carry to James' mother), James established an intermittent correspondence with his parents. Information from those letters let James maximize the profit from cargos that the *Jolly Roger* captured.

Years later, when Captain Scratch retired, the crew elected James to be captain of the *Jolly Roger*. He had been captain for just over a year when he and Peter Pan renewed their acquaintance.

The *Jolly Roger* was on course for Nosy Boraha, laden with plunder. The sky was a cloudless tropical blue. The wind was fair, the ship's sails were full, and the crew was as relaxed as a ship's crew can be when the vessel is under sail.

Smee, the bosun, was splicing two lengths of rope to make a longer rope. The cook was cracking coconuts that had been gathered on an island some days before. A group had gathered around him. Each time he cracked open a nut with a blow of his machete, he handed it around so that the men could drink the sweet coconut water.

James, in a philosophical mood, had been talking with Rumbold, a recent addition to the ship's crew.

Yes, that's the very same Rumbold that Holmes and Watson would later meet on their voyage to Madagascar. The pirate ship that had rescued Rumbold from the jungle island was the *Jolly Roger*.

Rumbold had joined the crew as the ship's doctor. James was glad to have him aboard—having a trained medical man on the crew made his ship more attractive to potential crew members. James also enjoyed Rumbold's company. They were well matched in temperament and attitude. They had quickly become intimate friends.

That sunny day, Rumbold had gone below to make a cup of tea when James heard the voices of children, laughing and shouting. James looked up and saw the Lost Boys landing in the rigging like a flock of birds. They laughed and called to each other.

James heard familiar names. "Make room, Tootles!" "Look out, Nibs, I'm coming in."

One figure, a boy no bigger than the rest, did not land. Still in flight, he circled the *Jolly Roger*, surveying the deck below. A twinkling light flew with the boy, barely visible against the blue sky.

The pirates stared up at the children, astounded at this intrusion. For a moment, James stood frozen, transfixed by the sight of children in flight, captured by a memory that usually came to him only in dreams. James remembered flying, skimming just above the ocean waves, soaring beside an albatross. Then he remembered his last flight with Peter when they attacked a pirate ship.

"To your weapons," James shouted to the crew. "Prepare for battle!"

The pirates responded instantly. Smee snatched up the marlinspike that he had been using to unravel the rope he was splicing—a foot-long metal spike with a nasty point. In the other hand, he held his hammer, a useful tool and an excellent club.

Skylights, who was never without his sword and his dirk, had drawn both, a weapon for each hand. The dirk had a heavy knob on the hilt, making that end as useful for cracking a skull as the other end was for stabbing and slashing.

Bill Jukes had snatched up a boarding ax. Alf Mason, who favored crushing over cutting, had a belaying pin in each hand. Gentleman Starkey, who preferred killing at a distance, had been cleaning his pistols. He loaded them swiftly and stepped into a protected position where he could shoot at leisure. Moments after the captain shouted, all were ready.

James preferred to avoid battle with the Lost Boys. Having once been one of them, he knew how hungry and desperate they were—and how ferociously they could fight under Peter's command.

James called out. "Hullo, Peter! Will you join us for tea? The cook is making coconut cake."

"Oooo," said the Lost Boys in the rigging, the involuntary moan of children promised a treat. For a moment, James thought bloodshed might be avoided. But Peter was not tempted.

"Tea with pirates? Never! Prepare for battle, boys!"

A moment's pause, then the boys responded with a ragged and unenthusiastic chorus. "Aye, aye, sir."

Peter swooped down to the deck, followed at some distance by the Lost Boys. Gentleman Starkey discharged his first pistol at Peter. He missed, but the shot scattered the boys in all directions.

Peter did not waver. "Put up your sword, pirate!" he shouted, then flew straight at James, sword drawn.

Over the years, James had become an expert swordsman. When Peter attacked with ferocity, James met the attack with an equally ferocious defense. Blades flashed as each tested the other and found himself well matched. Peter was quick, but James was just as quick. Peter fought from the deck, needing a firm footing to put power behind his blows, but he could fly when he needed to.

James had the advantage of a long reach and an understanding of strategy and positioning that the boy lacked. James was, however, distracted by memories of the distant past.

"We don't need to fight," James said, after the initial skirmish. "Don't you know me, Peter? It's Tootles."

Was there a flicker of recognition on the boy's face? If so, it was fleeting. Peter lived in the moment, blithely unencumbered by memories of the past.

"You aren't Tootles," called one of the ragged children who was hovering above the fray. "I am!"

Peter renewed his attack.

James used a blend of styles that would have baffled the most expert of sword fighters. He had the advantage of Peter when interference came from an unexpected quarter. Peter's fairy, that twinkling light that was really a tiny winged person, flew at James' face, blinding him. James stepped back, momentarily off balance.

Peter attacked with a sudden blow to the pirate captain's sword hand, a slash that cut through bone and muscle, removing the hand just above the wrist. The blow sent James' hand, still holding the sword, over the rail into the ocean waters. Stumbling, James slipped on his own blood. He fell to the deck, clutching the stump where his hand had been. Peter laughed with boyish delight and stepped in to deliver the final blow.

That could have been the end of James. But at that moment, Rumbold emerged from belowdecks, armed with his favorite weapon.

On the *Jolly Roger*, Rumbold had become intrigued by the pirates' methods of combat. Not an athletic man, he was attracted to a weapon that is not generally featured in fictional accounts of pirates. That inelegant weapon, a precursor to the modern grenade, was known among pirates as the stinkpot.

The name aptly describes this weapon. Originally developed by the Chinese and used against the British during the second Opium War, the stinkpot took a number of different forms. The original Chinese stinkpot was an earthenware pot packed with malodorous substances. Hurled aboard an enemy ship, it shattered on impact. Men had been known to dive overboard to escape the foul stench.

Over the decades, innovators had created variations on the original form: pots packed with gunpowder and equipped with a fuse that was set alight before launch, or leather bags stuffed with stink and coated with tar and set alight. Unfortunately, flaming stinkpots had a nasty tendency to set ships on fire, destroying valuable cargo.

Being scientifically minded, Rumbold had begun experimenting with stinkpots in their original form, making use of a source of stink that was readily available on many tropical islands. When the *Jolly Roger* visited an island to get provisions, Rumbold had visited a colony of seabirds nesting on a nearby spit of land. There he had collected several jars of guano, which he pulverized into dust.

The collection process had been unpleasant but brief. Carefully sealed, the glass jars had no unpleasant smell. Rumbold's theory was that a hurled jar would shatter, releasing a cloud of ammonia dust. Rumbold had not yet tried the experiment when Peter attacked the *Jolly Roger*.

Hearing the clamor of the battle overhead, Rumbold had tied a kerchief over his nose and mouth as an improvised gas mask and snatched up a guano-filled stinkpot. He emerged from the hatch just in time to see Peter Pan amputate James' hand with a slashing stroke. As James slipped and fell, Rumbold hurled the stinkpot, aiming at the deck where Peter Pan stood ready to deliver the killing blow.

The results exceeded Rumbold's expectations. The jar shattered, sending up a great gray cloud of guano dust. Even at a distance, the stench was impressive. It stung the eyes, attacked the throat, and offended the nose. Peter Pan and his fairy companion flew up, above the cloud.

Rumbold charged into the cloud, finding his way to where James lay on the deck. Rumbold heard Peter Pan call to the children. "Come away! We're done with these scoundrels. Back to Neverland and away from this stink."

Eyes watering, Rumbold knelt beside James, grateful for the breeze that blew away the stench and the dust. He worked swiftly, applying pressure to James' brachial artery and slowing the flow of blood. As he worked, he shouted to the crew, "Bring me a belaying pin!" With his belt and the belaying pin, Rumbold improvised a tourniquet.

CHAPTER 29
Like a Cat with a Mouse

MARY WOKE IN a comfortable bed at Ruby's. The night before, she had taken a bath, a luxury that hadn't been possible aboard the *Honest Trader*. Ruby had left a robe by her bed and Mary wrapped herself in it, relishing the feel of the soft silk against her clean skin.

Mary found Ruby in her office, where she was examining several lovely dresses. Ruby greeted her, with a smile and poured her a cup of tea from the teapot on her desk. "Did you sleep well?"

"Very well," Mary said. "I've come in search of my clothes."

"I've sent your clothes to be washed," Ruby said. She studied Mary thoughtfully. "And I suggest you change your wardrobe before you continue on this adventure."

Mary looked startled. "What do you mean?"

"Before the *Jolly Roger* comes in, you need a proper dress."

"A dress?" Mary had grown used to being Marty Watson. "I think I'm much better off continuing to dress as a man."

"That was a wise choice for the journey. You make a very convincing young man. But you're a small man, likely to be challenged by larger men. Is that not so?"

"I have my sword and I know how to use it."

"I have no doubt about that. But you will have to prove your skills repeatedly to those who challenge you. That's a waste of time and energy. I suggest you keep the sword—but change your men's clothing for a dress. Marty Watson is a young man in search of adventure—and young men in search of adventure are quite commonplace. You have a much more interesting story to tell, a much better character to play. It's time to reclaim your power as a woman—while keeping your sword at the ready."

"I can't fight in a dress," Mary protested.

"I'll find you a dress you can fight in," Ruby said. "And wearing a dress will give you a distinct advantage."

"What's that?"

Ruby smiled. "They'll think you don't know how to fight." Ruby reached out and took Mary's hand. "You can fight like a man. But you can also fight like a woman. A pirate thinks a small man with a sword is someone to challenge and overcome. A beautiful woman with a sword is someone to woo . . . and that's a position of power."

"You feign weakness, but not too much weakness," Mary said. "They think they can win easily, but first they will play with you, like a cat with a mouse. They think you are the mouse, but they're wrong. You are the cat." She noted Ruby's expression of surprise. "Miss Sanderson, my fencing teacher, told me this. She said that women made the best fighters, because men are often stupid when it comes to women."

"I think I would like Miss Sanderson," Ruby said. "Men can be very stupid indeed around a pretty woman. Not James, of course. But many men."

"Not James?"

"He appreciates women, but he prefers men."

Mary nodded slowly, taking that information in.

"But most men underestimate women, ignoring their intelligence and skills because men are distracted by other things. Now let us find a dress that you can fight in."

After much comparison of this gown and that, Mary was dressed in a way that satisfied both herself and Ruby. She wore a simple green linen dress with a split skirt. No frills or lace to get in the way, but a lovely trim in a paler shade of green. No pinch-waisted silhouette here—the garment's lines were that of the Aesthetic Dress movement, which advocated for clothing that was softer and more comfortable, yet still quite becoming.

The only concession to frills was her hat—broad brimmed to keep the tropical sun out of her eyes and decorated with silk ribbons and a tiny veil to add a touch of mystery. Had it not been for the sword that hung from the belt around her waist, Mary would not have looked out of place strolling in Royal Victoria Park at Bath.

She practiced various defensive and offensive moves to determine that she could fight wearing the dress. She had to admit that she rather liked the loose feel of the skirt. And freeing her breasts from the binding she had used to confine them was a great relief.

The two women, pleased with the results of their collaboration, were settling down to have lunch when they were interrupted. The young woman who had greeted Mary at the gate the day before came to Ruby's office in haste. "Ruby? There's a young man at the gate. He insists he has to see you. His name is Tom Watson."

Tom was no longer the lanky youngster who had gone to sea. He was taller, tanned, and far more muscular—a handsome young man. A thin scar on his forehead, running diagonally from left to right, did not detract from his looks. Combined with his confident grin, it gave him a rakish charm.

Mary recognized him immediately. "Tom!" she cried out. Tears ran down her cheeks. She held out her arms to hug her brother.

He blinked at her in confusion.

"Don't you recognize your own sister, Tom?" she asked.

He studied her face, startled. "Mary? How did you get here?"

She hugged him then. "Where have you been for all these years? I thought . . . I didn't want to think . . . when I never heard from you, I thought you were dead. Oh, Tom! How is it that we meet again, just when I need your help the most?"

Back in Ruby's quarters, as they ate spicy sweet potato stew with rice, Tom told them where he had been all those years. Mary knew the beginning of the story from Sam. Tom picked up from the point where he and Sam had parted ways. A captain had offered Tom a position as bosun on his merchant ship, the *Bold Adventure*. Tom had taken the job, even though there had been no position for Sam.

For a time, Tom had been happy on the *Bold Adventure*. But when the ship made port in Cape Town to take on cargo, it had sailed without Tom, leaving him behind.

According to Tom's account, here's what had happened: Tom saw a group of thieves attacking a young woman in an alley. Though outnumbered, he rushed to her aid. He succeeded in chasing the scoundrels away, but the encounter left him badly beaten. The woman, grateful for her rescue, had nursed him back to health, but before he could recover, his ship had sailed. The scar on his forehead, Tom said, was a souvenir of that fight.

The truth of the matter was a little different. When drunk, Tom had tripped and fallen in a brothel, gashing his head on the edge of a table. The ship had sailed when he was recovering from this injury.

Do not think the worst of Tom for lying about his past. Like many people, he had rewritten his past into a narrative that he liked a bit better than what actually happened. He had told these stories for so long that part of him really believed them.

When Tom had recovered from his injury, he found a berth on the *Lucky Penny*, a merchant freighter bound for Bombay. In the Arabian Sea, the freighter was captured by the *Mad Maggie*, a swift-sailing pirate schooner. As luck would have it, *Mad Maggie's* first mate had been a seaman on the *Jolly Roger* when Mary, Tom, and Sam had sailed with Captain Scratch. When the *Mad Maggie* set sail, leaving the freighter stripped of all that was valuable, Tom sailed with the pirates.

No need to know all of Tom's travels. He tended to change ships frequently, always looking for a more comfortable berth. But his words to Mary painted a picture of a romantic, swashbuckling life.

Mary listened to his story dutifully, nodding and making all the right sisterly sounds of sympathy. But she did not believe the tale in its entirety. She knew his ways. As a boy, Tom had often evaded punishment by telling stories that were not true. As the youngest child, he got away with it, indulged by their mother and father and, to some extent, by Mary as well.

"Why didn't you write to me, Tom?" Mary asked.

"I did write," Tom said, his tone that of a man who has been falsely accused. "In several ports, I gave letters into the care of ships bound for England. Didn't you get them?" He was lying, but he had learned long ago to be both specific and vague in his lies.

Mary chose to believe him, recognizing it was a choice. He may indeed have written. Letters from the other side of the globe often went astray. It was easier to choose belief than start an argument.

Tom had been a handsome and mischievous boy who got away with his mischief because of his golden curls. That pretty child had grown into a good-looking man, who was still getting away with mischief.

Ruby turned the conversation to more useful channels. "What brings you back to Nosy Boraha after all these years?"

Tom's eyes lit up and he leaned forward, smiling. "Treasure," he said. "Mary, do you remember the treasure that we buried on Neverland? I've run low on funds, and I thought it was time to dig that up."

"I think it is time you hear what has brought your sister to Nosy Boraha," Ruby said.

Once again, Mary told her story.

Tom did not share her dismay that Peter had taken the children. "I am sure they are having a splendid time," he said. "Living in the cave, hunting in the forest. I remember it well. What a lark it was!"

Mary shook her head, shocked at his reaction. "A lark? Do you remember when Curly and Nibs died in the pirate raid? You cried yourself to sleep that night."

"Cried myself to sleep?" Tom snorted. "Not likely."

"You were just a child," Mary said heatedly. "There is no shame in a child's tears."

"But it isn't true," Tom said. "I had a rousing good time in Neverland. Don't you remember? The battles with pirates, the mermaids' lagoon—what fun it all was!"

Ruby intervened before the disagreement became rancorous. (It was clearly headed in that direction.) "The question," Ruby said, "is what we do now. Have you a ship that will take us to Neverland, Tom? Do you have a chart to show the way?"

Tom admitted he did not.

"Your sister has worked very diligently to find a chart and . . ."

"Excellent!" Tom interrupted. "With that, I can find the way. All I need is a ship. Don't worry, Mary, I'll bring your children back to you."

Ruby spoke before Mary could respond to his assumption that he would take her work, fetch the children and the treasure, and leave her out of the entire affair. "Mary and I have already begun discussing possible ships. James Hook, captain of the *Jolly Roger*, has reasons to pursue Peter Pan."

Tom was taken aback. He had heard tales of the ruthless Captain Hook and his villainous crew. "Captain Hook? He'd slit our throats and take the treasure."

"Do you remember James, who helped us after we escaped Neverland?" Mary's voice was steady and calm, evidence of great self-control.

"James? Of course! Capital fellow—I remember him well."

"James is Captain Hook," Mary said.

"James?" Tom was shaking his head. "Surely you have that wrong. I've heard such tales of Captain Hook, so horrible I won't even tell you. I can't believe . . ."

"James is Captain Hook." Ruby repeated Mary's words with a note of impatience. "When the *Jolly Roger* makes port, you will see for yourself."

Ruby had heard far too many pirates' boasts to give any credence to Tom's grandiose accounts of his adventures. During the conversation, Ruby had been contemplating the problem at hand and formulating a plan. She stood and rang the bronze ship's bell that hung by the door.

Turning back to Tom, she took a softer tone. "You must be tired after your travels," she said. She glanced at the young woman who had come in response to the bell. "This is my friend Tom. I've kept him here talking for far too long. I thought perhaps you could show him around, offer him proper hospitality." She glanced back at Tom, who was smiling at the woman.

With Tom out of the way, Ruby returned to her seat to resume her conversation with Mary. "Now, let's get back to business," she said. "Your brother is a sweet boy, but he needs a bit of management."

CHAPTER 30
An Afternoon Tea

A S THE *Golden Dawn* entered the harbor at Toamasina, the main port city on the island of Madagascar, Watson stood at the rail with Rumbold, Holmes, George, and Sam.

A Malagasy pilot stood with the first mate, guiding the ship to a gap in the coral reef that encircled the harbor. Looking down, Watson saw a school of brilliant blue fish dart away from the ship. The afternoon breeze carried the scent of tropical flowers and fruit gone bad.

"It's an excellent harbor," Rumbold said. "The city, however, is rather more squalid than your usual African port. There's little point discussing the politics of the place—the tribal government is a great tangle of royalty with names so long you can never remember them. I hardly even try. Just now, the French are in charge, or so they believe. They've been wrong before. Personally, I think the rats and the fleas own the city."

Lady Emily Hawkins sat in a deck chair, putting the final touches on a botanical sketch of an orchid in the genus *Agrostophyllum*. Her steam yacht was moored near a private dock that belonged to her good friend, Monsieur Durand.

When Mary, Tom, and Peter Pan shared tea with Lord and Lady Hawkins in the Indian Ocean, Lady Hawkins had been a newlywed on her first trip with Lord Hawkins. Now she was a middle-aged widow.

Lord Hawkins had died four years before, bitten by a venomous sea snake. Ever curious about how the native people lived, he had gone fishing with a young man off the eastern coast of Madagascar. A sea snake caught in the fishing net had bitten Lord Hawkins as he helped pull the net in. The fisherman brought Lord Hawkins back to the beach, where he died in Lady Hawkins' arms.

After her husband's death, Lady Hawkins carried on with their work alone. She saw no need to return to London. She found London weather dreary and London society oppressive after the freedom she had enjoyed on their travels.

Lady Hawkins sent plant specimens to Kew Gardens, along with her illustrations of the plants in their original habitat. She shipped orchids to collectors in England. She wrote some articles for the *Strand Magazine* and published a book titled *A Lady Among the Flowers* about her travels with Lord Hawkins.

When the *Golden Dawn* arrived in Toamasina, Lady Hawkins smiled at the sight of the ship entering the harbor. She had a trunk filled with plant specimens and sketches, packed and ready to go to London.

Setting aside her sketch pad and pencils, Lady Hawkins picked up her spyglass, always close to hand. Through the glass, she studied the passengers on the ship's deck. One group caught her interest. First, she noticed the Newfoundland dog—the animal's paws were up on the railing and the dog was staring at the port city just like the humans. What a beautiful beast!

The man who stood on one side of the dog had the look of a British gentleman—broad shoulders, neatly trimmed moustache. He had one hand on the rail, the other on the dog's head. He looked like a friendly sort of chap—at home in a pub, always comfortable to be around.

The man on the other side of the dog was dark-skinned with curly blond hair, a combination Lady Hawkins had seen occasionally among South Sea Islanders. He was dressed like a sailor—loose trousers, cotton shirt, and a kerchief around his neck. A gray parrot rode on his shoulder, looking quite at home. The islander was chatting amiably with the British gentleman and the man on his other side—a thin fellow who looked more like an accountant than an adventurer.

A few steps away from the group was someone Lady Hawkins recognized: Rumbold. She had met him in Toamasina the year before, when he was waiting for a ship to London. She remembered that he was well-spoken and intelligent—very knowledgeable about plants, particularly those with medical properties. There was something a bit slippery about him though. A useful man to know, but not someone to trust.

Rumbold was talking to a tall man with a thin face and a hawk nose. The tall man seemed strangely familiar.

The tall man looked like someone who took himself entirely too seriously. She knew the type. He was, she guessed, very good at whatever it was he did—most likely something a bit out of the common run of things. Maybe a poet, maybe a musician, maybe an expert in some scientific field that only half a dozen people cared about. He probably thought he was a genius, and he might very well be right about that.

As she studied the man through her spyglass, Lady Hawkins realized where she had seen him before—in an illustration in the *Strand Magazine*. It was the detective Sherlock Holmes, the subject of a series of lively accounts of criminal investigations. As she watched, Holmes called out to the friendly looking man with the dog—Dr. Watson, she guessed.

It was convenient that the ship had come in on Thursday. On Friday, Lady Hawkins hosted a late afternoon tea party in the mansion of Monsieur Durand. Durand was a businessman who loved to host parties, but had no talent for arranging them. Lady Hawkins, on the other hand, was quite good at arranging parties, but had no home in which she could entertain. Monsieur Durand had a lovely mansion and a talented chef who set out an excellent repast. The tea party was a perfect alignment of Lady Hawkins' talents and Monsieur Durand's resources.

"Saro!" Lady Hawkins called. "Please bring my visiting cards. I must invite those gentlemen on the ship to Monsieur Durand's tea."

Always curious, Lady Hawkins wanted to know what brought Sherlock Holmes to Madagascar. She also hoped to hear the latest news from London—and she yearned to pet that sweet-faced Newfoundland dog.

Saro rowed to the dock in the yacht's dinghy and met the men as they disembarked. Rumbold received Lady Hawkins' card with a smile. Written neatly on the back of the card was a note:

My dear Mr. Rumbold,
Welcome back to Madagascar. I will be hosting an afternoon tea at Monsieur Durand's house tomorrow. I would be delighted if you and your friends could come. Please bring that wonderful dog along. I should be very pleased to see you again.
Yours sincerely,
Lady Hawkins

"Well, now—this is very nice. Lady Hawkins has invited us all to tea tomorrow afternoon," Rumbold told Holmes.

Holmes shook his head impatiently. His eyes were bright; his expression was alert. He had abstained from Rumbold's drugs for the last few days and his languor was a thing of the past.

Before Holmes could say that they had no time to waste on a tea party, Rumbold went on. "Lady Hawkins is very well-connected. I expect a number of French officials will be there along with many of the local businessmen. It will be an excellent opportunity to gather information on conditions we may encounter as we travel down the coast."

Watson responded to Rumbold's news with enthusiasm. "Lady Hawkins! What an honor!"

"You know her?" Holmes asked.

"Only through her writing," Watson said. "Her tales have been published beside my own work in the *Strand Magazine*. Her book was the talk of London."

"How is it she knows we are here?" Holmes asked Rumbold sharply.

Rumbold glanced at Saro.

"She has been waiting for the mail," Saro said. "And watching with the spyglass."

"The earliest we can depart is Saturday, so no time will be lost," Rumbold told Holmes. "Besides, there's an excellent meal to be had. Monsieur Durand's chef is marvelous!"

Holmes nodded, and Rumbold replied with a note on a page torn from Watson's notebook.

My dear Lady Hawkins,
I would be delighted to accept your invitation. I will be accompanied by my friends, Mr. George Darling, Mr. Samuel Smalls, Mr. Sherlock Holmes, and Dr. John Watson, along with our canine companion, Nana.
With fond regards,
Mr. Richard Rumbold

The next day, at the appointed time, the party entered Monsieur Durand's mansion on the edge of town.

Lady Hawkins greeted them. "Hello, Mr. Rumbold. A pleasure to see you again." Rumbold made introductions and Lady Hawkins welcomed them warmly, paying particular attention to Nana, who was looking her best. With Rumbold's assistance, Watson had acquired a hairbrush made of some sort of stiff native grass. With that, he had brushed Nana's shaggy coat.

He was glad he had taken such time with the dog's appearance when Lady Hawkins knelt to address Nana eye to eye and scratch behind the big dog's ears.

The gathering was all that Rumbold had promised. French government officials mingled with French, American, and British industrialists and businessmen. The tea itself was a splendid spread with sandwiches and scones and little cakes, some involving fruit jams or meats that you would never have found in England.

Watson fixed himself a plate of delicacies, then sat in an out-of-the-way corner of the large room, with Nana at his side. Holmes was deep in conversation with a pair of French officials. Rumbold and Sam were chatting with a group of Malagasy businessmen. George stood at the tea table, loading a plate with a second helping.

"Hello, Dr. Watson." Lady Hawkins approached, carrying a plate of cooked chicken. "I wanted to make certain that Nana was not left out of the festivities."

Nana waited politely while Lady Hawkins set the plate on the floor. The great dog offered thanks with her expressive eyes.

That taken care of, Lady Hawkins took a seat in the chair beside Watson. "I am delighted that you were able to attend, Dr. Watson."

"Thank you, Lady Hawkins," Watson said. "You have been too kind."

"I'm sorry to hear from Mr. Rumbold that your stay in Toamasina will be brief. I have read your stories in the *Strand Magazine*. It would have been lovely to discuss your work at length."

"I have read your work as well," Watson said. "A wonderful blend of botany and adventure." He was flattered by the attention of this beautiful and intelligent woman.

She nodded. "Since your time is short, I suppose I must ask you a question now if I am to have the chance to ask it at all. Who knows if our paths will cross again? It may seem an odd question, since Watson is not an uncommon name." She leaned forward, studying him with her brilliant blue eyes, a grave look on her face. "Do you happen to know a girl named Mary Watson? She has a brother named Tom. She has blue eyes and brown curly hair."

Watson was instantly alert. "You've seen Mary. When? Where?"

"Please calm yourself, Dr. Watson. Let's not catch the attention of the other guests. I'd prefer to keep this discussion between us."

Watson struggled to check his sudden emotion at the thought that Mary might be close at hand. "Of course," he said, trying to match her calm tone.

"So you do know Mary Watson?"

"Mary Watson is my niece. Tom, my nephew. Where did you see them?"

Lady Hawkins kept her voice low. "I have a strange story to tell, but it's for your ears alone. First, let me make certain we are speaking of the same Mary Watson. Your niece and nephew . . . do they come from Cooktown, Australia?"

"They grew up there."

Lady Hawkins' face lit up. "Very good! I would hate to make a mistake."

"Where did you see Mary? Was Tom with her?" Watson struggled to keep his voice low. "Please. We have come in search of her."

Lady Hawkins ignored his questions. "Clearly we must talk more, but not here. After the party, come with me to my yacht so we can talk in private." She thought for a moment. "I'll need an excuse. I know—one of my crew has fallen ill and I wish you to doctor him. Everyone knows I treat my crew as family. It will pass muster."

"But why—?"

Lady Hawkins interrupted him. "Not now. I will share my story later."

Watson was confused by her need for secrecy. "I'll tell Holmes. We can—"

"No," Lady Hawkins said decisively. "You mustn't tell him anything about this. You will come alone. What I wish to discuss with you will not fit into Mr. Holmes' view of the world."

"But my dear lady . . . " Watson began, but he faltered when he noted the look in Lady Hawkins' eyes. Earlier, those eyes seemed as placid and blue as the afternoon sky over the harbor. Now they had the glint of cold steel.

After her marriage to Lord Hawkins, Lady Hawkins had learned to give orders. She was of an amiable disposition, but she had learned that sometimes it was necessary to call on traits other than amiability.

"Holmes will not be part of this discussion," she said. "If you feel it necessary to discuss matters with Holmes after we speak, that's your business. I rather think you will choose not to."

Watson nodded a silent assent.

"Very good." She smiled, once again a gracious hostess. "I must leave you for a time to attend to my other guests."

She left him then, making her way across the room to greet a few late arrivals to the party. Watson remained where he was. A servant, directed no doubt by Lady Hawkins, replenished Nana's plate of chicken and brought Watson another drink.

The party was winding down when Sam joined Watson in his corner, taking the seat that Lady Hawkins had vacated. "I'll be joining you and Lady Hawkins when you go to the yacht to see to her crew member," he told Watson. "The fellow who needs your attention is from the Solomon Islands, so I can interpret for you."

Watson frowned. Was there really someone who needed doctoring? He deferred that question for another time. "You speak the language of that place?"

"One of the many languages of that place," Sam said. "There are many islands and many languages." Then he said something that sounded like gibberish to Watson.

"What was that?"

"I said, 'I have not forgotten the languages of my childhood. But I have had little need for them in London.'"

Watson was startled by this side of Sam. He had come to think of the man as an Englishman who just happened to have dark skin and a store of arcane knowledge. Watson knew where the Solomon Islands were on the map, but had never given their language (or languages) any thought.

They watched as guests began to leave the party. Watson was worried that Holmes would see through any lie he might tell, but there was no need for him to lie. From his seat, he watched Holmes leave the party with a well-dressed Frenchman—an exporter, he later learned from Rumbold, who came to their corner with George to say goodbye.

Rumbold raised a quizzical eyebrow at the news that Watson would be going to Lady Hawkins' yacht. His expression implied (without Rumbold saying a word) that Watson was the recipient of great good luck that he probably didn't deserve.

CHAPTER 31
Watson Adjusts His Thinking

L ADY HAWKINS LED Watson and Sam (with Nana in tow), from the mansion to the nearby dock, where her steam yacht was moored.

The *Salacia* was a beautiful craft—oak framed and planked in teak and pitch pine, with bronze fastenings, a lead keel, and copper sheathing. She had the lines of a clipper ship in miniature.

The main cabin, which served as living room and studio, reflected Lady Hawkins' long residence aboard. Initially, the room had been furnished as a Victorian parlor, but Lady Hawkins had made changes over the years. Parlor chairs had been replaced by sturdy Moorish armchairs with latticework backs. The camelback settee had given way to a wonderfully comfortable loveseat constructed from water buffalo horns and leather. Fabric adorned with floral prints had been replaced with African mudcloth painted with elaborate geometric patterns. The large teak desk that had once belonged to Lord Hawkins remained, but it had become Lady Hawkins' drawing table.

Saro brought wine and glasses. While she poured, Lady Hawkins waved Watson and Sam to the Moorish armchairs, then rummaged in a drawer of the desk. "Ah, here it is," she said, taking a document case from the drawer. She sat in the chair beside Watson and placed the case on the low table beside her. Nana, who had been watching Lady Hawkins, lay down on the floor between the two of them.

"Now we can talk," Lady Hawkins said.

"Yes," Watson agreed. "Please tell me where you saw Mary."

She regarded him steadily. "I saw her many years ago, when my late husband Lord Hawkins and I were en route from Mauritius to Madagascar."

"Many years ago!" Watson interrupted, leaning forward impatiently. "But . . ."

"Wait, Dr. Watson," Lady Hawkins said. "You, of all people, must realize that it takes time for a story to unfold."

Reluctantly, Watson settled back into his chair. He took a deep breath and a sip of wine. Only then did Lady Hawkins resume her tale.

"In 1883, my husband and I were on this yacht, making our way from the island of Mauritius to Madagascar. We were having tea on the deck when Mary and Tom Watson swooped down from the sky and asked if they might join us. They were dressed in their nightclothes, looking windblown and tired."

"Swooped down from the sky?" Watson said.

"It will take longer to tell the story if you keep repeating me," Lady Hawkins said tartly. "Mary and Tom were traveling with a boy named Peter Pan, who had taught them to fly. The children were delighted to share my biscuits and tea. Mary told me Peter was taking them to Neverland, the island where he lived. I tried to persuade the children to stay aboard the yacht with me. Peter did not seem like a reliable guide. Sweet-looking boy, but I didn't trust him."

"Then they flew away," Lady Hawkins said. "Mary didn't want to go, but Peter and Tom flew off. Mary went after her brother, saying she would be back. They never returned. Fortunately, before they flew off, Lord Hawkins got his camera. He had acquired it in London to document our travels and our research."

Lady Hawkins opened the document case that she had taken from the drawer earlier, revealing a set of photographs that she placed in Watson's hands. "Quite a remarkable instrument, that camera."

Watson studied the photographs. There was the young Lady Hawkins, sitting on a deck chair with one hand raised, as if to command someone to stop. The girl beside her was certainly Mary as a child; there was no mistaking her.

In the next photograph, Mary was leaping out of her chair. The cause for Mary's action was also in the frame. Tom was several feet above the yacht's deck. Flying, Watson thought. The photo also showed another figure—a boy was in the sky, higher and farther away than Tom.

In the third shot, the boys were two small blurs in the distance and Mary was flying after them, also blurry but still recognizable.

Lady Hawkins had given Watson photographic proof of children in flight. It was a seismic shift in his understanding of reality.

People generally do not welcome seismic shifts in their understanding of reality. Fortunately, Watson had a great deal of practice in rapidly adjusting his thinking. At the conclusion of each adventure, Sherlock Holmes rearranged Watson's reality as he explained the mystery. Whenever Holmes pointed out everything that Watson had overlooked, misunderstood, or ignored as inconsequential, Watson had to rearrange his thinking. Lady Hawkins' photograph had a similar effect.

Watson nodded slowly. Mary and Tom had flown with Peter Pan. His own experience had not been a dream.

Lady Hawkins studied his face. "You don't seem surprised. I thought you would say it was impossible for anyone to fly."

"Not at all. You see, I have experienced this myself."

"You have seen children fly?"

"No, my dear lady," Watson said. "I have flown." As Lady Hawkins leaned toward him, her eyes on his face, Watson stopped thinking of Mary and the children. He had a glass of wine, the full attention of a beautiful woman, and a good story to tell. "It's the fairy dust, you see," he told Lady Hawkins, with an air of authority. "That's why the children could fly."

Watson told Lady Hawkins of rescuing the fairy from the cat and of taking flight. He neglected to include Nana's role in rescuing him. The big dog regarded him with reproach at this omission, but Watson did not notice. He was reveling in Lady Hawkins' attention.

Lady Hawkins was the perfect audience; her face was filled with admiration. When married to Lord Hawkins, she had honed the skill of listening to men's stories at dinner parties.

"What did Mr. Holmes have to say about this?" she asked.

Watson shook his head. "I decided it was best not to share this with him. It seemed wise to be careful who I tell."

Sam, who was listening quietly, sipped his wine and smiled.

Lady Hawkins nodded with approval. "Holmes sees only what he wants to see. I think you made the right choice. Some of us choose to see a greater world, accepting that there are powers that are outside our experience, that we cannot explain with our current science. Holmes has a much more limited view of the world.

"I admire your patience with the man. It seems to me that being his friend would be quite difficult. He has such a pronounced disdain for the abilities of others and such unshakeable confidence in his own abilities. He seems to think he excels at every skill related to capturing criminals. Yet your stories reveal quite clearly that he does not."

Watson was taken aback. "Indeed? And where do you think his skills are lacking?"

"He excels at deduction. There's no question of that. But when it comes to actually catching the criminal . . ." She shook her head. "He makes elaborate plans, keeps them entirely to himself, then springs them on you with no time to change them. When things go awry, he says, 'Who could ever have predicted that?' Who indeed! Anyone with a grain of common sense!"

Watson shook his head, ready to protest, but Lady Hawkins did not give him the chance. "Take, for example, your tale—*The Hound of the Baskervilles*. An excellent story, I thought. Right up until the end."

"What do you mean?" Watson was stung. He thought the ending had displayed Holmes at his finest. "Only Holmes could have figured out the identity of the killer."

For those who don't recall the story, here's a quick synopsis: A Baskerville family legend told of a giant hound from Hell that stalked the Baskerville family because of the villainous actions of a long-dead ancestor. Sir Charles Baskerville died under questionable circumstances, and some blamed this legendary hound for his demise. People told of hearing a hound baying on the moor. They reported seeing this terrible beast. Holmes dismissed these tales as the idle chatter of superstitious peasants.

After Sir Charles died, Henry Baskerville, the heir to the Baskerville fortune, moved to Baskerville Hall. People continued to hear the hound on the moor. Was Sir Henry in danger from supernatural forces?

Holmes unraveled the mystery. A butterfly collector named Stapleton, who lived in a house on the moor, was actually a Baskerville. If Sir Henry died, Stapleton would inherit the Baskerville fortune. Stapleton was keeping an enormous half-starved hound locked up on the moor. He had scared Sir Charles to death with the beast, and he intended to set the hound on Sir Henry.

"I remember Holmes' plan quite well," Lady Hawkins continued. "It was ridiculous. He told Sir Henry to go to dinner at Stapleton's and then walk home alone across the moor. Holmes planned to wait by the path with you and Lestrade. The three of you were to stop the hound from killing his client. He didn't tell Sir Henry of this plan. He sprang it on you and Lestrade when it was too late to make any changes. Then the hound got past you, Holmes, and Lestrade. It almost killed poor Sir Henry."

"It would have been fine if the fog hadn't come in," Watson protested. "Because of the fog, we had to pull back to higher ground."

"If I recall the story correctly, that's what Holmes said." Lady Hawkins was having none of it. "Fog is a common occurrence on Dartmoor—it should have come as no surprise. If Holmes had discussed the matter with you and Lestrade, you could have found many other ways to handle the problem. One of you could have hidden near the shed where the hound was kept and shot the beast at the moment that Stapleton set it on Sir Henry's trail. Or the three of you could have intercepted Sir Henry, surrounding him so that you could kill the hound before it caught up with him. At the very least, one of your group could have remained with Sir Henry while the rest of you left in pursuit of Stapleton.

"Instead, Holmes left him sitting alone on a rock, shivering in the darkness beside the carcass of the hellhound, while the lot of you gave chase. It's no wonder the poor man suffered a nervous collapse."

Watson blinked, overwhelmed by her list of possibilities. She had clearly given his account a careful reading. Now that he thought about it, leaving Sir Henry alone beside the dead hound did seem rather heartless. "It wasn't completely dark," he muttered, feeling defensive. "The moon was up."

Sam, who had been listening with some amusement, spoke up then. "We seem to have gotten off the topic of Mary and Tom, fairies, and flying."

Lady Hawkins took a deep breath. "Quite true," she said. "I have told you my part of that story. But I have always wondered what happened after the children left me. For weeks, I watched for them, expecting them to return. Did they reach Neverland? How did they get home again?"

"I can tell you a bit about that," Sam said. "I was in Neverland when they arrived."

Watson listened in amazement as Sam described the children's time on the island, their escape by boat, eventual rescue by pirates, and return to Australia. "Henry Watson took me in and made me a member of his family. Eventually, Henry and Mary returned to London. Tom and I went to sea."

"But the story isn't over yet." Lady Hawkins turned to Watson. "You said you were in search of Mary. How has she come to be missing?"

Watson told of the night when Wendy, John, and Michael disappeared and of Mary's departure from London, with Sam filling in parts Watson didn't know.

"I arranged for her passage to Nosy Boraha, intending to accompany her," Sam said. "But things went awry and I was delayed. Her ship left on the tide, with Mary safely aboard. She is going to Neverland to rescue the children. We hope to find her in Nosy Boraha."

Lady Hawkins turned to Watson. "What does Mr. Holmes think of all this?"

"He hasn't said what he's thinking," Watson said. "Holmes suggested we follow Mary. He has not discussed more specific plans with me."

"Of course not. He never does."

"Whatever plan he has, I'm sure it's brilliant!" Watson felt compelled to defend Holmes.

Lady Hawkins shook her head, as if to dismiss Holmes from her mind. "I have additional information that may be useful to you. Last month, as I was returning to Toamasina from a trip along the southern coast, four children landed on my ship. Or perhaps I should say, three children plus Peter Pan. That would be Wendy, John, and Michael."

Watson was speechless.

"I suspect Peter remembered my yacht as a source of biscuits," Lady Hawkins added.

"How were the children?" Watson asked.

"Hungry. I was at breakfast when they landed. I fed them, of course. Like Mary and Tom, they were windblown and weary, but well enough for all of that.

"Wendy told me they were going to Neverland. She said that Peter claimed they had been blown off course by an unfavorable wind, but she wasn't so sure she believed him. She thought maybe he had been distracted by some mermaids and had flown off course to follow them for a time. Wendy likes the boy, but she is smart enough not to trust him entirely."

Lady Hawkins studied Watson's stunned expression and considered how she might help him process the startling news she had delivered. She decided that something stronger than wine was called for and asked Saro, who was waiting attentively nearby, to bring fresh glasses and a bottle of whiskey.

Watson looked miserable, clearly worried about the children. Lady Hawkins, having grown up in the rough conditions of a mining camp, had a great deal of faith in the children's durability. Mary had survived her adventure, and Lady Hawkins had confidence that Mary's children would do the same.

"You recognized Peter Pan?" Watson said. "It's been many years since you last saw him."

Lady Hawkins was sympathetic. Poor man, she thought. Having accepted the photographic proof that the children flew, he would have to struggle with the next impossibility. "Peter Pan is still a boy," she said.

"He is not a boy," Sam said. "He never was."

"What is he then?" Watson asked.

"A sort of spirit, I think," Sam said.

Watson frowned. "Really? Some sort of native spirit? You can't believe that, Sam."

"Oh, I don't think he's a native spirit," Lady Hawkins said. "He's very British."

Sam nodded. "I agree. Definitely British."

Watson looked from Sam to Lady Hawkins. They couldn't be serious. "A spirit? Ridiculous!"

Lady Hawkins tried to help him out. "Do you go to church?" she asked.

"Of course—every now and then."

"Do you believe in God?"

"Certainly!"

"And you believe in angels and saints and devils?"

Watson hesitated, sensing a trap. "Well, yes." Watson had never thought deeply about religion, but he had learned Bible stories at his mother's knee. He accepted the existence of angels, saints, and devils without question.

"You could think of Peter Pan as rather like an angel."

Watson shook his head. "This Peter Pan does not seem angelic. More like a devil than an angel."

"Think of him as a devil then. In any case, a being with magical powers—just like angels and devils. The Bible is filled with beings with magical powers."

"Not magical," Watson grumbled. "Holy."

"Different words, same thing," Sam said. "Powers that we can't fully comprehend." He lifted his glass. "Here's to God, the angels, and Peter Pan. All equally incomprehensible."

"God does not kidnap small children," Watson said.

Sam shook his head. "Kidnapping is the least of it. Have you read the book of Job?"

The conversation and the drinking went on.

CHAPTER 32
The Legend of Captain Hook

WHEN LAST WE saw James, he was lying in a pool of his own blood on the deck of the *Jolly Roger*. It was lucky for him that Rumbold was on board.

Rumbold's improvised tourniquet stopped the bleeding. Rumbold tied off the cut blood vessels and cauterized those that could not be tied off. He used a needle and thread from the sailmaker's kit to stitch up the wound. He painted the wound with honey to prevent infection, a trick he had learned from a Chinese healer. He soothed the injured man with morphine and reassured the crew that the captain would recover.

Rumbold's efforts speeded James' healing and ensured the resulting stump was as tidy and comfortable as a stump could be. Even so, it was a painful voyage back to Nosy Boraha. When the *Jolly Roger* reached the island, Rumbold immediately took James to Ruby's place.

Ruby and James had been friends ever since he had delivered Mary, Tom, and Sam to her care. James recognized Ruby's wisdom, her resourcefulness, and her connections. And Ruby knew a secret that James concealed from his fellow pirates: He had a kind heart.

For a month, Ruby and the women in her employ nursed the pirate captain back to health. With James' permission, Rumbold served as de facto press agent, providing the *Jolly Roger*'s crew with information about the process of the captain's recovery.

The fact that James' convalescence took place in a brothel provided a useful cover story. Had it been known that James was being coddled and cared for and tucked in each night, his reputation would have suffered.

Instead, Rumbold reported to the crew that the captain was keeping half a dozen women very busy. "He doesn't need both hands for that," Rumbold said with a leer. He did not mention that the captain had struggled to train his left hand to handle a spoon (let alone a sword) with any degree of skill.

Early on, Rumbold visited the local blacksmith, a muscular woman named Gwendolyn. She had (while disguised as a man and calling herself Gwyn) learned her trade in a London shipbuilding yard.

Rumbold described what James needed: an iron hook that could substitute for his lost hand. Gwendolyn crafted a wickedly beautiful hook with a socket that could be tightened to fit the captain's stump and a system of straps to secure it in place.

When the hook was complete, Rumbold assisted James in strapping on his new appendage. At breakfast, James experimented, using the hook as a substitute for a fork to spear a piece of mango. At that moment, James smiled for the first time since the battle. The smile, like the hook, had a wicked edge.

"Now we'll work on the story," Rumbold said.

"What story?" James asked.

"The story of how you lost your hand."

James looked baffled. "What do you mean? Peter Pan lopped it off, you threw a stinkpot, and . . ."

"The stinkpot is out," Rumbold said. "Not heroic enough. I've been telling people you fought him left-handed until he fled."

James blinked. "Not heroic enough? Heroic enough for what?"

Rumbold grinned. "For the legend of Captain Hook."

"Captain Hook?" James frowned thoughtfully. "That has a nice ring. So you are leaving out the stinkpot and saying I continued to fight left-handed. If I kept fighting . . ."

"You mean: 'When you kept fighting . . .'"

"Quite so. When I kept fighting after my hand was lopped off, blood would have been everywhere."

"Absolutely. The deck was slippery with it."

And so James became Captain Hook. The hook was the beginning of the transformation. The story took care of the rest.

By the time Captain Hook ended his convalescence, his legend was no longer a story, but a known fact. Every crew member had helped fill in details, describing the captain's brilliant swordsmanship, the ferocity of the battle, the screams of the attackers, and the courage of the crew. The smoke of the stinkpot had long since blown away.

For the most part, the *Jolly Roger*'s crew had waited for the captain's return, whiling away the days with drinking and whoring, along with recounting and embellishing their own roles in the shipboard battle.

Only one crew member had been too impatient to wait. While James was convalescing, Skylights decided he would take over as captain of the *Jolly Roger*. With the guidance of Rumbold, Gentleman Starkey (who recognized the value of being part of a legend) and Jukes (who was fiercely loyal to James) removed that threat. Starkey dispatched Skylights late one night. Jukes loaded the body into the ship's longboat and took it to a cove not far outside of town. He left it there, and the mud crabs—giant crustaceans that lived among the mangroves—made short work of it.

Ruby provided Captain Hook with clothes that befitted his legendary status. Black breeches and shirt, flame red vest, and a belt with a scabbard on the right for a left-handed draw.

James had been clean-shaven. He had kept his hair tied back in a single braid, neat and out of the way. His hair and beard had grown long during his convalescence. When he was well, Ruby shaved off his beard but left an elegant moustache. Rather than trimming his hair short or simply tying it back, Ruby braided it in many small tight braids, reminiscent of the braids that the infamous Blackbeard wore in his beard.

When he left Ruby's, James looked fit, wicked, and every inch a captain. He could handle a sword quite admirably in his left hand and could use the hook for close-in fighting. When he entered the tavern with Rumbold at his side, he was greeted with cheers. A few days later, the *Jolly Roger* set sail with Captain Hook at the helm.

Three years after James became Captain Hook and about a week after Mary had returned to Nosy Boraha, the *Jolly Roger* sailed into the island's harbor.

Though the day was fine, Captain Hook's mood was not. The cuffs of his shirt were filthy, and he hated feeling dirty. His stump itched. Worse yet, his right hand itched. Though the physical hand was gone, its ghost lingered, a phantom hand that sent messages of pain and discomfort to his brain.

He was on his way to Ruby's. The women at Ruby's would see to his laundry, draw a bath so he could be clean again, and provide a comfortable bed. Ruby would have a salve to stop the itch. At Ruby's, James could relax. If a letter had come from Rumbold, Ruby would have it. Rumbold had returned to England to tend to his elderly mother, but his last letter had suggested he would be returning soon.

He was following the path up the hill when a large man with a peg leg hailed him from the open door of a tavern known as the Dirk and Cutlass. "A word with you, Captain."

"I'm on my way to Ruby's, Slash." Captain Hook's tone was impatient, enough to make most men turn away.

But Slash persisted. He had once been Captain Slash, a fierce fighter noted for his ability with a cutlass. He had lost his leg when a stab wound from a barroom brawl became gangrenous, which necessitated a speedy amputation.

Slash was still a good man in a fight—as quick on his peg leg as some were on two feet—but he had mellowed after becoming proprietor of the Dirk and Cutlass. These days, he dressed in the cloth wrap that the native men wore in place of trousers. Even so, he retained the air of authority that suited a former pirate captain.

"Aye, Captain. But you might want to stop for a moment. There's a lady here that's been asking about you."

Captain Hook scowled. "I have no interest in tavern wenches."

Slash shook his head. "This is a proper lady. She says she has urgent business."

"A proper lady?" Hook repeated in a scornful tone. "There are no proper ladies on this island."

Slash reconsidered the word. "Maybe proper ain't the word. But she's no tavern wench. She came from London. She's drinking tea." That was, in Slash's mind, a significant distinction of ladies. "Says she has important business to discuss with you."

Intrigued despite himself, Hook followed Slash into the tavern. The doorway led onto a wooden deck with a view of the harbor. Woven grass mats covered the plank floor. The Dirk and Cutlass was the fanciest of the harbor taverns.

There were few patrons. A young pirate leaned against the bar, looking rather ragged—up all night most likely and wondering if going to bed was worth the trouble. An older pirate was easing into the day with Slash's grog, a mixture of light rum, lemon juice, cinnamon, and honey.

Hook saw the woman immediately. She sat in a bamboo chair by a small wooden table. On the table was a lovely china teapot and matching cup— no doubt looted from the captain's quarters of a well-to-do merchant vessel. For a moment, Hook was frozen by this apparition from another life. Then he became aware that the lady had another admirer. A mustachioed man was striding toward her table, a broad smile on his face. Hook recognized him: a Frenchman called Jacques Le Têtu, first mate aboard the *Golden Dagger.*

"Mademoiselle," Le Têtu exclaimed. "I am here to bring a smile to your beautiful face."

The lady's face was shadowed by her hat and Hook could not see her expression. "Thank you for your concern, sir," she said, her cool, clear voice loud enough to be heard across the room. "I don't need your assistance. I am waiting for—"

"You are waiting for me," Le Têtu said.

He reached out to take her hand, which was resting on the table. She withdrew it before he could touch her.

"I don't wish for your company, sir."

"Oh, my darling, don't be afraid." Le Têtu stepped closer, reaching out to touch her face.

Then many things happened quickly. The woman stood suddenly, stepping forward with a dirk in her left hand and a sword in her right. The tip of the sword was inches from the lace at Le Têtu's throat; the dirk was ready to thrust into his belly.

As Le Têtu was stepping backward—his eyes wide, his hands lifted in defense—Captain Hook recognized the woman. "Marty!" he said. "You have not forgotten my lessons."

He had taught her that move. He remembered saying, "Hold the dirk ready to thrust upward into the belly." She was doing just that.

"Yes, James," she said. "I remember your lessons well."

She did not take her eyes from Le Têtu. James had also taught her that. "Always keep watch on your foe," he had said. "Even a craven dog can turn on you."

Le Têtu, having backed away, was now out of range of the dirk. He glanced in Hook's direction and went pale. "Captain Hook," he stammered. "My apologies, sir. I did not know . . . I did not realize . . ."

Hook smiled, an expression designed to terrify any opponent. His left hand was on his sword, but Le Têtu's eyes were fixed on the iron hook at the end of his right arm. Every pirate on the island had heard tales of Captain Hook's skills with that weapon. He could use it to tear your sword from your grasp, to stab you, to rip your flesh.

"You have acted in error, Le Têtu," Hook said. His tone was mild, but held a hint of displeasure, as if he had noticed a fly in his glass of wine.

"My apologies, Captain." Now several steps away from Mary, Le Têtu had dropped his hands, attempting to regain his dignity.

"It is the lady to whom you should apologize," Hook said.

"My apologies, mademoiselle." Le Têtu glanced in her direction, trying to keep watch on both opponents at the same time. "*Je suis profondément désolé.*"

Le Têtu looked back at Hook, who had not drawn his sword. "It was a mistake," Hook acknowledged. "I am confident it will not be repeated."

"You may be certain of that." Le Têtu risked a small bow, at the same time letting his hand come to rest on his sword. "I am glad that you understand that this was a simple mistake. I would like to remain on very good terms."

"Indeed. *Au revoir,* Le Têtu."

As Le Têtu took his leave, Hook smiled at Mary—but this time, the smile was genuine, rather than threatening. "I recognized you by the way you held your sword and dirk."

She sheathed her weapons, returning his smile. "Will you join me for tea?"

They had a great deal to catch up on, but first there were niceties to attend to.

Mary waved to Slash for another cup and another plate of pastries. Hook apologized for his attire, mentioning the difficulty of staying clean aboard ship. Mary laughed, reminding him that she was familiar with the conditions aboard the *Jolly Roger.* She poured tea and offered him pastries, acting the perfect hostess.

Hook studied her. Her face was tanned. Her curly hair was very short—a becoming style, but unusual. "Why are you here?" he asked. "I had thought I would never see you again. I know nothing of what happened to you after you left for Australia."

She told him of their journey home, her return to England, her marriage, her children, and the terrible moment in the nursery. "I found the nursery window open and my children gone. The snow on the ground revealed that they had not left by the door, but there were marks in the snow on the windowsill."

"Peter Pan," Hook said. His tone was even, but his expression was grim. She nodded, the pain clear on her face. "I have come to find my children and take them home. I have a chart that shows the approximate location of Neverland. But I need a ship and a crew. I thought . . . I hoped that you might help. Just as you helped me so long ago."

He nodded thoughtfully. "This is not the place to discuss such things. I was on my way to Ruby's."

"That's where I am staying," she said.

"Then let us go." He offered her his arm.

Ruby took charge immediately, showing Hook to her best room. Moments after he arrived, a bath was prepared and a silk robe was ready for him to wear until his clothes were washed.

Later, in Ruby's courtyard, Mary, Hook, and Ruby sat in the shade of the trees and drank tea. Hook's long dark hair was clean and freshly braided. Ruby had provided a salve to ease the itch in his stump. He was relaxed and at ease.

"You've heard my story," Mary said. "What of yours? I have heard . . ."

"Don't believe everything you've heard. In my line of work, it is quite useful to have people believe you are cruel and bloodthirsty. My friend Rumbold and I came up with the best bits, then others added to the tale." He held up his hook. "You would be amazed at the things people say I can do with this."

"I've heard that Peter Pan fought with you, cut off your hand, and tossed it overboard to a crocodile. I also heard that the crocodile once swallowed a watch, so it is always ticking."

"The first part is true," James said. "My hand went overboard. Rumbold added the crocodile and the watch. I think he wanted to see just how much people would believe."

Mary considered this. "Quite a lot, I would say. I wondered though. Would a watch actually survive the gastric juices of a crocodile?"

James smiled. "Rumbold and I discussed that at some length. Rumbold contends that the watch's gold casing would survive for a time, protecting the inner workings. So the crocodile keeps ticking."

"The sound warns you of the beast's approach," Mary mused. "But the watch is running down. When it runs down, the stealthy beast can approach you unawares."

"That adds to the suspense." James sipped his tea. "Now, let's continue our discussion of Neverland. Perhaps we can find a way to add to my legend and provide you with a legend of your own. You are well on your way, after your encounter with Le Têtu."

"I was hoping Tom would be here," Mary said. She had told James that Tom was also on the island, though she had not provided any details. She turned to Ruby. "Do you know where he is?"

"I believe he is visiting Lila's," Ruby said, naming a tavern down by the dock.

"You said you had a chart that showed the island's location," James said.

Mary got the chart from her seabag and handed it to James. The exact location of Neverland was not marked on the chart. Rather there was a circle where the probability of finding Neverland was high.

"Where did you get this?" he asked her.

She explained the information that Annie Maunder had used in her calculations: Sam's memories of stars from that location, information Mary recalled from her flight to the island, and Mary's memory of Lady Hawkins' description of her yacht's location.

James listened, nodding. He accepted the anecdotal nature of the information. Though nautical charts had improved since he first became a pirate, there were still many areas that were unmapped, where the best information came from the vague memories of an old sailor who had visited the area before.

"This is where the *Jolly Roger* was when Peter attacked us." James tapped a location on the edge of the search area. Rumbold had noted the location in the ship's logbook. "That's a few days' sail from here, if the winds are favorable. Unfortunately, it's far from the usual shipping routes. Not likely we'll find a prize near there. But the crew will need to be paid somehow."

"That can be arranged," Ruby said smoothly, her voice taking on a businesslike tone. "There is treasure on the island. A share of that would compensate you and your crew."

"Treasure? What sort of treasure?"

"Show James what you have," Ruby told Mary.

Mary handed James the ring. He held it to the light, admiring the ruby's color and clarity. "Nice," he said. "Very nice indeed."

"We will need to agree upon appropriate shares," Ruby said. "And the crew must understand that the agreement is with me, as well as with Mary."

"A wise precaution," James said. "Can you tell me how many more gems like this are in this treasure?"

"It is all in a small chest," Mary said. "I remember there were several pieces of jewelry, some loose stones, and many gold pieces. We each took some coins, and we buried the chest on the island. I know exactly where."

"You buried it?" James repeated, shaking his head in amazement. Buried treasure was the sort of thing that landlubbers wrote about. He had never met anyone who had actually done it.

That was the moment when Tom returned. He had been drinking at Lila's all afternoon. He heard James say, "You buried it?" and mistook his amazement for admiration. "That was my idea," he announced in a drunken bellow. "All my doing! I buried it because I knew we'd be back for it later."

Tom grabbed a chair and sat down at the table. "Don't be giving away all our secrets, sister," he said to Mary, shaking his head. He surveyed the table. "You're drinking tea?" He snorted. "Rum is what we need here." He pulled a flask from his pocket and splashed rum into the teacup that Ruby had offered him.

The peace of the garden was shattered. Tom was boisterous and overbearing, cheerful and entirely annoying. He spilled rum on the chart and laughed. Then he grinned at James, thinking the man to be a friend of Ruby's. "Mop that up, will you, old man?"

In his silk robe, fresh from the bath, Hook did not look like a pirate captain to be feared. An observant man might have noticed that the right sleeve of Hook's robe seemed rather empty toward the cuff. But Tom was not an observant man.

Mary tried to tell him. "We were just talking about going to Neverland," she said. "Captain Hook—"

"Oh, hush, sister. Forget about Captain Hook." Tom waved a hand dismissively. "I wouldn't trust that bloke to get us there. Any man who'd let Peter Pan lop off his hand can't be much of a fighter. Don't you worry. I'll find us a ship."

Tom leaned back in his chair, the bamboo creaking under his weight. Clearly, he felt at ease, comfortable, and very much in charge.

"Tom, I don't think you realize . . ." Mary began, glancing at James.

"Don't fuss at me, sister. I'll take care of everything. There's nothing to worry about."

Mary fell silent. James—or perhaps I should say Captain Hook—was staring at Tom with narrowed eyes.

Captain Hook did not care for drunks. He did not tolerate fools. It was clear that Tom was both.

"You don't recognize me, Tom," Hook said evenly. "You knew me as James. These days, I'm known as Captain Hook." He lifted his arm and the cuff of his robe fell back, revealing the hook.

Tom's grin froze. He turned pale.

"I don't think that we need rum," Captain Hook went on. "I prefer to keep a clear head, and I would wager you've already had enough."

Ruby leaned forward. "You know, Tom, the girls in the salon were asking after you," she said.

"They were?" Tom's voice was barely a whisper.

"Oh, yes," Ruby said. "Perhaps you'd like to join them for a drink. I know they'd enjoy your company."

"What a fine idea!" Tom said, a bit louder. "I'd hate to disappoint them."

A few days later, the *Jolly Roger* set sail just as the sun was peeking over the horizon. Mary was aboard, but Tom was still abed.

Following their encounter in the garden, Captain Hook advised Mary that Tom would not be welcome on the *Jolly Roger*. With a combination of reluctance and relief, Mary had agreed that it would be better if her brother did not come along.

They had told Tom that the *Jolly Roger* would sail at dawn. Tom swore that he would be on board when the ship sailed. But Ruby, with her usual quiet efficiency, had arranged for Tom to meet a buxom and enthusiastic bed partner late in the evening before their scheduled departure.

Predictably, Tom was not on the *Jolly Roger* at dawn. When he stumbled down to the dock at noon, the *Jolly Roger* was long gone.

CHAPTER 33
You Prefer to Ignore Logic?

THE MORNING AFTER Lady Hawkins' tea party, Watson was feeling the aftereffects of overindulgence in wine, whiskey, and philosophical conversation. At breakfast, Rumbold offered him a hangover cure of exotic herbs. Watson opted for ginger tea and a light breakfast. His head ached. His time with Lady Hawkins had left him feeling quite muddled.

At breakfast, he sat quietly, listening to the others chat. Rumbold asked Holmes whether he had learned anything useful from the French industrialists. The detective waved a hand in impatient dismissal and said, "I learned that the best French brandy can only be found in France."

Rumbold nodded, then turned his attention to Watson. "So, Watson, did you learn anything useful from Lady Hawkins?"

Watson sipped his ginger tea, considering what to say. His unhappy stomach and throbbing head made the decision easy. "I learned that you can find excellent Scotch whiskey outside of Scotland."

Sam said nothing, and Watson was grateful for that.

Late that morning, Rumbold led them to the ship that would take them to Nosy Boraha, a gaff-rigged schooner carrying freight to the pirate island. The captain, a friend of Rumbold's, was a taciturn Malagasy man.

They set forth in the early afternoon. When the ship was underway, Watson found a spot by the rail, out of the way of the crew. It felt good to be by the rail in case his stomach decided that even his light breakfast had been too much. Nana sat beside him, a watchful and comforting presence.

Rumbold came to join him. "Let me know if I can bring you anything," he said. Then he leaned on the rail beside Watson in companionable silence. The fresh air soothed Watson's headache. His stomach settled and soon he felt a bit better.

Holmes, on the other hand, was growing more restless and irritable. He paced the deck. Watson watched as the detective passed them once, then twice.

The third time Holmes passed them, Rumbold spoke up. "We won't reach Nosy Boraha until late tomorrow. If there's anything I can do to make the passage easier, please let me know. To soothe the overheated brain, I would recommend . . ."

At that, the great detective exploded, like a bottle of shaken champagne suddenly uncorked. "My brain does not need soothing," he snarled. "What I need are facts—not foolish chatter and fairy tales. Data that I can work with. I need information." He was glaring at Watson as he spoke. "Watson, you might as well tell me whatever secrets you're keeping."

Watson did not ask how Holmes knew he had secrets. The good doctor was in no mood to hear all the tiny indications that had led the detective to know that Watson had something to hide. No doubt he had revealed himself in the way he sipped his tea, glanced at his watch, lit his pipe, or performed (or failed to perform) some other trivial action.

Watson took a deep breath, gathering his thoughts.

That pause gave Rumbold a chance to excuse himself, saying he needed to check on something. He made a quick escape from what he realized could be a difficult conversation.

When Rumbold was gone, Watson spoke. "I am withholding information that you will dismiss as foolish chatter and fairy tales."

"Allow me to decide what I will dismiss," Holmes snapped. "You are withholding information at a crucial time in my investigation."

Watson returned the detective's glare. "I can list many times that you have kept me in the dark, for no reason other than your desire to explain the entire mystery in one grand revelation. Many times, when you decided not to tell me what you had planned, preferring to control it all yourself."

"Always for the good of the investigation," Holmes said.

Watson could recount specific instances in which Holmes' preference to keep his own counsel had not served the investigation well. But he knew that the list would not change the detective's mind.

He took a deep breath before speaking again. "Does it surprise you that I might prefer to keep some information to myself until I can confirm it to your satisfaction? Do you understand why I prefer not to have my ideas dismissed and ridiculed out of hand?"

"Ridiculed?" Holmes looked shocked. "When have I ever ridiculed you, Watson? I value your help and your companionship."

Watson shook his head slowly, thinking of all the times when Holmes had asked his opinion, only to laugh at it. Holmes really didn't know, Watson thought. He did not even realize the impact his words had.

Watson met the great detective's gaze and resigned himself to the inevitable. "I will tell you what Lady Hawkins told me. She said that she met Mary back in 1883. Lord and Lady Hawkins were sailing their steam yacht from the island of Mauritius to Madagascar. Mary and Tom landed on her yacht, hungry and thirsty. She fed them tea and biscuits."

"They met when Mary was a child?" Holmes was frowning. "And you say the yacht was traveling between two islands? What sort of ship were Mary and Tom on?"

"No ship," Watson said. "Lady Hawkins said that Mary and Tom were flying. They swooped down from the sky. They were in the company of a boy named Peter Pan. Lady Hawkins has photos that her husband took. They show the children sitting with Lady Hawkins. They also show the children in flight. A bit blurry, but clearly in flight."

Holmes waved a hand, dismissing the photographs. "Obviously the photographs are fraudulent."

"The photographs were clear," Watson insisted. "Mary and Tom were flying, well above the ocean waves."

Holmes shook his head, chuckling. "It is very easy to use photography to deceive. American spiritualists have quite perfected the art of photographic fakery. Consider William Mumler, a specialist in defrauding grieving widows and bereaved mothers. His most famous photo is of Mary Todd Lincoln, with the ghost of her dead husband standing behind her. You can see Abraham Lincoln's ghostly hand on her shoulder. It's a double exposure, of course. Mumler was tried for fraud in 1869.

"Creating a photograph of Mary and Tom flying would be easy enough. You simply need a picture of the ocean and pictures of the children. You don't even need to be an expert photographer. One can produce convincing results by carefully cutting people from one photograph, pasting the cutout on another photograph, then taking a photograph of the composite.

Lady Hawkins is a talented artist, is she not? I have seen her botanical art. She has a great eye for detail."

Watson was offended on Lady Hawkins' behalf. "Why would she do such a thing? And where would she get a photo of the children?"

Holmes was looking more cheerful than he had in days. "Lady Hawkins told you that the children were Mary and Tom, but did you actually recognize them? After all, you did not meet your niece until she was older, and you have never met Tom. Lady Hawkins said the children in the picture were Mary and Tom, and you believed her."

Watson was appalled. "Why would Lady Hawkins deceive me? It makes no sense! This is too much, Holmes."

"Calm yourself, Watson. You like Lady Hawkins, so you believe she is honest. But emotions are incompatible with clear reasoning. The dishonest among us can be quite likable. I knew a man who—"

"I can't listen to this," Watson said. He knew that Holmes was about to tell him a story of a charming swindler who was dishonest but quite likable. Watson turned and walked away. He was glad that Holmes did not follow.

At the bow of the ship, Watson stood by the railing, watching the waves. The breeze from the ship's movement cooled him. The soft sound of water rushing past the ship's hull, the snap of the canvas when the wind shifted—the sounds were soothing. He could feel his heartbeat slowing.

He remembered sitting with Lady Hawkins last night—yes, it was just last night, though it seemed much longer ago than that. Was she a charlatan, intent on deceiving him for some mysterious reason? No, he could not believe that. And Mary—had she been fooling them all with her act as a grieving mother?

He heard soft footsteps on the deck as Sam approached quietly. "Do you care for company?" Sam asked hesitantly. "If you'd prefer to be alone . . ."

"I'd welcome your company." Watson continued watching the ship's bow wave. "I told Holmes that Lady Hawkins had met Mary when she was a child. I told him about the photographs. He said the photographs were fraudulent and that Lady Hawkins had created them." Watson glanced at Sam. "I didn't tell him that I had seen a fairy and I didn't say I had taken flight."

Sam leaned on the railing beside Watson. "Holmes understands the world of crime," Sam said softly. "He fits everything he sees into that world. He believes that everything can be explained with logic."

"What if I showed him a fairy?"

"It wouldn't matter if you did. He would capture it in a jar and look for a naturalist who could identify this strange insect." Sam shook his head. "Some people say that seeing is believing. That's not quite right. People don't believe what they see—they see what they want to believe. Fairies and Peter Pan have no place in his logical world."

"What if he flew, like I did?"

"Holmes will never believe that he can fly," Sam said flatly. "Therefore, he never can."

"But I could show him. I could fly . . ."

"You couldn't fly with Holmes watching," Sam said. "You have the capacity for belief, but his scrutiny would make you doubt. Once you doubt, you can't fly—not with all the fairy dust in the world.

"Holmes's logic is very useful," Sam continued. "It lets him deduce that a man with an air of importance and an anchor tattooed on his hand is a retired sergeant of Marines. That's a reasonable deduction. But embracing reasonable deductions can blind you to other possibilities. Perhaps the man is an anchor maker. Perhaps he's a swindler who preys on sailors and uses the tattoo to make himself seem like one of them. Maybe it's a birthmark in the shape of an anchor." Sam shrugged. "There are many unreasonable possibilities. The world is much stranger than Holmes imagines."

Later that day, when Watson was smoking his pipe on the deck, Holmes joined him. Watson acknowledged the detective with a nod, but did not initiate conversation.

Holmes did not apologize, but he did acknowledge Watson's feelings. "I realize that you are feeling wounded," he began. "But you know that was not my intent. My goal is to gather all the facts I need. Sometimes, that may involve listening to a fairy tale, and correctly reinterpreting it through the lens of logic. Lady Hawkins' photo is one such fairy tale. You have provided me with a missing piece of a complex puzzle."

Watson did not respond. He gazed at the waves, remembering his moment of flight. The wind had lifted him as if he were light as a feather. Only Nana's determination had kept him tethered to the ship. He had felt like a boy again, running down a hillside, arms spread as if they could catch the wind and carry him aloft. Yes, he did believe that he flew. He did not want Holmes to reinterpret that memory through the lens of logic.

"I see it differently," Watson said quietly.

"You prefer to ignore logic?"

Watson nodded slowly. "If logic dictates that Lady Hawkins is a fraud and that Mary is an accomplice in the abduction of her own children, I will ignore it."

Holmes frowned. "That makes no sense."

"Do you remember when I showed you my tale, *A Study in Scarlet?*" Watson asked. "You objected to what you called 'romanticism' and suggested that I should ignore the love story that was at the heart of the murderer's motive. I said that I could not tamper with the facts. And you replied . . . I remember your very words: 'Some facts should be suppressed, or at least a just sense of proportion should be observed in treating them.'"

"Yes, I recall that." There was a touch of impatience in Holmes' tone. "The only points in that case that deserved mention were those relevant to the analytical reasoning by which I succeeded in unraveling it."

Watson leaned on the rail, remembering the tales he had written about Holmes and his cases. "I understand that's what you believe," Watson said. "But you aren't writing the story. I am." He turned and faced his friend. "I suggest that we hold alternate theories of this case."

"You wish to believe in fairy tales. You wish to think that Lady Hawkins and her photo are genuine." Holmes shook his head. "I will take a more sensible approach."

"State it as you like," Watson murmured, gazing out to sea.

The next morning, they reached Nosy Boraha. Watson was very glad to get off the ship.

CHAPTER 34
I've Come to Take You Home

THE *Jolly Roger*'s crew was somewhat baffled by Mary. They knew that she was leading them to a treasure, and they had agreed to the division of the spoils. It was clear that Mary was somehow in business with Ruby, though she certainly did not work in the brothel.

Captain Hook had told them that Mary was to be treated with respect, and they did their best to comply. Gentleman Starkey called her Madam. When the cabin boy grumbled that a woman on a ship was bad luck, Bill Jukes corrected him sternly, explaining that Mary was not a woman—she was a lady, and that was very different. Cookie prepared special meals that he thought were "fit for a lady." The biscuits were free of weevils.

When James and Mary dined together that first night, she mentioned how startled she was by the crew's manners.

James laughed. "They have heard of your skill with a blade. When they look at you, they see a dangerous woman."

The story of how she had bested Le Têtu had grown in the telling. In the latest version, crockery had been smashed and tables overturned. Members of Le Têtu's crew had come to his aid, and Mary had taken them on as well. The epic battle ended with Mary's blade at Le Têtu's throat and two pirates dead.

Mary smiled, listening to James recount the story. It was quite a glorious tale, though perhaps a bit contradictory. Mary was not sure how she could be both a proper lady and also the very devil with a blade, but she was delighted that others could accept the contradiction.

"I've always wanted to be notorious," she said.

"You are well on your way." James refilled her glass of wine.

"I've been wondering about something," she said. "Do you know why Peter Pan attacked you?"

James leaned back in his chair. He and Rumbold had discussed that very matter at length. "For a time, I thought it was because I had been a Lost Boy and had left him. But I've decided he doesn't remember that at all.

"Here is my thinking on the matter," James went on. "Peter is not complex in his needs. He has the simple and immediate desires of a boy. He wants admiration—so he captures boys and brings them to Neverland where they will have no choice but to follow him. He wants love—so he dreams of his lost mother and captures girls who will serve as a surrogate for her."

Mary nodded. "When I was in Neverland, he would cry out in his sleep sometimes. I had to comfort him. And he would call me Mother, no matter how often I told him not to."

James nodded. "He also craves adventures—so he looks for trouble. And if there is no trouble, he creates it. He attacked me simply because I was a pirate captain."

"Didn't he recognize you?" Mary asked.

"I told him I was Tootles, the name he called me on the island. But Peter doesn't remember the past. Once an adventure is over, he forgets it."

Mary sipped her wine, thinking about her time in Neverland. "I wonder if he'll recognize me now."

"It seems unlikely," James allowed.

Their conversation turned to Neverland—to the accuracy of Mary's chart and the elusiveness of the island.

"Some say that you can find Neverland only if the island wants to be found," James said. He shrugged. "People say all manner of things."

"Sam told me things to watch for. Look for clouds, he said. They form over islands in the afternoon. Watch for land birds."

"Yes," James said. "Every sailor knows to look for those signs of land."

In the end, finding the island was easy. Perhaps it wanted to be found.

On the third day, Mary saw a distant puff of white—a single cloud in the relentless blue of the sky. Then a never bird, a species native to Neverland, landed in the rigging. Mermaids rose in the ocean waters, riding the ship's bow wave like dolphins. By that time, the lookout in the crow's nest had spotted the island.

The *Jolly Roger* anchored in the small cove from which Mary had left the island so many years before. The ship's longboat conveyed a landing party to the shore.

At last, Mary stood on the beach from which she and Sam and Tom had sailed away. Across the cove were the mangroves where Sam had found the boat and the dead pirate. Mary remembered climbing through a mangrove jungle, immense and dangerous. She saw a clump of trees, tiny compared to the enormous jungle she recalled.

Before she could go in search of the children, Mary had to find the spot where they had buried the treasure. She remembered the saying she had invented to remember the place: "Between the old wolf's teeth, the treasure lies." She walked up and down the beach, closely watched by the pirate crew, searching for a tall rock with a pointed top. She found it at last, half buried in the sand. She recognized the point at the top, still sharp as a tooth.

The second boulder—the smaller, more rounded "tooth"—had been buried in sand. But with a little digging, she found it.

"We buried the treasure between these rocks," Mary told James. "While your men dig it up, I'll go and find the children."

"Are you still determined to go alone?" James asked.

She nodded. She and James had discussed strategy on the ship. She insisted on going to the Lost Boys camp by herself. Peter would attack a party of pirates without hesitation. But she didn't think he would attack her if she were alone.

Once again she was wearing the men's clothing that she had worn on the *Honest Trader*. Her elegant dress would be a hindrance in the jungle, where every bramble and bush would catch at a long skirt. On this path, dainty silk slippers simply would not do. She wore George's old boots. She set off through the jungle with her sword at her side and a packet of mixed sweets in her trouser pocket.

Before leaving London, Mary had thought long and hard about her time in Neverland. She remembered longing for the comforts of home. Not so much for her comfortable bed or her mother's embrace. What she had dreamed of was food: eggs and bacon, shepherd's pie, roast mutton, and bread with cheese. More than anything, she had dreamed of candy: humbugs, barley sugar, and pear drops.

She hoped her children would be glad to see her. She thought they would be ready to come home. But the part of her that had once been a child knew that they would be even more delighted by the candy that she brought.

She remembered the hike from the mangroves to the Lost Boys camp as long and difficult. It was neither. It was a short walk along an overgrown trail.

A small band of fairies flew past. They were chattering among themselves—a cacophony of jingling bells. She knew they were talking about her. They flew off—maybe to tell Peter, but she didn't really think so. The fairies tolerated Peter, but did not serve him.

The Lost Boys camp was smaller and grubbier than Mary remembered. There wasn't much there: a fire pit, some stumps that served as chairs, the entrance to the cave where they slept. No one answered when she called out. For a moment, she stood in the middle of the clearing, trying without success to match her memories to what she saw. It was not just that the particulars were different. The emotions were all wrong.

She remembered Neverland as a place of great emotions. When night fell, she was terrified. When the sun rose and she woke to see another day, she was joyous. Anything could happen. Wolves could attack as you were walking to the lagoon. Peter might swoop down and say it was time to fight with pirates. Her emotions had been overwhelming, even terrifying.

Mary missed those feelings—not the great terrors, but the moments of joy and triumph, the sense that anything was possible. Each challenge she survived had made her stronger.

Standing in the Lost Boys camp, she remembered George as he had been back then—thoughtful, cautious, and always out of step with the other boys. She wondered whether he was still in Nana's kennel. What would he think of what she was doing?

He would ask her to be careful—and that wasn't bad advice. He would try to help—he wouldn't be good at it, but he would try. And when he wasn't worrying or trying to help, he would look at her as if she was the most amazing woman on Earth.

She followed the path through the jungle to the top of the bluff. From there, she looked down on the lagoon, an expanse of brilliant turquoise water, bounded on one side by a white sand beach, on the other by a coral reef. Out beyond the reef, the water was a deeper darker blue.

In the center of the lagoon was Marooners' Rock. The tide was low and the rock was well above the water. Half a dozen mermaids were basking on its sun-warmed surface, languidly combing out their hair.

Mary could see the sun glittering on the mermaids' scales. One mermaid turned her head to look in Mary's direction. Then the others did the same. Mary felt a flash of terror, a shadow of what she had experienced as a child, but enough to make her tremble. Then she touched her hand to her sword and glared at the mermaids. She was no child to be intimidated.

On the beach below, she could make out a pack of children running on the sand in a game of some sort. Another child sat in the shade of a palm tree, well away from the others.

Mary made her way along the top of the bluff to a zigzagging path that led down to the beach. When she was a child, she had run down this path, heedless of any danger. Now she walked down it very carefully. She was aware that rocks could slide, that she could fall, that she could die here on the island.

The edge of the path crumbled a little each time she took a step. Bits of rock and soil skittered down the steep slope. There were places where the path climbed, to make its way over a spot where the hill had given way in a miniature landslide of rocks and debris. It was a process, she thought: the slope tried to erase the path; the children made it again.

Always, she felt the mermaids' eyes on her, watching with amusement and anticipation. They wanted her to fall. They enjoyed watching people die.

Mary took her time navigating the path. She reached the beach safely and walked toward the place where the children were playing.

Wendy sat on the sand in the shadow of a palm tree. Her nightgown was filthy, marked with soot from the fire and red clay from the cave floor. An old rope tied around her waist served as a makeshift belt. Her hair was a mass of tangles. She looked up from the sandcastle that she was building and squinted at Mary, suspicious of this stranger.

"Wendy," Mary said, relief washing over her. "It's Mother."

"Mother?" Wendy sounded surprised, like someone who opened a kitchen drawer and discovered a frog among the spoons. "What are you doing here? Why are you wearing those clothes? You look like a pirate."

Mary sat on the sand beside her daughter, resisting the urge to sweep her into a hug. The great emotions she had felt as a child were not gone, but they were different. Rather than being centered on herself, the emotion she felt was about this little girl on the beach.

Mary took a deep breath before speaking. She did not trust her voice to be steady.

"I've come to take you home," she said. "I thought you might want to sleep in your own bed again. I thought you might be ready for supper with your father. I could make shepherd's pie." That was Wendy's favorite dish. "We miss you." Her voice started to break on the last sentence.

Wendy smiled at the thought of supper and her comfortable bed. "I asked Peter yesterday if he would take us home. I'd asked before, but he forgot. He said he couldn't take us just now because . . ." She frowned and shook her head. "I'm not sure why. But I was going to ask again."

"Of course you were," Mary said. "Where is Peter now?"

Wendy shrugged. "Off on an adventure, I suppose."

"I've missed you so much," Mary said.

Mary blinked back tears as Wendy leaned against her. "I learned to fly," Wendy said. "I met fairies and mermaids. They aren't very nice, you know."

"I know," Mary said. "I met them when I was your age." She put her arm around Wendy, feeling the warmth of the small body against hers.

"I met some very nice people on the other side of the island. They have a teepee and a long name I don't quite remember," Wendy said. With the painful and casual honesty of childhood, she added, "I didn't forget about you and Father. John and Michael did sometimes, but I reminded them."

"I'm glad you did," Mary said. "I know you did a great job taking care of your brothers."

"I'll have to say goodbye to Peter before we go."

Mary shook her head. "There's no time for that. We'll be leaving today. I'm sure he will come to visit you at home. He can fly there whenever he wants."

Wendy considered that. "How will we get off the island? I can't fly when Peter isn't here."

"I have a ship," Mary said. "It's a pirate ship."

Wendy frowned at this. "Peter kills pirates," she said.

"Peter will not kill these pirates," Mary said, her tone stern. "They're friends of mine."

Wendy took a moment to consider this information. Peter was a magical being who flew through the air and consorted with fairies. Her mother, on the other hand, had been the authority on all things since Wendy was a baby. Even Peter admitted that mothers were powerful.

Wendy nodded, confident in her mother's ability to make pirates and Peter Pan do her will. That matter disposed of, Wendy moved on to more immediate needs. "Do you have anything to eat?" she asked.

"There are biscuits and jam on the ship. I have humbugs and barley sugar in my pocket," Mary said. "Get the boys and you can have some candy now."

Wendy ran and got the boys—not just John and Michael, but all the Lost Boys. They stood in an untidy and uncomfortable circle around Mary, staring at her as if she were an exotic beast, more fantastic and unlikely than mermaids or fairies. Wendy introduced the Lost Boys to her mother: Curly, Nibs, Slightly, the Twins, and Tootles.

All the children were very dirty. Most wore the remnants of the clothes that they had been wearing when they flew away with Peter. One boy wore a man's shirt, several sizes too big for him. Bloodstains and a slash in the side of the shirt suggested that its previous owner had met an untimely end.

John and Michael, after a moment's hesitation, had approached her to be hugged. "Yes," John said hesitantly. "I remember you."

Michael frowned. "Peter said you had forgotten us. He said you'd have a new baby now."

"You are my baby and Peter is an idiot," Mary said firmly. "Peter doesn't know the first thing about mothers. I've come to take you home."

"Peter won't like it," Tootles said.

Mary studied Tootles for a moment. "I don't care what Peter likes," she said calmly.

All the children stared at her, stunned into silence.

Mary doled out the candy: one piece to each child for starters. Perhaps, long ago, their mothers had told Tootles, Nibs, Curly, Slightly, and the Twins to beware of strangers with candy. If so, that advice was long forgotten.

When the first piece was gone, Mary offered each child a second piece, then returned the bag to her pocket. By that time, John and Michael had given her genuine hugs. Wendy stood close by her side.

Mary stood then. "We'll be going home now," she said to Wendy, John, and Michael. "The ship is waiting."

"What ship?" Curly asked.

"The pirate ship that will take us home," Wendy said calmly. "The pirates are friends of my mother's. They have biscuits and jam for us."

Curly's eyes widened—startled by the idea of friendly pirates and enthusiastic at the thought of biscuits and jam. "Can I come?" he asked. Then all the boys were clamoring to go home with Mary.

She stood and dusted the sand off her trousers. "We will ask the captain."

The children followed Mary to the beach where the pirates had just finished digging up the treasure. They were busy reburying the skeleton of the dead pirate that Tom and Sam had buried atop the chest.

Captain Hook stood by the longboat, watching the group approach. "Rather more children than you anticipated," he said to Mary.

"This is my daughter Wendy and my sons John and Michael," Mary said. "Children, this is my friend James, also known as Captain Hook."

"Very pleased to make your acquaintance," Wendy said, curtseying after a fashion. She did a reasonably good job of it, considering she was wearing a tattered nightgown. John glanced at the hook and did not offer to shake hands. He bowed ever so slightly. Michael just smiled at him and said, "Hullo."

Mary gestured toward the other boys, who were hanging back and looking uneasy. "These young gentlemen say they would also like to come along."

Hook surveyed the group, remembering his own time as a Lost Boy. "Is that so? What do you say, young gentlemen? Would you like to come, or have you reconsidered?"

After an awkward moment when the boys looked at each other, Tootles stepped forward. "I am just Tootles," he said, "and nobody minds me. But I think . . ."

Hook interrupted him. "What's your name? Not Tootles. Tell me the name your parents gave you." His thoughtful expression had become a frown.

Tootles hesitated, looking confused. "My name? My mother called me Oliver."

"Oliver is a fine name," the captain said, his expression softening ever so slightly. "Go on, Oliver."

Though clearly flustered, Oliver continued. "I would like to go home," he said.

Hook nodded. "Now, Oliver—I imagine that Peter will pursue us. Suppose Peter flies aboard the ship and shouts, 'To me, boys!' What will you do then? Will you fight with Peter against me and my crew?"

Oliver blinked in sudden confusion, and the other boys looked startled. They had not imagined this possibility.

Hook went on. "I do not ask that you fight to save the ship that's taking you home. But you must swear you will not raise your hand against me or the crew."

Peter always chose the most thoughtful boy to call Tootles, Mary thought, watching Oliver. George had been Tootles, James had been Tootles, and now Oliver was Tootles.

"I've asked Peter to take me home lots of times," Oliver said. "But he always forgets." The boy straightened his back, holding his head high. "I won't fight against Peter. But I swear I will not raise my hand against you or your crew."

"Very good, Oliver. You are welcome aboard the *Jolly Roger*," James said.

The other boys were looking at Oliver, at each other, at the sand beneath their feet—looking everywhere except at Hook.

"What about the rest of you?" Hook asked. "Will you swear?"

They looked at him then, unable to avoid his gaze. Curly spoke up first. He was not as thoughtful as Oliver. He wanted to go home, but he felt the need to blame this decision on someone else. "I think my mother would want me to come home. In fact, I am sure she would. So I swear I will not raise my hand against you or your crew."

The other Lost Boys were nodding. As it turned out, every one of the Lost Boys was quite sure that his mother wanted him to come home and so every one of them swore that he would not raise his hand against Hook or his crew.

CHAPTER 35
You Are Surrounded by Forces
You Do Not Understand

O N Nosy Boraha, Rumbold acted as a local guide, declining offers of lodging at the tavern nearest the dock with a wave of the hand and an easy laugh.

"You'll be better off up the hill a bit," he told Holmes. "I'll take you to the Dirk and Cutlass. Slash has some acceptable rooms to let and you'll find him an excellent source of information."

The group followed Rumbold to the tavern, with Nana close at Watson's side and Captain Flint riding on Sam's shoulder.

Slash had two large airy rooms that he was delighted to rent to the group. When asked if he had seen a young woman from London, possibly dressed as a man, he told what he knew.

"Dressed as a man? Not when I made her acquaintance. She was a lady and dressed as such," Slash declared. He recounted, with enthusiasm, the tale of her battle with Le Têtu. Slash's version of the story included some acrobatics that James' version had omitted. (Who would have imagined that Mary could leap atop a table from a standing start?) He also recounted Le Têtu's impassioned speech begging for mercy.

"Such a lovely lady—who would suspect she knew how to fight?" Slash said. "She was magnificent."

"Yes," George murmured. "She is magnificent."

Slash went on. "The next thing I knew, she was sailing off on the *Jolly Roger* with Captain Hook and his villainous crew."

The color drained from George's face. "She sailed with Captain Hook?" he gasped.

"She did! The two of them seemed to be old friends. Thick as thieves, you might say." Slash grinned.

Holmes nodded. "Accounts say that Captain Hook can be quite the gentleman."

"He can," Slash agreed. "But he is never more dangerous than when he is most polite. They say he always smiles when he claws a man with his hook." Slash clawed the air with a hooked finger, still grinning.

Slash, you might be interested to know, had been a failed actor before he became a pirate. When the occasion called for it, he was quite willing to embrace the drama of a situation.

Rumbold, who had been fetching himself a glass of grog, rejoined the group in time to catch the end of this exchange. He patted George on the shoulder, frowning and shaking his head at Slash. "I am glad to hear that Mary has the help of my friend James—Captain Hook, that is. I want to reassure you, George, that James will see that no harm comes to your wife. I often sail on the *Jolly Roger* as the ship's surgeon. A fine ship and a very competent crew." He turned to Slash. "This gentleman is the lady's husband."

Slash's eyes widened. "Her husband?" He regarded George with greater respect, clearly reevaluating his initial impression of the man.

"One question for you," Rumbold continued. "Did the lady stay here when she was on the island?"

Slash shook his head. "She stayed at Ruby's. They are old friends, from what I've heard."

The group left their baggage at the Dirk and Cutlass and followed Rumbold up the hill to Ruby's. They followed a meandering path through the town.

It was midday, but the town was still waking up. A rooster crowed from the coop behind a brothel, his cry answered from another coop. A woman in a silk robe stood in a doorway, gazing after a sailor who was headed for the harbor. Then she shifted her gaze to the group of men walking up the hill and smiled at them.

At the top of the hill, Ruby greeted Rumbold with a cordial smile and Sam with an embrace. "Welcome back, Sam. So wonderful to see you again. All my chicks have come home! You must tell me how you've been."

She served them tea in the private courtyard by her house, but Sam did not have a chance to tell her of his life in London. Holmes took charge, with an air that some might regard as masterful and others might consider quite rude.

Holmes questioned Ruby about when Mary had arrived on the island, her purpose in coming to the island, and the ship she had sailed on. "Did she leave the island willingly with Captain Hook?" Holmes asked.

"Willingly? Of course! She was eager to find her way to Neverland and rescue her children. James Hook is an old friend, and he was happy to help. He has a score to settle with Peter Pan, you know."

Ruby saw no reason to discuss the business arrangement regarding the treasure. She was aware that Sam knew about the treasure, but she thought it best to discuss the particulars of Mary's bargain with him in private.

"Have you seen the children?" Holmes asked, studying her closely.

Ruby eyed Holmes, frowning. "No, I have not seen them. I've never been to Neverland, nor would I care to go from the tales I've heard."

"This Peter Pan—I've heard he's a pirate," Holmes said.

Watson knew what Holmes was doing. Stating misinformation often led a witness to correct him, telling him far more than he would otherwise have learned.

"If you believe that, you're a fool." Ruby had no patience for the sort of game Holmes was playing. She glanced at Sam. "Sam, you told him better, didn't you?"

Sam shrugged and raised his eyebrows in an expression that said quite eloquently—he wouldn't listen to the likes of me. And he won't listen to you, either.

Ruby gave Holmes a hard look. "Peter Pan is not a pirate. He looks like a boy and he has the thoughtless cruelty of a boy. Perhaps he is an island spirit that has adopted the ways of your people." She shrugged. "Let others argue about that. He can fly and he can give others the power to fly."

Holmes frowned. "You're a hardheaded woman of business. Yet you tell us these fairy tales."

Ruby regarded Holmes with a level gaze. "I suggest you be cautious, Mr. Holmes. You are not in your own land. You are surrounded by forces you do not understand." She reached for the teapot. "Would you care for more tea?"

They had another cup of tea. Ruby was still the perfect hostess, but her expression was no longer quite so open and amiable. Though Holmes continued his questioning, he got no additional information. Finally, the detective said, "Thank you for your time, madam."

As Holmes stood to leave, Watson remained seated. "You go on," he said. "I'll join you shortly. I would love to have another cup of tea."

Holmes nodded curtly and headed for the gate. Rumbold followed.

Sam glanced at Watson. "Shall I stay?"

"No need," Watson said.

"I'll try to keep Holmes out of trouble," Sam said, then followed Rumbold.

George hesitated, then quietly settled back into his chair. Nana stayed with the two of them, leaning against Ruby's leg as if making her allegiance clear. Ruby reached down to scratch the big dog's ears.

Back at the Dirk and Cutlass, Holmes found another source of information. Tom was there, in a mood that Mary would have described as sulky. He had been drinking and brooding ever since Mary left on the *Jolly Roger*. He had run out of money and was living on the promise of future treasure.

After Mary's departure, Ruby had offered him a room in exchange for some help around her compound—repairing a fence, fixing a stone wall. Tom had dismissed those chores as beneath him, preferring to seek lodgings elsewhere.

He had found a place to sleep at one of the brothels where the owner had an unused room and was willing to gamble that Tom would pay up eventually. But Tom was sleeping alone in a house full of pretty women. The women had heard too many promises of future payment that never materialized to be willing to take a chance on Tom. This made Tom feel quite put upon.

Tom spent his time visiting various taverns where he could tell stories and cadge drinks. He was nursing a drink and staring out at the harbor when Holmes, Rumbold, and Sam entered the Dirk and Cutlass. Parrots have long memories, and Captain Flint recognized Tom immediately. "Ahoy, matey!" the parrot shrieked. "Ahoy!"

Sam followed up on the parrot's greeting. "Is that you, Tom?"

Tom responded with enthusiasm—greeting Sam as a long-lost brother. Soon the group was settled at a table with a round of drinks.

Holmes was glad to meet Mary's brother. Though it was clear that Tom was a drunkard and a rascal, he could still be a useful source of information.

Holmes listened as Tom told Sam about how his sister had stolen away to Neverland to get the treasure that they had buried long ago.

"She sailed off with Captain Hook and left me behind," Tom said in an aggrieved tone.

"She went to rescue her children," Sam said. "Your niece and nephews."

Tom shrugged. "The children are fine. Mary knows that. They're on an adventure. It's the treasure that makes the trip worthwhile."

"Tell me about this treasure," Holmes said, his keen gaze focused on Tom.

Tom smiled at Holmes. With the wiliness of a longtime drunk, he had identified the detective as an excellent source of a few more rounds. Holmes wanted information, and Tom would supply that in abundance—a mixture of truth and fabrications, all told in the form of rambling stories fueled by rum.

Ruby was not surprised that Watson and George lingered behind the others.

"There are things I need to ask you," Watson said.

"Yes," George said. "I have questions, too."

"I am happy to speak with you further," Ruby said. "But there is no need to rush. Your friend, Mr. Holmes, is very . . ." She hesitated, choosing her words carefully. ". . . very determined to get his questions answered." Again, she paused. "Even when he is not asking the right questions and he chooses not to believe the answers."

"Yes, of course," Watson said. "But . . ."

Ruby held up a hand. "Hush," she said. "Take a moment. There is no hurry, here on the island. Arranging for a ship to go in search of Mary will take time, no matter how quickly Mr. Holmes wants to move. Sometimes, it's best to move slowly and welcome an occasional moment of silence."

Watson nodded, fighting the urge to speak, to get up and rush after Holmes, to do something, anything. But he remained silent. He could hear women in the distance—laughing and talking among themselves. A bird fluttered down from the tree overhead to eye the plate of fruit Ruby had set out when her visitors arrived. Ruby took a slice of mango and set it on the ground for the bird, then covered the remaining fruit with a cloth.

George broke the silence. "Please," he said. "I am worried about Mary. How did she seem to you?"

Ruby studied George. "What she's doing is dangerous and you are right to be worried. But she is smart and determined, and good with a sword. She said she had plenty of time to practice en route."

"I wanted to keep her safe," George murmured. He looked miserable. "You can't do that by keeping her at home." Ruby regarded him with some sympathy.

"I didn't know what else to do," George said. "I wanted to help. But I didn't know what to do."

"You could try asking Mary how you could help," Ruby suggested.

George hung his head.

Another moment of silence. The bird that was eating the mango had been joined by another bird who wanted a share. The two were engaged in a dispute that involved much posturing and flapping of wings.

"It's clear that Mr. Holmes does not believe in fairies or Peter Pan," Ruby said at last. "But I would like to know your feelings on these matters."

It's worth mentioning here that Ruby already knew a great deal about Watson and his feelings. The captain of the ship that had brought them to Nosy Boraha was one of Ruby's many cousins. While Watson and Holmes had been settling in at the Dirk and Cutlass, the captain had climbed the hill to Ruby's, where he always stayed when in port. The captain, who understood far more English than he admitted to, recounted conversations he had overheard. He told her that Watson and Holmes had argued about Lady Hawkins and the photographs she had taken—that Watson and Sam had discussed fairies and flight.

"It's complicated," Watson said slowly.

"I think it may be quite simple." Ruby folded her hands in her lap, allowing a moment of silence. "I think maybe you have seen things that you can't explain."

Still Watson hesitated.

"Oh, just admit it!" George exclaimed in a sudden burst of fury. "You saw a fairy. You flew. I've done that myself. I've been to Neverland and I don't care who knows it!" He glared at Watson.

"I saw a tiny woman with wings," Watson said slowly. "Sam said it was a fairy. I remember flying, but that could have been a dream."

"There are many things here in the islands that might seem like a dream. I suggest, for your own safety, you accept them as real." Ruby rather liked Mary's uncle and her husband. They were foolish men, but well-meaning. She stood up. "I think we've had enough tea. Let me get something a bit stronger."

She went inside to fetch some whiskey, leaving the men alone in the peaceful courtyard. The birds that had been squabbling over the fruit had been quiet for a time. A breeze rustled the leaves overhead.

"Listen," George said suddenly. "Do you hear that?"

Watson heard a soft jingling of bells. Nana, who had been lying by his feet, sat up, suddenly alert.

Aribelle flew down from the treetops and landed on Watson's shoulder. "Where have you been, you silly ass?" she said in the jingle of bells that is fairy speech. "I have come to grant your wish. What do you want?"

Fairies are all about bargains. If you've read fairy tales, you know that. Save a fairy's life and that fairy is under an obligation to you. When she was pinned by the cat's paw, Aribelle had offered to grant a wish to whoever saved her. When Watson failed to take advantage of that offer, she had dismissed the matter of obligation. Surely she wasn't responsible for the big fool's stupidity. But the sense of obligation unfulfilled had nagged at her.

And so had the mermaids. They knew about the incident with the cat. There was little that happened on or near the ocean that they did not know about. When they sat on Marooners' Rock, combing out their hair, they talked about Aribelle and the cat and the human who saved her. They laughed at Aribelle and called her "Cat Food."

For their own amusement, the mermaids had kept track of Watson's whereabouts, noting when he reached Madagascar and when he was en route to Nosy Boraha. They listened in on his discussions at the railing—with Holmes, with Sam, and with George. Gleefully, they reported juicy tidbits of those conversations to Aribelle.

"The tall man who thinks he knows everything says you don't even exist," one mermaid told Aribelle. All the mermaids laughed at this. "The thin man who is often sick says that you are nasty and wicked and not to be trusted. He's right about that. You can't be trusted to keep your promises."

"Don't you worry about that obligation," said the oldest of the mermaids. "Your man friend can hear us singing. He'll come for a swim with us soon enough. And that will be the end of him."

The mermaids all laughed, thinking this was a very good joke.

Finally, Aribelle decided she had had enough. When the mermaids told her that Watson had reached Nosy Boraha, she decided to go to the island, find him, and grant his wish, whatever it was.

It was a long flight to Nosy Boraha. Fairies are not built for long-distance flight. The wind can easily push them off course. By the time Aribelle reached Ruby's garden, she was tired and angry. But she was determined to take care of this matter.

"I'll grant your wish," she repeated in a fit of temper and a cacophony of bells. "What do you want, you mutton-headed foozler?!"

Fortunately for Watson, George had listened carefully to the fairies when he was in Neverland. Rather than ignoring fairy speech like the other Lost Boys, he had often asked Peter what a fairy was saying. He had learned to recognize three phrases: "Give me that!" "You silly ass!" and "I'll grant your wish." The first two were very common. The third was vanishingly rare, but George had asked Peter about it specifically. It seemed like a useful thing to know.

"She says she'll grant your wish," George said. "Tell her to take us to Mary."

"Will you take me to Mary?" Watson asked. "Is that why you've come?"

Aribelle flew around Watson's head three times, sprinkling him liberally with fairy dust. Then she grabbed his ear and pulled upward until Watson stood.

"I'll take you to Mary if that's what you want. Come along, you great gallumpus!"

George was on his feet. He grabbed Watson's hand. "Tell her that I must go with you," he said. Nana was up, too, staring at the flickering light.

Aribelle fluttered her wings, releasing another cloud of fairy dust. The dust showered Watson, George, and Nana.

"Come on!" she said again. "Push off, you cork-brained looby!" She gripped Watson's ear with both hands and yanked upward as hard as she could.

The painful pinch made Watson raise up on his toes—just enough of a push to lift him off the ground. At that moment, Nana lunged to grab Watson's trouser cuff, just as she had on the ship. Nana, a solid, no-nonsense sort of dog, would have remained earthbound had she been certain that dogs could not fly. But seeing Watson take flight on the ship had convinced her otherwise. If Watson could fly, Nana knew that she could too. When she lunged to grab Watson's trouser cuff, she took off, passing Watson as he was hauled upward by the ear.

Unlike Watson, Nana was graceful in flight. As a young dog, growing up on a farm, she had sometimes leapt from the bank of the farm pond to land with a tremendous splash in the water. The leap that carried her upward was like that—but without the water and the splash. It was a leap that went on and on, carrying her upward and forward and onward to find and rescue Mary and the children. Hind legs outstretched, front paws reaching forward, she was in a classic diving pose, or as close an approximation as a large shaggy dog can manage.

George pushed off as well. Remembering the long-ago night when he had followed Peter Pan, he soared.

As Watson left the ground, he kicked his legs and waved his arms in search of something solid to grab hold of. His hand brushed a palm frond, and he almost got a grip on it. But Aribelle yanked him to one side, scolding him in a jangle of bells. "Stop that! I am taking you to Mary whether you like it or not."

"Don't flail about!" George shouted. "This is the best part. Just soar. Let the wind take you!"

Ruby returned to the courtyard just in time to see Nana, George, and Watson clearing the tops of the trees. "Tell Holmes!" Watson called down to her. "Tell him we've gone to rescue Mary."

CHAPTER 36
It's Hook or Me This Time!

THE *Jolly Roger* was en route to Nosy Boraha, making good time. They had left Neverland late in the afternoon and had sailed all night. It was a fine sunny morning with a steady wind. The sunlight glittered on the ocean swells. Earlier, a pod of dolphins had escorted the ship, surfing in the ship's bow wave. There were mermaids among the dolphins, but no one noticed them.

Wendy, her brothers, and all the Lost Boys were at the bow of the ship, discussing pirates and eating biscuits. They had finished breakfast two hours before, but Cookie had brought them a plate of biscuits to share. The children had decided that the pirates, particularly the cook, were misunderstood.

James had watched the cook take the plate of biscuits to the children.

"They're a very hungry lot," Cookie had said as he passed the captain.

James had nodded his approval, remembering how many biscuits he had eaten in his first few days on the *Jolly Roger*. History, he thought, does not give cooks enough credit. Frederick the Great once said that an army marches on its belly, and James agreed. But Fredrick had not commented on the ones who kept that belly fed. The cooks, James thought, are the unsung heroes of any fighting force.

"Peter told us lies about you pirates," John confided to Cookie, as he helped himself to a biscuit from the plate.

It was at that moment that the sailor in the crow's nest called out, "Flying boy!"

Peter Pan swooped down from the clear blue sky. He landed and posed for a moment. His head was high, as if he knew the Lost Boys were watching him with admiration. (They were not. They were munching biscuits and thinking about how nice it was to be somewhere that there were biscuits to munch.)

"Stand back, boys! Leave Hook to me!" he shouted, as if the boys were rushing to attack Captain Hook. (They were not.)

James—or Hook, if you prefer—had his left hand on his sword and his hook held ready. Unlike Peter, he did not relish this fight. All he wanted was a peaceful trip back to Nosy Boraha with the children and the treasure.

"There's no need for us to fight," Hook said.

"We have biscuits, Peter!" Michael called from the bow of the ship.

"Very good biscuits," John added. "Come have some, Peter!"

"Yes, do join us, Peter!" Wendy added her voice to the others.

Peter ignored them all and drew his sword. "It's Hook or me this time!" he shouted. He was quite determined—a bold boy who looked every inch a hero, ready to do battle with his enemy.

That was when a slender pirate in a red cap stepped between Peter and Hook.

"No!" said the red-capped pirate. "It's not about you and Hook. It's about you and me, Peter. It's high time we met again."

Peter was momentarily baffled. He didn't recognize this pirate. "No one stands between me and Hook," Peter said.

But Peter was wrong about that. The slender pirate met the first sweep of Peter's sword with an elegant parry and returned a thrust that Peter barely deflected. Peter attacked again, a volley of blows intended to overwhelm his foe, but the pirate slipped aside, flowing like water, wriggling like an eel, never where Peter thought he would be.

"Stand and fight," Peter said.

The pirate laughed. "Fight like a man? Is that what you mean to say? I fight like a boy. I learned by watching you."

Peter shook his head, refusing to acknowledge the pirate's words. Could this be a Lost Boy, returned to taunt him for some forgotten reason? There had been so many Lost Boys, each one with him for a time and then forgotten.

Peter advanced again, slowly this time, a contrast to his earlier impetuous charge. He was testing his opponent and playing to his audience. For a time, the attention of the onlookers had shifted to this interloper and Peter did not like that. He grinned more broadly each time the pirate met his blow and stepped back.

Then the red-capped pirate attacked for the first time, with a whirlwind of blows and spins and leaps almost as flashy as Peter's own, though perhaps the comparison is a bit unfair. The pirate was bound by gravity, whereas Peter was often in flight.

The pirate drove Peter back, as quick as the boy—but having the advantage of longer arms and legs. Whenever Peter's feet left the deck to fly, the pirate's blade flashed over the boy's head, driving him down.

Peter's blade slashed at the pirate's head, looking certain to connect. But no—the pirate ducked. The blade caught the red cap. A flash of red—not blood, just the cap—flew from the pirate's head, releasing a tumble of curly hair.

Even as she ducked, Mary Darling's blade flashed toward Peter, catching his sword and flicking it away to follow her cap. As quick as her flashing blade, she closed the gap between them, dropping the sword and grabbing him by the ear.

Yes! She grabbed him by the ear, as if he were a wayward child rather than a hero, a magical being, a god. In her left hand, she held a dagger at the ready.

"You will kill me now," Peter said, bearing the pain of his twisted ear. "Do it, then! To die will be an awfully big adventure."

Mary stared at the boy, frozen. She had imagined this fight many times. But now what? Her imagination had never taken her this far. Kill him? No, she couldn't do that.

He was just a little boy. Yes, he was a supernatural creature—a god or spirit of some sort. But he was also a little boy—self-absorbed as children are. She had been angry with him for so long, resenting and at the same time envying his brash confidence, his freedom, and his certainty that the world revolved around him. Gazing at Peter's face, she knew she would never get satisfaction from this child. He was what he was: innocent and heartless and eternally young.

Over the course of the long trip from London to Neverland, her anger had cooled. Memories of her time on Neverland had shifted and mellowed. She knew that she would not be the woman she was if she had not spent time on Neverland.

She had a grip on his ear, but now what could she do?

Then Watson arrived, landing on the deck with a thump, followed by George and Nana. Watson and George took in the scene on the deck, trying to make sense of it all: a hook-handed pirate, a villainous crew, and a band of ragged children. In the middle of it all, Mary Darling, dressed in men's clothing and wielding a dagger, gripped a grubby boy by the ear. Fortunately, Nana knew exactly what to do.

Dogs are not bound by the social rules that people follow. Nana was very much a nursemaid but also very much a dog. She leapt forward and knocked Peter over, yanking his ear from Mary's grasp. With two large paws on his chest, she held him down and bathed him, washing his face with a large tongue as if he were a misbehaving puppy. His face really did need washing and Nana was just the dog to do it.

It is difficult to look heroic in a situation like that. At best, you can look stoic, but that really wasn't in Peter's nature. He squirmed, trying to get away. He made faces. Peter turned his head to escape Nana's determined tongue, but that only served to give the big dog access to his ear, which she bathed with enthusiasm.

Mary laughed. If that weren't bad enough for Peter, the children all laughed, too. Wendy, John, and Michael had all been bathed by Nana at one time or another. Watching as this magical boy was subjected to that same treatment was strangely satisfying.

"I have beaten you, Peter Pan," Mary said in a ringing voice. The occasion seemed to call for a speech of some sort. "I have beaten you in a fair fight. Fly away now, and leave me and my children be."

George clapped his hands and shouted, "Hear! Hear!" Wendy cheered and the other children joined in. It had been a splendid fight.

James sheathed his weapon and picked up Peter's sword, removing the danger that the boy might reclaim it. Then the pirate captain made a speech about fighting fair and about the heroism of mothers and a great deal more. It was a fine speech, though perhaps a bit long. James was a good speaker—he had a deep voice and perfect diction. Everyone cheered again when he was done.

Everyone except Peter. Listening to James, Nana sat back on her haunches, releasing the boy. He sat up, his face red and wet with dog spit and perhaps tears. He did not look like a hero or a god. Rather, he looked like a child who had been weeping in a passion because he had not gotten his way.

Peter leapt to his feet, doing his best to recover his poise. James had finished his speech. Watson and George had rushed to Mary, standing on either side of her protectively.

"Foul pirate!" Peter said. "Prepare to fight."

"Oh, stop it, Peter!" Mary said in exasperation. "Just stop it!"

She felt sorry for him, but not so sorry that she would put up with his nonsense. In her mind, he had changed from a dangerous opponent to a willful and spoiled child. In fact, he was both and had always been both.

"If you keep this up, I'll put you to bed without any supper," she went on, taking a step toward the boy.

Peter did what any child wishes they could do when catching the wrong end of a mother's temper. He flew away.

Wendy, John, and Michael ran to Nana and hugged the big dog. George went to Mary. She caught a glimpse of his face before he swept her into an embrace. He was smiling, but his eyes were wet with tears. "You are magnificent," he murmured into her ear.

Then the children ran to George, pulling him away from Mary for a cacophonous reunion. All three talked at once about their adventures.

While the children mobbed their father, Watson put his arm around his niece's shoulders. "Where did you learn to fight like that?" he asked.

I wish I could say Watson's tone was one of admiration. Maybe there was a touch of awe, but the overwhelming tone was that of confusion.

Mary smiled at him. "I could equally well ask you where you learned to fly like that, Uncle John."

"One does what one has to do," Watson murmured.

"Exactly so," Mary said. "Exactly so."

It wasn't until that evening, when the children were sleeping under Nana's watchful eye that George and Mary had a moment to themselves. They stood by the rail, watching the moon on the water.

"I was astonished when I saw you and my uncle," she murmured. She turned and studied his face. "You came to rescue me. That was very brave of you."

"I had to come. Even though I am no good at this sort of thing." He did not look at her. "You were doing very well on your own, but I had to come."

"I'm glad you did," Mary said.

George kept his eyes on the ocean swells. "I shouldn't have tried to keep you at home. I'm sorry. I . . ."

"You wanted to protect me," Mary said. "I know that." She leaned against him and put her head on his shoulder. He held her close, comforted and comforting.

When the mermaids came to swim alongside the ship, George interrupted their song. "Push off and leave us alone," he said rudely. "You're not wanted here."

The next day, George made a point of thanking Captain Hook for helping his wife. James accepted the thanks graciously and made it quite clear that he and Mary were good friends, nothing more. Somehow, during the course of that discussion, the two men discovered that they had both been called Tootles by Peter Pan, and they bonded over that shared history.

"I hated it," James said.

"As did I," George agreed. "Peter would not use my name, no matter how often I told him. So of course all the other boys called me Tootles."

"But look at us now," James said, smiling. "I am a pirate captain. You have a marvelous wife and three brave children. And Peter has fled to Neverland."

George nodded, suddenly proud to have shared a name with the man who became Captain Hook. Perhaps being Tootles was not so shameful after all.

Nearby, the Lost Boy who had most recently been dubbed Tootles by Peter Pan overheard the two men talking. Like James and George, Oliver had hated being called Tootles. Such a foolish name, he had thought, a name for a clown or a fool. But now he smiled, knowing that he was in illustrious company.

CHAPTER 37
Some Choose to See a Greater World

WHEN LAST WE saw Sherlock Holmes, he was at the Dirk and Cutlass with Sam and Tom. He had interviewed Tom at length. Tom believed in fairies and Peter Pan. He talked of buried treasure and of how his wicked sister had run off with Captain Hook, leaving him behind. His conversation was a rich mix of fairy tales and grievances.

Watson and George had not returned by nightfall, but Holmes had not been troubled by their absence. Rumbold had assured him that Ruby would take very good care of them. "She is, after all, in the business of hospitality," Rumbold said, managing to deliver this line without a trace of a leer.

Holmes woke early, anticipating that Watson might have returned with news. But Watson and George were not there. He met Rumbold and Sam, who were having breakfast. At that moment, a young woman stepped into the Dirk and Cutlass. "I have a note from Ruby for Mr. Holmes," she told Slash. The message was simple:

Dear Mr. Holmes,
 Not long after you left last night, Dr. Watson and Mr. Darling met a fairy in the garden and flew away with her. Dr. Watson asked me to tell you that he and Mr. Darling had gone to rescue Mary.
 Regards,
 Ruby

Holmes went to Ruby's with Rumbold and Sam in tow. Ruby repeated what she had written in her note. Holmes questioned her and she stuck to her story. Then Holmes proceeded to conduct an extensive investigation in Ruby's courtyard, examining the ground for footprints while Ruby looked on with great interest.

Best to leave Holmes to his work. He will be busy for some time, searching for clues that would lead to an explanation that do not involve impossible fairy tales.

The next day, Lady Hawkins' steam yacht set anchor in the harbor at Nosy Boraha. When the *Jolly Roger* returned to port, Lady Hawkins took photographs of the ship's return using Lord Hawkins' camera.

In the first photograph, you can see a cluster of people on the deck, blurry in the distance. They are clearer in the second photograph. Mary and her children are waving. Watson and George Darling stand behind the group. Watson is smiling. George has lifted one hand in a tentative wave; the other rests on Mary's shoulder, as if he wants to make sure she is still there. Nana is beside them, grinning as only a happy dog can grin. On the other side of Nana are the Lost Boys. Nana had taken charge of them, and their faces were clean as a dog could make them.

Having spotted the ship from the Dirk and Cutlass, Sam, Holmes, and Rumbold hurried to the dock to meet their friends. It was a triumphant return.

Watson greeted Holmes with enthusiasm, shouting joyfully, "Holmes! We've done it!" In response, Holmes managed a thin smile and tolerated Watson's boisterous embrace.

James was delighted to see Rumbold after his long absence.

Saro rowed Lady Hawkins to the dock, where she greeted Mary like a long-lost daughter. Wendy, John, and Michael cheered for Lady Hawkins—or perhaps for the memory of biscuits aboard her yacht.

That evening, at an impromptu celebration at Ruby's, the returning adventurers told their tales. James recounted the efforts to find the island of Neverland. Watson told of how he and George and Nana had flown to the *Jolly Roger*. George described the battle between Mary and Peter, detailing every leap and flourish with great enthusiasm.

Mary smiled but said little. Ruby had provided her with a bath and clean clothes. Dressed as a lady once again, she was content to sit back and listen to the others hold forth. (She had already made plans with Ruby and Lady Hawkins to breakfast together so that she might share her version of the tale with them.)

At some point, Tom joined them, entering into the party as if he had been there all along. (Within the week, he was telling the tale as if he had.) A little later, Mary noticed that James and Rumbold had quietly slipped away together.

"Perhaps we should put the children to bed," George said softly to Mary. Michael had already fallen asleep on Mary's lap. Wendy, who had begged to stay up for the party, was rubbing her eyes and John was yawning. All the Lost Boys were slumping in their chairs.

The party broke up. Tom went off to the bordello where he had been staying, eager to begin spending his share of the treasure. Watson and Holmes returned to the Dirk and Cutlass.

Nana led the way to the room that Ruby had prepared for the children. Mary and George followed. It felt so strange and at the same time so natural, Mary thought, to carry Michael in her arms again, his head resting on her shoulder. George gave one hand to Wendy and the other to John, and the Lost Boys followed behind.

Mary and George said good night to the children, then Nana took charge, keeping watch as each child found a sleeping mat. The children were so tired that they didn't even ask for a bedtime story.

Ruby had given Mary and George a room at the back of the house. Their bed was a splendid four-poster double bed with a luxuriant silk canopy. When they looked at that bed, they both hesitated for a moment, feeling suddenly shy with each other—long married, but suddenly strangers.

Mary spoke first. "I was surprised that you remembered my sword fight with Peter Pan in such detail," she said softly.

"How could I forget?" he said. "I was terrified watching you."

She turned to look at him. "I'm not the woman you married, George. You need to know that."

George took both her hands in his. "I know that," he said. "I traveled halfway around the world to find my wife, but instead I found the girl that I fell in love with when I was in Neverland so many years ago. Watching you fight Peter, I recognized that girl. I was in love with you then, and I'm in love with you still."

It was a beautiful moment, but George wasn't very good at beautiful moments. He let go of one of Mary's hands so he could fumble in his pocket. When he didn't find what he was looking for, he let go of her other hand and fumbled in his other pocket. Then he brought out the wedding ring she had left behind in London. "I brought this in case you wanted it," he said.

Mary studied his face. This was the George who had asked her to marry him, she thought. Over the years of their marriage, he had become someone else—someone who fretted about what the neighbors would think and worried about whether people respected him. Now, as he held out the ring, he looked like the sweet and awkward boy she had met on Neverland.

"I am not respectable," Mary said, determined to make sure he really understood how she had changed. "I don't think I will ever be respectable again."

"I know that," George said. "I never really liked being respectable." He believed it when he said it, and maybe it was true. "Who cares what the neighbors think!"

"If we go back to London, we'll have to be respectable. But we don't have to go back." Mary spoke as if the idea had just occurred to her, though actually, she'd been thinking about it for some time. "We could stay here."

The shadow of a frown crossed George's face. "I'd rather not have any more adventures," he said hesitantly. "I'm really no good at them."

"You managed this one quite splendidly. But you don't have to have any more if you don't want them."

She held out her hand. George slipped the ring onto her finger, then pulled her into his arms. There's a time when conversation ends, and that moment was the time.

I won't tell you all of what happened in that double bed—this isn't that sort of story. But I think it was like coming home after being away for a long time—familiar, comfortable, and sometimes surprising as you discover pleasures you had almost forgotten.

After the others left, Sam and Ruby lingered in the garden, having a nightcap. "And what will you do with your share of the treasure, Sam?" Ruby asked as she poured two glasses of rum. "Will you go back to London? Or will I need to find another way to fence the pirates' plunder?"

In the distance, Sam could hear drunken men singing a sea chanty to a ukulele accompaniment: *"Rolling home, rolling home, rolling home across the sea. Rolling home to dear old England. . ."*

Listening, Sam smiled and shook his head. "England is not my home. I left my head rat skinner in charge of the business. He's a fine young man and he has all the contacts he needs to fence the goods for you. He can keep on making and selling gloves. I'll be staying here."

While Sam and Ruby chatted in the courtyard at Ruby's, Holmes and Watson sat at a table overlooking the harbor at the Dirk and Cutlass. Watson had a glass of whisky and a cigar. He was feeling mellow and content.

"On that day in London when Mary ran away, I could not imagine a happy ending to her story," he said. "Yet here we are. Mary and George are happy. The children are happy. Sam is happy. And I am very happy."

"You are too easily satisfied, Watson." Holmes had been silent and watchful during the festivities at Ruby's. But now he had a few things to say. "I listened to the fairy tale that you and George told. Are you really content to believe that nonsense?"

"Yes," Watson said. "Having lived through it, I do believe it."

"A flying boy who kidnaps children? Fairy dust that makes you fly?" Holmes shook his head, smiling in disbelief.

Watson held his temper. "I know what I have seen and what I have done. If I did not fly, how else could I have reached the pirate ship so quickly? And it's not just me. The children talk of their flight to Neverland. George flew there with me. Sam says . . ."

Holmes waved a hand, dismissing these eyewitness accounts as irrelevant. "Allow me to provide an explanation based on logic, not fantasy."

Watson almost protested, then stopped himself. He recognized the expression on his friend's face—the happy eager look Holmes had when he was about to explain his solution to a mystery. Holmes needed to tell his version of the story, Watson realized. It was not just for his own glory and ego, though that was part of it. But more than that, Holmes wanted and needed to make sense of the world using facts and logic. Holmes would explain the strange occurrences and thus, to his way of thinking, set the world right.

Holmes continued. "Chemical compounds found in the leaves and roots of jungle plants can give a man dreams of flight so convincing that he will swear he had flown. Ask Rumbold about that. Or ask your friend Lady Hawkins. With her knowledge of botany, she certainly knows of these plants. She planted the suggestion of flight in your mind with her photos of flying children. Then all it took was a dose of the right plant extract, perhaps administered by Ruby. Your brain did the rest. You and George were drugged and taken aboard that pirate ship."

"How could that be?" Watson said. "The *Jolly Roger* set sail before we arrived in Nosy Boraha."

Holmes chuckled. "The ship left this harbor, but that doesn't mean it sailed for Neverland. Slash tells me there are several nearby coves where a ship can anchor. The *Jolly Roger* set sail—then anchored at the nearest cove and waited for our arrival."

Watson shook his head, frowning in disbelief. "That suggests Hook knew we were coming and planned all this."

"My dear Watson, of course he knew. Remember—Captain Hook's friend Rumbold was traveling with us. Rumbold suggested we attend Lady Hawkins' afternoon tea, which gave him just enough time to get a message to Captain Hook. Knowing that we were on our way, Hook made his plans. He made a grand show of setting sail for Neverland, but stayed close and left behind a couple of sailors and the ship's longboat. Once you and George were drugged and unconscious, the men brought you to the *Jolly Roger*."

Watson sipped his whisky, remembering the discussion he had with Sam. Holmes, Sam had said, believes that everything can be explained with logic. Fairies and Peter Pan have no place in his logical world.

Watson remembered flying. He believed he had flown. He did not want to reinterpret that memory through the lens of logic.

Holmes was hitting his stride. "What was not clear to me earlier was why anyone would want us to believe in a fairy-tale world. How could anyone profit from that?

"Your nephew Tom provided me with the missing motive. Tom is a drunk and a braggart—and he is quite indiscrete when he has been drinking. After he had consumed the better part of a bottle of Slash's finest rum, Tom mentioned that he had once helped bury a chest filled with jewelry and gold on a tropical island." Holmes smiled. "Tom said that he and Mary knew right where the treasure was buried—and told me that Hook and Mary had gone to dig it up."

"How would Mary know anything about buried treasure," Watson asked.

"A very good question," Holmes said. "To answer it, I must bring up my inquiries into Mary's past, which you objected to so strenuously back in London. With the help of Australian authorities, I obtained a very interesting article from the Cooktown newspaper. According to the newspaper, Tom and Mary were kidnapped as children. They were picking wildflowers by the river when they were snatched by pirates. Though the children escaped their initial captors, they ended up on the *Jolly Roger*, under Captain Scratch. That good captain, sympathetic to the children's plight, arranged their passage home.

"James Hook had been first mate under Captain Scratch. Evidently James Hook learned of the treasure from Tom when the boy was on the *Jolly Roger*. When Hook became captain of the ship a few years ago, he decided it was time to dig up that long-buried treasure. He located Tom, but Tom's memories of where the chest was buried had been addled by years of drinking. So Hook needed Mary to find the treasure.

"I have not yet traced the particulars on how Mary's children were snatched from London, but I know why they were taken. Hook needed Mary to find the treasure—and what better way to lure a mother than to capture her children?

"Sam had a hand in it, of course. As did Lady Hawkins. But Captain Hook was the mastermind behind it all."

Watson took a deep breath and remained silent. As he sipped his whiskey and listened to his friend carefully construct a logical sequence that could explain all that had happened, Watson remembered something Lady Hawkins had said: "Some of us choose to see a greater world, accepting that there are powers that are outside our experience, powers we cannot explain with our current science."

It is possible, Watson thought, to believe two things at the same time. He believed in gravity, yet he knew that birds could fly. Yes, he knew that air was involved and that the interaction of air and the bird's wings somehow kept the bird aloft. But did that make the bird's flight less amazing? Surely not. And before people knew of air, how did they explain birds in flight? With magic? Or did they just accept that birds fly because it is in their nature?

Watson decided that he believed in gravity and he believed that he had flown to the pirate ship. He also believed that it was best, at that moment, to keep his beliefs to himself. Holmes would never accept that there were things that he could not explain. Holmes could not believe in fairies, in mermaids, nor in magical boys who remained eternally young. For Holmes, the lights in the trees would always be exotic insects, the songs from the ocean waves would always be whales.

CHAPTER 38
Whose Story Is It?

And so the story comes to an end.

For those who are curious about exactly what happened next, here are the particulars.

Watson and Holmes returned to London. Sam arranged their passage on a merchant ship sailing from Nosy Boraha. With them went Slightly and Curly and Nibs and the Twins and Tootles (who was now going by Oliver). Mary paid the Lost Boys' fare and gave Watson the task of reuniting them with their families.

Watson and Holmes never spoke of this adventure again. Watson refrained from writing about it. But he maintained a correspondence with Lady Emily Hawkins for many years.

Sam met a notorious woman pirate named Black Jenny and fell in love. That's Sam's story to tell, should he choose to do so. I hope he does. But just so you don't worry about Sam, I'll tell you here that Sam and Jenny lived happily ever after.

George wrote to the London firm that employed him, explaining that he was exploring investments in Madagascar and would advise them further when he knew the date of his return to London. That time never came.

Mary's share of the treasure made her a lady of considerable means. With George, their children, and their faithful nursemaid Nana, Mary made a happy home on Nosy Boraha.

Mary consulted Lady Hawkins on how she might best invest her new fortune. Lady Hawkins—Emily, as Mary came to know her—became Mary's confidant and advisor in many things. With Lady Hawkins' assistance, Mary achieved some success as an author, writing about her life on Nosy Boraha. Mary never wrote about Peter Pan. Another account, the one written by J. M. Barrie, is the best-known tale of Mary Darling and her family.

In writing that account, Barrie relied on information he recalled from that long-ago dinner party where George met Mary and also on the reminiscences of Captain James Hook. When James retired as a pirate, he and Rumbold relocated to London, where James gained a reputation as a poet. He composed in a form he had learned from a Japanese sailor. Hook's best-known work was titled "Apparent Contradiction":

> Some have one eye,
> One leg, one hand. The complete pirate
> Has some parts missing.

James was celebrated in literary circles. Though everyone knew he was a famous pirate captain, he maintained a polite fiction that he was a merchant and explorer. (After all, piracy was illegal.)

He and Rumbold were quite in demand as dinner guests. At one such dinner, James Barrie made their acquaintance and learned, to his delight, about Mary's adventure.

As every author does, Barrie interpreted what he learned, matching it with his understanding of the world. And it is quite clear to me that Barrie had a terrible view of growing up and a very skewed view of women. In Barrie's account, Peter is fascinating, Wendy pines for him, and Mary Darling is a perfect mother and an accommodating wife.

I don't believe any of that for a minute—and I should know. I'm Wendy's daughter Jane, all grown-up now. I've written this book to correct Barrie's account. I may not have gotten it all quite right, but I'm sure I did better than Barrie. After all, it's my family and my history. I set out to tell the story of my grandmother, Mary Darling, and now I've done it.

There are many other stories to tell, and I hope someone else will someday tell them. This is not Sam's story, though he has an important place in it. I would like to hear Sam's story, but I know that I don't know enough to tell it. Ruby has a story to tell—many stories, I would guess—but someone else will have to tell those. I can only relay the bits and pieces that I heard at my grandmother's knee, and I'm not even sure I would get those right. Perhaps some young woman of the Kanien'kehá:ka could tell the story of the woman J. M. Barrie dubbed Tiger Lily, though that was certainly not her name. (The island had no tigers, no lilies, and certainly no tiger lilies.)

I will admit that J. M. Barrie did get a few things right. He wrote that Wendy grew up, got married, and had a daughter named Jane. He wrote that Wendy's family lived in number 14, the house from which Peter had taken Wendy and her brothers. He wrote that Jane was fascinated by stories about Peter Pan. And one night Peter flew in the window and took Jane to Neverland.

All that is correct. Wendy, my mother, eventually married an Englishman, after an introduction made by Lady Hawkins. Edward, my father, was a botanist at Kew Gardens who had traveled to Madagascar to meet with Lady Hawkins, a recognized expert on the plants of the island.

My parents married and returned to London. My grandparents' London home, number 14, had been rented for many years, under the capable supervision of Mrs. Hudson. With the blessing of Mary and George, Wendy and Edward set up housekeeping there. I grew up in the nursery from which my mother left for her adventure so many years ago.

When I was ten years old, Peter Pan flew in the nursery window. I had been thoroughly prepared for this visit by my mother and my grandmother (who still lived in Nosy Boraha). When I was seven, I had started fencing lessons with Miss Sanderson, who was elderly but still quite spry. The following year, I spent six months in Nosy Boraha with my grandmother.

By the time I returned to London, I could build a fish trap, paddle a canoe, shoot with a bow and arrow, and locate constellations useful for finding my way. Ruby taught me to identify edible and medicinal jungle plants. Back in London, at my grandmother's urging, my Granduncle John Watson taught me first aid basics, so I could bandage a wound, splint a broken bone, and wrap a sprained ankle. It was my choice to decide whether I would fly off with Peter, but they all wanted to make sure I was prepared, should the occasion arise.

In a canvas rucksack that I kept by my bed, I carried a nautical chart and a compass, a fishing line and hooks, a needle and thread, a clean shirt and trousers, a sharp hunting knife, an excellent pocket watch (a gift from Granduncle John), a bar of soap and a small towel, a pack of hard candy, a box of matches, a notebook, a pencil, and a leather canteen filled with fresh water.

My grandmother had made the rucksack for me. Every pocket on it was held shut with a flap that could be fastened closed with a strap and a buckle. "That's so you won't lose anything when you do a somersault in midair," my grandmother told me.

She was quite right. I tested the rucksack in the nursery as soon as Peter taught me to fly. The pockets remained shut and I did not lose a thing.

Peter was exactly as my mother and grandmother had described him. Charming, quite full of himself, and clearly unreliable. After a few practice flights around the room, we flew out the window in search of adventure.

That's another story. I might write it someday, but it doesn't belong here. This tale belongs to Mary Darling, my grandmother, brave, true, and in these pages forever young.

EPILOGUE

Dear Jane,

Over the years, I have come to realize that writing the "truth" is far trickier than I ever imagined. Reading your work, I realize how much my stories reflect my point of view—that of a British army doctor born in 1852. When I wrote about the exploits of Sherlock Holmes, I believed without question that a woman's place was in the home. I believed that the British empire brought civilization to people all over the world. I believed the world was better because of that.

I have come to question those beliefs. Many years ago, you took me to task for the ways I wrote about women. Lady Hawkins did the same. Sam reproached me for my descriptions of people with skin as dark as his. I have listened to all of you and I am trying to change the habits of a lifetime. Not an easy task, but I am trying.

You live in a different world than the one I grew up in. You see the world through different eyes. And your story reflects that.

As for the thoughts and words you gave my character, I still contend that you have an excellent imagination. In some places, I was shocked by how close you came to my feelings. In other places, you missed the mark.

But I would not change a word of this story. I'm proud of you.

With much love,
Your antique granduncle,
John Watson

P.S. I have long wondered why you were so determined to learn the basics of first aid at age nine. I did not really believe you when you told me it was a requirement for a Girl Guides badge, but even then, I knew better than to question you!

AFTERWORD

I AM WRITING this afterword for those who want to know:

1. Is this history? Or did you make it all up?
2. Why is Neverland so very grim?
3. Whose history is this anyway?

1) IS IT HISTORY?
I have a good imagination. That's a prerequisite for being a novelist. But I don't have a good enough imagination to invent all the weirdness that is history. History is weirder and crueler and funnier than most people realize.

Lest readers give me credit for far too much imagination, I want to let you know that many events and characters in this novel are based on or taken directly from history.

Consider the list below. According to historical records, all of the items in the list are true—except for one. Can you identify the untrue item?

* In 1891, Professor Hartl brought his Corps of Viennese Fencing Ladies to London, where they performed at the Empire Theatre, an exhibition of swordsmanship that included duels with rapier and dagger.
* Sir James Matthew Barrie, author of *Peter Pan*, enjoyed reading penny dreadfuls—cheap, sensational story books popular in the Victorian era. *The Coral Island*, the book Sam reads in chapter 14, was one of Barrie's favorites.

* ABC tea rooms, run by the Aerated Bread Company, were the only establishments where respectable women could lunch without a male escort in Victorian London.
* In the early 1900s, Miss Sanderson developed a system of umbrella and parasol self-defense. She instructed suffragists on self-defense techniques.
* In the late 1880s, pirates based in Madagascar preyed on vessels in the Red Sea and Indian Ocean.
* Richard Dadd, a Victorian-era painter famous for his depictions of fairies and fairyland, did most of his work while locked up in psychiatric hospitals.
* In the late 1800s, performers from the indigenous nations of North America ("Indians" in the parlance of the time) organized their own Wild West shows and successfully toured Europe and South Africa.
* In 1880, at an agricultural fair in Little Falls, New York, Mary Meyers took off on a solo flight in a balloon and traveled for twenty miles before coming down in a farmer's field. Over the next decade, she made many demonstration flights and was known as "Carlotta, the Lady Aeronaut."
* In the late nineteenth and early twentieth century, hundreds of rich American heiresses married cash-strapped British aristocrats, just as Lady Hawkins did.

Have you made your choice?

It saddens me to reveal that the untrue item is the time period of the pirates. The Golden Age of Piracy was from 1650 to 1730 (or thereabouts), more than a century before the events of this novel. James Matthew Barrie, the author of *Peter Pan*, was willing to put in pirates wherever they were needed, without regard for history. Since Captain Hook is an essential character for any story featuring Peter Pan, *The Adventures of Mary Darling* includes pirates who are misplaced in time. Their home port, the island of Nosy Boraha off the coast of Madagascar, was a popular spot for pirates during the Golden Age of Piracy.

Perhaps you wondered about Lady Emily Hawkins. Lady Hawkins herself is a character from my imagination—but there were many impoverished British aristocrats who married American heiresses in the late nineteenth and early twentieth century. There were also many orchid hunters during the same period. I'd like to believe there could have been an overlap between these categories resulting in an American heiress/orchid hunter.

Lady Hawkins' steam yacht is based on historic vessels. In 1876, the Right Honorable Lady Brassey traveled around the world with family and friends on the steam yacht *Sunbeam*. Lady Brassey's account, *A Voyage in the 'Sunbeam', our Home on the Ocean for Eleven Months*, was a bestseller.

Like Lady Emily Hawkins, Chief Laughing Bear's performing troupe was inspired by history. You may be familiar with Wild West shows run by Buffalo Bill Cody, Texas Jack, and other white men. Those shows often employed indigenous people. But there were also groups of indigenous performers who produced and starred in their own shows, with dances, scripts, costumes, and sets of their own creation.

Perhaps the best known of these shows was The Famous Deer Brothers, Champion Indian Trick Riders of the World, a family of performers from the Kanien'kehá:ka nation. In the early 1900s, they toured Europe, the United Kingdom, and South Africa as the Deer Family Wild West Show.

Another performer who was famous in the 1880s was Gowongo Mohawk of the O-non-dowa-gah nation (dubbed the Seneca tribe by colonists). Gowongo Mohawk wrote her own shows, cross-dressed to star as the male lead, and performed all her own stunts, including trick riding and shooting. Her shows were an enormous success in both the United States and Europe. At a time when government and cultural forces were trying to erase indigenous peoples, Gowongo Mohawk, the Deer family, and other indigenous performers refused to be erased, challenging the notion of the "vanishing Indian" prevalent at the time.

So Chief Laughing Bear's Amazing Indians are based on history. I am sorry to say that the descriptions of life on the reservation are also based on historical accounts. Reading about residential schools and the governmental efforts to separate children from their native culture gave me a new (and horrifying) perspective on American and Canadian history.

I could make a much longer list of elements of the novel that come from the historical record. Yes, the rest cure was implemented as I have described it. Yes, ABC tea shops were extremely important to the women of Victorian London, serving as meeting places for suffragettes. Yes, there are blue-eyed, dark-skinned people among the Solomon Islanders. Yes, British orchid hunters roamed the world in search of rare flowers. Yes, there were articulated artificial legs in Victorian England. Yes, it is possible to make leather from rat skins (though I did not find records of any ratskin glovemakers in Victorian London.) The poor children of London—the crossing sweepers, mud larks, flower girls—are all well documented in history.

After researching this book, my view of the past has been forever changed.

2) Why is Neverland so grim?

Some may think that my view of Neverland is too grim. If you feel that way, I recommend you read James Barrie's novel. It's most decidedly dark. Here are a few quotes from the novel that capture a bit of that darkness:

When Barrie introduces the Lost Boys, he notes:

> The boys on the island vary, of course, in numbers, according as they get killed and so on; and when they seem to be growing up, which is against the rules, Peter thins them out . . .

Clearly death is very much a part of life on Neverland. So is killing. When Wendy, John, and Michael first fly over the island, Peter and John have this exchange:

> "There's a pirate asleep in the pampas just beneath us," Peter told [John]. "If you like, we'll go down and kill him."
> "I don't see him," John said after a long pause.
> "I do."
> "Suppose," John said, a little huskily, "he were to wake up."
> Peter spoke indignantly. "You don't think I would kill him while he was sleeping! I would wake him first, and then kill him. That's the way I always do."
> "I say! Do you kill many?"
> "Tons."

My thinking about the lack of food on Neverland was shaped by a few lines about Peter Pan and make-believe:

> . . . to him make-believe and true were exactly the same thing. This sometimes troubled [the Lost Boys], as when they had to make-believe that they had had their dinners.

If they broke down in their make-believe, he rapped them on the knuckles.

And if you think I exaggerate the pressure on Mary to be mother to the boys, read this passage describing Wendy's experience of the underground room where the Lost Boys lived:

> Really there were whole weeks when . . . she was never above ground. The cooking, I can tell you, kept her nose to the pot, and even if there was nothing in it, even if there was no pot, she had to keep watching that it came aboil just the same. You never exactly knew whether there would be a real meal or just a make-believe, it all depended upon Peter's whim . . .

My description of pirate battles was shaped by a scene in the book where the Lost Boys fight the crew of the *Jolly Roger*. The pirates were stronger than the Lost Boys . . .

> . . . but they fought on the defensive only, which enabled the boys to hunt in pairs and choose their quarry. Some of the miscreants leapt into the sea; others hid in dark recesses, where they were found by Slightly, who did not fight, but ran about with a lantern which he flashed in their faces, so that they were half blinded and fell as an easy prey to the reeking swords of the other boys. There was little sound to be heard but the clang of weapons, an occasional screech or splash, . . .

Death is part of Neverland, but it's easy to forget that. That's what Peter does. When Wendy reminds Peter of past battles, he simply doesn't remember them. "I forget them after I kill them," he says of past enemies.

In forgetting about the death, we are simply following Peter's lead. It's all fun and games until someone is gutted and tossed overboard.

3) Whose history is this, anyway?

The most difficult part of writing this novel was telling the stories that are not my own. I began this project with the notion of reimagining James Barrie's novel, *Peter Pan,* from the point of view of Mrs. Mary Darling.

Though *Peter Pan* and Neverland have long fascinated me, I have always been annoyed by the roles provided for women and girls. In the novel, girls and women alike adore Peter Pan. They want to mother him. They want him to love them.

I don't want either. I want to go on the adventure. I don't want to be the mother who takes care of everyone and tells them when to go to bed.

That was my starting point. I felt comfortable taking Mary Darling's viewpoint. I could write parts of Mary Darling's story from authentic experience. I know what it's like to be expected to dress and behave in a certain manner. I know what it's like to have Sherlock Holmes explain things to me as if I didn't have a clue. (Oh, all right—it wasn't Sherlock Holmes himself, but people who simply could not conceive that I knew more about a topic than they did. Close enough.)

Peter Pan reflects the views of the time and place in which it was written—in England at the height of the British Empire. It is a boys' adventure book in the spirit of British imperialism, a literary cousin to the penny dreadfuls of the time, in which anyone who was not white was smashed into a stereotype. I had to deal with those stereotypes to create authentic characters of the time.

My ancestors were Irish and Ukrainian, and I was raised in suburban California. I have no firsthand knowledge of life in the Solomon Islands, nor on a reservation in 1900, nor on Madagascar. So I did research. And more research. When I could, I talked to people from the cultures I wanted to represent. I read books by authors from those cultures. I read histories.

I've always known that words can be very tricky—but I have a new understanding of how terribly tricky they can be. Many of the names we use for indigenous cultures reflect historic inaccuracy and disrespect. I've introduced some of the names that people call themselves—Haudenosaunee rather than Iroquois, Kanien'kehá:ka rather than Mohawk. But to give readers who are unfamiliar with the correct nomenclature a context, I have used the historic terms as well. Not a perfect solution, but the best I could come up with.

All that is to say: I've tried to get things right. Like Watson, I realize my version of the "truth" reflects my point of view. But the story does not need to end here. As Jane suggests in the last chapter, I invite others to write the truth as they see it, telling the stories of characters who deserve to be celebrated and remembered.

Pat Murphy
Boulder City, 2025

ACKNOWLEDGMENTS

THERE'S A PERSISTENT myth that writing is a solitary profession. When it comes to putting words on the page, I suppose writing can be considered a solitary job. But when it comes to getting those words out the door, it takes a crowd.

I want to thank everyone who cheered me on, contributed ideas and inspiration, and generally helped me keep on writing. Special thanks to Jeanne Gomoll. After hearing me read the dinner scene in which Mary spills her glass of water on Sherlock Holmes, Jeanne would not rest until I let her read a completed (though far from final) draft of the book.

I am very grateful to everyone who read and commented on the entire manuscript (sometimes more than once)! That list of heroes includes: Eleanor Arnason, Debbie Daughetee, Meg Grant, Eileen Gunn, Manjula Menon, Aaron Micheau, Nancy Jane Moore, Ellen Neuborne, Therese Pieczynski, Michaela Roessner-Hermann, Nisi Shawl, Diane Silver, and Erin Van Rheenen. Special thanks to Leslie Klinger, who reviewed the entire manuscript in search of Holmes-related copyright issues.

I also want to thank those who helped me better understand the culture of the Kanien'kehá:ka nation. Salt and Sage Books' sensitivity reader Lune Dube helped me see Peter Pan from a Kanien'kehá:ka perspective and, with their questions and ideas, strengthened the book in so many ways. Erica Gray taught me so much in her Level 1 Mohawk language class, offered through the Kanatsiohareke community. I also relied on information supplied by many organizations, including Kanien'kehá:ka Onkwawén:na Raotitióhkwa Language and Cultural Center, Iroquois

Indian Museum, and the Native North American Traveling College. All that I got right is thanks to them. Anything I got wrong is on me—I am still learning and expect to continue learning for the rest of my days.

Of course, without the efforts of my agent Jennifer Weltz, my publisher Jacob Weisman, and my editor Jaymee Goh, this book would still be a file in my Google drive and an unruly pile of printouts on the bottom shelf of my bookcase. Thank you all!

Finally, thanks to my patient husband, Officer David Wright, who has been living with this book for as long as I have.

THE MARY DARLING BOOK CLUB
BOOK SYNOPSIS AND OVERVIEW

J. M. BARRIE's *Peter Pan* and Arthur Conan Doyle's Sherlock Holmes reflect the attitudes of the time they were written—when every girl was destined to become a mother, and the sun never set on the British Empire. *The Adventures of Mary Darling* reimagines and combines these stories, questioning their underlying assumptions.

Mary Darling is the mother of Wendy, John, and Michael, the children who fly away with Peter Pan. From her point of view, the children have been kidnapped. She even knows where they have gone. As a child, Peter Pan took Mary to Neverland, a dark and dangerous place.

Mary Darling is also the niece of Dr. John Watson, friend of Sherlock Holmes. When Mary discovers the children are gone, her husband seeks help from Mary's uncle. Uninvited, Sherlock Holmes takes on the case, applying logic to a mystery that's rooted in the fantastic. Mary becomes his prime suspect.

To save her children, Mary must flee London and travel halfway around the world, pursued by Watson and Holmes. As Mary gathers allies among people indigenous to the lands Britain claimed, this adventurous romp reveals the realities that the past held for women and indigenous peoples.

QUESTIONS ABOUT THE BOOK AS A WHOLE
1. Would you recommend the book to a friend? How would you describe the story if you were to recommend it? What kind of reader do you think would most enjoy this book?

2. Was there any part of the plot or aspects of the characters that frustrated or upset you? If so, what and why?

3. If you could talk to the author, what question would you want to ask?

4. Did you read the Afterword? Did it change your thinking about the book? If so, how?

5. Did you highlight or bookmark any passages from the book? Did you have a favorite quote or quotes? If so, share which and why.

QUESTIONS ABOUT THE CHARACTERS

1. How did focusing on Mary Darling's point of view change the way you think about the Peter Pan story? How did it affect your view of Sherlock Holmes?

2. Which character in this book would you be most likely to get into an argument with? Why?

3. Which character would you like to take home to meet your family? Why?

4. Which character would you trust to take care of your children? Why?

5. Who was your favorite character? Were there any characters that you disliked? Why?

6. Which character would you like to be stranded with on a desert island?

7. If the author were to write a sequel, which character would you like to read more about? Captain Hook, Ruby, Lady Hawkins, Polly River (also known as Tiger Lily), or someone else? Why that character?

8. Sherlock Holmes is a well-known character, from the original stories and from many spin-offs. Do you think this book is fair to Sherlock Holmes?

QUESTIONS INVOLVING TRICKY DECISIONS

1. Jane Darling, the novel's narrator, says, "This book tells the true story." Does knowing that Jane is telling the story change how you think about it? Do you think Jane has succeeded in telling the truth? Do you think it is possible to tell a story that is equally true for all readers? Do you think all the characters in the book would agree with this assertion? Is a family member the best person to tell the "true story" of a family?

2. How does *The Adventures of Mary Darling* comment on the underlying assumptions of the original stories?
3. Mrs. Hudson tells Mary, "I learned long ago that it is far better not to tell your husband everything that you think and do." Do you agree? Why or why not?
4. Watson remains silent as Holmes explains away events that Watson has experienced—such as meeting a fairy, flying to the pirate ship, and hearing the song of the mermaids. What would you have done in Watson's position? Would you have argued with Holmes or remained silent? How would your decision have made you feel?
5. Mary flees London to rescue her children, leaving her husband behind. In the end, Mary and George reunite. What do you think Mary sees in George? Why does she love him?
6. In this novel, Polly River (also known as Tiger Lily) and her family are members of a Wild West show that is based on the Famous Deer Brothers, a show that toured Europe in the early 1900s. Did anything about these characters surprise you or change your view of Native Americans?
7. This novel introduces minor characters whose lives were changed by the spread of the British Empire: Sam Smalls, a Solomon Islander whose village was destroyed by contact with Western civilization; Ruby, a Malagasy woman on an island that everyone thinks is run by pirates (although it's actually run by women); and Polly River and her family. What did you think of these characters? Would you like to know more about any of them? Why?

QUESTIONS ABOUT YOUR READING EXPERIENCE

1. How did you feel right after you finished reading the book?
2. Which place in the book would you most like to visit and why? Neverland? Nosy Boraha? London in 1899?
3. Which scene resonated with you most on a personal level and why? How did it make you feel?
4. This book is a *mashup*. It was created by combining elements from two different sources. If you were going to make a mashup, what fictional characters would you want to combine?

ABOUT THE AUTHOR

PAT MURPHY IS the Nebula, Philip K. Dick, Seiun, Theodore Sturgeon, and World Fantasy Award-winning author of science fiction and fantasy short stories and novels, including *The Falling Woman, Points of Departure, The Wild Girls,* and *The Shadow Hunter.* Murphy also has written and edited numerous art, science, and craft books and elementary school curricula. She has written for the acclaimed Exploratorium; the popular children's publisher Klutz; and the academic publisher Mystery Science. Her nonfiction has won awards from the American Institute of Physics and the American Association for the Advancement of Science.

Murphy has taught writing and science fiction at Stanford University, the University of California at Santa Cruz, and the Clarion Speculative Fiction Workshop. She is a cofounder of the Otherwise Award (formerly known as the Tiptree Award), which is presented annually to works of speculative fiction that explore and expand gender.

Murphy currently lives in Nevada. She is a black belt in kenpo karate and her favorite color is ultraviolet. Find out more at PATMURPHY.NET.